By R. Chᵢ

LOOKING FOR
SOMETHING TO SUCK

THE VAMPIRE STORIES OF

R. CHETWYND-HAYES

Edited with a Foreword by
STEPHEN JONES

Illustrated by
JIM PITTS

VALANCOURT BOOKS

Looking for Something to Suck: The Vampire Stories of R. Chetwynd-Hayes
Originally published in hardcover by Fedogan & Bremer in 1997
First Valancourt Books edition 2014

Published by Valancourt Books, Richmond, Virginia
http://www.valancourtbooks.com

ISBN 978-1-941147-31-3
Also available as an electronic book.

All Valancourt Books publications are printed on acid free paper
that meets all ANSI standards for archival quality paper.

Set in Dante MT 11/13.2

CONTENTS

ACKNOWLEDGMENTS

Special thanks to Linda Smith, James D. Jenkins, Jim Pitts, Seamus A. Ryan, Mandy Slater, Jo Fletcher, Dorothy Lumley, Phillip J. Rahman and, of course, Ronald Chetwynd-Hayes, for their help and support in compiling this collection. All stories reprinted by permission of the Estate of R. Chetwynd-Hayes.

Foreword:

NEVER BEASTLY TO VAMPIRES

by Stephen Jones

'ME AND VAMPIRES have always got on well together,' said Ronald with a smile. And he should have known. In a writing career that spanned more than four decades and literally hundreds of short stories, he wrote about the undead often enough – even making up his own unique variations on the theme whenever he felt the need.

'I've often thought about whether vampires really exist,' he revealed. 'After all, there are stories about them in every age. Perhaps it is some form of madness, a terrible urge to drink blood? I don't think we shall ever find a Count Dracula anywhere, but there are probably people who have an unholy lust to consume blood.'

R. Chetwynd-Hayes (1919-2001) was known as 'Britain's Prince of Chill', and his numerous collections of genteel and humorous ghost stories filled the shelves of almost every public library in Britain during the 1980s. In 1989 he was presented with Life Achievement Awards by both the Horror Writers of America and the British Fantasy Society, and he was a special guest at the 1997 World Fantasy Convention in London.

Ronald Henry Glynn Chetwynd-Hayes was born in Isleworth, West London, on May 30, 1919, the son of Henry (a movie theatre manager) and Rose May. After appearing as a schoolboy extra in a number of pre-War British movies, he followed his father into the Army at the start of World War II. Rising to the rank of Sergeant in the Middlesex Regiment, he was evacuated from Dunkirk and returned to the beaches of France on D-Day.

When he came out of the Army, he joined the furniture department of Harrods as a trainee buyer. Four years later he moved to an exclusive furniture emporium in Berkeley Street as a showroom manager.

Throughout this period, he read voraciously and was soon convinced that he could do better himself. He began writing his own stories – everything from romances to his favorite genre, historical fiction – and along the way garnered numerous rejections from magazines and book publishers.

'I used to try to write the great novel,' he lamented. 'Try to be another Brontë. But, of course, nobody wanted to publish it. Then when I looked on the bookstalls and saw all these supernatural titles, I thought that was obviously the market to aim for. I'd always been interested in the supernatural anyway.'

In fact, his first published work was a science fiction novel, *The Man from the Bomb*, which appeared from Badger Books in 1959. 'I sent that all over the place,' explained the author. 'Badger offered to take it, so I let them have it. They paid me £25.' That was followed in 1964 by a novel about reincarnation, *The Dark Man* (repackaged as a romantic Gothic, *And Love Survived*, in America), but only after it was rejected by nineteen other publishers.

By the early 1970s, his short fiction could be found in numerous anthologies, a number of which he also edited, and his first collection of stories, *The Unbidden*, appeared in 1971. 'In those days, everything to do with the supernatural sold,' he recalled. 'At one time I had six volumes with my name on them in bookshops.'

Ronald's tales of terror are often notable for a disarming sense of humour, which the author readily admitted that he couldn't help. 'I've always got this terrible urge to send the whole thing up. It just slips in, I have never been able to stop it.' However, his skill as a horror writer also resided in his ability to bring new perspectives to familiar themes . . .

'Having of course read *Dracula*,' he explained, 'I sometimes think Bram Stoker could have done a better job than he actually did. Everyone says what a great novel it is.

'Count Dracula was actually a very kind, educated aristocrat in many ways. Do you remember that when Jonathan Harker first turned up at the castle, the Count said, "Welcome to my house. Come freely. Go safely; and leave something of the happiness you bring!" That was a nice thought. Of course, it's a pity he didn't keep that up!

'For me, the most horrific piece of writing ever is when Harker looks out of the window and sees the Count climbing head-first down the wall of the castle. Perhaps the only thing more eerie than that is when Harker wakes up in that moon-lit room surrounded by those three women, giggling, deciding which one should have the first sip.

'The Count was apparently very versatile too. He was obviously a cook – those three women didn't do it! He could also make beds, because Harker saw him doing it. So when you think of him doing little jobs like that, he loses some of his terror.

'Vampires really are human beings. If you're not very careful, a vampire is just a normal human being with a longing for blood. Where you and I would like a lamb chop for dinner, a vampire would like a pint of fresh blood.'

When asked about his favourite movies, Ronald cited *Mark of the Vampire* (1935) as the most terrifying vampire film ever made. 'I remember that scene with a man in a horse-and-cart who has an oil-lamp which casts a circle of light as his vehicle advances. Suddenly he comes across two creatures dressed in shrouds, standing by the road. And they don't smile, they don't glare. Afterwards, you see them looking in through a window, and I used to think that was the most horrifying thing I'd ever seen as a teenager.'

In 1972, while still selling furniture in London's West End, Ronald was approached by Milton Subotsky of Amicus Productions, who wanted to film some of his stories. 'We'd just been taken over and I'd got the sack,' he recalled, 'so it was marvellous. I became a freelance writer on the strength of it. It terrified me – I suddenly realized I had to live on my own wits – but it was something I wanted to do. Look at the books I turned out as a result of that!'

Following the successful anthology format they had established in 1965 with *Dr. Terror's House of Horrors*, Amicus adapted four of Ronald's stories in *From Beyond the Grave* (1973), directed by Kevin Connor and starring Peter Cushing, Donald Pleasence and David Warner. 'Needless to say, I was delighted with the all-star cast,' remembered the author.

Seven years later, Ronald was again contacted by Subotsky, who wanted to make a film of his collection of connected tales, *The Monster Club*. 'Milton Subotsky was the kindest man I ever met, but he should never have made a film. His idea of humour was silly. He had to crack a walnut with a sledgehammer. In *The Monster Club*, he had that business where Richard Johnson gets up out of his coffin and says, "I was wearing my stake-proof vest", then turns to his wife and says, "Look, ketchup!" They could have made it much funnier.'

During the shooting, Ronald visited the set and met the stars of the film, Vincent Price and John Carradine. 'Poor old John Carradine played me in the film,' explained the author. 'That was Milton's idea of a joke because I had put him into the book as "Lintom Busotsky", an anagram of his name. When I saw Carradine he was seventy-four years old and crippled with arthritis. At the preview, a man came up to me and said, "I'm so sorry you suffer from arthritis." I said, "I don't, that's John Carradine!"

'Vincent Price played a vampire in *The Monster Club*, and he was good. He was such a nice man, and he would tell me some wonderful stories about Hollywood. It's sad, they're both dead now.'

Over the years, Ronald contributed a number of memorable tales to the literature of the undead. 'Amongst my favourite vampire stories I've written is "My Mother Married a Vampire",' he revealed. 'She did, you know. That vampire's hunting ground was on the London Underground. I've always thought that all horror takes place on the Underground. Try travelling on it during the rush-hour in the summer, and you'll suddenly realize that there are very few places on this earth that are worse than that! I've always had the urge to put these bizarre happenings in commonplace surroundings.

'I sent a copy of "The Labyrinth" to a producer at Hammer Films, who said he had never before read such an original vampire story in his life.

'When I showed "Looking for Something to Suck" – which was about a shadow that couldn't go into the light or it would be destroyed – to an editor, she said, "Well you know they're all going to get the wrong idea." And I said, "That's too bad, people shouldn't have such horrible minds!"

'Then, of course, there was "The Werewolf and the Vampire". That was about an ordinary boy who hears a dog howling somewhere in the woods and he thinks it's been caught in a trap. But there's a thing with a long wet nose there, and it bites him. Of course, he doesn't know it, but he's now got the virus in him of a werewolf. While he's in Hampton Court Palace he meets Carola, who happens to be a vampire.

'Carola, by the way, was based on a lady who used to work for Tandem Books. It was such a fascinating name, that I've hung on to it ever since. The story finishes up with a fight between so-called good and evil. Good is supposed to be the Reverend and the evil is supposed to be the werewolf and the vampire. But of course you realize that it's nothing of the sort, it's the other way around.

'It's the bad that always triumphs in my stories. I'm on the monster's side. The good is all right, but the bad is always more interesting.'

When this present collection was first published by Fedogan & Bremer in 1997, it didn't include 'The Great Indestructible', which features Count Dracula himself. Back in 1976, Ronald was commissioned by publisher New English Library to edit and write the entire contents for a children's magazine entitled *Ghoul*. For reasons that are not entirely clear, NEL cancelled the title before the first issue even appeared on newsstands.

That now rare and very collectable one-shot featured the story under the title 'I Meet the Great Indestructible' and was credited to the pseudonymous 'Hans Clutcher' (Ronald could never resist a bad pun). When I eventually rediscovered the story, I reprinted it under its original title in the author's posthumous collection *Frights and Fancies* (2002); however, it more properly belongs in this volume, and I am delighted to include it in this first paperback edition.

Ronald always said that he could write a story about any subject but, back in the 1990s, even he believed that the market was in danger of being flooded with too much vampire fiction. 'I've always had a motto: never be beastly to vampires,' he explained, 'but there are far, far too many vampire stories being published. We'll soon have to think of something else. That's why my idea of sending them up or asking who does the laundry was an attempt to add something extra.

'There are different ways you can treat the subject. Anything that feeds off a human being could be classed as a vampire. For example, in my 1980 novel *The Partaker*, the young cub is taken care of by an old woman who is covered with fleas. And he realizes that these are small partakers, who were partaking of her blood and showing an unholy interest in him. So he wills them to see a lump of wet meat, and all the fleas leave her and go for this imaginary piece of meat. Down they come, thousands of them, crawling over her face. So you see, in a way, a flea is a vampire.

'Whatever few pennies I've made as a writer, I suppose have come from vampirism in some form or another. Being a vampire is a form of immortality, so long as you can keep out of the way of clergymen and boy scouts – either of those two will put a stake through your heart in no time at all!

'I'm writing for the future. I hope in a hundred years' time some editor will find one of my old books and decide it will fill up a gap. And so I shall live again. In that respect, I suppose being a writer is very much like being a vampire . . .'

THE BASIC RULES OF MONSTERDOM

Vampires – sup; Werewolves – hunt; Ghouls – tear;
Shaddies – lick; Maddies – yawn; Mocks – blow;
Shadmocks – only whistle.

– from *The Monster Club*
by R. Chetwynd-Hayes

MY MOTHER MARRIED A VAMPIRE

She did.

I ought to know because – the vampire – was my father and what that makes me is anyone's guess. A humvam maybe, although I have never felt the urge to take up the old man's line of business. I can't say I ever noticed anything unusual about him, not when I was a kid at any rate, although he was a bit on the pale side and never put in an appearance before sunset. I assumed he worked at nights (as he did), probably as a head waiter or something, for he always left the house a little after lighting up time, immaculately dressed in a well-pressed dinner jacket and smelling of rose-water.

My mother – may the earth lay lightly on her bones – worked very hard to get him ready for the nightly trip round the local necks; laying out a fresh starched dicky, polishing his patent-leather shoes, making sure there was a good supply of handkerchiefs in both jacket pockets, for his profession was a messy one and she was rather afraid he might be mistaken for a butcher. I remember on the rare occasion when he took us both out – a wet dinner and a show afterwards – he wore a gold star attached to a blue ribbon round his neck, and my mother once informed me that this symbolized his noble status.

'Your father is really a count,' she said proudly, 'which means of course that I am a countess and you – well – you must be a viscount.'

Naturally I couldn't keep information like this to myself and passed it on to a crowd of my contemporaries on the way home from school.

'I'm a viscount,' I said.

They chucked me in the local canal and most of them were for leaving me there, maintaining that such a white-faced, bulging-eyed little brat was of no account and should have been drowned at birth. Fortunately a passing clergyman grabbed my hair as I was going down for the third time, then did the necessary arm-pumping-belly-pushing business, which brought me back to gasping life.

'Why did those little limbs of Satan do this to you?' he asked, when I was in a condition to answer questions.

'Because I'm so ugly, I guess,' I replied.

He looked me up and down and quickly dismissed an expression of deep distaste with a gentle smile.

'We all have our crosses to bear. A rough exterior often conceals a heart of gold. Let me see you home.'

Unfortunately I was not aware of my father's built-in repugnance for parsons and gladly accepted this offer of ecclesiastical protection, there being the distinct possibility that my persecutors were waiting to complete their water cure. When we reached my house, which was surrounded by an overgrown garden, the clergyman knocked smartly on the front door, then eyed the flaking paint, the blacked out windows and the large hideous door knocker – it was a brass satyr with pronounced essentials – while frowning with marked disapproval. Then my mother opened the door and was standing with a bright light behind her; a vision that had made my father realize that a monster need not live by blood alone. My reverend rescuer removed his hat and replaced his frown by the smile of one who might – if his profession allowed him to dare. He said:

'Madam, this young man is possibly your son . . .'

Mother shrieked. 'Marvin! What on earth have you been doing?'

'I fear a small mishap . . .'

'They threw me in the canal,' I interrupted, 'and I would have drowned if it had not been for this parson.'

Mother pulled me over the doormat, lifted me up into a bone-crunching embrace, assisted possibly by muscles that had been hardened during fifteen years of putting an over-sated father to coffin. Then I was carried into the front parlour and hastily stripped and wrapped in a velvet tablecloth and deposited in front of the fire. Then we became aware that the Reverend Gentleman had invited himself in and had been watching my mother's quick denuding operation with unstinted admiration.

'What a lucky little lad he is,' he observed. 'My word, if only I had had a beautiful mother to administer to my needs, when I was his age.'

My mother turned pale and looked anxiously at the open doorway.

'Goodness gracious, he'll soon be up!' she exclaimed. 'I'm sure that dog's collar will give him a nasty turn.'

Either the clergyman did not hear or decided she was referring to an agnostic in dire need of spiritual guidance, for he advanced across the room with outstretched hand.

'Allow me, dear lady, to introduce myself. Martin Pickering. Your humble vicar.'

My mother accepted the hand with some reluctance and murmured, 'Mrs – that is to say – Countess de Suc-Little. My husband will be up any time now . . .'

'Ah! A member of the nobility! There is nothing like blue blood as I'm sure your husband will agree.' A faint sound drifted up from the lower regions and Mother sighed deeply. 'Oh, I don't think he minds what colour it is.'

Mr Pickering smiled broadly and gave vent to a deep, fat chuckle. 'A sense of humour! I really must remember that one. Madam – Countess – do you suppose your husband would consider joining the altar dressing committee? A title would be such an asset . . .'

It was then that my father entered the room and stood staring at the visitor with an expression of horrified astonishment. He had a very presentable appearance, being tall, with a long lean face, dark melancholy eyes and dark hair that was slightly grey at the temples. Apart from his extremely pale face and rather pronounced eye-teeth, there was little to betray his line of business – so long as no one waved a cross at him or tried to find his reflection in a mirror. He could have easily have been mistaken for a high-class waiter or a conservative member of parliament.

But at the moment he was displaying the natural repugnance that might be expected from a bishop who finds himself confronted by a red-hot communist. Mother tried to pour soothing oil on very troubled waters.

'This gentleman pulled Marvin out of the canal. He saved his life.'

But my father could only stare at the offending clerical collar with horrified amazement and enquire weakly:

'How did it get in?'

It would seem that the Reverend Mr Pickering assumed that this objection to his presence was the result of lack of faith and therefore should be treated as a challenge.

'My, dear Sir,' he said heartily, 'we brothers of the cloth are not members of a different species, although at times appearances may suggest otherwise. The only difference between you and I, Sir, is I have so much to give. Indeed I have an overabundance of richness, which, if you will only drink from the fountain will guarantee everlasting life.'

Father allowed a thin rivulet of moisture to seep out from the left corner of his mouth.

'I cannot believe,' Mr Pickering went on, 'that you do not thirst after righteousness. Do you not wish to partake . . . ?'

It was at this point that my mother grabbed him by the left arm and pushed him with more haste than politeness towards the front door.

'Thank you for everything,' she said. 'Sorry to rush you off but my husband is anxious to get to work.'

'But, dear lady, we were about to get to grips with . . .'

'Yes, I know. But he has very decided views on a certain subject and nothing you can say will alter them.'

'I will call again, dear lady, of that you can be sure.'

The door slammed and Mother came back into the dining-room. She seated herself at the bottom of the table, poured Father a glass of red stuff from an earthenware jug, then spoke her mind.

'Now, Manfred, I was well aware of what you were – and your strange little ways – when we married. I have no objection to you taking a little from those who have lots to spare, and possibly at times of dire need, from those not so well endowed. But the church is out. Apart from anything else, you never know what a clergyman may be wearing.'

If Father could have turned pale, he would have done so.

'You don't mean a – C.R.O.S.S.?'

Mother nodded. 'Almost certainly. A clergyman without – you know what – is like a sausage without seasoning. Then where would you be if you got your teeth stuck into one of those?'

Father appeared to be quite overcome by the prospect and almost choked on a lump of black pudding, which I may say, was the only solid food he could keep down. But of course they had both overlooked one important factor that often escapes the attention of parents. Namely, I could, within certain limits, spell. I asked a simple and to my mind innocent question.

'Mother, why should Father be frightened of a cross?'

Father slumped down in his chair and had to be revived by a generous draught of the red stuff, which in my innocence I had always assumed to be tomato juice. When he was in a condition to do so, he looked at me with an expression of sad reproach.

'To think that a son of mine should use such language!'

'He wasn't to know,' Mother protested. 'I always said the boy should be told the facts of death long since. And you should have been the one to tell him.'

'That's all very well – but can he keep his big mouth shut? You know how people feel about my profession. I don't want – you know who – round here with hammers, stakes and a sack of garlic.'

Now I wasn't all that stupid and had seen more than my full ration of horror films and the combination of crosses, stakes and garlic, plus the fact that Father slept in a coffin, was sufficient to give me an inkling of the truth. 'Father,' I exclaimed, 'you're not . . . not a vampire?'

Father flinched and Mother said gently:

'We prefer to think of him as a partaker. It is much more refined. Your dear father lightens the burden of those who have too much and is rewarded by certain nutritious benefits for his trouble. Moreover donators rarely realize that they have been privileged to . . .'

'A nip, a suck and never let 'em feel a thing,' Father interrupted, his voice trembling with emotion. 'Feed without Greed – that's always been my slogan. The rush hour trains and the after theatre crowds provide a rich harvest for them that knows their business.'

Mother permitted a tiny frown to mar her smooth forehead.

'I do not think, dear, there is any need to reveal your working procedure. A gentleman – not to mention a nobleman – does not mix his business and home life. Sufficient that Marvin now knows that he has an unusual father who has some claim to the title of benefactor.'

'But keep the good news to yourself,' Father warned me.

Having experienced the kind of treatment the common herd dish out to a sprig of the nobility, I had no desire to find out what might be in store for the offspring of a vampire. So I shook my head vigorously and gave the required undertaking.

'I will never breathe a word.'

Mother gave a deep sigh of relief. 'Well, that's settled. Now, Manfred, you must hurry or you'll miss the five-thirty from Oxford Circus. That is the train which I seem to remember affords you the greatest nutritious value.'

Father rose and dashed upstairs where he washed and shaved and generally smartened himself up so as to present an immaculate appearance before setting about his beneficial business. I of course was most anxious to know why, how and where.

'Mother, why did you marry a vampire?'

'The attraction of the opposites, my dear. I was somewhat anaemic – your father at the time of our first meeting – singularly well-endowed.'

'How did . . . ?'

'That is not a question I am prepared to answer.'

'Where did . . .'

'On the Brighton express one foggy November night. Your father had been on his annual holiday. Now, that's enough. It's time for your bath.'

That night I lay awake trying to imagine my quiet, unassuming sire, like a dark nocturnal fly, gathering red pollen from the metropolitan garden. How strange that people never knew that they had donated that precious drop that was so important to my father's well being. I wondered how he did it. Did he hypnotise them first? A few passes with his long-fingered hands? Or a whispered word that caused their minds to send out a smoke screen of forgetfulness? And how was it that no one saw him do – whatever it was he did?

Then I heard my mother sobbing.

It was a low, almost imperceptible sound that I could not have heard had I still been in the state of blissful ignorance. Perhaps she cried every night. Was held back from the arms of sleep by the knowledge that the one she loved was not only earning his living, but in constant danger. I got up, put on a dressing gown and went into her bedroom.

She was fully dressed, lying on top of the bed and looking like a beautiful Hero mourning the loss of her Leander. She sat up when I entered and wiped her eyes on a black lace handkerchief.

'Son, what are you doing up?' she asked. 'You need so much beauty sleep.'

I sat down on a bedside chair. 'Why are you crying? Is it because of Father?'

She did not answer, but began to cry again and I – who am usually so undemonstrative – took her hand and tried to find some words of comfort from a forest of unimaginable fears.

'But he's so clever. No one can know – what he is – not after all this time. Otherwise – well – we would know.'

After a while Mother whispered. 'The authorities know. At least, they know his kind exist. But it's a state secret. They're afraid of a panic if ordinary people found out. There's a special branch of the special branch at Scotland Yard. It's called the B. Squad. The Bleeny.'

Even in the midst of my deep concern, I was delighted to be the recipient of such thrilling information. Naturally I wanted to know more.

'What do they do? The B. Squad I mean.'

Mother shuddered. 'The squad is comprised of undercover agents. They might be anyone. The butcher, baker – stockbroker. But when they – go into action – they carry violin cases. That's the right length to hold the sharp stakes. Son, tremble if you see men carrying violin cases.'

I promised to be very wary of anyone I saw so equipped, then suggested I should make a nice cup of tea with lots of sugar, a beverage to which my mother was very partial. Mother said I was a good boy, even – despite my unprepossessing exterior – a beautiful one, and not to add too much milk. Later, while we were warming our hands on large earthenware mugs, she revealed how beauty and grotesque had come to be mated.

'I was courted by those who carry the rolled umbrella,' she said. 'Proposals rolled off tongues that were accustomed to uttering – tiresome platitudes. My name was linked with a number of revolting words that included chaste, respectable, decency, angelic, soulful, moral and others which, due to my association with your dear father, I will not repeat. Suffice to say, that I came to the conclusion that modern society hides its many sores under a thick coating of whitewash.'

She paused, then after a deep sigh, continued:

'Then he came out of the darkness. Pursued by the B. Squad persecutors, brave, made noble by the grey-tinted coronet of evil; it was love at first fright. Together we fled from the respectability-tainted atmosphere of Liverpool and took up residence in the much more salubrious confines of Great London. Here your father has been permitted to progress from the slender throats of shorthand typists, to the red bull-necks of property tycoons. Such are the advantages of a free society.'

I wiped a solitary tear away with the cuff of my pyjama sleeve. 'That's the most beautiful love story I have ever heard. Don't worry. Father will come home to us in the morning.'

He did.

In fact he came safely home for many mornings, and I was fifteen before I saw three men wearing dirty raincoats and carrying violin cases enter our street. I ran into the kitchen where Mother was making a giant black pudding for Father's birthday (I never did find out how old he was) and blurted out the news.

'They're coming. The B. Squad.'

Mother turned as white as raw pastry and looked anxiously at the kitchen clock.

'It's three hours till sunset and nothing under heaven can waken him. We must tell many lies, Son. Do anything to keep them from going down into the cellar before sunset.'

They stood in the porch and looked at us with unblinking eyes, each holding his violin case in one hand, while hiding the other in a raincoat pocket. The one in the centre – the one with a built-in smile – spoke in a low, carefully controlled voice.

'Might we come in, Mrs de Suc-Little? Won't take up a moment of your time. Pure routine, you understand.'

There was no keeping them out. So Mother stood to one side and they all filed into the hall, then looked at the door leading to the cellar with hungry eyes. Mother pushed them into the front room, then stood with her back against the door.

'Well?' she demanded.

The one in the middle acted as spokesman. He produced a bright red card and murmured:

'Blood Squad. A Division. I am Detective Sergeant Fixer. These gentlemen are Detective Constables Mooney and Watson.'

They all bowed most politely and at Mother's invitation sat down in a neat row on the sofa. She drew a chair in front of the door and proceeded to play mouse-in-the-hole with sleek cats.

'How can I help you?' she asked.

'Ma'am,' Sergeant Fixer said, pulling a document from his breast pocket, 'we have reason to believe that you are cohabitating with a known vampire.'

'I live with my husband and young son,' my mother replied calmly. 'The son is before you, my husband is out.'

The sergeant said, 'Ah!' and the two constables shared 'Ho!' and 'Hi!' between them. The sergeant suddenly removed his polite mask and replaced it by what I can only describe as a leering sneer.

'I'm willing to bet my Sunday boots, Ma'am, that the 'orrible monster is at this moment a kipping in his wooden overcoat somewhere in the lower regions.'

'I have not the slightest idea what you are talking about,' my mother said quietly. 'And I find your manner objectionable.'

'This document is a search warrant,' the sergeant stated, 'and I must ask you to open all doors and cupboards.'

'What makes you think that I am harbouring a vampire? Always supposing such a creature exists.'

'Oh, he exists all right, ma'am. We spotted him on the eight-thirty-two out of Cannon Street. Followed him to this house. Would have paid you a visit earlier, but had to check up with the local B. Squad Chief Super. He'll be along any time now.'

Mother cast a quick glance at the mantelpiece clock and the sergeant chuckled.

'Several hours to sunset, Ma'am. Vampy won't be poking a leg over the coffin walls for sometime yet. Mind you, once the old stake is driven home, he'll come alive. Just for a moment. They always do. Did you know? Sort of jump up and yell like a scalded cat.'

'Say, Sarge,' Constable Mooney contributed his mite of sick humour, 'do you remember that one in Gothic Villas. The posh one. Ran round with the stake sticking out its chest. Rare sight that, wasn't it?'

Sergeant Fixer nodded. 'Sure was. Didn't last long though. Crumbled up over a wine barrel.'

Further reminiscences were curtailed by a polite tap on the front door and the sound made me shiver. For although the underlings might be crude, unthinkingly cruel – high authority would be coldly efficient; go about its unsavoury business without pity, rancour or pleasure. Constable Mooney got up and walked towards my mother who sat unmoving in her chair in front of the door. He said, 'Excuse me, ma'am,' and lifted her – chair and all – to one side.

He went out into the hall, we heard the front door open, the murmur of voices, then the tread of approaching footsteps.

The Reverend Mr Pickering entered the room and beamed benignly at Mother and myself.

For a moment hope flared up in my terror-numb brain, for the Reverend Gentleman had paid us several visits over the past few years (always in daylight) and we never had occasion to believe he was other than he seemed. A kindly, somewhat simple clergyman.

'Mr Pickering,' I screamed, 'you must stop them. They are going to murder my father.'

The smile died, the eyes grew hard and a completely alien voice barked:

'Not murder, lad. Exterminate. Erase. Blot out. It has taken a long time to nail him – if I may be permitted the pun – for he was one of the cleverest it's been my privilege to track down. I was hoping he would have a go at partaking from me. But he was too smart. Right, lads, down in the cellar. Bring your kit.'

'Right, Super,' Sergeant Fixer nodded. 'Pleasure to work with you, Sir.'

Constables Mooney and Watson gave the impression that they were considering kneeling down and licking the great man's boots, until the sergeant snapped:

'Don't let's hang about, then. We've another job at the teaching college before sunset.'

Mother screamed and threw herself at Chief Superintendent Pickering, who promptly pushed her into Constable Watson's arms without interrupting his march towards the door.

'Bring her – and the brat – along,' he commanded. 'The law demands that immediate followers witness execution.'

We were manhandled across the hall, down the cellar steps and to the curtained alcove where my father rested. Mother had made it cosy. Shaded lamps, an enlarged print of Count Dracula over the coffin; a vase of freshly picked flowers on a bedside cabinet. Father looked so peaceful; so still, pale, handsome; a faint smile parted his lips and revealed even white teeth. A soiled handkerchief which peeped out from his breast pocket was the only sign to betray his calling.

Constable Mooney opened a violin case and took out a steel rod which tapered down to a sharp point, and a large coal hammer. At least that is what it looked like. Sergeant Fixer cleared his throat.

'Will you do the honours, Sir? After all, this is your manor.'

When the Superintendent removed his jacket, Mother called out. 'Manfred – wake up. Wake up.'

No one took any notice – least of all the still white figure in the coffin – and Mr Pickering placed the sharp point in position, just over my father's heart, raised the hammer – and brought it down with a resounding thud.

A cascade of crimson rose up like a glorious fountain and turned the neat alcove into a blood-drenched cave. Then Father's face came up over the coffin walls; his eyes bulging, his mouth wide open – while he bellowed like a wounded bull. Superintendent Pickering nodded slowly.

'A strong one, lads. Don't panic, he won't last long. The stake has gone right through him.'

It was then that Father reached out and grabbed the B. Squad commander by his large ears and pulled him down into the coffin. The three men ran forward and did all they could to free their chief; pulled, kicked the coffin to splintered planks – and after a long, long while they succeeded. They unclamped the grinning skull from the superintendent's neck, carried the twitching body into the main cellar, then stood back and looked down at my father's final achievement.

It was not pretty. The right side of Mr Pickering's neck was raw. Mangled, as though a starving crocodile had been interrupted at the beginning of a much needed meal. But the superintendent was still conscious.

'Get an ambulance, Sergeant. Don't stand there.'

Mother laughed. A loud, terrible sound that made us all shudder – including the man against the wall.

'You'll need more than an ambulance. Manfred didn't just nip – suck – take a trickle of refreshment. He bit deep. You know what that means? Now, you're one of his kind, Mr Pickering. You'll have to be staked by your own men.'

For a moment no one spoke, then the sergeant said quietly:

'She's right, Sir. The virus is in you. Come sunset and you'll be on the rampage. We'll have to do our duty, Sir. Sorry.'

Mr Pickering looked up at his subordinate with fear-glazed eyes. 'You don't mean that, Sergeant! I'm Pickering. The departmental legend. Good God, man, I've nailed over two thousand vamps! You can't mean to . . .'

The sergeant sighed. 'You wouldn't want us chasing you through the underground, Sir. Wouldn't be respectful. Now, Sir, if you could see your way clear to laying out flat like, Mooney here will have the old doings through your gizzard – begging your pardon for the expression, Sir – in a giffy.'

Mr Pickering was up on his feet and making good speed for the cellar steps, when Constable Watson brought him down with a flying tackle.

When Mother and I left them, they were fighting over their fallen chief, like dogs over a succulent bone, and I was relieved to realize that the blind goddess brings down her chastising hand on 'them' and 'those' alike.

Mother was dead within a month and went to join Father in that land where monsters and rolled umbrella carriers dine at the same table.

As for me – I am now looking forward to being Chief Tax Inspector for the Greater London Area.

In a way, you could say I am following in my father's footsteps.

A FAMILY WELCOME

S<small>IR</small> C<small>HARLES</small> W<small>ALTON</small> <small>WAS</small> <small>BURIED</small> on Wednesday; two weeks later he was up and about.

That he was dead there was no manner of doubt. The heart had ceased to beat, his blood had congealed, and on the day of the funeral, a full six days later, the corpse was already giving out a cloying sickly odour. Old Doctor Bartholomew said Charles Walton was dead, and the doctor knew a dead man when he saw one, even if at times he was not all that sure what killed him. He signed the death certificate 'Gastro-enteritis' without hesitation, and hurried back to his interrupted breakfast, after absentmindedly patting the grieving widow on her well-shaped bottom. At the bedroom door he hesitated, then spoke over one shoulder.

'I'll telephone Fleming from the surgery. He'd better put things in shape for you.'

Mr Fleming was the undertaker, and on his arrival at the manor house some three hours later he found various things needed to be put into shape. He amended 'Gawd Strewth' to 'Dreary Me' just in time, when he first saw Sir Charles's face twisted up into what can be best described as a bestial snarl. The pale blue eyes were wide open and seemed to be in imminent danger of bursting forth from their sockets; the yellow teeth were bared in a ferocious grin, and the eye teeth, which were unnaturally long, looked as if they would snap at the first hand that came within biting distance. To make Mr Fleming's work even more distasteful, one leg was bent double, the bony kneecap stuck up above the bedclothes like a weather-bleached piece of driftwood.

'Leave it all to us, me lady,' he addressed Madeline Walton, 'we'll have him looking as peaceful as a sleeping babe.'

She murmured 'thank you', and turned her full dark eyes on to the undertaker, who pondered on the advantages of being rich, even if you were sixty-five. He escorted the beautiful young widow to the door, before removing his jacket and turning to his young assistant who was gazing at the corpse with an expression that proved he was as yet new to the profession chosen for him by his father.

'Looks a sight, don't he?'

'Well, he ain't what you might call a kiddie's idea of Santa Claus,' Mr Fleming admitted, 'and he's going to be the devil's own job to get into shape. ''Ere, grab hold of his ankle and give it a good tug.'

The young man reluctantly gripped the skinny ankle and obediently tugged; the corpse slid a little way down the bed, but the leg remained obstinately upright. Mr Fleming scratched his head.

'Rigor mortis has set in. The old devil must have had a heart spasm. Get the mallet.'

The lad gulped. 'What yer going to do?'

'Break the thigh bone of course, got to flatten 'im out somehow. Now don't hang about, lad. Give us the mallet.'

It took two hard blows to get Charles Walton's leg straight, but finally the job was done, then the undertaker turned his attention to the grinning face.

'Surgical spirit, Harry, and some cotton-wool.'

He never did succeed in obliterating the grin. The yellow face was soused with surgical spirit, and Mr Fleming kneaded and pressed; he pulled, patted, and finally punched, but all to no avail. Sometimes the grin turned into a leer, at others it became a ferocious smirk, but the creases refused to be smoothed out. The undertaker padded the cheeks with cotton-wool and Charles Walton assumed a well-fed, sleek, self-satisfied look; the smirk became a smile of anticipation. Then the eyes refused to remain shut. The undertaker fastened them down with transparent sticking plaster, but scarcely had he stepped back than there was a faint ripping sound, and the lids snapped open to reveal that disturbing glare.

'We've got to best him, lad.' Mr Fleming wiped his brow on a towel. 'Half the county gentry will be coming to have a look at

him, and he's no advertisement as he is. Get out the needle and thread.'

Downstairs in the large, overfurnished drawing room, Madeline was being consoled by an extremely handsome young man who, as the other mourners were soon to be informed, was a distant cousin. They were seated on the sofa and the young man was demonstrating his cousinly affection by long ardent kisses; a sight that would have left the observer, had there been one, with the impression that his heart was in the right place. Madeline was the first to break off the engagement.

'Harold, he looked so awful.'

'Yes,' murmured Harold, 'he would do.'

'Doctor Bartholomew signed the certificate "Gastro-enteritis".'

'No reason why he shouldn't,' Harold said, his fingers toying with the buttons on her dress. 'He's been treating the old devil for tummy trouble for years.'

'Harold, stop it. This isn't the time. It would look dreadful if someone came in.'

'Yes, I suppose you're right.' Harold put the erring hand into his pocket. 'Well, he's dead now, and you get the lot.'

'Harold, don't be so vulgar.'

'What's vulgar about half a million, to say nothing about this house? Worth five years of marriage, wasn't it?'

'I don't know.' She shuddered. 'He was an awful old man.'

'Never mind.' He drew her to him again. 'It's all over now. He's dead. Soon he'll be locked away in the family vault, and that's the last you'll see of him.'

'Yes,' Madeline agreed, 'he's dead – dead.'

On reflection Madeline decided she could have no doubts at all that her husband was dead. Two grains of arsenic was more than ample to put the old man under, but she had used three, just to be on the safe side.

Harold put his lips to her delicate white ear.

'Did you get rid of the tin?' he whispered.

The funeral was a grand affair; quite the most impressive display that the inhabitants of Walton-on-the-Lee and surrounding districts had enjoyed in a long while. Although the deceased had been thoroughly detested during his lifetime, as Mr Fleming had rightly forecast, half the county turned up to give Sir Charles a rousing send-off.

Madeline, when escorted by her distant cousin into the large drawing room where Sir Charles lay in state prior to being screwed down, had to admit Mr Fleming had done a first-class job in making the departed one look presentable – when one considered the difficulties it represented. The eyes were now fast shut and the lids darkened with blue make-up; the face had a creamy texture, while the padded cheeks were faintly flushed, but of course the grin remained. A replete, sardonic, anticipatory grin, but a vast improvement on the grimace that haunted Madeline's memory. She thought the evening suit made the old man look distinguished; when this was brought into line with the darkened eyelids, pink cheeks, and replete smile, he looked a little like a tailor's dummy which had strayed from a high class shop window.

'He looks very peaceful,' Madeline murmured to Mr Fleming who stood respectfully to one side. 'I'm sure this is the way he would have wished to have looked.'

'You're too kind, me lady.' Mr Fleming bowed his head while thinking yearning thoughts about the screwdriver that nestled in his hip pocket. He could not entirely dismiss the fear that those carefully inserted stitches were not sufficient to hold the eyelids down. He had a vision of them popping open just as old Sir Gregory Maining, whose age and appearance suggested he might require Mr Fleming's professional services at any time, came forward to pay his last respects.

'Do I have to . . . ?' Madeline did not complete the question, and the undertaker suppressed a shudder.

'It would not be advisable, me lady.'

'No,' he told himself, there would be no chaste kisses on foreheads, not with all that pancake make-up, and those not-to-be-trusted eyelids. He trembled when Sir Gregory bent over the coffin, but relaxed when he realised the ancient baronet was only short-sighted.

The distinguished assembly shuffled by, then when the last one had passed out of the room, Mr Fleming whipped out his screwdriver and waved his assistant forward. 'Snappy, lad, the lid.'

There was really no need to worry, the stitches on the eyelids were holding nicely.

Thirty-two carriages followed the hearse, and most of the villagers trailed behind the carriages, for someone had spread the completely unfounded rumour that there was free beer for one and all once the service was over. Madeline and the distant cousin sat in the Walton family pew, and listened to the Vicar who was endowing the departed one with all the virtues his imagination could devise, and his conscience permitted. It was midway during this discourse when the congregation was disturbed by a late-comer. One oak, nail-studded door creaked open and a little old lady dressed in a rusty black dress, with a frayed veil covering her face, came shuffling down the aisle. With lowered head and bowed shoulders, looking to neither left or right, she moved slowly forward, her old cracked shoes beating out a tattoo on the paved floor. She did not pause until she reached the Walton pew, then one black gloved hand reached out, opened the low door, and Madeline could only stare with startled astonishment as the black-clad bundle seated itself beside her. The little head, completely masked by the thick, frayed veil, turned slowly, and a low, hollow whisper reached Madeline's ear.

'His sister. Come to pay my last respects.'

The Vicar finally decided he had stretched truth to very near breaking point, and informed the congregation it would now sing hymn five hundred and thirty-seven: 'Peace, perfect peace, in this dark world of sin.'

Everyone got to their feet, all save Sir Gregory who looked as if it were scarcely worth his while going home; the organ thundered out the tune, the congregation sang more or less in time, and Madeline could hear a hollow little voice at her side droning a completely unrecognisable dirge, except when everyone else sang 'sin', the old lady intoned 'tin'.

The Walton family vault stood behind the church; a massive granite structure with solid teak doors, which had an inscription etched out in the stonework above them. Harold nudged Madeline while they waited for the coffin to be carried through the doorway, and together they deciphered the weather-blurred letters.

HERE YE WALTONS SLEEPE
GOD GRANT THEY ALL LYE DOWN

Within the vault a flight of stone steps ran down to a crypt some twenty feet beneath the churchyard; a long room, perhaps thirty feet by fifteen, with stone shelves lining the walls from ceiling to floor, each one divided into niches capable of accommodating a single coffin. Madeline looked round and gripped Harold's arm while the Vicar said all that remained to be said. Most of the coffins were in a remarkable state of preservation, although some of the older ones looked as if they might give way if interfered with. One sagged ominously, while another had its lid displaced; Madeline watched as Charles was put into an empty niche, then with more haste than dignity followed the vicar up the steps to the blessed daylight outside.

Without waiting for an invitation the little old lady, who had stood in the churchyard during the interment, clambered into the Walton carriage and sat between Harold and Madeline; a black motionless little figure, that once the door closed gave off a faint musty smell. Madeline found she must either speak or scream. She decided to speak.

'I was not aware that Charles had a sister. He never spoke about you.'

The veiled head turned, and Madeline wondered why the old horror wore no hat.

'I don't suppose he would have, dear.' It was a strange voice, hollow, as though the speaker were in a vast empty room. 'You see, we've been parted a long while, and I was much older than he.'

'I see. Do you live far away?'

There was a suggestion of a chuckle; a rasping crackle.

'Not all that distant, dear.'

Madeline felt slightly relieved; she had been troubled lest this creature might expect to be put up at the manor. The old woman appeared to have read her thoughts.

'Don't worry yourself about me, dear. I've got me own key.'

The young people exchanged glances, and Harold touched his forehead with an expressive finger.

'No,' the hollow voice went on, 'I only want to look at the old place again, and pick something up.'

'Pick something up!' Harold spoke for the first time. 'What? Everything belongs to Madeline now. There were no bequests.'

Again there was a rasping chuckle.

'Oh, nothing valuable, dear. Just something small, but very necessary.'

There was no further conversation for the remainder of the journey, and when they arrived at the manor Harold put out a hand to help the old lady down, but she brushed it aside.

'Thank you, dear, but I'll manage. I don't like being gripped by a young hand. You see . . .' slowly she clambered down to the ground, '. . . I'm a bit fragile.'

The old lady was forgotten once the post-funeral guests arrived. They sat or stood in the east drawing room, drinking Madeira and munching sandwiches, while discussing Madeline and her distant cousin in respectful undertones.

'A barmaid,' observed one straight-backed dowager, 'or at the very best, a chorus girl.'

'Shouldn't be surprised.' Her son fitted a monocle into his perfectly normal right eye. 'Well set-up little filly though. Wouldn't mind trying my luck there. I mean to say – half a million.'

There was only one small incident before the assembly broke up. Mr Fleming appeared in the doorway, not of course daring to actually enter the room; he looked anxiously from left to right. Harold was the first to notice him.

'What is it, Mr Fleming? 'Fraid we can't offer you a drink. We have no beer.'

'That's all right, Sir. But you see I've lost something, and it was valuable as such things go. It had a solid silver handle.'

'What?' demanded Harold, waving a hand in an extravagant gesture, for with a pint of Madeira inside him he was now quite mellow. 'What have you lost?'

Mr Fleming's face was quite comical in its distress.

'Me screwdriver, Sir. Somebody's pin . . .' He restrained himself just in time. 'I've mislaid me presentation screwdriver. I put it down on the 'all table, now it's gone.'

*

Madeline and Harold were having tea when the old lady made her next appearance. The young man was expressing his desire for a cash advance from the estate, and Madeline was wondering if she could bear to change her title for a plain Mrs, when she saw his jaw drop. Turning around she almost screamed. The little black figure was shuffling across the carpet having made a silent entrance through the french windows. She was still clad in the decrepit black dress, the thick frayed veil still hiding her face, and in one gloved hand she clutched a silver-handled screwdriver. She laid it on the tea table, then lowered her frail body into a chair before speaking in that disturbing hollow voice.

'I've brought it back, dear, as I said I would.'

'Thank you.' The young widow stared at the silver handle that was dull and smeared, and decided that nothing on earth would make her touch it, then became aware of the musty smell. It was stronger than when she had first noticed it in the carriage, and the old woman must have seen her look of distaste.

'Warm, dear. Very warm today. I shouldn't be out and about in weather like this, if you understand. Not before sunset really.'

Conversation lagged for a little while; Harold looked at his plate and gave the impression he might be sick, given the slightest encouragement: Madeline gulped and wondered how quickly they could get rid of this most unwelcome visitor. The old woman looked round the tea-table.

'Cakes for tea!' It was more of a statement of fact than a question.

'Would you . . . ?' Madeline began, but was interrupted by a low crackling chuckle.

'No, dear, I can't keep solids down.'

There was another awkward silence, then the girl asked:

'Is there anything I can get you?'

'Yes, dear. Two things. First – a pair of scissors.'

'Scissors!' Madeline's voice was only just above a whisper, and Harold echoed her:

'Scissors!'

'Just a small pair; such as you might cut your nails with – or small stitches.'

'I've got a pair in my handbag.'

The black head nodded its approval.

'Get them, dear.'

Madeline rose, went over to the sideboard and presently came back with a pair of nail scissors; they disappeared somewhere in the folds of that black, foul dress.

'Thank you, dear.'

Again, there was a long silence; Madeline could hear the marble clock on the mantelpiece tick away the seconds, then:

'You wouldn't have a crutch about the house?'

Such a question could not be answered by words; Madeline shook her head.

'I thought not.' A harsh, rasping – something – that bore some comparison to a sigh followed. 'What about a broom?'

'A broom!' Madeline managed to repeat the word: Harold appeared incapable of saying anything.

'Yes, dear. A broom. A useful substitute for a crutch, specially if it's got a nice soft head. You see, an old party I know has a broken leg. Very nasty, just over the knee, and it stops him getting about. And he badly wants to get about tonight.' She cackled again. 'A sort of – family outing.'

Madeline said 'Ah!' and Harold made a guggling noise.

'Yes, it wouldn't be right if he couldn't – rattle along with the rest. A little walk after sunset will do him a lot of good; he'll rest much easier afterwards. So a broom, dear, if it's not too much trouble. Perhaps your young man wouldn't mind popping down to the kitchen.'

Harold gasped, sounding very much like a puppy that has had its tail trodden on. The veil turned in his direction and the hollow voice was raised slightly.

'I wouldn't like to use nasty words, dear. Words like, arsenic, tin, that wasn't buried deep enough, murder, that could lead to a very nasty word called – rope. Run along and get a nice broom, there's a good boy.'

Harold's white face turned slightly green, as he retreated backwards, seemingly unable to take his eyes from that sinister black figure, and flinched when Madeline screamed:

'Don't leave me alone with her.'

The small black hand seized her wrist in an iron grip, but the hollow voice was still gentle, only now it was faintly mocking.

'You wouldn't leave your old auntie, would you, dear? The young man won't be long, because if he is I'll think of some more nasty words. Like, hangman, neck, grave . . .' The unseen eyes again looked at Harold. 'Are you still here, dear?'

Harold disappeared so quickly an observer might have been forgiven had he supposed the young man had suddenly acquired invisible wings. Madeline tried to pull her wrist free, but to no avail.

'Charles is not happy, dear,' the black head was shaken in mock reproof, 'not what you might call happy at all. I mean, arsenic, so crude, so – forgive me, so working-class. A little something on the stairs he might have understood, not forgiven you understand, but appreciated. Cold steel would have aroused his admiration, for no gentleman can complain about being killed with cold steel. But poison! Such a nasty, underhanded way of doing someone dirt.'

'It was Harold's idea,' Madeline sobbed. 'I was all for pushing him out of the window, but Harold said that as Charles was suffering from stomach trouble, the doctor would never suspect anything was wrong.'

'But Charles did.' The old woman nodded so vigorously, Madeline experienced a fresh spasm of fear lest that veil fell off. 'The moment he felt the death rattle coming on, he knew. Why, bless your heart, the Waltons have suffered from upset tummies ever since Great-great-great-Grandfather Roderick came back from Transylvania in 1763. But it never killed them; the trouble was their diet, dear. They should never have taken solids. At least never eaten on an empty stomach.'

Harold came back with his broom; the old lady took it handle foremost.

'You haven't been long, dear. Now I best be getting back, in this warm weather, I'm apt to get a little sticky.'

She walked very slowly to the french windows using the broom as a staff; just before she went out into the garden she paused and spoke without turning her head.

'There'll be a full moon tonight, and we like doing our business by moonlight.' She moved forward, and they could hear her hollow voice still intoning: 'By moonlight – by moonlight.'

There was a dull thud: Harold had fainted.

The sun set, and they had not come to the all-important decision; they argued the whys and wherefores; then when the moon rose fear had its cold, clammy way with them, and they ordered the carriage, packed two small bags, and prepared to depart.

The servants collected in small groups, so many whispering shadows; and Soames the butler carried the bags down to the carriage, his face as unrevealing as a blank sheet of paper. The coachman, heavy, bemantled, looked gloomily over the horses' heads, and there was unspoken suspicion in the air.

'To the station, hurry.' Madeline's voice was made sharp by fear, and the coachman muttered, 'Right, me lady,' as Soames closed the offside door.

Within five minutes the village was left behind and the flat moorland lay out beneath the moon; bleak, sad, and even on this summer night, wind-swept. The mournful cry of an owl – or something – was a warning, or a signal, and the girl clutched her companion's arm, but he needed comfort as much, if not more, than she.

Jenkins the coachman sat high up on his box and allowed his thoughts to feed upon what he knew, guessed or plainly surmised.

'Making a bolt for it,' he muttered. 'I wonder if . . .'

Then he shuddered and remembered what his father, long dead, had said he saw; and how the old women of the village wise in the knowledge of 'Rather not be seen at any price', related with grisly relish what they had seen, heard, or only sensed. It was not good to recall such memories when sitting high up on a coach box with the open moor spread wide around one, knowing full well that the churchyard was but a mile away.

'God grant that they all lie down.' The quotation slipped, unbidden, into his mind, and he crossed himself, as had his forebears for three hundred years. A small black figure was crossing the moor over to his far left; a dog, he hoped, or a stray sheep, but there was little comfort in the supposition, for the figure bobbed up and down, suggesting the use of two feet instead of four, and was making for a position in the road where it would intercept the carriage. He shook the reins but the horses seemed to be reluctant to go faster, and his shudder turned to violent trembling when he saw other figures rising from the heather. Then, black-clad creatures that covered the ground with astonishing speed. One, supported by a crutch, was fairly bounding along, and as the coach drew nearer to this hideous pack, the horrified man heard his name called out by a hollow but – now his teeth rattled – recognisable voice.

'Jenkins – Jenkins . . .'

'By the saints – the old man.'

He gasped out the words, and pulled hard on the left rein, swinging the coach round in a wide arc, determined to race back along the road he had come. But the voice became a howl of rage.

'Jenkins – Jenkins . . .'

The horses stopped of their own accord and stood trembling, and neither rein or whip would make them move.

'Jenkins,' Madeline's voice was a plaintive cry, 'why have we stopped?'

There was a sound of breaking heather, plus a strange, heart-stopping cracking, such as leg sockets might make when they have not been used in a long while, and a flapping of scarecrow rags, and occasional crackling laughter. Jenkins came to a decision.

'Get out.'

He fell, rather than clambered down from his seat, and wrenched open the carriage door. 'Get out, it's you two they want, not me.'

He was mad with fear, his normal strength trebled by terror. Madeline was pulled savagely from her seat and flung on to the ground; Harold clung to the far door, and Jenkins had to half climb into the coach and brutally club the gibbering wretch with his clenched fist before he could be yanked free.

'It's your sin,' Jenkins spared a glance at the sprawling figures, 'may God help you.' Then he was up in his seat, and the horses, now free from their paralysis, leapt forward, and the carriage tore away down the road to the village.

The old woman arrived first, peering down at them through her thick veil; an old man came next, his face black skin, his eyes white marbles; one might have been a young girl – once. Her face was leper white, but her eyes were yellow, like a hungry wolf. Another man was silver-haired, red eyed, with green patches on his yellow skin; but one thing they all had in common was – teeth. White, gleaming in the moonlight, the eyeteeth unnaturally long; fangs that dimpled their chins. They all stood in a circle, thirty or forty of them; Madeline did not try to count.

'We have all matured,' the old woman observed, 'in our different ways.'

One figure stepped forward – or bobbed, or hobbled; he was supported by a broom, its soft head nestling snugly under the left armpit; one leg swung to and fro, and his well-fed smirk shrank to a hungry grin as he spat out cotton-wool. Tiny cotton threads hung down over the bulging eyes, but he was well dressed; quite the smartest one present. The grin did not shift, the rouge red lips did not move when he spoke:

'Poisoner – adulteress . . . The last meal you gave me was bitter, this one will be sweet. Sweet and warm.'

'Charles,' the old woman said gently, 'you must have patience. She took life, now she will give life – of a kind. The young man too, and him we will drain dry.' Her black hands – they were not gloved after all – came slowly up to her veil. 'My, but they are succulent morsels. We'll all feel the better for them both.'

The circle closed in, and the old woman muttered angrily as Harold screamed: 'Don't push, my dears, there's enough for all.'

The last thing Madeline saw this side of the vault was the old woman's black bloated face, and the last words she heard were:

'Welcome to the family, my dear.'

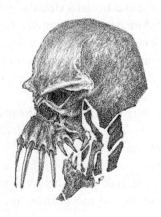

RUDOLPH

Since you insist on my telling all – as the saying goes – I'll start from the beginning. Yes, I think that's best. Someone should know what's going on, even if I can't believe half of it myself. But I've got to, seeing as how most of what I'm going to tell you happened to me. Me, Laura Benfield, who at thirty-seven years and three months, lived quite comfortably on a small income my mother had left me, together with the house.

Then I did a part time job, nothing strenuous you understand, for I'm not all that strong, just addressing envelopes for a mail order firm three days a week. Then that bastard Michel Adler came into my life and lit a bomb under me.

What? No, I don't mean literally. For God's sake! But it would have been kinder if he had. Handsome bastard he was. Looked like Errol Flynn in *Captain Blood* that I saw on telly twice. And charm! He could bring the birds down from the trees and worms out of the ground and get 'em to play hop-scotch together.

I met him at the Byfleet Social Club when I was sweating on a full house at bingo. I was just one number missing – legs eleven it was, but of course with my luck a cow from Tyburn Avenue got it. Not legs eleven, but five and three, fifty-three, which filled her house for her.

Then I hears this voice, all soft and gentlemanly like, say:

'Damn bad luck, old dear,' and turning I sees him for the first time.

You know I went right weak at the knees, there and then, me who normally would never talk to a strange man. He had grey eyes, the sort that sort of twinkle and seem to be full of mischief. Know what I mean?

Well, not to make mincemeat out of a cold sausage, when he suggested we have coffee in the club room, I accepted like a shot and made sure Maud Perkins saw me hanging on to the arm of this sexpot, although when we were seated side by side near a ruddy great mirror that some sadistic bastard had stuck on the wall so that it took in the entire room, I began to ask myself where the catch was.

I mean, every woman there from sixteen to eighty was giving him the what-about-it sign and I – let's be honest – had nothing bed-wise to offer. There again they do say beauty is in the eye of the beholder, so I thought maybe my eye was missing out on some of my beauty. Any road that was the only explanation I could think of, for boy, did he give me the treatment.

After pouring coffee down me, he suggests dinner in some quiet restaurant wouldn't be out of place, he having not eaten since breakfast, due to being run off his feet by business commitments. It seemed that he had popped in the bingo club to unwind, for hearing numbers shouted out over a loud speaker had a relaxing effect on him. He also said it was the play of my features that directed his attention to me, suggesting as they did I had a beautiful soul, which was reflected in my eyes.

No one has ever talked to me like that before and although you may think I'm a silly 'apporth to be taken in by stuff like that, just you remember that in every plain, dull woman, there's a beautiful, interesting one trying to get out. And he knew how to order a good dinner and wines with names I couldn't even pronounce, and when he left the waiter two pounds as a tip, I thought he must really be on the top shelf spondulicks-wise.

Then he took me home and I felt awful about inviting him in, for the place hasn't seen a decorator's brush since my mum died and truth to tell, I'm no great dab at housework. But he – Michel – only laughed and said the house had character and personally he had no time for your spotless and everything in its place living unit, where it was impossible for anyone to feel comfortable.

Well, I had nothing in the house in the booze line, except for a few bottles of brown ale and I couldn't offer him that after all the wine and liquors he'd lashed out for on me. But he said he'd just as soon have a cup of tea, which he made, after telling me to sit down and put me feet up.

Then we talked. Even now, I have to admit that man had a wonderful brain. He told me all about the stars and how this world is only one among millions of suns and things and there must be billions of civilisations and one day clever, but funny-looking creatures will either visit us or we'll visit them and . . .

Sorry. I didn't mean to break down like that, but when I think how things could have been if he hadn't turned out to be a crook, me heart's fit to break.

Anyway he came to see me quite often and took me out once or twice a week, always somewhere swanky, but there was one thing I thought was strange. After he'd paid the bill, he entered the amount in a little black book. He said it was so he could claim it back against tax, which didn't sound right, for a friend once told me that you can only get tax rebate for entertaining foreign buyers, but I didn't say anything, just supposed he knew his business best.

Then he got to talking about money, saying that lots of people did not realise they were sitting on thousands, until the matter was brought to their attention.

'Let's take your case, Laura,' he said, 'that house of yours, you could raise forty thousand quid on it any day. Invested by someone who knows his business, you could double it within six months, pay back the mortgage and use the extra thirty thou for further investments. That kind of thinking has laid the basis of many a fortune. I know – that's the way I started out.'

Honestly it sounded right, particularly the way he put it, and when I said I wouldn't like to mortgage my mum's house, he said fair enough, he was only talking about what could be done, but God forbid he should influence me in any way. But if I should ever consider the idea, he'd be pleased to help me.

The seed had fallen on fertile ground, if you get my meaning. All of us could do with some more money, and the very thought of having thirty thousand nicely invested made me feel good. So one day I said I'd like to investigate the possibilities a little further – and that was it.

He cleaned me out in three weeks.

He did all the paperwork – all I had to do was sign, the milkman witnessing my signature. First the mortgage on the house, then liquidating my little investments, for Michel said they were only chicken feed and he'd do much better for me. He explained for tax reasons all the money would be paid into a bank account under his name . . .

Thank you for the handkerchief, sir, these little lace things he brought me are no good when you shed buckets as I've been doing over the past few months.

What? Of course . . . well I had to get myself a proper job, didn't I? I mean I was down on my uppers. The house gone, me in a shabby bed-sit and not a penny coming in. I got taken on by a local store, but I wasn't really fitted for it. Me ankles swelled up with all that standing and when the customers got nasty, I answered back, which didn't please their mightinesses on the sixth floor, so I was soon out on my ear.

Then I read this advertisement. See? I've got the newspaper cutting here?

COOK HOUSEKEEPER required by single gentleman. Live-in all found. Salary by negotiation. Ring Mr Rudolph Acrudal 753.9076.

As I've said I'm not all that good at housekeeping, but I'm not all that bad at cooking, so long as no one expects anything fancy. And with a single gentleman there's no woman to find fault – so why not?

The voice that answered the phone sounded genteel, which reassured me, for I find educated gentry are more easily pleased than your jumped-up-come-by-nights, and it was agreed I should come round right away, so I gave Mr Acrudal (pronounced Ac-ru-dal. I must say it took a bit of getting used to) my name and hired a taxi, for it's just as well to give the impression that you're not hard-up when applying for a job, and got myself driven to the address the gentleman had given me over the phone.

An old Victorian terrace house it was, four storeys high including the basement, with a flight of cracked grey steps leading up to the front door. The place didn't look so much run down as

neglected, and I could imagine an old bachelor who just couldn't
be bothered to have it done up.

He answered the door – Mr Rudolph Acrudal – a tall lean man
who could have been any age. Honestly, I couldn't make up my
mind if he was a worn-out thirty, or a young seventy. He had a
mass of black hair sort of sprinkled with white, as though he had
been painting the ceiling and splashed white paint over his hair.

High cheekbones and a hooked nose and two long eye-teeth that
dimpled his lower lip, which I might as well say were black. The
lips I mean. His ears tapered to a sharp point at the top, making
him – what with sunken black eyes – look like those old prints of
the devil. He wore a tight-fitting black suit that included stove-pipe
trousers. True. I swear on oath. He jerked his head back and forth
several times and then said in a rusty kind of voice:

'Miss Benfield – yes? Good. Come in – don't just stand there.
The sun may come out at anytime and that won't be good for my
health.' And he all but pulled me into a hall that stunk of damp
and what could have been burnt fat, and where every floorboard
creaked when you took a step forward, to say nothing of the odd
flake of plaster that floated down from the ceiling, particularly
when Mr Acrudal slammed the front door.

He led the way into a front room that looked even worse than
the hall, being mostly dominated by a giant old desk and a mixture
of books and papers that lay everywhere. Honestly I thought for a
moment it was the dumping area for Let's-have-all-your-old-books-
and-newspapers-week. But he upended one wooden armchair, so
that everything on it – including a huge tom cat – slid on to the
floor. He half sat on the desk and gave me the doings.

'My wants are simple. Breakfast – black pudding on toast. Lunch
– pig's blood mixed with lightly done mince. Dinner – the same.
Nightcap – a glass of pig's blood.' He looked at me intently. 'How
does that strike you?'

I spoke boldly – it always pays in the long run: 'Well, sir, it
wouldn't suit me, but if that's what you want – I'll try to make it
as tasty as possible.'

He jerked his head up and down and I could swear he was dribbling as though the very thought of his favourite diet had started
his mouth watering. 'Good. The last housekeeper I had, heaved up

when she saw me shovelling in the mince and blood. That's settled
then. You have a free hand. Make sure I'm fed and moistened three
to four times a day and you can do what you like.'

I said, 'Thank you, sir. I can see there's plenty to do. And where
will my quarters be?'

'Wherever you care to make them. Plenty of empty rooms on
all floors. I use this one and the one next door. No need for you to
go in there. As for money . . .'

'I was about to mention that, sir.'

He bent down and brought forth a large old carpet-bag from
beside the desk, which he dropped in my lap. When I opened it
I found wads of bank notes – fifty pounds, tens and fivers. Mr
Acrudal waved a dirt-grimed hand.

'Pay yourself a hundred a week, then take whatever is needed
for housekeeping.'

I shook my head firmly. 'That won't do at all, sir. We won't
know where we are. I'd like you to keep this bag somewhere safe
and pay me whatever is required each week.'

His face – white as a pig's belly – took on a real bad-tempered
expression and I thought to myself: I wouldn't like to cross you,
me lord, that I wouldn't. For now, his face from dead white turned
to a light grey. Very off-putting it was. Never seen anything like
it before. Then he kind of spluttered out words it took me some
time to understand.

'Don't . . . ar . . . r . . . g . . . u . . . e . . . with . . . me . . . m . . .
m . . . e . . . w . . . o . . . m . . . m . . . a . . . n . . . D . . . o . . . o . . . o
. . . a . . . s . . . I . . . say.'

He scared the wits out of me and I was about to give him a
piece of my mind and then walking out, when I remembered the
cold bed-sit and the two quid and small change in my handbag,
so I nodded like an idiot and said: 'All right, sir . . . calm down. I'll
make a note of all the money I take and let you have a statement
once a week.'

He did calm down, but appeared to be tired out as though the
outburst had drained him.

I got out of the room as fast as my legs would take me and after
I had cooled down a bit, began to explore the house. The kitchen I
found in the basement, if the grease-lined hell-hole could be iden-

tified in any way as a place for preparing food. Do you know there was an old rusty iron range that heated an antiquated boiler with a tap on one side. A plain deal table collapsed when I tried to move it. Damp rot had done its worst to the floorboards and I almost broke an ankle when my foot sank into rotting wood. I made up my mind then and there – the kitchen was a write-off.

I chose a room two floors up that commanded a view of the overgrown back garden and decided to take a thick wad of notes from the bag and buy a portable oil stove and a complete set of saucepans.

But number one question. When did the old devil want feeding next?

I looked at my watch and saw that the time was twelve-fifteen, so it would be reasonable to suppose that lunch – pig's blood and mince – should be served around one o'clock. Frankly I lacked the courage to ask Mr Acrudal where the nauseating mixture could be found – or obtained, but finally I went down into the hall and found a gold-coloured round tin that contained about three pints of thick blood and a bulging newspaper parcel.

I could sympathize with my predecessor who heaved when she saw her employer tuck into this muck, particularly when my nose told me the mince – and maybe the blood as well – was most definitely off.

I washed an iron saucepan as best I could, bunged the soggy mess into it and actually managed to stew it over an old hurricane lamp I found in one corner of the so-called kitchen.

I did my best to flavour this horrible concoction (boiling blood explodes into evil-smelling blisters) with pepper and salt, plus a nutmeg I found the large cat playing with, while pretending fat healthy maggots weren't being done to death down below.

At one o'clock precisely I carried a tin tray on which slid back and forth a deep bowl containing bubbling, flavoured, blood-seeped, spice mince. I had also succeeded in washing a dessert spoon, and after pushing the door open with my right knee, lurched across the littered floor to where the old-young man sat behind his desk. He really brightened up when he saw me with the tray and when I bunged it down in front of him, he grabbed the spoon and began shovelling the mess in.

It was a dreadful sight and sound. Slop-slub-lip-smacking with what missed the target dribbling down his chin. When the bowl was half empty he paused for breath and expressed sincere appreciation.

'The best blushie I've tasted in years, Miss Benfield. You are talented . . . so talented. Just give me the same for dinner and we'll get along famously. I knew by your smell that we'd haunted the same track.'

I said primly, 'So pleased to give satisfaction, sir,' and backed out of the room. I didn't know what he meant by smell and could only regard the remark as some kind of insult.

Having taken care of my new employer's requirements, I began to sort out my own. I explored the house from attic to basement and confirmed my original opinion that neglect had resulted in devastation, but a few weeks' hard work could make the place at least livable again. But not by me. As money seemed to be no object, I decided to dig well down into that carpet bag and hire a cleaning firm; the kind of organization that takes care of offices and showrooms. In the meanwhile I turned out a small bedroom on the third floor, took over a quilted double divan that must have cost a pretty penny when new, shook the dust out of some red blankets, unwrapped pink sheets and pillow-cases that sometime in the past had been sent to a well-known laundry.

I uncovered three bedrooms – literally – and threw their contents out of a landing window and watched them land in an enclosed dank area. Two tubs had to be written off as what appeared to be cinders and wood ash had been thrown into at least six inches of water, resulting in corrosion that in some places had eaten through the metal. But one was still in reasonable condition and I managed to scrape it clean and plug two holes with putty that I found clinging to the banisters. By five o'clock that part of the house that I would be using was at least clear of surface rubbish and filth and I was free to think of my own needs.

I visited Mr Acrudal and to my disgust found he had licked the bowl clean and by his greedy enquiring look clearly thought I had brought a replacement.

I said, 'Sir, I will need money, mainly for food for myself and having this house cleaned from top to bottom.'

He put his head on to one side and looked not unlike an intelligent dog that is trying to understand what it is being told to do. Then there came from his throat what I can only describe as growled words.

'Cleaned . . . from . . . top . . . to . . . bottom?'

'Yes, sir. If you'll forgive me for saying so, the place is a disgrace the way it is. I was thinking of engaging a cleaning company.'

'More than two strangers . . . strangers . . . in . . . the . . . house?'

'Well, there's no way I can do all the work myself and we can't leave it the way it is.'

He reached down and produced that carpet bag again and dumped it on the desk. He fumbled around inside for a few moments and brought out a bundle of fifty pound notes that must have totalled at least seven hundred pounds. Then for the first time so far as I was concerned, he got up and eased his way round the desk, clutching the money in one hand and supporting himself with the other. I think there was something wrong with the left foot – or rather I thought so then. In fact as he drew nearer I couldn't dismiss the thought that he was in some way deformed, terribly deformed, although a slight limp was the only outward sign.

Then he was close up – breathing on me.

I all but choked on the stench of decay that might have seeped through water-logged churchyard loam. I retreated back one step, before his right hand formed a band of steel round my left arm and jerked me forward until our faces were only a few inches apart. Then he smiled, a strangely sweet smile that revealed beautiful white teeth and instantly I forgot his grotesque appearance, the foul breath and the oddness abut him; instead I became aware of a rising wave of excitement that later made me distrust my own senses. His voice came quivering from his open mouth as a thrilling whisper.

'Do whatever you wish . . . at all times the house is yours, but never . . . never . . . allow strangers . . . to cross my threshold.' His smile became more pronounced and such was my fascination I could even ignore those long eyeteeth. 'Please understand that. If work is too much . . . leave it. Confine yourself to preparing the so excellent blushie and I will demand no more.'

He released me, thrust the money into my hand, then returned to his chair and became engrossed in reading what looked like an old document.

After a while my limbs became once again capable of movement, so I bolted back into the hall and took refuge in the room I had requisitioned for my own use. The bundle of money still clutched in my left hand forbade all thoughts of decamping and making for the nearest YWCA for even the most incorruptible soul must surrender to greed when loot is constantly thrust into its vicinity.

But there was another reason why I would find it increasingly more difficult to leave this house, no matter how fearsome it might become.

Mr Rudolph Acrudal was without doubt ugly, repulsive and sinister, but I knew now he radiated some kind of charm that sooner or later I would find irresistible.

I got some kind of routine working – and surprised myself.

Mr Acrudal's rations came from the local butcher, who dumped can and parcel on the top step each morning, plus whatever I ordered for myself. I may add my spiced blushie so pleased my employer that he would eat nothing else – not even the black pudding, a fact that aroused the interest of the butcher when I paid him every Friday morning.

Having done things to an elaborate cash register, I was given a printed receipt, before a red face creased into a wide confidential grin.

'Tell us the truth, love. What the 'ell does he do with all this blood and mince? I mean it's not as though it comes from fresh meat. From the beginning I was told it must be high. Straight up. Warm, runny and smelly. And the blood – thickish.'

I always started out by giving the same answer: 'That's Mr Acrudal's business and mine,' but after a while the need to talk to someone who is nice to me, got the better of discretion and I finally admitted I had to cook the horrible mess which Mr Acrudal was so kind as to say he enjoyed. And although Mr Redwing – that was the butcher's name – expressed disbelief, I could see he wanted to believe and pass on what he believed to an enthralled public.

Then while carving me a nice piece of topside: 'No one seems to know what he looks like, him never coming out in daylight. Is it true he has 'orns under his hair?'

Of course I could only gasp. 'Of course not. It's not as bad as that. Don't be silly.'

I think it was about then that I became aware that the house was being watched. Not openly, but sometimes from a parked car, or the shadow cast by an old tree. Dark, squat, round-shouldered men was the only impression I got, never actually seeing them close-up, you understand. I wasn't all that worried, assuming that such was the interest as to what took place in the house, some nosy parker – or parkers – were hoping to catch a glimpse of Mr Acrudal at one of the windows.

I started another kitchen on the first floor, buying one of those elaborate oil stoves complete with oven and grill; and a table-high frig and sink unit. Getting the sink connected up without letting Mr Acrudal knowing, took a bit of organizing, but I did it by donning a boiler suit and putting in an occasional appearance in the Master's room, complaining how wrong it was for a woman to have to do this kind of work without help.

He never commented, but tried to hide behind a massive tome that looked as if it had been stored in a damp cellar for a few years. In fact all the books in that room gave me that impression. Any road by the end of the first month I had made myself as comfortable as the surroundings would permit and more or less adapted to what could only be called a bizarre situation. But that failing that my dear mother had so often stressed – had killed the cat – namely curiosity – would not give me any peace.

For example: he had never allowed me to see his bedroom or so much as move a book in that awful room where he spent so much of his time.

So I gave the rest of the house a good going over, and got the impression Mr Acrudal had been there a long time.

I found newspapers going back to 1870, some announcing the abdication of Napoleon III. Cupboards were crammed with them, some seemingly unopened, others with rectangular holes where paragraphs and entire columns had been cut out. I unearthed books bound in plain covers lacking both title and author, the script in some foreign language which I would never understand in a thousand years.

I was about to replace one when I saw a piece of paper sticking out from the middle pages, thrust in hurriedly I would imagine as a book marker, which turned out to be a letter written – thankfully – in English.

I would have you believe, Sir, that I do not as a rule pry into other people's correspondence; my mother raised me properly, but when you're eaten up by curiosity and badly want to know who – what – your employer is, you'd be a saint – which I beg leave to say I'm not – not to read a few lines scrawled on a piece of paper.

I can remember every word.

Rudolph, a word of warning: Total abstinence of essential fluid will age a body that should retain youth for nigh on eternity. Waste not the gift our sire gave you. The blushie diet will only sustain. H

And that was all. I put the paper back in the book, then settled down to have a good think. When I was a kid my dad was always swearing to practise Total Abstinence, which meant not drinking booze in any form whatsoever. His good intentions were usually drowned in about fourteen days.

But I had never heard booze called essential fluid – although my dad might have thought it was – and certainly couldn't entertain the idea *not* drinking the stuff would age the body. Quite the contrary I would have thought.

And my employer's diet was mainly blood and rotten meat. Blushie. To my mind the only nourishing meal he ever ate was his early morning black pudding – or blood sausage as I've heard it called. But now he'd given that up.

Blood!

It would seem that my employer needed blood in some form or another to sustain life, but according to H he wasn't getting it in the right quantities – or quality. In other words he wasn't getting the right kind of blood.

Yes, sir, I've seen my ration of horror films and my mind came up with the question: What kind of being needs a diet of blood to exist? – and supplied an instant answer.

A vampire.

And it was no use calling myself a silly twit and repeating 'Vampires don't exist' over and over again, for my bloody brain came up with another question: How do you know they don't exist? And I remembered the long eye-teeth and suddenly imagination created a fantasy-picture, complete with sound, touch and colour. I was being held by one large hand while the other tore my dress leaving my throat bare, hot stinking breath on my skin; then came a sharp pain and I became as a virgin on her wedding night, terrified, gasping – and shuddering with ecstasy.

'We were reckoning the other day,' Mr Redwing said, adjusting his straw hat to a more becoming angle, 'that your boss must have eaten his weight in rotten mince several times over. Doesn't he have any vegetables? Or salad?'

I'm not good at lying so I just shook my head.

'Thought not. My missus says if you just eat meat and nothing else, you're in line for scurvy. Like they did in Nelson's navy. Hope you look after yourself, love.'

'I do that. Plenty of salad and fruit. But is that true about scurvy?'

'Sure thing. Ask any doctor. Must have a balanced diet.'

After the lapse of three days I had come round to ridiculing the very idea of Mr Acrudal being a vampire. Or at least half convinced myself I was ridiculing the idea, which is almost the same thing. But certain facts could not be erased, particularly my employer's strange diet and the damned letter, which for my peace of mind, I should have never read.

Now Mr Redwing's little snippet of information had set fire to the dry grass of conjecture, highlighting the fantastic more vividly than ever. If a hundred percent protein diet resulted in scurvy, then Mr Acrudal should have been dead long ago. If one thought about his health at all, the only reasonable assessment must be neither good or bad, but Acrudal-normal.

So far as I knew he took no exercise, the only movement being from workroom to bedroom, with periodical visits to the bathroom. Presumably he washed there, but I was willing to swear he never took a bath or shaved. I assumed that his hair must grow, that is to say on his head, but his face remained smooth, which made me wonder if there was any hair on his body at all.

I had been in the house just over three months when Janice turned up.

She let herself in the front door, having it appeared her own key. A pretty, impudent teenager – or so she seemed – dressed in a white jersey with red stripes and a pair of well-washed jeans. Black, wind-blown hair, thick eyebrows and dark sparkling blue eyes. A broad intelligent face that seemed to be always lit by a faintly mocking smile, and really beautiful white skin that positively glowed with obscene good health. I noticed she had large well-shaped hands. When she spoke her voice had a brittle quality, enhanced by a slight foreign accent.

'Hallo, don't tell me you're the new cook and bottle-washer! I'm Janice, sort of niece to old thingy.'

I said, 'I'm pleased to meet you, miss. I've been Mr Acrudal's housekeeper for three months now. I'll inform your uncle you're here.'

She laughed, a lovely soul-warming sound in that dreadful house, and shook her head until the black hair bounced.

'No need. I'll surprise the old sod.'

And while I was shaking my head, for I've no time for bad language, to say nothing of disrespect for elders and betters, she pranced along the hall and without so much as a tap on the door, entered her uncle's room.

I heard a roar that had much in common with a lion suddenly spotting an extra and quite unexpected meat ration. When I arrived at the open doorway, I was greeted by a spectacle that both shocked and angered me.

She – Janice – was sitting on his lap and he had pulled the jersey down from her left shoulder and was pressing his lips into the white flesh, and she – brazen hussy – was laughing with head well back and turned towards the door, so that she was looking directly at me. To this day the picture is etched on my memory. The young girl with laughter expressed in every line on her face and Mr Acrudal pressing his lips into her bare shoulder, as though he were preparing to eat her.

And another smell had been added to those which already

pervaded the house – the smell of lust. But not the healthy lust that even a left-on-the-shelf type like me can understand, but something alien – foreign I think that means, sir – that made my flesh crawl. But I couldn't move, just stand there watching them; and gradually there came to me another emotion that filled me with self-disgust.

Jealousy.

I wished with revolting envy he was doing it to me.

The spell was broken when that wool jersey ripped exposing most of her back, for then she flowed off his lap, rolled across the floor, then sprang to her feet with one graceful bound that would not have disgraced a sleek, well-conditioned cat. She stood staring down at Mr Acrudal in his chair, her hands raised, the palms facing him.

'Steady on.' Her voice held a hint of menace. 'I'm one of the family, remember? So far – so good – or bad. And humey eyes are watching and the thing is going green.'

And she turned her head and grinned at me in such a fashion my hand itched to decorate her smooth white cheek with my finger-prints. But at least anger had set me free and I was able to run up to the makeshift kitchen and there whisk two eggs with a fork, consoling myself with the thought that if the young bitch wanted lunch, she could get it herself.

She came up some ten minutes later, the jersey pinned together with a safety pin, but still not doing much to cover the left shoulder.

I said, 'Yes, miss, anything I can do for you?' in a tone of voice that suggested I'd prefer her room to her company. At least that's what I intended to convey, but it didn't have any effect. She gave me another impudent grin, then sat on the table, swinging one leg.

'Have you got hot pants for the old sod? Don't get aereated, they all do, even if he is off-putting. You'll go crawling back regardless.'

'You insolent slut.'

She leaned over and actually tickled me under the chin. 'Am I? I expect you'd like to belt me, wouldn't you? But don't try it on, I could break your back in three different places before you'd raised a hand.' She giggled and put her head on to one side and I couldn't help admitting how pretty she looked. 'Funny how you humes pretend horror, but drop your knicks when one of the Count's by-blow's breathes on you. It's the smell what does it. Gets the old glands going.'

I sat down on a chair and took a shuddering breath and although I knew the veil must be torn from the face of truth, nevertheless curiosity fought a bitter battle with dread. Eventually I asked.

'What's all this in aid of, miss?'

How the little bitch laughed. Came right up close and ran one large beautiful hand down my leg, so that the desire I had kept so well under control, broke free and flooded my loins with liquid fire. And the safety pin must have come unfastened, for the torn jersey slipped down from her shoulder and I could see one rounded breast – and oh, my God! I didn't know where I was or what kind of machinery was ticking away in my body, and the house was saturated with evil – well it must have been, only what the hell is evil? – because how else were such thoughts belting around in my brain. Then her low, thrilling voice with its slight accent, spoke again.

'Oh, come off it. Don't tell me you don't know the score. Been in the house for three months or more, looked at him, smelt him, and not known him for a second generation vampire? The count's son? Sooner or later you'll be down under him taking the shagging of a lifetime, so that in around a year you'll drop a little humvam.'

I screamed, 'No!' and her laughter should have choked her.

'Yes. Yes . . . yes . . . yes. He likes the over-ripe, retarded type. The spark in the belly waiting to erupt into a mighty flame. After a session with my Lord the Prince Rudolph, my sort-of uncle, a stallion won't satisfy you. But,' she leaned over and inserted one long finger into the crease between my breasts, 'guess what. He, descended from the most ancient line in the world, is ashamed of being what he is. Son of the vampire king. He won't partake from the neck, or even intake vital essence from a bottle. Makes do with pig's blood and rich mince. That's why he looks so weird. And all he's got to do is imbibe once – and, oh boy, you'll see the difference. He almost gives way when I get to work on him, but no way. I don't mind slap bot and fumble, but no give with the vital. Well, it wouldn't be decent.'

I took a firm grip of my reeling senses, drove a shaft of iron through my quivering soul and transformed a spoonful of courage into a little spear of anger.

'You're a dirty little trollop, miss. At least that's what my old mum would have called you. You must have a mind like a cesspool, only it's probably so twisted you can't tell the difference between fact and fancy. Me, I'm going to hang on to my sanity and assume that dirty old man is over the edge, or if you prefer, up the pole, then get the hell out of this place.'

She patted my cheek and I smacked her hand away. 'You can't. No way. You've let him come real close and the smell of him is in your blood. And just supposing you were real strong and managed to get away – the pack would get you. The pack of shadmads. Or maybe as you're someone special – vammads. They've been watching the house since you arrived. Looking after you. Once they get on your track they never let up until you're a flabby bag of nothing in the gutter. No hume ever lives to spill the beans on the family.'

I closed my eyes and muttered a kind of prayer.

'Let me disbelieve now and know I am protected by invisible angels and can never be pulled down. Never.'

Her giggling flooded my being with cold wavelets and for the first time I knew my soul was confined in a castle that crouched half way up a flame-tipped mountain, where it waited for death to set it free. And in the valley there waited the demons, the unnamed, who feed on immortal essence, and breathe their fire-dreams into our sleeping brains.

Large beautiful hands stroked my naked thighs and I screamed total, absolute surrender.

'Take me to him,' I screamed. 'Take me to him.'

She purred a soft little chuckle.

'That's why I came. Uncle Rudolph must be up and around soon, there's so much for him to do. Help bend time for example. And he must have that what is essential for him to look young again.'

She was behind me, her hand on my breasts, guiding me out of the room, down the stairs. Realization of what lay in store made me struggle when we crossed the hall, and the mere sight of him – immortal son of Dracula – seated on the desk, exploded a fear bomb in my stomach and I passed into a fire-streaked darkness where the five senses merged into one, or took on an extra.

Tell me, sir, you might know, is it possible for all of us to have extra senses that sleep within our bodies, but could be awakened if the conditions are right – or wrong?

They – Mr Acrudal and the young bitch – did something to me, for it seemed as if I slid down a tunnel through days, weeks and months, even years, and only allowed me to pop my head up through a ventilation hole, once now and again.

Did they bury me? If not, then how is it I can still remember the cloying dampness pressing on me everywhere; breathing rich soil that gave me a joyous half-sleeping life. Every now and again I became aware of one of their faces gazing down at me, his grown strangely young, glowing with a special kind of beauty that I suddenly realised had always been lurking just beneath the surface.

My blood gave a deeper red to his lips, my vital essence lit candles in his eyes; weakness fought tingling strength in my veins; blood had been replaced by something more interesting. Strangely, I cannot remember during that twilight period being other than happy. Or if not happy, then blissfully content. I became dimly aware that somewhere along the road to eternity I would take a dark turning and never come back, but even that prospect could not mar the safely insulated present.

I came to understand, sir, that fear and even dread can so easily change from black to bright red. Can you understand that?

The birth pangs were muted.

Like having a tooth pulled when the cocaine hasn't quite taken effect. I mentioned that dread had changed from black to bright red, well, during the birth I existed in a red mist. I could see the young bitch (only she wasn't young), moving about, feel her hands on me, forcing my legs apart, but when she and Mr Acrudal spoke, their voices seemed to come from a long way off and I couldn't understand a word they were saying.

The explosion that tore my guts apart rocketed me into full consciousness for around two minutes and I felt the agony, the pure seething terror and knew . . . knew – knew actually what I was giving birth to, but then he, Mr Acrudal, Prince Rudolph, filled my brain with wonderful pictures, so that fear, the pain, the knowledge, were banished and I was permitted to sink back into my nice cosy insulated happiness.

I awoke in my own bed.

That which had come from my body was confined to a black wooden cradle and when it raised its head and spat at me, I screamed and strained at the broad straps which only permitted limited movement. Even now, sir, when more immediate horror whimpers just beyond that door, a cold shudder sends limb-freezing dread down my body, when I think of that tiny face twisted up into a grimace, hissing like a snake, then spitting . . . No, please don't ask me to describe it. Please don't . . . Thin and white, two jutting teeth, black gleaming eyes . . . yes, like those of a snake? a black mamba . . .

Rudolph was very gentle with me – the young bitch had disappeared for the time being – and he explained over and over again that it would improve beyond recognition in time, become beautiful, as did the entire race down to the fourth generation. The right nourishment took care of that. But . . . but – I will be all right, sir, in just a minute – but I must tell you . . . must . . . he said for the first few weeks I must . . . feed . . . feed it . . . but . . . he explained wonderfully . . . it was not milk it needed . . . so it wouldn't suck . . . but bite . . . chew . . . chew . . . sometimes nibble . . . nibble . . .

After two weeks they took the thing I had bred away from me, which may have saved the remnants of my sanity, for it had begun to develop tiny claws on fingers and feet, although I was assured that they would soon disappear, being in fact the equivalent of milk teeth.

Rudolph – how beautiful he had grown – fed me on stewed mince and maybe because I didn't think about it too much, it tasted quite nice and most certainly did me good. I put on weight and when I was quite strong – and not before, for he really was most considerate – the Prince took my left hand in his and explained all I needed to know.

Actually all he wanted was to live a quiet eternity writing a history of his illustrious family, but it would seem it was his duty once now and again, to father an offspring, which would be a half-breed, but help spread the Dracula blood among the humes. Only a woman who could remain in that dreadful house for not less than three lunar months, was suitable for vam breeding.

Rudolph bared his sharp white teeth in an engaging smile that I found to be so irresistible. 'You are to be congratulated, my dear. Many were interviewed, few were chosen.'

'And what happens to me now?' I asked.

He sighed deeply. 'Why did you have to ask that question? Whatever answer I give is certain to hurt. I should put you down, but I lack the necessary ruthlessness. So, I am going to set you free. Whatever happens will not be the result of my action. Take my advice, get well away from the house. Travel by day. The pack are not happy in daylight and whimper most piteously when caught under the naked sun. I cannot give you hope for a long life, for that on reflection will not be desirable, but you may derive some satisfaction in evading the pack for a quite considerable period.

'Tell someone of your experience if you so wish and it eases your mind by doing so. No one will believe, but a version may be passed on and that will give birth – in the fullness of time – to an interesting legend. But of course should someone even half believe and start to investigate – more work for the pack.'

The pack.

He always pronounced that word in a peculiar way, as though it were distasteful to him and its implication something no gentle-man would ever consider. Oddly enough, I did not even think about it, although at the back of my mind I knew what eventually my fate would be. The young bitch had told me plainly enough.

Instead, I began to wonder who prepared the wonderful meals that were served up on a wooden tray and came to the conclusion it must be Rudolph. A gifted family and, when necessary, domesticated. After all, the original count cooked excellent meals for Jonathan Harker and made his bed into the bargain. Yes, he actually gave me *Dracula* to read.

Then came the morning when he kissed me on the lips and as always my legs turned to jelly and you would never believe how young and beautiful he looked.

My luggage stood in the hall, but I couldn't really believe I'd have a use for it – not now. The young bitch opened the door and I ignored her impudent grin, but I will confess I'd go to my end more happily after an hour alone with her, just supposing she was tied down or something.

'Goodbye,' Rudolph whispered. 'There's plenty of money in your handbag. More than you'll ever need.'

A taxi stood waiting and someone – Rudolph I suppose – carried my luggage out and piled it at my feet. Then I was away and again knew nothing until the cab drew up outside a rather dingy hotel. The driver spoke over one shoulder.

'The Imperial, ma'am. That was where I was told to bring you.'

I must have blacked out or maybe time-jumped forward a few hours, for I remember nothing more until finding myself lying on a double bed looking up at a cracked ceiling.

And you want to hear something really weird? I was homesick for that awful old house and Rudolph and the young bitch. I think I must have passed around three days eating and sleeping, and quite possibly have remained in that hotel until my money ran out, if I had not seen them from my window.

It must have been early evening for the street was silver-gold with lamplight and I could easily see the black car standing opposite with three or four figures leaning against it, staring up at my window. Dressed entirely in black, with long dog-like faces; jutting mouths, black lips, flattened noses, tapering ears and gleaming red-tinted eyes. I breathed one word:

'The pack!'

I'd forgotten them.

I sat by the window and watched them all night. So far as I could see not one moved until the first streak of dawn lit the grey roofs. Then they all piled into the car and drove away.

I left the hotel ten minutes later and have been more or less on the move ever since. But the pack have never really been far behind and I've no doubt are somewhere in this vicinity now. I've seen them several times, but they keep their distance, because I suppose I'm not quite ready for the kill yet. When I leave, sir, it might be well if, for your own sake, you waited for a while before leaving. Don't let them think you're at all interested in me. But you may

be safe enough, for Rudolph said I could tell my story, but it's best
not to take risks.

Well I'll be on my way. Thank you for being such a good lis-
tener – and, yes, buying me that drink after that silly fainting spell.
They'll be calling time soon, so you can go out with the crowd.
Lovely full moon tonight . . . wolf moon I've heard it called. Good
luck, sir . . . good luck . . .

THE LABYRINTH

THEY WERE LOST. Rosemary knew it and said so in forcible language. Brian also was well aware of their predicament but was unwilling to admit it.

'One cannot be lost in England,' he stated. 'We're bound to strike a main road if we walk in a straight line.'

'But suppose we wander in a circle?' Rosemary asked, looking fearfully round at the Dartmoor landscape, 'and finish up in a bog?'

'If we use our eyes there's no reason why bogs should bother us. Come on and stop moaning.'

'We should never have left that track,' Rosemary insisted. 'Suppose we get caught out here when night falls?'

'Don't be daft,' he snapped, 'it's only mid-day. We'll be in Princetown long before nightfall.'

'You hope.' She refused to be convinced. 'I'm hungry.'

'So am I.' They were walking up a steep incline. 'But I don't keep on about it.'

'I'm not keeping on. I'm hungry and I said so. Do you think we'll find a main road soon?'

'Over the next rise,' he promised, 'there's always a main road over the next rise.'

But he was wrong. When they crested the next rise and looked down, there was only a narrow track which terminated at a tumble-down gate set in a low stone wall. Beyond, like an island girdled by a yellow lake, was a lawn-besieged house. It was built of grey stone and seemed to have been thrown up by the moors; a great, crouching monster that glared out across the countryside with multiple glass eyes. It had a strange look. The chimney stacks might have been jagged splinters of rock that had acquired a rough cylindrical shape after centuries of wind and rain. But the really odd aspect was that the sun appeared to ignore the house. It had baked the lawn to a pale yellow, cracked the paint on an adjacent summerhouse, but in some inexplicable way, it seemed to disavow the existence of the great towering mass.

'Tea!' exclaimed Rosemary.

'What?'

'Tea.' She pointed. 'The old lady, she's drinking tea.'

Sure enough, seated by a small table that nestled in the shade of a vast multi-coloured umbrella was a little white-haired old lady taking tea. Brian frowned, for he could not understand why he had not seen her, or at least the umbrella, before, but there she was, a tiny figure in a white dress and a floppy hat, sipping tea and munching sandwiches. He moistened dry lips.

'Do you suppose,' he asked, 'we dare intrude?'

'Watch me,' Rosemary started running down the slope towards the gate. 'I'd intrude on Dracula himself if he had a decent cup of tea handy.'

Their feet moved on to a gravel path and it seemed whatever breeze stirred the sun-warm heather out on the moors did not dare intrude here. There was a strange stillness, a complete absence of sound, save for the crunch of feet on gravel, and this too ceased when they walked on to the parched lawn.

The old lady looked up and a slow smile gradually lit up a benign, wizened little face, while her tiny hands fluttered over the table, setting out two cups and saucers, then felt the teapot as though to make sure the contents were still hot.

'You poor children.' Her voice had that harsh, slightly cracked quality peculiar to some cultured ladies of an advanced age, but the utterance was clear, every word pronounced with precision. 'You look so hot and tired.'

'We're lost,' Rosemary announced cheerfully. 'We've wandered for miles.'

'I must apologise for intruding,' Brian began, but the old lady waved a teaspoon at him as though to stress the impossibility of intrusion.

'My dear young man – please. You are most welcome. I cannot recall when I last entertained a visitor, although I have always hoped someone might pass this way again. The right kind of someone, of course.'

She appeared to shiver momentarily, or perhaps tremble, for her hands and shoulders shook slightly, then an expression of polite distress puckered her forehead.

'But how thoughtless I am. You are tired having wandered so many miles and there are no chairs.'

She turned her head and called out in a high-pitched, quivering voice. 'Carlo! Carlo!'

A tall lean man came out of the house and moved slowly towards them. He was dressed in a black satin tunic and matching trousers and, due possibly to some deformity, appeared to bound over the lawn, rather than walk. Brian thought of a wolf, or a large dog that has spotted intruders. He stopped a few feet from the old lady and stood waiting, his slate-coloured eyes watching Rosemary with a savage intensity.

'Carlo, you will fetch chairs,' the old lady ordered, 'then some more hot water.'

Carlo made a guttural sound and departed in the direction of the summerhouse, leaping forward in a kind of loping run. He returned almost immediately carrying two little slatted chairs and presently Brian and Rosemary were seated under the vast umbrella, drinking tea from delicate china cups and listening to the harsh, cultivated voice.

'I must have lived alone here for such a long time. Gracious me, if I were to tell you how long, you would smile. Time is such an inexhaustible commodity, so long as one can tap the fountainhead. The secret is to break it down into small change. An hour does not seem to be long until you remember it has three thousand, six hundred seconds. And a week! My word, did you ever realise you have six hundred and four thousand, eight hundred seconds to spend every seven days? It's an enormous treasure. Do have another strawberry jam sandwich, child.'

Rosemary accepted another triangular, pink-edged sandwich, then stared open-eyed at the house. At close quarters it looked even more grim than from a distance. There was the impression

the walls had drawn their shadows above themselves like a ghostly
cloak, and although the house stood stark and forbidding in broad
daylight, it still seemed to be divorced from sunshine. Rosemary of
course made the obvious statement.

'It must be very old.'

'It has lived,' the old lady said, 'for millions upon millions of
seconds. It has drunk deep from the barrel of time.'

Rosemary giggled, then hastily assumed an extravagantly serious expression as Brian glared at her. He sipped his tea and said:
'This is really most kind of you. We were fagged out – and rather
scared too. The moors seemed to go on and on and I thought we
would have to spend the night out there.'

The old lady nodded, her gaze flickering from one young face
to the other.

'It is not pleasant to be lost in a great, empty space. Doubtless,
if you had not returned before nightfall, someone would have
instigated a search for you.'

'Not on your nelly,' Rosemary stated with charming simplicity.
'No one knows where we are. We're sort of taking a roaming
holiday.'

'How adventurous,' the old lady murmured, then called back
over one shoulder. 'Carlo, the hot water, man. Do hurry.'

Carlo came bounding out of the house carrying a silver jug in
one hand and a plate of sandwiches in the other. When he reached
the table his mouth was open and he was breathing heavily. The
old lady shot him an anxious glance.

'Poor old boy,' she consoled. 'Does the heat get you down, then?
Eh? Does the heat make you puff and pant? Never mind, you can
go and lie down somewhere in the shade.' She turned to her guests
and smiled a most kindly, benign smile. 'Carlo has mixed blood
and he finds the heat most trying. I keep telling him to practise
more self-control, but he will insist on running about.' She sighed.
'I suppose it is his nature.'

Rosemary was staring intently at her lap and Brian saw an ominous shake of her shoulders, so he hurriedly exclaimed:

'You really live all alone in that vast house? It looks enormous.'

'Only a small portion, child.' She laughed softly, a little silvery
sound. 'You see the windows on the ground floor which have

curtains? That is my little domain. All the rest is closed up. Miles upon miles of empty corridors.'

Brian re-examined the house with renewed interest. Six lower windows looked more wholesome than the others; the frames had, in the not-too-distant past, been painted white and crisp white curtains gave them a lived-in look, but the panes still seemed reluctant to reflect the sunlight and he frowned before raising his eye to the upper storeys.

Three rows of dirt-grimed glass: so many eyes from behind which life had long since departed, save possibly for rats and mice. Then he started and gripped his knees with hands that were not quite steady. On the topmost storey, at the window third from the left a face suddenly emerged and pressed its nose flat against the glass. There was no way of telling if the face were young or old, or if it belonged to a man, woman or child. It was just a white blur equipped with a pair of blank eyes and a flattened nose.

'Madam . . .' Brian began.

'My name,' the old lady said gently, 'is Mrs Brown.'

'Mrs Brown. There's a . . .'

'A nice homely name,' Mrs Brown went on. 'Do you not think so? I feel it goes with a blazing fire, a singing kettle and muffins for tea.'

'Madam – Mrs Brown. The window up there . . .'

'What window, child?' Mrs Brown was examining the interior of the teapot with some concern. 'There are so many windows.'

'The third from the left.' Brian was pointing at the face, which appeared to be opening and shutting its mouth. 'There is someone up there and they seem to be in trouble.'

'You are mistaken, my dear,' Mrs Brown shook her head. 'No one lives up there. And without life, there can be no face. That is logic.'

The face disappeared. It was not so much withdrawn as blotted out, as though the window had suddenly clouded over and now it was just another dead man's eye staring out over the sun-drenched moors.

'I could swear there was a face,' Brian insisted, and Mrs Brown smiled.

'A cloud reflection. It is so easy to see faces where none exist.

A crack in the ceiling, a damp patch on a wall, a puddle in moon-light – all become faces when the brain is tired. Can I press you to another cup?'

'No, thank you.' Brian rose and nudged Rosemary to do the same. She obeyed with ill grace. 'If you would be so kind as to direct us to the nearest main road, we will be on our way.'

'I could not possibly do that.' Mrs Brown looked most distressed. 'We are really miles from anywhere and you poor children would get hopelessly lost. Really, I must insist you stay here for the night.'

'You are most kind and do not think us ungrateful,' Brian said, 'but there must be a village not too far away.'

'Oh Brian,' Rosemary clutched his arm. 'I couldn't bear to wander about out there for hours. And suppose the sun sets . . . ?'

'I've told you before, we'll be home and dry long before then,' he snapped, and Mrs Brown rose, revealing herself as a figure of medium height, whose bowed shoulders made her shorter than she actually was. She shook a playful finger at the young man.

'How could you be so ungallant? Can you not see the poor girl is simply dropping from fatigue?' She took Rosemary's arm and began to propel her towards the house, still talking in her harsh, precise voice. 'These big strong men have no thought for us poor, frail women. Have they, my dear?'

'He's a brute.' Rosemary made a face at Brian over one shoul-der. 'We wouldn't have got lost if he hadn't made us leave the main track.'

'It is the restless spirit that haunts the best of them,' Mrs Brown confided. 'They must wander into strange and forbidden places, then come crying home to us when they get hurt.'

They moved in through the open french windows, leaving the hot summer afternoon behind them, for a soft, clinging coolness leapt to embrace their bodies like a slightly damp sheet. Brian shivered, but Rosemary exclaimed: 'How sweet.'

She was referring to the room. It was full of furniture: chairs, table, sideboard, from which the sheen of newness had long since departed; the patterned carpet had faded, so had the wallpaper; a vase of dried flowers stood on the mantelpiece and from all around – an essential part of the coolness – came a sweet, just perceptible aroma. It was the scent of extreme old age which is timidly approaching death on faltering feet. For a moment, Brian had a mental picture of an open coffin bedecked with dying flowers. Then Mrs Brown spoke.

'There are two sweet little rooms situated at the rear. You will rest well in them.'

Carlo emerged from somewhere; he was standing by the open doorway, his slate-grey eyes watching Mrs Brown as she nodded gravely.

'Go with him, my dears. He will attend to your wants and presently, when you have rested, we will dine.'

They followed their strange guide along a gloom-painted passage and he silently opened two doors, motioned Rosemary into one, then, after staring blankly at Brian, pointed to the other.

'You've been with Mrs Brown a long time?' Brian asked in a loud voice, assuming the man was deaf. 'Must be rather lonely for you here.'

Carlo did not answer, only turned on his heel and went back along the passage with that strange, loping walk. Rosemary giggled.

'Honestly, did you ever see anything like it?'

'Only in a horror film,' Brian admitted. 'Say, do you suppose he's deaf and dumb?'

'Fairly obviously,' Rosemary shrugged. 'Let's have a look at our rooms.'

They were identical. Each held a four-poster bed, a Tudor-style chest of drawers and a bedside cupboard. The same faint odour prevailed here, but Rosemary did not seem to notice it.

'Do you suppose this place runs to a bath?' she asked, seating herself on Brian's bed.

Before he could answer, Carlo's lean form filled the doorway and he made a guttural sound while beckoning them to follow him. He led the way down the passage and at the very end opened a door and motioned them to enter the room beyond. It was empty save for a very ancient hip-bath and six leather buckets lined up against one wall.

They began to laugh, clinging to each other for support. Their silent guide watched them with an expressionless stare. Brian was the first to regain his powers of speech.

'Ask a silly question,' he gasped, 'and you'll get a ridiculous answer.'

'I rarely eat.'

Mrs Brown was sipping daintily from a glass of mineral water and watching the young people with lively interest as they each consumed a large steak and a generous helping of fresh salad.

'When you are my age,' she went on, 'one's fires need little fuel. A sip of water, an occasional nibble, the odd crumb.'

'But you must eat,' Rosemary looked at the old lady with some concern. 'I mean – you have to.'

'Child – ' Mrs Brown beckoned to Carlo who started to collect the empty plates, ' – food is not necessarily meat and vegetables. Passion will feed the soul and nourish the body. I recommend love as an *hors d'oeuvre*, hate as the *entrée* and fear as a chilly dessert.'

Rosemary looked nervously at Brian, then took a long drink of water to hide her confusion. The young man decided to bring the conversation back to a more mundane plane.

'I am most interested in your house, Mrs Brown. It seems a shame that so little of it is used.'

'I did not say it was not used, dear,' Mrs Brown corrected gently. 'I said no one lived in the region that lies outside this apartment. There is, as I am sure you will agree, a difference.'

Carlo returned, carrying a dish of large, pink blancmange; this he deposited on the table after giving the girl and young man a long, expressionless stare.

'You must forgive Carlo,' Mrs Brown said while she carved the blancmange into thin slices. 'It is some time since we entertained guests and he is apt to stare at that which he is not allowed to touch.'

Brian nudged Rosemary, who was watching the blancmange carving with undisguised astonishment. 'Mrs Brown, you say the rest of the house is used, but not lived in. I'm sorry, but . . .'

'Does anyone live in your stomach?' Mrs Brown asked quietly.

He laughed, but seeing no smile on the wrinkled face opposite quickly assumed a serious expression.

'No, of course not.'

'But it is used?' Mrs Brown persisted.

He nodded. 'Yes indeed. Quite a lot.'

'So with the house.' She handed Rosemary a plate that contained three thin slices of blancmange and the girl said 'Thank you' in a strangled voice. 'You see, the house does not require people to live in it, for the simple reason that it is, in itself, a living organism.'

Brian frowned as he accepted his plate of sliced blancmange.

'Why not?' The old lady appeared surprised that her word should be doubted. 'Do you begrudge a house life?'

They both shook their heads violently and Mrs Brown appeared satisfied with their apparent acquiescence.

'After all, in ordinary houses, what are passages? I will tell you. Intestines. Bowels, if you wish. And the boiler which pumps hot water throughout the body of the house? A heart – what else could it be? In the same way, that mass of pipes and cisterns that reside up in the loft, what are they if not a brain?'

'You have a point,' Brian agreed.

'Of course I have,' Mrs Brown deposited another slice of blancmange on Rosemary's plate. 'But of course I was referring to ordinary houses. This is not an ordinary house by any means. It really lives.'

'I would certainly like to meet the builder,' Brian said caustically. 'He must have been a remarkable chap.'

'Builder!' Mrs Brown chuckled. 'When did I mention a builder? My dear young man, the house was not built. It grew.'

'Nutty as a fruit cake.' Rosemary spoke with strong conviction while she sat on Brian's bed.

'True,' Brian nodded, 'but the idea is rather fascinating.'

'Oh, come off it. How can a house grow? And from what? A brick?'

'Wait a minute. In a way a house does grow. It is fathered by an architect and mothered by a builder.'

'That's all very well,' Rosemary complained, 'but that old sausage meant the damned thing grew like a tree. Frankly, she gives me the willies. You know something? I think she's laughing at us. I mean to say, all that business of carving blancmange into thin slices.'

'A house is an extension of a man's personality.' Brian was thinking out loud. 'In its early life it would be innocent, like a new-born baby, but after it had been lived in for a bit . . .' He paused, 'then the house would take on an atmosphere . . . could even be haunted.'

'Oh, shut up.' Rosemary shivered. 'I'm expected to sleep here tonight. In any case, as I keep saying, the old thing maintains the house grew.'

'Even that makes a kind of mad logic.' He grinned, mocking what he assumed to be her pretended fear. 'We must reverse the process. The atmosphere came first, the house second.'

'I'm going to bed.' She got up and sauntered to the door. 'If you hear me scream during the night, come a-running.'

'Why bother to go?' Brian asked slyly. 'If you stay here, I won't have to run anywhere.'

'Ha, ha. Funny man. Not in this morgue.' She smiled impishly from the doorway. 'I'd be imagining all manner of things looking down at me from the ceiling.'

Brian lay in his four-poster bed and listened to the house preparing for sleep. Woodwork contracted as the temperature dropped; floorboards creaked, window frames made little rattling noises, somewhere a door closed. Sleep began to dull his senses and he became only half-aware of his surroundings; he was poised on the brink of oblivion. Then, as though a bomb had exploded, he was blasted back into full consciousness. A long drawn-out moan had shattered the silence and was coming at him from all directions. He sat up and looked round the room. So far as he could see by the light of the rising moon that filtered through his lace curtains, the room was empty. Suddenly, the groan was repeated. He sprang out of bed, lit his candle, and looked wildly around him. The sound was everywhere – in the walls with their faded pink-rose wallpaper, in the cracked ceiling, the threadbare carpet. He covered his ears with shaking hands, but still the mournful groan continued, invading his brain, seeping down into his very being, until it seemed the entire universe was crying out in anguish. Then, as abruptly as it began, it ceased. A heavy, unnatural silence descended on the house like a great, enveloping blanket. Brian hastily scrambled into his clothes.

'Enough is enough.' He spoke aloud. 'We're getting out – fast.'

Another sound came into being. It began a long way off. A slow, hesitant footstep, married to squeaking floorboards, a laborious picking up and putting down of naked feet, interspersed with a slow slithering which suggested the unseen walker was burdened with the tiredness of centuries. This time there was no doubt as to where the sound was coming from. It was up above. The soft, padding steps passed over the ceiling and once again the house groaned, but now it was a moan of ecstasy, a low cry of fulfillment. Brian opened the bedroom door and crept out into the corridor. The moaning cry and the slithering footsteps merged and became a nightmarish symphony, a two-toned serenade of horror. Then, again, all sound ceased and the silence was like a landmine that might explode at any moment. He found himself waiting for the moan, the slithering overhead footsteps to begin all over again – or perhaps something else, something that defied imagination.

He tapped on Rosemary's door, then turned the handle and entered, holding his candle high and calling her name.

'Rosemary, wake up. Rosemary, come on, we're getting out of here.'

The flickering candle-flame made great shadows leap across the walls and dance over the ceiling; it cut ragged channels through the darkness until, at last, his questing eye saw the bed. It was empty. The sheets and blankets were twisted up into loose ropes and a pillow lay upon the floor.

'Rosemary!'

He whispered her name and the house chuckled. A low, harsh, gurgling laugh, which made him run from the room, race down the long corridor, until he lurched into the dining-room. An old-fashioned oil lamp stood on the table, illuminating the room with a pale orange light and revealing Mrs Brown, seated in an armchair, calmly darning a sock. She looked up as Brian entered and smiled like a mother whose small son has strayed from his warm bed on a winter's night.

'I would put the candle down, dear,' she said, 'otherwise you will spill grease all over the carpet.'

'Rosemary!' he shouted. 'Where is she?'

'There's really no need for you to shout. Despite my advanced years, I am not deaf.' She broke the wool, then turned the sock and

examined her work with a certain pride. 'That's better. Carlo is so
hard on his socks.' She looked up with a sly smile. 'It is only to be
expected, of course. He has hard feet.'

'Where is she?' Brian set down the candle and moved closer to
the old woman, who was now closing the work-basket. 'She's not
in her room and there are signs of a struggle. What have you done
with her?'

Mrs Brown shook her head sadly.

'Questions, questions. How hungry youth is for knowledge. You
demand to know the truth and, should I gratify your desire, how
distressed you would become. Ignorance is a gift freely offered by
the gods and so often it is spurned by misguided mortals. Even I
sometimes wish I knew less, but . . .' Her sigh was one of sad res-
ignation. 'Time reveals all to those who live long enough. I should
go back to bed, dear. The young need their sleep.'

Brian advanced a few steps, then spoke in a carefully controlled
voice.

'I am going to ask you for the last time, Mrs Brown, or whatever
your name is – what have you done with Rosemary?'

She looked up and shook her head in sad reproof.

'Threats! How unwise. A sparrow should never threaten an
eagle. It is so futile and such a waste of time.'

Mrs Brown carefully placed her work-basket on the floor, then
snapped in a surprisingly firm voice: 'Carlo!'

There came, from somewhere to Brian's rear, a low, deep growl.
Such a menacing sound might have issued from the throat of a
large dog whose mistress has been threatened, or a she-wolf
protecting her young, but when the young man spun round, he
saw Carlo standing a few feet away. The man had his head tilted
to one side and his large, yellow teeth were bared as he growled
again. His stance was grotesque. He was leaning forward slightly
as though preparing to spring and his fingers were curved, so that
with their long, pointed nails, they looked uncannily like talons;
his cheeks seemed to have shrunk and his black hair lay back over
his narrow skull like a sleek, ebony mane.

'Will you believe me?' Mrs Brown said, and her voice was less
harsh – much younger. 'I have only to say one word and your
windpipe will be hanging down your shirt-front.'

'You are mad.' Brian backed slowly away and Carlo moved forward, matching him step for step. 'You are both mad.'

'You mean,' Mrs Brown came round and joined Carlo, 'we are not normal by your standards. That much I grant you. Sanity is only a form of madness favoured by the majority. But I think the time has come for you to meet truth, since you are so eager to make her acquaintance.'

'I only want to find Rosemary, then get out of here,' Brian said.

'Find your little friend? Perhaps. Leave here? Ah . . .' Mrs Brown looked thoughtful. 'That is another matter. But come, there is much for you to see, and please, no heroics. Carlo is on the turn. He is apt to be a little touchy when the moon is full.'

They filed out into the hall, Mrs Brown leading the way with Brian following and the grim Carlo bringing up the rear. To the right of a great staircase was a black door and this Mrs Brown unlocked, then entered the room beyond, where she proceeded to light a lamp from Brian's candle.

The light crept outwards in ever-increasing circles as she turned up the wick, revealing oak-panelled walls and a cobweb-festooned ceiling. The room was bare, except for the portrait hanging over a dirt-grimed marble fireplace. To this the young man's eyes were drawn like a pin to a magnet.

The background was jet-black and the face corpse-white; the large black eyes glared an intense hatred for all living things and the thin-lipped mouth was shut tight, but so cunningly had the portrait been painted that Brian had the feeling it might open at any moment.

'My late husband,' Mrs Brown stated, 'was a partaker of blood.'

The statement did not invite comment and Brian made none.

'It must be the best part of five hundred years since they came down from the village,' Mrs Brown continued. 'Chanting priests looking like black ravens, mewing peasants huddled together like frightened sheep. I recall it was night and the mists shrouded the moors and swirled about their thrice-accursed cross as though it wished to protect us from the menace it represented.'

She paused and Brian realised that she looked much younger. The face was filling out, the shoulders were no longer bowed.

'They did not consider I was of great importance,' Mrs Brown went on, 'so I was merely tied to a tree and flogged, thereby providing entertainment for the herd of human cattle who liked nothing better than to see a woman writhe under the lash. But him . . . They dug a hole, and laid him flat, having bound his body in cords that were sealed with the dreaded sign. Then they drove a stake through his heart . . . Fools.'

She glared at Brian and clenched her small fists.

'They left him for dead. Dead! His brain still lived. The blood was only symbolic, it was the vital essence we needed – still need: the force that makes the soul reach out for the stars, the hammer that can create beauty out of black depravity.'

She went over to the portrait and stroked the white, cruel face with hands that had become long and slender.

'When they buried his beautiful body they planted a seed, and from that seed grew the house. A projection of himself.'

'I don't believe you.' Brian shook his head. 'I won't – can't believe you.'

'No!' She laughed and Carlo howled. 'Then feel the walls. They are warm, flesh of his flesh. Moist. The body fluids seep out when he is aroused. Look.' She pointed to a great double door set in one wall. 'Look, the mouth. When I open the lips, food pops in. Succulent, living food and we all benefit. I, Carlo, who sprang from the old people – I still let him roam the moors when the moon is full – and, of course, He. The House. He needs all the sweet essence he can get. He sleeps after meat and no longer moans. I do not like to hear him moan.'

'Where is Rosemary?' Brian asked again and knew what must follow.

'She passed through the lips an hour since.' Mrs Brown laughed very softly and Carlo made a whining sound. 'Now, if you would find her, there is not really much alternative. You must follow her through the great intestines, down into the mighty bowels. Wander and cry out, trudge on and on, until at last your will is broken and He can take from you what he needs.'

'You want me to go through those doors?' Brian asked, and there was a glimmer of hope. 'Then go wandering through the corridors of an empty house? When I find Rosemary, we will break out.'

The woman smiled as she motioned to Carlo.

'Part the lips, Carlo.'

The man, if indeed that which crept forward was a man, silently obeyed; the great doors groaned as they swung inwards and Brian saw a murky passage, lined with green tinted walls. A warm, sweet, cloying odour made his stomach heave and he drew back.

'She's waiting for you,' Mrs Brown said softly, 'and she must be very frightened wandering through the labyrinth, not exactly alone, but I doubt if she will appreciate the company. Most of them will be well digested by now.'

Carlo was waiting, his hand on the handle of one door; his eyes were those of a hungry wolf who sees his prey about to be devoured by a lion. Brian, without a sideways glance, passed through the entrance and the doors slammed to behind him.

There were no stairs. The corridors sometimes sloped upwards, at others they spiralled down; there were stretches when the floor was comparatively level, but the corridors were never straight for long. They twisted, crossed other passages, suddenly split, leaving the wanderer with a choice of three or more openings; occasionally they came to a blank end, forcing him to retrace his footsteps. Light was provided by an eerie greenish glow radiating from the walls and ceiling and sometimes this light pulsated, suggesting it originated from some form of decay.

Brian stumbled onwards, shouting Rosemary's name, and his echo shocked him, went racing on ahead until it became a faraway voice calling back along the avenues of time. Once he stumbled and fell against the wall. Instantly, the moist, green surface contracted under his weight and there was an obscene sucking sound when he pulled himself free. A portion of his shirt sleeve remained stuck to the wall and there was a red mark on his arm.

When he had been walking for some thirty minutes he came upon the window passage. There was no other word to describe it, for one wall was lined with windows, each one set about six feet apart, and he gave a little cry of joy, certain this was the place from which he and Rosemary could make their escape. Then he saw – them. Before each window stood one, occasionally two, forms – hideously thin, scarecrow figures that pawed at the window panes with claw-like fingers and emitted little animal whimpers.

Brian approached the first window and gave a quick glance through the grimy panes. He was two floors, if that was the right expression, up, and he saw the lawn then, further out, the moors, all bathed in brilliant moonlight. Even as he watched, a great hound went bounding across the lawn. It cleared the low wall in a single leap, then streaked out across the moor. Something touched Brian's arm and he spun round to face one of the creatures that had silently crept along from the next window. He saw at close quarters the skeleton face covered with brown, wrinkled skin, and the vacant blue eyes that stared up at him with mute, suffering appeal. He judged the man to have been a tramp, or possibly a gypsy, for he wore the remnants of a red shirt and brown corduroy trousers. The claw-hands plucked feebly at his arm, the mouth opened, revealing toothless gums, and a hoarse whisper seeped out.

'The old cow said come in.'

'How long have you been here?' Brian asked, uncomfortably aware that a number of other grotesque bundles of rag and bones were leaving their posts by the windows and slithering on naked feet towards him. The whisper came again.

'The old cow said come in.'

'Have you seen a young girl?' Brian shouted. 'Have any of you seen a girl?'

The man tried to grip his arm, but there was no strength left in the wasted frame and he could only repeat the single phrase:

'The old cow said come in.'

They were all clustered round him. Three bore some resemblance to women, although their hair had fallen out, and one, a tall beanstalk of a creature, kept mumbling: 'Pretty boy,' while she tried unsuccessfully to fasten her gums into his neck.

'Break the windows!' Brian shouted, pushing them away as gently as he could. 'Listen, break the windows, then I'll be able to climb down and fetch help.'

'The old cow said come in.' The man could only repeat over and over the six ominous words, and a wizened, awful thing, no higher than a child, kept muttering: 'Meat,' as it tried to fasten its mouth on Brian's right hand.

Unreasoning terror made him strike the creature full in the face and it went crashing back against the wall. Instantly, the green surface bent inwards and a deep sigh ran through the house, making the ghastly pack go slithering along the corridor, their remaining spark of intelligence having presumably warned them this sound was something to be feared. The small, child-size figure was left, stuck to the wall like a fly on gummed paper, and, as the green light pulsated, the creature jerked in unison.

Brian pulled off one of his shoes and smashed the heel against the nearest window-pane. He might just as well have struck a slab of solid rock for all the impression he made, and at last he gave up and continued his search for Rosemary. After an hour of trudging wearily along green-tinted passages, he had no idea how far he had travelled, or if indeed he was just going round in a perpetual circle. He found himself dragging his feet, making the same hesitant, slithering footsteps that had so alarmed him in his bedroom, centuries ago.

The corridors were never silent, for there were always cries, usually some way off, and a strange thudding sound which came into being when the green light pulsated, but these offstage noises became as a murmur when the scream rang out. It was a cry of despair, a call for help, a fear-born prayer, and at once Brian knew who had screamed. He shouted Rosemary's name as he broke into a run, terrified lest he be unable to reach her, at the same time in dread of what he might find. Had she not screamed again he would doubtlessly have taken the wrong passage, but when the second shriek rang out he ran towards the sound and presently came to a kind of circular hall. They were clinging to her like leeches to a drowning horse. Their skeleton hands were tearing her dress, their toothless mouths fouled her flesh, and all the while they squealed like a herd of hungry pigs. He pulled them away and the soulless bodies went hurtling back against vibrating walls; bones snapped like frost-crisp twigs and despairing whimpers rose to an unholy chorus.

He took Rosemary in his arms and she clung to him as though he were life itself, clutching his shoulders in a terrified grip while she cried like a lost child. He murmured soft, unintelligible words, trying to reassure himself as much as her, then screamed at the pack who were again slowly moving in.

'Don't you understand, this is not real. It's a projection of a mad brain. A crazy nightmare. Try to find a way out.'

It is doubtful if they heard, let alone understood what he was saying, and those that could still move were edging their way forward like rats whose hunger is greater than their fear.

'Can you walk?' he asked Rosemary and the girl nodded. 'Good, then we must make our way downwards. The woman's apartment is on the ground floor and our only hope is to batter those doors in and escape across the lawn.'

'It's impossible.' Rosemary was clinging to his arm and they were leaving the creatures behind. 'This place is a labyrinth. We will wander round and round these corridors until we drop.'

'Nonsense.' He spoke sharply. 'The house can't be all that big and we are young and fit. So long as we go down, we're bound to find the doors.'

This was easier said than done. Many corridors sloped down, only to slant up again, but presently they came out into a window passage and found they were somewhere at the rear of the house, but only one floor up.

'Now,' Brian kissed Rosemary, 'only one more slope to go and we're there.'

'But we're the wrong side of the house,' Rosemary complained, 'and even if we find the doors, how are you going to break through them?'

'One step at a time. Let's find them first, then, maybe, I'll use you as a battering ram.'

It took an hour to find the next downward slope and then only after they had retraced their steps several times, but at last they were moving downwards. Rosemary shivered.

'It's getting colder.'

'Yes, and that damned stink is becoming more pronounced. But never mind, we'll soon be there.'

They went steadily downwards for another five minutes and then Rosemary began to cry.

'Brian, I can't go on much longer. Surely we've passed the ground floor ages ago? And there's something awful down here. I can feel it.'

'It can't be more awful than what's up above,' he retorted grimly.

'We must go on. There's no turning back unless you want to finish up a zombie.'

'Zombie!' She repeated dully.

'What did you imagine those things were, back there? They died long ago and only keep going because the house gives them a sort of half life. Mrs Brown and Carlo appear to be better provided for, but they died centuries ago.'

'I can't believe all this.' Rosemary shuddered. 'How can a place like this exist in the twentieth century?'

'It doesn't. I should imagine we stumbled across the house at the right, or in our case, the wrong time. I suppose you might call it a time-trap.'

'I don't know what you are talking about,' Rosemary said, then added, 'I very rarely do.'

The passage was becoming steeper, spiralling round and sloping down until they had difficulty in remaining upright. Then the floor levelled out and after a space of about six feet came to an end.

'Earth.' Brian felt the termination wall. 'Good, honest earth.'

'Earth,' Rosemary repeated. 'So what?'

Brian raised his eyes ceilingwards and then spoke in a carefully controlled voice. 'So far we have been walking on a floor and between walls that are constructed of something very nasty. Right? Now we are facing a wall built or shovelled into place – I don't care – of plain, down to earth – earth. Got it?'

Rosemary nodded. 'Yes, so we have got down to the house foundations. But I thought we were looking for the doors.'

Brian gripped her shoulders.

'Say that again.'

'Say what again? Look, you're hurting me.'

He shook her gently. 'The first bit.'

She thought for a moment. 'So we have got down to the house foundations. What's so important about that?'

He released her and went up close to the wall, where he stood for a few minutes examining its surface, then he came back and tilted her chin up so she was looking directly into his eyes.

'Will you try to be very, very brave?'

Fear came rushing back and she shivered.

'Why?'

'Because I am going to break down that wall.' He spoke very slowly. 'And on the other side we may find something very nasty indeed.'

She did not move her head, only continued to gaze up into his eyes.

'Isn't there any other way?' she whispered.

He shook his head.

'None. None whatsoever.'

There was a minute of complete silence, then:

'What are you going to use as a shovel?'

He laughed and went back to the wall which he pounded with his fist.

'I could say you have a point there, but I won't. Let's take an inventory. What have we that is pick- and shovel-worthy? Our hands, of course. Shoes? Maybe.' He felt in his pocket and produced a bunch of keys and a penknife. 'This might start things going, then I can pull the loose stuff out with my hands.'

He sank the penknife blade into the soft, moist earth and traced the rough outline of a door, then he began to deepen the edges, digging out little lumps of earth that fell to the ground like gobbets of chewed meat. Brian then removed his shoes and used the heels to claw out a jagged hole.

'If I can work my way through,' he explained, 'it should be an easy matter to pull the entire thing down.'

He dug steadily for another five minutes, then a glimmer of light appeared and, after a final effort, he was able to look through an opening roughly six inches in diameter.

'What can you see?' Rosemary asked, her tone suggesting she would rather not know.

'It seems to be some kind of large cave and it's lit up with that green light, just like the passages. I can see hunks of rock lying about, but not much else. Well, here goes.'

He thrust his right hand through an aperture, curled his fingers round the inner wall and pulled. A large chunk came away, then he began to work with both hands, pulling, clawing, and the entire wall came tumbling down. He wiped his hands on already stained trousers, then put on his shoes.

'Now,' he said, 'for the moment of truth.'

They were in a rough, circular cavern; it was perhaps twenty feet in diameter and an equal distance in height. Loose lumps of rock littered the floor, but there was no sign of anyone – alive or dead – and Brian gave a prolonged sigh of relief.

'I don't know what I expected to see, but thank heavens, I don't see it. Now, we must start looking for a way out. I'll go round the walls, you examine the floor. Never know, there might be a hole going down still further.'

He turned his attention to the irregular walls, leaving Rosemary to wander miserably among the large rocks and boulders that formed a kind of fence round the centre of the cavern. He looked upwards and saw, some twenty feet from the ground, a fairly large hole. Deciding it would be worth investigating, he began to ascend the wall and found the task easier than he had supposed, for projecting rocks made excellent footholds. In a few minutes he had reached his objective. The hole was in fact a small cave that was about seven feet high and five across, but alas there was no exit.

He was about to descend and continue his search elsewhere when Rosemary screamed. Never before had he realised a human throat was capable of expressing such abject terror. Shriek after shriek rang out and re-echoed against the walls, until it seemed an army of banshees were forecasting a million deaths. He looked down and saw the girl standing just inside the fence of stones looking down at something he could not see; her eyes were dilated and seemed frozen into an expression of indescribable horror.

Brian scrambled down the wall and ran over to her; when he laid hands on her shoulders she flinched as though his touch were a branding iron, then her final shriek was cut off and she slid silently to the floor.

A few feet away there was a slight indentation, a shallow hole, and he experienced a terrifying urge not to look into it, but he knew he must, if for no other reason than a strange, compelling curiosity.

He dragged Rosemary well back and left her lying against one wall, then he returned, creeping forward very slowly, walking on tiptoe. At last he was on the brink of hell. He looked down.

Horror ran up his body in cold waves; it left an icy lump in his stomach and he wanted to be sick only he had not the strength.

He had to stare down, concentrate all his senses and try to believe.

The head bore a resemblance to the portrait in Mrs Brown's ante-room; it was dead-white, bloated, suggesting an excess of nourishment consumed over a very long period. The hair was at least six feet in length and was spread out over the loose rock like a monstrous shroud. But the torso and arms grew out of the ground. The shoulders and part of the forearms were flesh, but further down the white skin assumed a greyish colour and, lower still, gradually merged into solid rock. Most horrifying of all was the profusion of fat, greenish, tubelike growths that sprouted out from under forearms and neck and, so far as Brian could see, the whole of the back. Obscene roots spreading out in every direction until they disappeared into the black earth, writhing and pulsating, carrying the vital fluid that circulated round the house.

The eyes were closed, but the face moved. The thin lips grimaced, creating temporary furrows in the flabby fat. Brian withdrew from the hole – the grave – and at last his stomach had its way and allowed him to be violently sick. By the time he returned to Rosemary, he felt old and drained of strength. She was just returning to consciousness and he smoothed back her hair.

'Are you fit enough to walk?' he asked.

She gave a little strangled gasp.

'That . . . that thing . . .'

'Yes, I know. Now listen. I am going to take you up there.' He pointed to the cave set high up on the opposite wall. 'You'll be all right there while I do what must be done.'

'I don't understand.' She shook her head. 'What must you do?'

'Mrs Brown told me her husband was a partaker of blood. In other words, a vampire, and centuries ago the local lads did the traditional things and drove a stake through his heart. She said something else. It wasn't his body they should have destroyed, but his brain. Don't you see? This house, the entire set-up, is a nightmare produced by a monstrous intelligence?'

'I'll believe anything.' Rosemary got to her feet. 'Just get me out of here. I'd rather walk the passages than spend another minute with that . . . thing.'

'No.' He shook his head. 'I must destroy the brain. The only point is, when I do . . .' He looked round the cavern, then over to the entrance of the green-walled passage. '. . . anything may happen.'

'What about you?' she asked.

'So soon as the job is finished, I'll join you.'

He might have added, 'If I can,' but instead guided Rosemary to the wall and assisted her up to the cave.

'Now,' he instructed, 'stay well back and don't, in any circumstances, so much as put your nose outside. Understand?'

'God, I'm petrified,' she said.

'Don't let it get around,' he nodded grimly, 'but so am I.'

He came to the hole like a released spirit returning to hell. As he drew nearer, the terror grew until it required a desperate effort to raise one foot and put it down before the other. Only the memory of Rosemary up there in the cave kept his spark of courage alive. At last he again gazed down at that horrible growth; it groaned and the sound raced round the cavern and up through the house. The face grimaced and twitched, while the green tubes writhed like a nest of gorged worms. Brian selected a rock which was a little larger than the bloated head and, gripping it in both hands, prepared to hurl it down. He had tensed his muscles, and was turning slightly to one side, when the eyelids flicked back and he was staring into two pools of black hate.

The shock was so intense he automatically slackened his grip and the rock slid from his fingers and went crashing down somewhere behind him. The mouth opened and a vibrant whisper went racing up through the house.

'Elizabeth . . . Carlo . . .'

The words came out slowly, rather like a series of intelligible sighs, but from all around, from the walls, the floor, the high roof – never from the moving lips.

'Would . . . you . . . destroy . . . that . . . which . . . you . . . do . . . not . . . understand?'

Brian was fumbling for a rock, but he paused and the whispering voice went on.

'I . . . must . . . continue . . . to . . . be . . . I . . . must . . . grow . . . fill . . . the . . . universe . . . consume . . . take . . . strength . . .'

A padding of fast-running paws came from the passage entrance and a woman's voice was calling out.

'Petros, drink of his essence . . . will him into walking death.'

There was a hint of fear in the terrible eyes. The whispering voice again ran through the house.

'He . . . is . . . an . . . unbeliever . . . he . . . is . . . the . . . young . . . of . . . a . . . new . . . age . . . why . . . did . . . you . . . let . . . him . . . through . . . ?'

The great dog leapt over the loose earth and emerged from the passageway; it was black as midnight, like a solid shadow newly escaped from a wall, and it padded round the cavern before jumping up on to a boulder and preparing to leap. Brian hurled a rock at it and struck the broad, black snout. The beast howled and fell back as Mrs Brown spoke from the entrance.

'You will not keep that up for long. Carlo cannot be killed by the likes of you.'

She had been transformed. The once white hair was now a rich auburn, the face was as young as today, but the glorious eyes reflected the evil of a million yesterdays. She wore a black evening dress that left her arms and back bare and Brian could only stare at her, forgetting that which lay behind him and Rosemary, up in the cave. All he could see was white flesh and inviting eyes.

'Come away,' the low, husky voice said. 'Leave Petros to his dream. He cannot harm you and it would be such a waste if Carlo were to rip your nice body to shreds. Think of what I can offer. An eternity of bliss. A million lifetimes of pleasure. Come.'

He took one step forward, then another, and it seemed he was walking into a forbidden dream; all the secret desires that up to that moment he had not realised existed flared up and became exciting possibilities. Then, just as he was about to surrender, go running to her like a child to a beautiful toy, her voice lashed across his consciousness.

'Carlo . . . now.'

The dog came snarling over the rocks and Brian fell back, suddenly fully aware of the pending danger. He snatched up a piece of jagged rock and threw it at the oncoming beast. He hit it just above the right ear, then began to hurl stones as fast as he could pick them up. The dog leapt from side to side, snarling with pain and rage, but Brian realised it was coming forward more than it retreated and knew a few minutes, at the most, must elapse before he felt those fangs at his throat. By chance his hands closed round the original small boulder – and it was then he understood what must be done.

He raised the rock high above his head, made as though to hurl it at the dog, which momentarily recoiled, then threw it back – straight at the head of Petros.

The house shrieked. One long-drawn-out scream and the dog was no longer there; instead, Carlo ran towards his mistress, making plaintive, guttural cries, before sinking down before her, plucking frantically at the hem of her black dress.

Brian looked back and down into the hole and saw that the head was shattered and what remained of the flesh was turning black. The green tubes were now only streaks of deflated tissue and the life-giving fluid no longer flowed up into the body of the house. From up above came a deep rumbling sound and a great splintering, as though a mountain of rocks were grinding together. Brian ran towards the far wall and, quickly scrambling up into the cave, found Rosemary waiting to welcome him with outstretched arms.

'Keep down,' he warned. 'All hell is going to break loose at any moment.'

They lay face down upon the floor, and Brian had to raise his head to see the final act. The green light was fading, but before it went he had a last glimpse of the woman staring blankly at the place where Petros had lain. She was patting Carlo's head. Then the ceiling came down and for a while there was only darkness filled with a mighty rumbling and crashing of falling rock. Fantasy tumbling down into the pit of reality. Time passed and the air cleared as the dust settled and presently, like a glimmer of hope in the valley of despair, a beam of light struck the entrance to the cave. Brian looked out, then up. Twenty feet above was a patch of blue sky.

They came up from the pit, bruised, clothes torn, but happy to be alive. They trudged hand-in-hand out across the moors and after a while looked back to see a pile of rocks that, at this distance, could have been mistaken for a ruined house.

'We will never talk about this to anyone,' Brian said. 'One does not talk about one's nightmares. They are so ridiculous in the light of day.'

Rosemary nodded. 'We slept. We dreamed. Now we are awake.'

They walked on. Two figures that distance diminished until they became minute specks on a distant horizon. Then they were gone.

The early morning breeze caressed the summer grass, harebells smiled up at a benign sky and a pair of rabbits played hide and seek among the fallen rocks. To all outward appearances the moors were at peace.

Then a rabbit screamed and a stoat raised blood-dripping jaws.

THE SAD VAMPIRE

THE HOUSE WAS BIG, very old and stood on the edge of a desolate moor. John's mother said it was far too large and heaven above knew how she would keep it clean. But his father was of the opinion that it was picturesque and had a wonderful old-world atmosphere.

'And what about heating?' Mrs Glendale asked. 'It will cost a fortune. To say nothing of decorating. The place is awfully run down.'

'Only about six or seven rooms are in use,' her husband consoled her. 'The rest are shut up. But honestly, it's a wonderful old house, and remember, it's been in my family for generations.'

'Well,' Mrs Glendale sighed, 'I was quite happy with our semi-detached in Surbiton, but since you and John are set on living in this place, I suppose I'll have to make the best of it.'

John, being only fourteen years old, thought Glendale Grange the most exciting house he had ever seen. His father had inherited it from a very ancient uncle who had recently died, together with a sum of money that would just about pay for its upkeep, so long as they lived simply. The main part of the house had been built during the reign of the first Elizabeth, but various generations of Glendales had added to it over the course of the past four centuries, so that now it was a low, rambling building, with doors opening in all sorts of unexpected places and long, rambling passages that made the house into a kind of exciting labyrinth.

Along with a household of beautiful antique furniture, John's father had also inherited a housekeeper. She was a very old woman, with a mass of white hair and a shrivelled brown face that reminded John of a pickled walnut. She was waiting in the large, oak-panelled hall when they opened the front door. She examined the small family with a cold, cynical eye.

'Ah, Mrs Combs!' Stafford Glendale said heartily. 'This is my wife – Mrs Glendale – and my son John.'

Mrs Combs hitched up a spotless white apron. 'Pleased to meet 'em, I'm sure. Do you all intend to live in the Grange?'

John's father grinned, then frowned. 'Yes. Why – have you any objection?'

Mrs Combs shrugged. 'It's all the same to me. But do you know what you're letting yourself in for? This is no ordinary house.'

Mrs Glendale decided to say a few words. John could see she was annoyed at the old woman's manner, which was, he had to admit, rather rude.

'Thank you, Mrs Combs, but we are very well aware that this is an old and large house, and I'm sure we'll manage quite nicely. Now, I'd be obliged if you would make us a nice cup of tea. After the long journey we could all do with one.'

Mrs Combs turned abruptly and shuffled towards the door, which John presumed led to the kitchen. In the entrance she paused and looked back over one shoulder.

'Tea is it? Well, let me say this. It's more than tea you'll want before you've been here long.'

'What an awful old woman,' Mrs Glendale gasped, once the door had been slammed by the departing Mrs Combs. 'Stafford, I don't believe I can take much of her.'

But her husband grinned indulgently. 'Bit of a character. We will have to make allowances for her funny ways. She looked after my uncle for over fifty years and probably considers the house to be her personal property. I suppose, from her point of view, we are intruders.'

'That's all very well,' his wife grumbled, 'but she could try to be civil.'

The rest of the day was spent settling in. As the Grange was fully furnished, they had disposed of almost all their own furniture to the buyer of the town home. The few items that John's mother could not bear to part with were coming down in a removal van the next day. So all they had to do was unpack a few suitcases and prepare two bedrooms for immediate use. Then Mrs Combs announced that dinner was ready and they made their way to the long, cool dining-room.

The meal was well cooked and greatly appreciated, even if the old woman did serve it with a certain amount of ill-grace, shaking her head in a manner of grim warning. It was not until coffee had been served that she dropped her bombshell.

'Everything satisfactory?' She addressed Mrs Glendale, who was not very happy at the way the coffee-pot had been crashed down in front of her. 'There are no complaints?'

After some thought John's mother shook her head.

'None that I'm prepared to mention at the moment. The dinner was very nice. You are a very good cook.'

The old woman drew up a chair and sat down, an action that earned her a glare from Mrs Glendale and an amused grin from John's father. She ignored both and, after clearing her throat, began to speak.

'Now, I don't suppose any of you will take any notice of what I am going to say, but that can't be helped. I'm going to say it anyway. This house has got a vampire.'

Mrs Glendale gasped and her husband tried hard not to laugh. As for John, he could only gape in speechless astonishment. At length, his mother rediscovered her voice.

'What did you say?' she asked.

'I thought I spoke clearly enough,' Mrs Combs said coldly. 'But in case you're a bit hard of hearing, I'll say it again. The house has got a vampire.'

John jumped up and down in his chair, his eyes wide with excitement.

'You mean . . . a *real* vampire? One that sucks blood and comes out of its coffin at sunset?'

Mrs Combs smiled. 'He comes out of his coffin at sunset all right. Don't you have any doubts on that score. As for sucking blood . . . Your uncle and me never gave him the opportunity, but I've no doubt that if we had been careless, he would have drained us drier than old orange peel.'

Mr Glendale made a great effort to speak with suitable gravity.

'And what precautions do you suggest we take, Mrs Combs?'

The old woman almost smiled and nodded with reluctant approval.

'I'm glad you've got the sense to ask. Well, first of all, shut your bedroom windows and doors and make sure the catches are fastened and the keys turned. Then lay garlic flowers – your uncle and me planted a whole crop of 'em in the kitchen garden – over all the cracks. And – yes, wear crucifixes round yer necks. If you take these simple precautions, you'll be as safe as a cup of water in a river.'

'But . . .' John did not really believe in vampires, but he wanted to. '. . . How did the house come to have a vampire?'

Mrs Combs shook her head grimly. 'You may well ask. It's your great-great-great-grandfather who wouldn't stay at home like a respectable body, but went gallivanting about in foreign parts. Got bitten, he did, by a Count Somebody-Or-Other and he's been a vampire for the past hundred and fifty years.'

Mrs Glendale gave John a warning glance. 'I think that is quite enough. The boy will be having nightmares – and so will we all, for that matter . . .'

'He'll have more than nightmares,' Mrs Combs interrupted, 'if you don't do what I say. Now, do you want me to fetch the garlic flowers?'

Mr Glendale made a strange choking sound behind his hand, but his wife smiled politely.

'I am sure you mean well, Mrs Combs, but I do not think your – er – precautions will be necessary. You may be assured that my husband is well able to deal with any intruder that may prowl round the house during the dark hours.'

'Please yourself.' Mrs Combs got up. 'You might be lucky – for a little while. Come to think of it I haven't heard him stalking round this part of the house for some time. But you can't say you haven't been warned. Well, I'm off. I barricade myself in my bedroom every night at sunset and stay there until morning.'

Scarcely had the door closed than Mr Glendale burst into a fit of uncontrollable laughter, and even Mrs Glendale found it hard not to smile.

'Did you ever hear the like?' John's father said at length. 'A vampire! Garlic flowers in the bedroom! The old dear is as mad as a March hare.'

'Maybe so,' his wife remarked quietly, 'but I am not at all sure she is the kind of person I care to have about the house. Heaven only knows, John has a vivid enough imagination as it is, without having that awful old woman filling his mind with vampires and goodness knows what.'

'Oh, come.' Her husband smiled. 'You mustn't take it all that seriously. I'm sure John has enough common sense not to believe in vampires.'

John hastened to qualify his fund of common sense.

'Of course I don't believe that real vampires exist. But . . .'

'But what?' his mother demanded.

'Well, it would be fun if it were true. I mean a real vampire with long eye-teeth . . .'

'There you are!' Mrs Glendale explained triumphantly. 'I told you so. He'll be having nightmares as sure as fate.'

But John's father shook his head. 'Nonsense. There's no such thing as horror to a boy of his age. Only adventure.'

Mrs Glendale shuddered. 'Well, I wish as much could be said for me. Heaven forbid that I should believe in vampires, but such talk makes one uneasy. Let's change the subject.'

John woke suddenly.

His room was flooded with moonlight; cold silver light that made every item of furniture stand out like shadows on a floodlit screen. He was instantly wide awake and found himself straining his ears for the sound which had roused him from a deep sleep. From far away he heard the hoot of an owl. But it was not this that had disturbed him. He waited, aware that his nerves were tingling with excitement and every one of his five senses was strangely alert. Then it came again and John sat bolt upright.

A long-drawn-out moan.

It came from some distance away, and he might not have heard it if his hearing had not been so acute and the sleeping house so quiet. After the lapse of a few minutes, the moan was repeated, and now it carried an undertone of almost unendurable despair. John got out of bed, put on his dressing-gown, slid his feet into slippers and crept towards the door.

The passage that lay beyond was gloomy, lit only by such light as could find its way through a window set in a wall at the far end. John moved very slowly towards this window and, when he at length reached it, peered out on to the garden below. A soft breeze stirred the grass, and the towering trees that stood like mighty sentinels on the edge of the moor shook their heads, as though disclaiming any responsibility for mysterious moans. Then the moan was repeated for the third time.

There was no manner of doubt. It came from somewhere to John's left – from beyond the end of another passage that led into the disused part of the house. After some hesitation, because suddenly he realised there might be danger, John entered the passage, walking slowly over floorboards that were thick with dust, and tried to peer out of windows that had not known the application of a wash-leather for many a long year.

The passage terminated at a door that was festooned with thick cobwebs and looked as if it had not been opened since the house was built. When John at length succeeded in turning the large, brass handle, the ancient hinges groaned their protest and seemed determined to combat his entrance. But at last the door was open, and John stepped into a large room, which must have been situated at one corner of the house, as two walls – each running at right angles to the other – were lined with tall windows.

The moonlight, which was thus permitted entry from two sides, bathed the room with a cold, silver glow and enabled John to see the damp-stained walls, the carpet of dust that coated the bare floorboards, and the high, cracked ceiling. He was also able to see – and hear – the man who sat in one window bay.

He was so awfully thin. He had a long, narrow face, covered with loose, white – oh, so white – skin, framed by long, matted black hair, and lit by a pair of large, sad eyes. His skeleton-thin body was covered by a threadbare black suit and there was a bunch of rotting lace at his throat. His feet were bare and the toenails were extraordinarily long – as indeed were his fingernails. But the one aspect about this terrifying figure that drew John's full attention was his teeth. The two eye-teeth were so long, they extended over his lower lip and dimpled his chin.

He was sobbing. Terrible, body-shaking sobs that made his thin

frame tremble like a wind-rocked tree, and every once in a while
he broke into a low, but perfectly audible moan. John – who was by
now very frightened – was about to withdraw, when the vampire
(for what else could it be?) swung its head round and stared at him
with tear-filled eyes. Then it sprang to its feet and went scurrying
over to the nearest corner, where it crouched, trembling in every
limb. John forgot his own fear and was only aware of a deep pity
for this terrified, forlorn creature, that was not behaving at all as
a vampire should. He moved forward a few steps and the huddled
figure cringed and emitted a wail of terror.

'Please,' John said softly, 'don't be afraid. I won't hurt you. I
promise.'

The vampire spoke with a low, husky voice. Rather as though
he had a bad cold.

'You aren't going to wave a cross at me?'

John shook his head. 'No. I haven't got a cross.'

The vampire seemed a little happier, for he ceased to tremble,
though he continued to watch John with a wary eye.

'You're sure? Everyone I've met in the past hundred and fifty
years has either waved a cross at me, or smothered me with garlic
flowers, or – worst of all – tried to drive a stake through my heart.
Everyone is rotten and mean – all because I have the misfortune
to be a vampire.'

'Well – ' John scratched his head, for he had never considered
a vampire's point of view before. 'I expect it's because you frightened them. I mean to say, you do go round sucking blood, and
people are not keen on that kind of thing.'

The vampire, realising, no doubt, that he was in no immediate danger, came out from his corner and reseated himself in the
window bay. 'It's not my fault. I don't really like blood. How would
you like it, if you had to eat – well, sausages for instance, for your
breakfast, dinner and tea, every day for a hundred and fifty years?
Anyway, I haven't moistened my lips for over fifty years. That's
why I'm so thin.'

John shook his head to express his deep sympathy.

'I am sorry. I can see it must be awful for you.'

'Another thing,' the vampire went on, 'I can't go out during the
day, but have to sleep in a rotten old coffin, which I may say is very

cracked and extremely damp. On top of everything else, I've got rheumatism in my knee joints. I can always tell when it's going to rain, because they play me up like billy-o.'

'How absolutely dreadful. My grandfather has rheumatism and he used to rub his joints with camphor. Would you like me to get you some?'

The vampire shook his head. 'That's very kind of you, though really, I doubt it would do much good. The fact is I need nourishment, but I'm determined never to suck blood again. The only trouble is, I can't swallow anything else.'

There was a short silence while John pondered on the vampire's seemingly insurmountable problems.

'Perhaps,' he said at last, 'I can get Mrs Combs to make you some black pudding. I mean to say, that would have the right ingredients. And it would be most nourishing.'

Something like a smile lit the vampire's white face.

'That's an idea. Never thought of that. But do you think the old lady will oblige? Up to now she has shunned me like the plague and bolts herself in her room every night and puts garlic flowers and crosses everywhere.'

John thought about this question for a little while.

'I think I can talk her round. I'm sure that under that forbidding manner she's got a kind heart. Also, I hope you don't mind my mentioning it – but your suit is really awful.'

'What's the matter with it?' the vampire asked. 'It was very fashionable in my day. I was buried in it.'

'Yes, I know. But it is in an awful state. Look, I can probably find you an old suit belonging to my father. It may be a bit large, but you can always roll up the trouser legs and fasten it here and there with safety pins. But however it looks, it will be an improvement on what you are wearing now.'

'You really are most kind,' said the vampire, rising slowly and painfully to his feet, 'and I can't thank you enough. It's nice to know that not everyone has sharpened stakes on the brain. Well, I've a feeling that the sun isn't far below the horizon, so I'd better be getting back to my old box. Do you suppose you could be here tomorrow night? Just in case the old lady sees her way clear to making me a black pudding.'

John nodded, pleased that his new friend had decided to trust him.

'Of course. By the way, what is your name? I can't just call you "Vampire".'

'Archibald,' the vampire confessed with some embarrassment. 'Sorry about that, but my father thought it was a very respectable name, and he wasn't to know I was going to be bitten by Count Thingumbob.'

'I think it's a very nice name,' John said.

'Well, it's a matter of taste. Would you mind opening one of the windows? I don't feel like trudging all the way back to the churchyard. My knees are playing me up.'

It took John some time and a great deal of effort before he was able to raise one of the sashes, but finally there was a gap some two feet high, through which crept the cool night wind.

'That's enough,' said Archibald. 'Now, help me up on to the window-sill.'

'Surely you're not going to jump!' John exclaimed. 'It's all of twenty feet to the ground.'

'Bad hells, no,' Archibald replied. 'Not these days, although I can remember the time when a little drop like that would not have troubled me.'

John heaved, jerked and pushed; a not very pleasant job, because Archibald was so thin that there was a danger some of his bones might break if pressed too hard. But at length he was doubled up between the window and sill. Then he said:

'Thanks very much. I'm all right now. See you tomorrow night.' The thin body shrank, the elbows jutted out on either side, and suddenly a bedraggled, extremely lean bat went fluttering out over the garden. It seemed to have some difficulty in keeping airborne and once or twice appeared to be in danger of nose-diving into a bed of stinging nettles. But, just in time, a strong breeze sprang up and the sad-looking bat glided behind some trees and was lost from sight.

John closed the window, and, after deciding that there was nothing more for him to see that night, went contentedly back to bed.

*

'Will I make what?' Mrs Combs inquired in a loud voice.

'A black pudding,' John repeated his question. 'A big one.'

The housekeeper seated herself on a kitchen chair and watched her young visitor with shrewd eyes. 'I'd be surprised if your mother has an appetite for a black pudding. Or your father either, as for that matter. Don't tell me you want it all for yourself.'

'No.' John hesitated, then said quickly, 'It's for a friend.'

The old woman nodded slowly. 'So, that's the way of it! You've been wandering round the empty rooms, haven't you? Meeting someone you shouldn't. It's a miracle you've got a drop of blood left in your body.'

'But he doesn't like sucking blood any more,' John explained, 'and I suggested that a black pudding might do as well and be just as nourishing.'

Mrs Combs patted his shoulder. 'You're a brave lad, I'll say that for you. There's not many who could face the vampire of Glendale Grange and then be concerned with what might fill its stomach. Well, if a black pudding keeps it away from me, I'll make one with pleasure. But, you'd better not tell your parents about it, or they will scream to high heaven, and that's a fact.'

'This will be a secret between you and me,' John promised. 'But Archibald is really quite harmless and is very frightened of people. He thinks everyone wants to drive a stake through his heart.'

'I'm not in favour of driving stakes through hearts as a rule,' Mrs Combs confessed, 'but I'll not say it might not be a happy release. He can't be very happy wandering about by himself in those empty rooms. Now, you run along and let me get on.'

John next approached his father concerning a suit of old clothes.

'What do you want it for?' Mr Glendale inquired.

'Er . . . there's a poor man living nearby, who has hardly a thing to wear. I said I'd try and find something for him.'

John's father frowned. 'Where did you meet this – this poor man?'

'Oh, I sort of bumped into him.'

'I don't want you talking to perfect strangers, but I'm pleased to see you are taking an interest in people less fortunate than yourself. You may take my old tweed suit. You'll find it in the big wardrobe.'

That night, when everyone was asleep, John, armed with his father's old suit and Mrs Combs's black pudding, crept down the passage and let himself into the empty corner room. Archibald was sitting in a window bay and rose quickly when his young friend entered.

'Have you got the black pudding?'

'Yes.' John handed him the black, thick, sausage-shaped object, and in no time at all the vampire had sunk his long eye-teeth into its rich substance and was chewing with every indication of satisfaction.

'That's good,' he said, after he had swallowed the first mouthful. 'Not quite as refreshing as the real thing, but it has got the right ingredients.'

'And I've brought you one of my father's old suits.'

Archibald took another bite of black pudding.

'That's nice.'

John then asked a question that had been bothering him all day. 'What happens to your clothes when you change into a bat?'

Archibald chewed, while creasing his brow into a puzzled frown. 'I've never thought about it. I suppose they must shrink and change into fur.'

'Oh!' John digested this item of amazing information for a while, then asked: 'What do you do with yourself all night?'

Archibald stuffed the last piece of black pudding into his mouth and was incapable of speech for a full minute.

'Mooch around,' he said at last. 'Sometimes I go for a little fly about, but I'm not up to any great effort these days. Rheumatism in me wings, you know.'

'Wouldn't you like to go . . . somewhere else?' John asked.

'You mean join my ancestors in heaven?' Archibald nodded. 'Indeed I would. But I can't bear the thought of this stake-through-heart business. And as far as I know, that is the only way we vamps can leave this world, so here I stay.'

John realised that this must be a very painful subject for his friend and quickly changed the subject.

'Look, I hope you don't mind my mentioning the matter – but when did you last have a bath?'

The vampire looked at him in astonishment. 'A what?'

'A bath. You know – wash all over.'

Archibald shook his head in bewilderment. 'Certainly not for a hundred and fifty years. I mean to say – well – vampires don't. For some reason we're not keen on water.'

John could scarcely believe his ears and expressed his horror by speaking loudly.

'That's awful. You haven't washed for a hundred and fifty years! Why, everyone should have a bath at *least* once a week. Don't you feel – well – dirty?'

Archibald shook his head. 'No. I suppose I must have got used to it.'

John got to his feet and assumed an expression of great determination. 'You're having one right now. You'll have a shower bath before you put my father's suit on.'

'Honestly, I'd rather not . . .' Archibald began, but John did not allow him to proceed further.

'Not another word. We've got a jolly good shower bath at the end of the passage. It's well away from my parents' bedroom, so no one will hear you. Come along.'

Archibald looked most unhappy, but he was clearly the kind of person who always does what he is told, for he followed John out into the first passage, even though he continued to voice his misgivings.

'I know that it's silly of me, but I could never abide water. I even get the shivers when I see rain running down the window-panes. Do I have to take a bath?'

'Yes, you do.' John nodded vigorously. 'You should be ashamed of yourself. Afraid of water! Why, I could spend all day in the river or swimming baths during the summer.'

With Archibald trailing miserably in his rear, John led the way into the occupied part of the house, and presently, after putting a finger to his lips to signify the need for silence, he opened the bathroom door. He went over to a small cubicle and turned on two taps that were fixed to the left hand wall. He waited until the water was nicely warm, then turned to the trembling vampire.

'Don't be so silly. Take those dreadful clothes off, get under the shower and give yourself a good scrub with this nice bar of pink soap. In the meantime I'll go to my bedroom and fetch a comb and a pair of scissors. Your toe- and fingernails most certainly need cutting.'

Archibald looked doubtfully at the hissing shower, then made a great effort to pull himself together.

'I suppose you're right. I will feel much better after a good wash. It's wrong of me to make all this fuss, after you have taken so much trouble.'

'That's what I wanted to hear,' said John. 'Now, I'll leave you to it. Won't be long.'

He went out and closed the door, then hurried to his bedroom, where he gathered up a pair of nail scissors, a comb, a hairbrush and, after some thought, a toothbrush, then he made his way back to the bathroom, where, after tapping on the door, he turned the handle and entered.

'Archibald,' he called out, 'I'm back. How are you doing?'

There was no answer. Just the continued hissing roar of the shower, which sounded like a violent rainstorm. John tried again. 'Archibald. Are you all right?'

As there was still no reply, he peered into the cubicle, although he was not at all keen to see Archibald with no clothes on. The cubicle was empty.

'This really is too bad,' John said out loud. 'He's run away. And after he promised me he'd take a bath.'

Then he noticed that the vampire's filthy old clothes were draped over the bath and Father's tweed suit hung next to them. The first waves of alarm were creeping across his brain when he reached into the cubicle and turned the taps off. He looked down and saw the pile of grey dust that was swirling into the plughole. Urged on by a feeling of blind panic, he ran from the bathroom and tore down the stairs that led to the lower regions where Mrs Combs had her bedroom.

After he had hammered on the door for some time, he heard her voice shout: 'Go away, you foul monster. I made you a black pudding, but you'll not have my blood.'

'Mrs Combs,' John called out, 'it's me – John. Please come quickly. I think something dreadful has happened.'

There came the sound of bolts being withdrawn and presently the door was opened to reveal the scowling face of Mrs Combs, who clearly was not at all pleased about being disturbed.

'Well, what is it? I have had to upset a rule of a lifetime because of you. I've never opened this door before sunrise before.'

'You don't understand,' John pleaded. 'Archibald – he's disappeared. His clothes are there, but he has gone. Please come.'

'Oh, very well.'

The old lady, after putting on a faded pink dressing-gown, followed John with exasperating slowness back to the bathroom. There she looked at the grey powder and examined the vampire's discarded clothes with much distaste. Then she nodded grimly.

'You mean to say you made him go under a shower bath?'

'Yes.' John nodded. 'He was so dirty. He hadn't washed for over a hundred and fifty years.'

'Don't you realise,' Mrs Combs asked scornfully, 'that running water is fatal to a vampire? He must have disintegrated.'

'Oh, no!' John was near tears. 'He said he was frightened of water. And I made him go in it.'

'I don't suppose he knew what hit him,' Mrs Combs said with a certain amount of satisfaction. 'The minute he stood under that running water – poof – he was a heap of dust being washed down the plughole.'

'Are you sure? He felt no pain?'

'Not a bit of it.' Mrs Combs shook her head. 'A happy release. And he won't bother anyone again.'

John felt much happier. 'He said he wanted to join his ancestors, but he couldn't bear the thought of having a stake driven through his heart. I'm certain he's happy now.'

'So far as I'm concerned,' said Mrs Combs, picking up the late vampire's suit on the end of a bathbrush, 'his ancestors are welcome to him. Now, you'd best get back to bed and let me get back to mine. Not a word to your parents. They don't believe in vampires, and as the old saying goes: "where ignorance is bliss, 'tis folly to be wise".'

John went back to his bed and was soon fast asleep. Next morning he remembered a strange dream. He had seen Archibald, attired in a beautiful white suit, looking very clean, and surrounded by a group of admiring ancestors. And that was not all. He was seated by a table and before him, on a golden plate, was a fat, gleaming, succulent and extremely large black pudding.

AMELIA

ANTHONY KNIGHT WAS TWELVE YEARS OLD when he first saw
Amelia Rohan and had never forgotten her. She had been brought
to his birthday party by Aunt Mildred, a gushing lady who was
prone to forming intense friendships with her own sex, although
no one ever suggested that anything untoward took place. On this
occasion she first gave Anthony his birthday present (an illustrated
book of wild birds), then said with a simpering smile:

'This is my dear friend, Amelia Rohan.'

Even a twelve year old knew he was looking upon an excep-
tionally beautiful woman. Midnight-black hair framed an oval
face, limpid dark eyes reflected a variety of expressions that
ranged from sadness to mischievous, while the full red lips were
frequently parted in an enigmatic smile. A long-fingered hand held
Anthony's small paw and a delightfully husky voice manufactured
words.

'Happy birthday. I do hope you have many, each one more exciting than the last.'

Anthony's parents and various uncles (mostly fictitious for in
those days all adults were given the courtesy title of uncle or aunt)
displayed signs that they were aware of the beautiful stranger;
paying her elaborate compliments, pressing her to partake of cake
and wine, and assuming expressions that the aunts afterwards
described as fatuous. Amelia Rohan appeared to accept these trib-
utes as no more than her due and distributed smiles and murmured words with unruffled graciousness, that made Anthony her
slave for life.

After an hour or so she departed with an ecstatic Aunt Mildred and Anthony did not see her again.

At least not for twenty-five years.

'His Majesty King Chance,' said Frederick the Great, 'does three-quarters of the business of this miserable universe.' Certainly if Anthony Knight had not missed his bus and therefore decided to walk the short distance to his flat, he would not have bumped into the extremely lean man who came reeling out of a narrow alley, while emitting a most disconcerting, continuous moan.

Anthony managed to clasp the tottering figure before it collapsed to the ground and found himself staring into a pair of bloodshot eyes that bore an unpleasant resemblance to red-streaked marbles. There was a revolting smell of stale sweat, plus the merest sugges-tion of perfume, and Anthony, despite his natural concern for the fellow's obvious distress, was suddenly aware of an ominous heave in his stomach. He pushed the man away and watched him slide down a wall to become a crouched shape on the pavement, still moaning and shaking his head from side to side.

Anthony forced himself to speak, but for some reason was unable to raise his voice above a hoarse whisper.

'What's wrong with you? Do you want me to fetch help? An ambulance or something?'

The gaunt head came slowly up and words slipped out over black lips.

'I'm done for. But . . . you . . . you get out of here before she comes . . .'

Anthony had never seen anyone die before, but even so there was no mistaking the sudden glazing of those awful eyes, or the terrifying stillness that transformed a once living creature into an inert object. He dared to prod one bony shoulder with a shak-ing forefinger, then started back when the corpse fell sideways. Conscience has not got a chance when confronted by fear, and Anthony Knight, after a quick glance along the deserted street, took to his heels, and without actually running, left the scene of his strange encounter with undignified haste.

Later, when safely back in the familiar surroundings of his flat, conscience re-established its demands.

'I should not have run away,' he told himself. 'It would not have harmed me to inform the police or someone. Damn it, the fellow might have been murdered or something.'

Then he remembered the dying man's words.

'. . . get out of here before she comes.'

She! A homicidal wife? A vengeance-seeking mistress? Or most likely a nurse whose charge had escaped from her surveillance.

Conscience received a sharp rebuff.

'I'm well out of it,' Anthony declared with growing conviction. 'Damn it all, the fellow was dead. There was nothing I could do.'

For the next three days Anthony sought in vain for some reference in the newspapers, about the discovery of a dead man in the entrance to a narrow alley. It seemed impossible that such an event would not have merited at least a paragraph in the local journal, that usually reported everything from a man fined for not having a dog licence to the customary row in the town hall.

Conscience came back onto its own when he was forced to consider the possibility that the fellow had not been dead at all, but had eventually got up and wandered off, or was once again in the clutches of the mysterious 'she' for whom he appeared to entertain such dread. And possibly not without reason, for had he not displayed all the symptoms of starvation? Memory recreated a mental picture of the reeling figure, with its sunken cheeks and skeletal body, plus – now he came to think about it – a certain suggestion of bloodlessness. Bones, skin and wasted muscles.

It must be confessed that Anthony was a worrier, cursed by a need to meet his troubles at their source, fired by a hope they would then disappear. The lean man had reeled out of an alley, therefore it was reasonable to assume he had emerged from some house which stood somewhere beyond that shadow-haunted passage. After three weeks spent in fruitless conjecture, Anthony decided to retrace his footsteps and return to the scene of his crime of omission.

He wisely chose a sunny day for his conscience-inspired pilgrimage and thus was able to walk boldly into a passage that was not in the least sinister. Merely a paved path some four feet wide, flanked on either side by a tall wall. Moreover it was perhaps thirty feet long and gave access to a broad, tree-lined street that created the impression of seclusion, blended with a kind of well-bred silence.

This phenomenon was hard to define. Anthony imagined that a rag and bone man would have been struck dumb in such a street. No hawker would dared have opened one of those wrought-iron gates and ventured into a green-tiled porch, let alone pushed a white bell-button to summon a glacial-eyed housewife, who would promptly slam the door. Each house glowered behind a well-tended lawn, every window glared its cold, soulless arrogance.

And the lean man had escaped, staggered or simply been pushed out of one of these extremely desirable residences.

Anthony Knight walked slowly along the left pavement, feeling rather ridiculous, realising that unresponsive house-fronts would not betray the secrets of those who lived behind them, and he shrank from the possibility of knocking on doors and making inane enquiries. He paced up the street, then down the opposite side, and for all the information that short journey had afforded him, he might as well have gone straight home.

Then the first house on the left displayed signs of life. The front door opened and an old woman, stern of visage, upright of figure, dressed in a severe black gown, marched briskly down the garden path and to Anthony's disconcertment, halted by the garden gate and stared at him with unblinking eyes.

The first impulse was to flee; take to his heels and run, but his brain, a cautious, well-trained organ, informed him that such an action could be interpreted as the result of nefarious intent, so he continued to walk slowly, looking inquiringly at each house, like one who is not certain of his surroundings. When he came opposite that first house, the old woman, still staring at him, with deep-set eyes, asked:

'You are looking for someone?'

His tongue gabbled the first words that poured into his brain.

'Yes. I'm looking for a brother . . . that is to say . . . a friend who was taken ill some while back. But I can't seem to find his house.'

The old woman nodded.

'I thought that might be so. I happened to glance out of the upstairs window and I said to my mistress, there is a man who is looking for someone.'

There was an indefinable accent, suggesting a mid-European origin, and it had a strange seductive quality that was not in keeping with the unlovely exterior. Anthony said:

'I guess I'll never find him now. So I'll go home.'

The old woman bared surprisingly white teeth in a mirthless grin.

'Aimless feet wander far. My mistress, who is an invalid, you understand, thinks you are familiar. Is that the right word? Someone she has met before and wonders if you would be so kind as to take tea with her.'

'I really don't know. I'm pressed for time . . .'

'You would be doing a kindness. One passes this way but once, is it not so? And any kindness will be one more paving stone on the road to eternal nourishment. It is well to think of the future.'

'I cannot impose . . .'

'My mistress will cry all night if you do not enter. Her health is delicate and distress can be so unbeneficial, do you not think? I ask for but a few minutes. A few sips of fresh brewed tea. Maybe two nibbles of a cucumber sandwich.'

Anthony Knight sighed deeply and surrendered. It was the most momentous decision of his health.

'Very well. But only for a few minutes.'

'You are extraordinarily kind.'

He followed the grim guide up the garden path and into the house; took note of the small hall that was flanked by a number of doors and had a wide staircase in the centre, before being led into a comfortably furnished room that looked out onto an unkempt garden.

'This,' the old woman announced, 'is the stranger you requested.'

Anthony, after a quick glance round the room, turned his full attention to the lady who had caused him to be lured in from the street. For a while disbelief battled with credibility, but finally he was forced to accept the evidence provided by his eyes.

Reclining on a sofa was Amelia Rohan.

There was no mistaking the lush beauty, the pale oval face, framed by midnight black hair, the limpid dark eyes – the vision which had haunted his memory for twenty-five years.

Only the girl on the sofa could not possibly be Amelia Rohan –

or should not be. Twenty-five years plus twenty-five – take or give a year – makes fifty, and it would be gross slander to suggest this lovely creature was a day over twenty-two.

But poor Anthony Knight who had nurtured and embellished a dream, could only stare, temporarily struck dumb by a lovely smiling face, then strangled an impulsive gasp when that never-to-be-forgotten voice created a smooth flow of words.

'How kind to take pity on a lonely and sick woman. What must you think of me? But the mere sight of a nice-looking man with compassionate face . . . I had to meet him. Can you forgive me?'

Anthony made a strange noise that could be accepted as acquiescence and tried to detect some subtle difference that would convince him that this was not Aunt Mildred's long ago friend. Certainly she looked younger than he remembered, but that might be due to the simple white dress and the gold band that confined the dark hair and gave her a youthful, vulnerable appearance. He experienced a ridiculous urge to pat her head and murmur comforting words.

She spoke again and motioned to an adjacent chair.

'Please make yourself comfortable. Greta, you may serve tea.'

The old woman, with suspicion of a smirk on her lean face, left the room and Anthony, after seating himself, had so far recovered from his initial shock as to arrive at a reasonable conclusion. This young creature must be a relative of Amelia Rohan. Perhaps a daughter. He ventured to make himself known.

'My name is Anthony Knight. May I ask . . . ?'

She shook her head in mock reproof, then clasped her hands in a most delightful way.

'How rude of me, I have not introduced myself. You must think I'm dreadful, what with inviting a perfect stranger in from the street and all. Then forgetting to say who I am. My name is Amelia Roland.'

Anthony started and exclaimed, 'Good Lord!' then, before he could master his excitement, added, 'Roland! Are you sure it isn't Rohan?'

The charming smile died and became a rather disturbing grimace, while what can only be described as a steely glint marred the beautiful eyes. Suddenly the comfortable room, with its heavy

old fashioned furniture, seemed to assume a sinister aspect; and
Anthony could not quite dismiss the notion that the temperature
had dropped ten degrees. Then Amelia Roland asked in a quiet
voice:

'Why should you imagine my name is Rohan, when I distinctly
said it was Roland?'

'Well – to be frank – I once met someone who looked just like
you, years ago when I was a child and her name was Amelia Rohan.
Honestly, you might be her double.'

He had said the right words, for the eyes lost that alarming
glitter and the adorable mouth parted in a teasing smile.

'And tell me, Anthony, how do you explain this dilemma? Clearly
I cannot be this lady that made such an impression upon you so
long ago. I wonder what the explanation can be?'

Anthony presented a reasonable conclusion.

'Amelia Rohan was or is a relative. Your . . . mother perhaps.'

Again the white hands came together and a joyous little laugh
drifted across the room, causing Anthony to forget his disquiet of
a few minutes before.

'You are clever. Really you are. My dear mother was Amelia
Rohan before her marriage. Imagine remembering what someone
looked like that you only met as a child.'

'I can never forget her,' Anthony confessed. 'But, forgive me for
asking – is your mother still alive?'

Again the smile died and was replaced by a sad expression; the
eyes seemed bright with yet to be shed tears.

'She . . . she died. Together with my dear, dear papa. In a motor-
ing accident, you understand. Apart from Greta, who has looked
after me these many years, I am quite alone.'

Anthony made sympathetic noises and only just restrained
himself from running over to the sofa and flinging a comforting
arm round the slim shoulders. He was also aware that this glorious
child-woman was having a disturbing effect on him; sufficient to
make him entertain hopes that he might be permitted something
more than polite conversation.

He almost at once dismissed the unworthy idea. She was too
artless, so clearly a gently nurtured young creature, who acted
on impulse, prompted by loneliness and possibly an unsuspected

sexual urge. No decent man could take advantage of such a situation. At least so Anthony told himself on this occasion.

The sad mood soon passed and she greeted Greta with a happy smile when the old woman entered, pushing a loaded food-trolley.

'That's right, Greta dear, in front of me, so I can be mother. Oh good! You have made some of your nice cucumber sandwiches!'

'Which,' Greta instructed with a ferocious frown, 'you will not touch. Dinner will be ready in an hour from now and I will not have you spoiling your appetite.'

Amelia screwed up her face into what Anthony thought to be a most delightful expression of mock exasperation, then sighed deeply.

'I am always being bullied. I can never have what I want. You are a monster, Greta.'

'I speak only for your own good.'

Anthony found himself trying to decide her real age, for during the last five minutes she appeared to have shed six years. Gone was the young woman of some twenty-two or three; now he was watching what must be a young girl who could not be possibly a day over sixteen. She giggled, then grabbed Greta's arm and after a smiling 'Excuse me,' to Anthony, whispered softly into the old woman's ear.

Greta jerked upright and pulled her arm free, then spat out a fierce denial.

'No . . . no . . . you must not. It is too soon.'

Amelia pouted, shrugged and generally behaved like a beautiful pampered child who has just suffered the rare experience of being denied something on which she had set her heart. Then she seemed to remember the presence of her guest and shot him a glowing, almost amorous glance, before saying:

'Anthony – you don't mind my calling you Anthony? – would you mind awfully eating all these sandwiches yourself, as this dreadful dragon will not let me have anything.'

'You are indeed exceedingly kind, but . . .'

'I will be awfully hurt if you do not, for then I will know you are offended.'

Greta turned quickly and Anthony thought he detected a gleam of fear in the deep-set eyes.

'You will ignore her. She is in a contrary mood. Eat what you please, leave what you will.'

After delivering this caustic advice she stumped from the room and Amelia poked her tongue out when the door was slammed. Anthony rose to accept his cup of tea and a plate on which lay three triangular sandwiches, then went back to his chair, where he sipped, nibbled and was gently interrogated.

'Were you looking for someone in this street? I saw you walking up and down, staring at each house.'

'Yes. A few weeks ago I found a man who was very ill – or rather I bumped into him at the end of the passage. I assumed he came from one of these houses . . . Silly really, because I have no idea which one.'

Amelia was nursing a cup and saucer and occasionally she raised it to her lips. She seemed to have recaptured the lost years and now looked fully twenty-five.

'How kind of you. You bump into a sick man, then come back with the intention of finding out if he had recovered. Did you tell anyone? Fetch a doctor? Notify the police?'

Anthony shook his head and realised that he was no longer interested in the lean man's fate.

'No, and that omission was troubling my conscience. You see, I thought he was dead. Perhaps he was. But I wanted to know.'

Amelia sighed and stared sadly at her tea cup.

'Poor man. But if he is dead, then there was nothing you could do for him, and if he got better, then that's all right. There is really no reason for you to worry either way.'

'You are very comforting.'

Amelia was now stirring her tea with a silver spoon.

'Tell me about yourself, Anthony. Are you married with lots of lovely children?'

'No. I never met anyone who looked the least bit like your mother. Anyway – not up to now.'

Maybe a faint flush stained the pale cheek, or perhaps this was only wishful thinking on Anthony's part, but the gentle interrogation continued.

'You doubtlessly have a family who care for you. Parents perhaps, brothers and sisters.'

'No. My parents, like yours, are dead. I may have one or two aunts around, but I lost touch with them years ago.'

For a while she made no further comment, but sat perfectly still as though this information required careful thought; indeed it did appear that she had suddenly become oblivious to her surroundings, temporarily lost in some deep abyss of conjecture. Her face was now in repose, had become a white mask devoid of all expression, and to Anthony's consternation bore some resemblance to that of a corpse. He coughed and was about to enquire if she had been taken ill, when she abruptly jerked her head up and gave him another dazzling smile.

'Fate would appear to have brought us together. Isn't it wonderful? You come looking for a sick man, I glance out of my window and feel a terrible urge to invite you in. Our meeting was planned long, long ago, when the world was young.'

Normally Anthony would have been acutely embarrassed by this purple rhetoric, but it had been delivered with such an air of conviction, he found himself agreeing that Providence may indeed have had a hand in arranging this fortuitous encounter. Afterwards he was forced to admit that when in her presence, he had little or no faith in his own judgement, and soon dismissed the unpleasant misgivings of a few minutes before, as pure imagination.

This first visit – if it could be so designated – was brought to an abrupt end by Greta entering the room and announcing that her young lady must now rest, she being far from well. Anthony wondered from what kind of illness she was suffering, or if she was no more than a female who enjoyed a permanent state of ill-health. But of course his young hostess pouted, and the Greta-monster always interfered just as she was beginning to enjoy herself, and begged Anthony to come again.

'I am sure,' Greta stated with apparent deep conviction, 'this gentleman has something better to do than waste time on the merest chit of a girl, who knows not her own mind from one minute to the next.'

Amelia did shed tears. Two. One crystal clear liquid diamond slid from each eye and glided down the snow-white cheeks; while her enchanting voice strangled a sob as she pleaded for understanding.

'I am so lonely and Anthony is so kind, absolutely on my wavelength – if that is the correct expression. If he does not come again I will die of grief, just like that lady on the lake, who could only see Sir Lancelot's reflection in the mirror.'

Greta addressed Anthony with more amity than she had so far displayed and even ventured a grimace that looked dangerously like a smile.

'Well, if the gentleman can find the time and has indeed the goodness of heart to waste it on a wayward child, I will open the door.'

The sun shone after a brief rain-storm and Amelia clasped her hands, jumped up and down on the sofa and now gave the distinct impression she was not more than fourteen, although Anthony was certain disappointment would age her fast.

'I will be happy to call again,' he said. 'Most happy.'

Amelia gave a squeal of delight and Greta whispered:

'She is becoming too excited and will not sleep this night. You had better go.'

And without further waste of time he was hustled out into the hall, then to the front door, where an affable Greta waved to him from the porch.

He walked home on light feet, in fact was close on several occasions to dancing along the suburban pavements, enjoying that rare period of madness that men call happiness, even though he was not at all certain what he had to be happy about.

Later, when cold calculating sanity returned, he began to think.

Temptation can only be kept at bay by the threat of consequences.

Anthony told himself over and over again that Amelia Roland was most certainly unbalanced, for all he knew under the age of consent (in fact her exact age was still a matter for nagging concern) and he would do well to keep well away from that fatal alley. But of course his weaker self was quite capable of putting up a contrariwise argument, pointing out that there could be no possible harm in spending an hour or so with a sick girl, and even stressing that a gentleman (which Anthony hoped he was) must always keep a promise.

★

Temptation might have succumbed to iron determination, had not Amelia Roland taken to invading his dreams. Normally Anthony was not a dreaming person, or perhaps to be more accurate, did not remember what he dreamed about. But two weeks after his disturbing adventure he had the most vivid dream that could not possibly be forgotten. Next day he tried to analyse this nocturnal experience, and came to the conclusion it must be the result of an over-excited imagination creating a wish fantasy in the sleeping brain.

He had suddenly woken up in that comfortable sitting-room; had seemingly been blasted into full awareness, knowing that he occupied a body that was a perfect duplicate of the one that he used during the daylight hours, which was at that very moment sound asleep in its respectable bed.

Amelia Roland was laying on the sofa stark naked.

A beautiful study in black and white, with a pale sad face that wore a melancholy smile, the slightly husky voice was as real as a train siren on Monday morning.

'Anthony, why have you not come to see me? I have waited so long.'

Anthony could feel his heart thudding in a most alarming fashion, fully aware that this was some kind of three-dimensional dream, and the everyday body was struggling to wake up. He advanced towards the sofa, stumbled, and was about to reach out shaking hands, when he suddenly sat up in his own bed. His heart was still thudding and it seemed as if that pale, sad face was a slowly dispersing vision that drifted like moon-tinted mist back towards the door. His fumbling hand found the bedside lamp switch and light shattered the darkness, although menacing blocks of shadow still lurked in obscure corners and behind the dressing-table.

Anthony heard his voice shout:

'I won't go. Oh, dear God, I must not go.'

A boisterous wind chased fallen leaves along the pavement when Anthony Knight paid his next visit to that neat house, which welcomed him with gleaming, discreetly curtained windows and wide open front door. Greta was waiting for him in the porch.

'So, you have at last decided to keep your promise and come.
She has been very difficult, sitting by the window all day and night,
crying like her heart was breaking. It is ridiculous, but she has
always been the same. But never as bad as this. Come in and wipe
your feet, I have but recently brushed the carpet.'

The joy, the blessed relief of surrendering to temptation. The
battle was over, the colours hauled down and maybe his soul was
damned, but before retribution, would come full payment for his
capitulation. Amelia Roland was again reclining on the sofa, her
face a veritable picture of tearful delight; and this was not the time
to wonder why, pay heed to a tiny warning voice that tried to mar
the perfection of this wonderful wide-awake dream. Anthony sank
down on to one knee and kissed one white hand; a courtier paying
tribute to his lovely, virgin queen.

Greta coughed and backed towards the door.

'I will leave you together. I will make tea.'

Amelia swung her legs off the sofa and patted a cushion.

'Dear Anthony, sit beside me, so I can scold you for not coming
before. Oh, why did you not come?'

To be seated beside her was an exciting, and – for some inexplicable reason – a rather fearsome experience. Her hand which
slid so naturally into his, was soft and warm, but she gave out –
Anthony struggled for the right definition – a subtle suggestion of
perpetual coldness. Rather as though she were nothing more than
an animated doll, heated by a faulty mechanism, that might at any
time break down.

Even at near proximity her beauty was flawless. She clearly did
not use make-up, but her lips were bright red, her white skin clear
as that of a child; not one line suggested maturity. Again her age
could have been anything from eighteen to twenty-two.

She raised one slim eyebrow.

'I am waiting, Anthony. Why did you not come before?'

'I thought perhaps you were only being polite when you asked
me to call again. After all I am thirty-seven, while you are little
more than a child. I have not much to recommend me, neither
looks . . .'

'You have great beauty.'

He blushed and pulled his stomach in.

'And not much to say for myself.'

'But I can see into your mind. It is a vast storehouse of wisdom. You have no need to clothe your thoughts with words.'

Now she was talking like a Victorian novelette, but Anthony was in no mood to be critical, although that irritating small voice would insist in pointing out that flattery is only tendered by those who want something more substantial in return. Only – what had he to give this glorious young creature?

'I want what you can take,' she said simply.

He shrank back and thought for a moment that he must have spoken out aloud. She smiled gently, then laid her head on his shoulder and when her hair brushed his nose, it seemed that he detected a faint smell of corruption. Immediately, as though to negate the rising wave of revulsion, it changed into the merest suggestion of some sweet smelling perfume. His right arm crept around her shoulders and he felt guilty, exhilarated and frightened, all at the same time.

Her voice assumed a soft, lilting quality.

'Now you are stumbling through a dark passage, but soon there will be light and you must not be frightened. Fear breeds death and you must not die.'

Two burning desires warred in his brain; one to break free and run from this house, never to return, the other to tear the dress from her back, ravish, dive deep into a black sea that would stain his soul for all eternity. In fact he did neither, but sat looking down at her, afraid to move or speak, lest he be forced to take decisive action. And it was no use telling himself that she was more than a little deranged, for he was straying near to the borderline of madness himself.

Then just as her mouth was opening and she appeared about to whisper into his ear, the door opened and Greta entered, pushing the trolley, forcing them both to draw apart, and Anthony found that his brow was streaming with perspiration. The old woman said nothing, but eased the trolley in front of Amelia, before turning abruptly and leaving the room. But in the doorway she paused and shot the girl one swift glance, that might have been intended as a warning.

'You do not mind cucumber sandwiches again, Anthony?'

Amelia asked. 'You are probably partial to ham, but the smell of meat makes me sick.'

Anthony muttered, 'Good Lord!' then said aloud, 'I love cucumber ... love it,' and grabbed a triangular sandwich, thrusting it into his mouth as though to demonstrate his partiality for this delicacy.

Amelia poured tea into two cups, added milk, a spoonful of sugar into one (Anthony could not remember telling her that this was his customary amount), then sank back and idly stirred with a small silver spoon.

'But she won't drink the tea,' that damnable tiny voice told Anthony. 'Or eat anything.'

He sat eating one sandwich after another, sipping from his cup, feeling like a schoolboy who has been invited round for a slap-up tea.

'You have a good appetite,' Amelia remarked.

In fact Anthony had never felt less hungry in his life, but eating and drinking filled in time and provided an excellent excuse for not doing anything else. It kept both of his hands occupied and enabled him to edge a little further along the sofa, thus creating a respectable gap between them. This was an irrational action of course, because one part of him wanted to get much closer, while the other was prepared to manufacture a scream if she so much as touched him.

When only two sandwiches remained on the large plate, he blushed and became uncomfortably aware that he had committed an impolite misdemeanor, and such was his character, all else was momentarily forgotten.

'I say, I'm awfully sorry! What must you think of me?'

'Should finish them, if I was you,' Amelia suggested playfully. 'There's no point in letting them go to waste.'

'But what about you?'

'I must not spoil my dinner, or the dragon will scold.'

There seemed little else to do, but follow this suggestion, then accept another cup of tea, well aware that the girl had not touched her first.

'Are you full up now?' she asked.

'Yes, absolutely. Could not eat another scrap.'

Amelia Roland produced a handkerchief from somewhere and leaning over, wiped his mouth.

For a while he did not speak but sat staring at the empty plate, trying to muster strength and resolution to rise and walk from the room. To take such a liberty she must be completely mad and he had been a fool to come back; a weak fool who could not fight temptation. She was edging across the gap which separated them, nuzzling her head against his shoulder, whispering . . . whispering . . .

'Know yourself . . . dear . . . dear . . . vampire.'

A white arm slid around his neck, the hand forced his head to the right and all he could see was a round, pulsating neck. He experienced a sensation that had much in common with a rug being pulled from beneath his feet. The whispering voice began to explain.

'There are those who take and those that give. Both form an intricate whole. Do you understand? No . . . no . . . do not turn your head, but listen. I have searched for years and years, and sometimes I have found one who seemed to be one of us – like the poor dear you bumped into – but the strain is often weakened by generations of interbreeding, and they were quite unable to adapt. Refused to take nourishment and quite literally starved to death. And I had to make do with the dragon. Can you imagine?'

Anthony struggled, albeit weakly. The arm became as a steel band round his neck. Amelia Roland – or Rohan – continued.

'You see by taking you also contribute. Some kind of virus that will give me nourishment. Then we will both live forever. Is not that exciting? Neither of us will ever die. Oh, Anthony dear, it is long past my milking time.'

Anthony stammered, 'I'm not . . . not . . . not . . .'

'Oh, yes you are. I spotted you as an embryo vam years ago, when your poor Aunt Mildred took me to your birthday party. By the way she was not your real aunt and was quite unable to adapt. Remember, you never saw her again.'

Anthony did not answer; he could not, being fully occupied in staring at the white neck. He was slowly realising that he had never seen anything quite so beautiful, desirable – or biteable in his entire life. The door opened and Greta entered. Her voice was not quite steady when she spoke.

'Do you need any help? Has he got what it takes or do we have to bury him with the rest in the cellar?'

'No, dear monster, I do believe we have – what is the expression? – hit pay dirt this time.'

Greta emitted a vast sigh of relief.

'Good, I will clear away these obnoxious tea things. May the Black One bless you both.'

At first reluctantly, then with fast mounting excitement, Anthony opened his mouth, allowed long eye-teeth to slide down over his lower lip – and bit. When one remembers he had never sucked blood before, he did a remarkably good job.

Anthony and Amelia were both well fed and enjoying – for want of a better expression – an after dinner nap, when Greta returned. She had the appearance of one who is looking forward to a long awaited treat and would under no circumstances be put off. Anthony eyed her with some disquiet, while Amelia giggled.

'Greta, you monster! Really, you must give him time to digest his intake. The poor darling is simply bloated.'

Two rivulets of moisture seeped down over the old woman's lips.

'I can see he is. He won't be for much longer.'

It took some little while for Anthony to understand the situation, but when he did a dash for the door seemed to be a good idea. Greta tripped him up with one outstretched foot. Amelia's laughter-choked voice came to him from the sofa.

'Anthony dear, you must not be greedy. I give, you take, Greta shares. All so nice and cosy. Do you not think so?'

He screamed when Greta fell on him.

ACQUIRING A FAMILY

CELIA WATSON EXAMINED the front of her new house with a critical eye, but could detect nothing lacking. The five windows – three up and two down – gleamed as only freshly cleaned glass can; the red brickwork looked as if it had been washed and sanded in the not too distant past, while frames, guttering and front door glittered with recently applied green paint.

Celia had dreamed of such a house for a long time and it was only the event of an ancient uncle's demise and the acquisition of his money, that had enabled her to buy this one. She was grateful for the late uncle's thoughtfulness in leaving her the where-withal to enjoy not only this dream house, but sufficient funds to never again have to consider the dire prospect of gainful employment.

She took a large key from her handbag, fitted it into a keyhole, then flung the door open.

The pseudo antique furniture suited the small house, ranging as it did from a credence table and umbrella-cum-hat-stand in the tiny hall, to the looming Tudor-style wardrobe and bed in what might be called the main bedroom. The last owner had decorated all the walls with light brown emulsion paint, and although this served as an excellent background for the furniture, it did have a rather depressing effect when viewed for the first time, but even this Celia managed to ignore. She had seen the interior of the house before of course and agreed to take it as it stood, furniture, decor and all; she hoped she would live there for many years and die contented – if not happy – in the vast Tudor style bed.

Such is one of the illusions that make up the foundation of that great fantasy we call life.

Celia Watson spoke aloud: 'This is what I have always wanted. Thanks to God I am not too old to enjoy it.'

She was fifty-three, an age that has escaped from the chains of youth, but has not yet slid into the iron cage of old age. At such a time of life one should be in a position to benefit from experience while still enjoying clear mental powers and – hopefully – good health.

Celia enjoyed both.

But she was alone. A strange distaste for any form of close intimacy with persons of either sex, resulted in her never marrying, or as for that matter encouraging anything more than superficial friendships, so that now – while still enjoying her own company – there was a fear-germ – a nagging thought – that she might have missed out on something essential to her well-being.

She swept, brushed, polished, arranged pictures and knick-knacks to her satisfaction, then manhandled heavy furniture from one place to another. But the time came when all that could be done was done and the bright hues of novelty died; then the fear-germ returned, a little larger, stronger than before.

Alien thoughts chased each other down the rarely explored avenues of the brain and eventually congregated into a ridiculous notion.

She should have had children.

Before moving into the cottage she would have laughed such an idea to scorn, for had she not ridiculed the premise that a woman's primary role was that of mother? 'In this over-crowded planet,' she often maintained, 'I at least have not made the situation worse by brat production. Pity there's not a few more like me.'

Now, while seated on a well padded chair, she would splutter up from a shallow sleep, almost certain that she had been awakened by tiny fingers tugging at her skirt or the sound of laughing child-ish voices coming from the next room. Nonsense of course. The result of a wobbly tummy, plus the excitement of moving into her new home.

Perhaps it would be better to get out more, join a literary appre-ciation group or something. After all she was now at that time of life when one wanted to be taken out of oneself – whatever that might mean – and it was most important not to pander to – well – fancies. She could remember one or two lukewarm friends who had gone distinctly funny after entering the fifties.

She joined the Ladies' Tuesday Afternoon Group, where the latest TV programme (if it were decent), the prime minister's latest misdemeanour, the prospect of an atomic war and other worthwhile subjects were discussed. As Celia prided herself on being an outspoken person who was not afraid of expressing her opinion, she had soon dethroned the current chairperson and made herself extremely unpopular, which as everyone knows, is the seal of success.

Then she took to attending evening classes, organized by the local county council, where she became proficient in basket-making, early Victorian letter writing, pottery and raising a garden in window boxes.

All this activity kept her as active as anyone could wish – or in many cases would want – and succeeded in taking her out of herself in no uncertain manner. There was no time for morbid *fancies* and hence no danger of her going distinctly funny.

For a while at any rate.

Basket-making became a boring pastime, early Victorian letter writers revealed themselves to be nothing more than persons with a penchant for not using one word when ten would do; pottery was a messy business, and as she already had an extensive garden, raising one in window boxes was a waste of time. Moreover the Ladies' Tuesday Afternoon Group grew restless under her dictator-ship, successfully organized a palace revolution, replaced her as chairperson by the wife of a coal merchant, which in effect meant she was sent into exile.

So it was that once again – as the time-honoured expression has it – time hung heavily on her hands, and she took to sitting in a comfortable armchair, trying to read a novel, which inevitably slipped from her hands, when she sank into a shallow sleep.

Almost every time she was awakened by tiny fingers tugging at her skirt, or the sound of laughing childish voices coming from the next room. But she could no longer say with hand on heart: 'Nonsense of course.'

Sometimes the tugging – the childish laughter took place when she was on the verge of awakening. She was in fact almost fully aware that four or five children were involved, possibly two by her knees and three in the next room. On occasion they made quite a clamour and it was this that rocketed her up from the pit of sleep, hurtled her into full awareness – then all sound and tugging stopped.

The phenomenon had an eerie effect, became more than a little disturbing and Celia again began to wonder if she was indeed becoming distinctly funny and if the house, after all, was going to suit her.

Then she began to see. Only a glimpse at first.

After a particularly noisy session, shrill laughter, stamping of feet, the slamming of a door, plus violent tugging, Celia cried out, opened her eyes, then fell back in her chair.

She had a glimpse of a tiny figure attired in a white dress dis-appearing round a door frame. A fleeting vision that might have been a vestige of a dream, or maybe an illusion created by the wakening brain (always supposing that organ ever sleeps), there were all manner of explanations, but when this last occurrence was matched up with the sounds, one's wondering invaded a new plane of conjecture.

A few days later she was permitted more than a glimpse. A good long look.

Sleeping again, but this time in her bed, with a bedside lamp sending a golden circle of light across the room, for the eerie, distinctly funny disturbances made total and even partial darkness unpleasant, to say the least. Lying on her left side, cheek nestled deeply in a plump pillow, her eyes sprang open, and she saw a child, a little girl, standing a few feet away, looking at her, attired in a white dress, with auburn hair groomed into tight ringlets, hang-ing down to her shoulders. Dark, limpid eyes gazed into her own and for a while it seemed as if time was frozen and Celia Watson would spend eternity staring at a child, while cold fear crept slowly up from her feet, like the soul-releasing chill that announces the approach of death.

Perhaps that good long look lasted two minutes – or five seconds – but it seemed as if time had stood still before the child vanished – ceased to be – became as never was.

But its image remained imprinted on Celia's brain, persisted in lurking behind her eyes, and when she closed the lids, there it was standing against a blazing red background.

Fearful to look upon, dreadful to consider – but – appealing.

When fear had unlocked its shackles, Celia leapt out of bed, ran out on to the landing and raced into the bathroom, this being a sure place of refuge back in the innocent days of childhood, it being assumed that no one would dare invade its privacy once the engaged bolt had been slid into position. So far as she could remember experience had never disproved this theory.

Seated on the lavatory pan she gave the matter her full attention and came to the conclusion that she might have over-reacted to the situation, fearsome though the experience had been. Had not her late, extremely wise Papa always maintained, 'There is always a rational explanation for every extraordinary experience if only we take the trouble to look for it.'

Therefore it stood to reason there was a rational explanation for all these sounds and visions, be they ghosts . . .

Celia shuddered on the lavatory seat and regurgitated that horrible little word:

'Ghosts!'

Her old new house was haunted!

She had never thought about ghosts before, save on the occasion when she read *The Turn of the Screw* by Henry James, and that did rather offer a rational explanation. The governess might have been distinctly funny. Had anyone asked her: 'Do you believe in ghosts?' the answer undoubtedly would have been a head shaking 'don't know,' which might have been a cover up for: 'Maybe I do.'

Now, sitting on the lavatory pan, she most certainly did.

She must leave the newly acquired house at the very break of day and never come back. Get the nice estate agent to put it on the market, then buy a well appointed flat nearer town. That was what she must do.

Most certainly.

She shifted her behind into a more comfortable position and gave the matter some more thought.

'Why?'

Why give up this lovely new-old house, just because of some noisy ghost children?

After all, they only seemed to manifest when she was on the point of waking up and that surely could be borne. Repetition was already veneering the phenomenon with the gloss of familiarity, which in due course might well breed a kind of contempt.

Children? She should have had children if only their production had not necessitated a rather revolting physical function. Now she might acquire some without any effort on anyone's part: children that did not require feeding, clothing, cosseting, washing or any other beastly service.

Dream children. Ghostly waifs.

Celia rose from the lavatory pan, automatically pulled the chain, then bravely walked out of the bathroom. She crossed the landing and stood (for no particular reason) looking down over the bannisters. She cleared her throat three times, before calling out in a singsong voice:

'Come on . . . children. Come to mummy. Come to mummy.'

This language had always worked with a kitten she had once owned, but the ghost children seemed to be unimpressed. Not a sight or sound greeted eye or ear and presently Celia went back to bed, there surprisingly to fall into a deep sleep and not awake until the morning sun had turned the window into a golden square.

'Ghost children,' Miss Broadfield-Blythe said gently, tapping Celia's knee with a pointed forefinger, 'are the most harmless of wraiths. You see, my dear, they are seeking love.'

Celia refilled her guest's cup and replaced a blue woollen cosy on the teapot.

'Is that so?'

'Indeed it is. No doubt during their brief lives they never experienced that precious emotion and are now spending eternity looking for it.'

'I've only seen one child,' Celia pointed out, 'although I've heard others. I think there's four or five.'

Miss Broadfield-Blythe closed and opened her watery blue eyes, then rubbed her long nose.

'Bound to be more than one, but not more than six I'd say. Never in my long experience have I known there to be more than six ghost-children in one group. When I received your most interesting letter, I said to Mildred – we've worked on many a case together – I said, Mildred, a mass juvenile haunting, but not more than six, I'll be bound. Tell me, Miss Watson . . . It is Miss?'

Celia nodded.

'How sensible. Tell me, Miss Watson, how did you come to contact me? Did someone recommend me?'

'No, I saw your advertisement in the tobacconist's window. As I've made no progress myself, I thought an expert might be more successful.'

Miss Broadfield-Blythe screwed up her face into an expression that might have denoted puzzlement and asked:

'Progress? Success? I'm not with you, dear. What kind of progress had you in mind?'

'Well, to bring the children out of hiding. I mean – I only hear or see them just before I wake up. Properly wake up, that is. I want to – well – make contact. See and hear them when wide-awake.'

'For what reason, dear? Not to experiment I hope. Our spirit friends are not at all happy when experimented with.'

Celia fluttered her hands. 'No, indeed. I want . . . want . . . to sort of adopt them.'

A wonderful smile spread slowly over Miss Broadfield-Blythe's face and for a while lent it a kind of beauty. 'That's simply gorgeous, dear. Simply heart-stopping.' She pulled forth an enormous handkerchief from a patch pocket. 'Want to adopt poor, love-seeking spirit children! God bless you, my dear.' She patted her eyes several times, then resolutely put the handkerchief away. 'But let's get down to our muttons. What can I do to help you?'

Celia put on her little-I'm-lost-girl act, which had never been known to fail when dealing with masculine-inclined middle-aged spinsters. 'I rather hoped you'd be able to do something that will bring them out. Let me see and talk to them.'

The lady medium looked thoughtful. 'I will do my best, dear.

Can't do more. No one can. I'll see what can be done with the atmosphere. Sort of taste it.'

She pushed her teacup to one side, laid her hands palms uppermost on the table, then closed her eyes. Presently she giggled, 'One of them is tickling me. Right in the centre of the right hand. How charming.' She called out in the same sing-song voice that Celia had used a few days earlier.

'Come to me, children dears, come to your Auntie Ag, who you need not fear. Put your tweeny hands in mine and we'll say hullo to your mummy-to-be. Won't that be nice? Yes, it will. Yes, it will.'

A loud crash came from above stairs, which sounded as if the cut glass perfume container that resided on Celia's dressing table had been knocked – or thrown – on to the floor. But that was all.

Miss Broadfield-Blythe intoned other inducements, but for all the response they received, she might as well have saved her breath. Presently she released a gentle sigh and said:

'Well, I'm sure I've stirred them up. Brought them to the surface, so to speak. You'll probably get results after I'm gone. Nothing startling at first. It takes time for this kind of thing to get really under way. But so far as I'm concerned there doesn't seem to be much more I can do. Not for today at any rate.'

'I can't thank you enough,' Celia replied. 'If nothing else, you've put the entire business on a commonplace plane, which is truly remarkable. At least I won't be frightened now, no matter what I see or hear.'

'Frightened! Why on earth should you be frightened? Those who have passed over, have no wish to frighten us. No wish at all. Just one little point, dear. My fee is ten pounds.'

For several days after Miss Broadfield-Blythe's visit, Celia saw and heard nothing, which was both a relief and a disappointment. A relief because she had by no means lost that inner dread which affects everyone who comes face to face with the unusual; disappointment, because she wanted to play the game of adopting dream children. One of those fantasies which it would be well if it never come to fulfillment.

Then one Sunday morning when the time-erupting sound of church bells was disturbing the dust of long dead memories, a ripple of childish laughter came from the landing, followed by the thud of footsteps running down the stairs. Celia, who was about to open the front door, spun round, but there was nothing untoward to see. Nothing at all.

So she went out into the porch, double locked the front door behind her, then went to church – a weekly social event she always enjoyed.

The old church with its stained-glass windows and lingering aroma that was comprised of burnt candles, prayer books and damp, made her for some reason think of crumbling tombs and deep underground vaults, where the noble dead have slept for centuries. Then the sunlight was filtered through the stained glass and did something wonderful to a young girl's hair, even while it revealed the gaunt face of an old man, and caused a shadow mask to form round his deep sunken eyes.

Choirboys' high-pitched treble voices sent a melody of sound up to the ancient rafters, before crashing open doors in Celia Watson's brain, and an impression of long-long ago childhoods came drifting out on multi-coloured clouds, even as dust-motes drifted along light beams formed by sunlight and stained glass.

The brain was quite unable to deal with this experience and closed down its awareness, so that Celia's next impression was that of shaking hands with the vicar who had hastened to the front porch for that purpose. She walked home in a not unpleasant be-mused state, even though she knew – positively knew – something exciting was about to happen.

When she opened her front door, she could not be certain if three or four small shapes raced up the stairs and disappeared on the landing, but the brain suggested in an abstract sort of way that such may have been the case. She removed her hat and coat, went into the kitchen, there opened the gas oven door and inspected the fillet end of a leg of lamb, which had been sizzling gently on a low heat for two hours. Almost ready. The roast potatoes had also acquired a rich crisp brownness, and it only remained for her to ignite the gas ring under a saucepan of garden peas, for Sunday lunch to be well on its way towards full preparation. She had long ago dispensed with apple pie and custard, which had been a per-manent feature of childhood Sunday dinner, but those were the days when plumpness was considered to be a sign of good health.

She turned, reached out for a towel on which to wipe her hands – and saw them.

The little girl – the one she had seen before – and a slightly older boy dressed in a blue velvet suit – were standing in the kitchen doorway, watching her.

First the dread-chill which ran up from her feet and threatened to paralyse her heart; then the wonderment – the suggestion of joy – and the realisation she was viewing two ghosts (hateful word) in full daylight, while wide-awake and at close quarters. And it was no use trying to quell the racing heart and rub sweaty hands on the skirt of her dress, for the blend of emotions was sending some kind of current down through her nerve grid and she was laughing and crying, both at the same time, and the two children continued to watch her, the hint of a smile on their angel faces.

With one hand she wiped tears from her streaming eyes and stretched out the other towards the two apparitions, half-hoping, half-dreading to make some kind of contact, but they continued to stare at her, the smile more pronounced, verging on deri-sion. Then they started to drift away from her, back through the doorway, across the hall until the two shapes were nothing more than splodges of coloured light on the far wall – the product of sunshine and glass.

Celia called out: 'Come back . . . come back,' and as though in derisive reply, the sound of childish laughter came from above stairs.

She slept hardly at all that night, the habit of trying to look in every direction at once, which she had acquired during the daylight hours, became even more pronounced once the sun had set. To lie in bed with the lights full on, jerking the head from side to side, straining the ears to catch every sound, became nerve-racking to say the least, particularly when fear became stronger than the desire to acquire ghost-dream-children. To Celia it seemed noth-ing short of ridiculous that she should dread and desire. It was a state of being that surpassed being distinctly funny and verged on insanity.

Not until the sun sent its first infant shafts of light through the window curtains, did she relax on to her sweat-moist pillows and slip into an uneasy sleep. When she awoke much later in the morning, she was in time to see a small arm and shoulder disappear round the half-open door and experienced the by now familiar feeling of pleasure blended with fear.

No further phenomenon manifested for the next few weeks, and such was Celia's anxiety, she often forgot to eat, wash or change her clothes. In consequence people – particularly those who did not like her – began making half-pitying, half-scornful remarks and generally conjecture why this lapse from pride-in-appearance had taken place. The vicar decided it was his duty to investigate.

'The place is in an awful mess,' Celia objected.

The vicar, a tall handsome man with thick white hair, gave her a most charming smile and said: 'But I've come to see you, dear lady, not your house. Please, I have walked a long way this morning and really would appreciate a cup of coffee.'

This request – some might call it a command – for hospitality from a man of the cloth, could not be ignored, so Celia could do no less than stand to one side and allow the reverend gentleman to enter. He gave the living room a quick glance and had to agree the place was indeed in an awful mess, for apart from an accumulation of dust, screwed up balls of writing paper lay on the floor, table, chairs and mantelpiece; one half sheet which seemed to have unrolled itself, caught his eye and he managed to decipher the words scrawled with a black ball point pen: 'COME TO ME CHI'

But if the room was in an awful mess, the woman could be aptly described as a wreck of her former self. Grey hair – strangely he could not remember seeing a single grey hair on her head before today – hung in rat-tails round and over a white-lined face; heavy blue pouches drooped under watery eyes, which seemed to be in danger of running down sunken cheeks. A slight but persistent tic quivered at the right of her mouth, while there was a distinct tremor of the right hand.

This she raised and waved in the direction of a deep armchair. 'Seat yourself, vicar, and I'll fetch you a cup of coffee.'

The clergyman shook his head. 'No, allow me to get you one. The kitchen is through there – ' he in turn pointed to an open doorway – 'as I remember. I used to visit this house in the days of Mrs Fortescue.'

'Really, I could not possibly allow you to . . .'

'Nonsense. You are clearly unwell and I'm quite capable of wait-ing on myself and you. Now you seat yourself. I'll find everything.'

Celia did as she was bid, but watched the vicar disappear into the kitchen with great concern, and once called out: 'It's in an awful mess . . . The coffee jar is on the shelf over the sink and there should be milk in the fridge . . .'

He returned after a lapse of ten minutes, carrying two mugs of steaming coffee and wearing an expression of deep anxiety.

'I found the coffee, but the milk in your refrigerator seems to have gone off, but fortunately I managed to unearth a tin of condensed. In fact your supply of fresh food seems to be – well – rather in the same state as the milk. Due no doubt to the sultry weather. But I do think someone should do something about clear-ing out – the debris – and restocking. I do really. But first drink this coffee. I did find some biscuits, but they were distinctly soggy.'

'I'm so sorry, but I've been very busy lately, I've rather let things go . . .'

The vicar seated himself on the edge of the chair and took a tentative sip from his mug of coffee. 'Please, no apologies are necessary. My job is to help and understand. Miss Watson – Celia – you are without doubt sorely troubled. Trouble shared is trouble halved. Please allow me to halve your trouble, then possibly dis-card the remainder.'

This rather puzzling offer was accompanied by such a charming smile, Celia for the first time in a long while dared to hope that a male might have the necessary acumen to give sound advice and even understand what must be an unique situation. But still she hesitated.

'I'm not sure, Mr . . .'

'Rodney, Celia. Please.'

'Yes, well yes, Mr. . . . Rodney. I mean I'm not sure if you'll fully understand my problem. You see . . .'

'Yes, Celia?'

'The fact is this house is . . . well . . .'

'Rather lonely for one person?'

'No, far from it. No . . . it is haunted by the ghosts of at least five children.'

The Reverend Rodney emptied his coffee cup and placed it gently on a nearby low table, then took one of Celia's hands in his.

'Dear Celia, let us take one point at a time. Firstly we know that ghosts – as such – do not exist. When the body dies the soul goes straight to heaven, or – sadly – straight to the place of atonement. There can be no lingering.'

Normally Celia would have accepted this dogma from a man of the cloth as literal truth, but now, having some first-hand evidence of ghosts, she was inclined to question the reverend gentleman's logic.

'But Mr . . . Rodney, cannot some souls, such as children's souls, be not quite ready for such an extreme – grand place as Heaven – the other place being out of the question – and prefer to – well – stay where they were in life. Right here. It makes some sense to me.'

'What makes sense to us, Celia, need not make sense to the Almighty. This is the plane of sin and flesh. I need hardly point out how the two go together. Above is the world of light. Below the world of darkness. There are no age groups in eternity.'

Celia took a deep breath and released a flow of words that revealed the truth as she saw it.

'But I have seen and heard the ghosts – disembodied souls of children. Here in this house – this room. First as dream figures – then as clearly as I see and hear you. And they need love. And I have so much to give, having sort of saved it up over the years. Please don't lie and tell me they don't exist.'

The Reverend Rodney assumed a very grave expression and clearly thought deeply before answering. Then he cleared his throat and after regaining possession of Celia's right hand (which she displayed signs of wanting to withdraw), said in his deep attractive voice:

'Dear Celia, I am not going to dismiss what you have told me as the result of a fevered, even neurotic, imagination, brought about by loneliness and frustration – for I have heard stories about this house, which up to this time I never credited as being other than complete moonshine. But now . . .'

He paused for a while, then went on. 'So far as I can gather, this house – a long while ago – was inhabited by a couple called

Ferguson – Jacob and Sarah Ferguson. And they did have five children – four boys and a girl. That must be admitted. There were
five children. All ranging from five to thirteen years. The parents
practised what they and some of their contemporaries called the
old religion. In other words the black arts, devil worship – witch-
craft. The children were corrupted from birth and in time – for
young minds are malleable – became even more evil than their
parents. No one knows how the end came about, but it is assumed
that the children killed their mother, then the father massacred
them, before committing suicide himself. But there is one school
of opinion that maintains it was the other way round. The children killed both parents, then themselves by some secret ritual,
which ensured their souls would be withheld from torment and
confined to the walls of this house. This I must disbelieve, but in
view of your experience I am inclined to believe some personality
residue, or manifestation of past evil, still lingers here. There can
be no doubt you must leave this house at once. Leave it and never
come back. It seems possible you have the kind of mind that can
pick up impressions, time debris . . . I don't know. But you must
leave this house.'

Celia gazed upon the vicar with mounting anger, all her mis-
trust of the opposite sex revived. When he had finished speaking
and given her hand a final squeeze, she remained silent for some
little while, before saying in a carefully controlled voice:

'First of all, vicar, I do not believe a single word of that horrid
story. If there is a basis of truth in it, then the wicked parents left
the poor little things to die of ill-treatment, and now their innocent souls are demanding – demanding, do you hear? – the love
and protection that was never theirs in life. I intend to remain here
and provide that love and protection.'

'Celia . . .'

'My name is Miss Watson.'

'Celia, you are dreadfully mistaken. This house is bad for you.
Believe me. I am convinced that is the truth. A hundred other
people might be able to live here undisturbed. But not you. Come
to the vicarage until . . .'

'I would be obliged if you would leave now.'

'You must allow me to convince you . . .'

'I do not wish to be rude. Please leave now. And do not come back.'

He conjured up a very wry smile. 'I do hope I'm wrong and sincerely apologize if I have needlessly upset you. I should not have told you that ridiculous story, but if you can see and hear . . .'

'Shut the door behind you as you go out.'

'I hate . . . simply hate . . .'

'Pull the door sharply to or the Yale lock will not engage. I believe the wood is warped.'

The slam of the front door was a prelude to an unnatural silence and the ensuing loneliness (a state she had never known before) possibly the reason for the sudden fit of crying. Her shoulders shook, tears poured down her cheeks, and it seemed as if the grief of a lifetime had suddenly found an outlet and was now smashing down all the carefully erected barricades of indifference.

But the fit passed, she wiped her eyes, gulped back one last sob and went into the sitting-room.

All five ghost children were waiting for her. The tallest one – blond hair, bright eyes, dressed in a green suit – standing by the window: the next – not so tall, auburn hair, dark eyes, in a long brown coat – to the left of the doorway. The little boy and girl she had seen before – to the left of the doorway: and another boy, of medium height, dressed in black, a long robe affair, his black eyes glittering in a rather alarming fashion if one looked at them too long. His black hair hung down to his shoulders.

Not one moved. Not so much as a blink or the merest movement of a finger. Motionless effigies. Three dimension shadows of what had been. Images recreated from personality debris by her brain and projected by her eyes. Maybe the vicar had instinctively pinpointed the truth of the matter, but she could not believe these five shades had anything evil in their make-up. That must be impossible.

Now to give them life and make them her own.

She called softly. 'Come, children. There's nothing to fear in this house now. I will be a mother to you all. Take from me the essence you need to live again. To be always with me, awake or asleep. So I can hear your voices, your footsteps – if possible feel your hands touching me.'

The little boy and girl (they might have been twins) were the first to move. They glided to her and came to rest some two feet away, heads tilted, eyes looking up into hers. But she could not detect a glimmer of intelligence. Merely the glitter that might be reflected in the eyes of some animal. Then the tallest came to her and stood behind the twins (if such they were) and looked into her eyes (or so it seemed). Then came the lad in brown who took up a position to her right; finally the one in black – all save the dead white face.

Her fearful-hopeful dream had been fulfilled. She was half surrounded by the five ghost children.

Now what to do with them?

She turned and after saying: 'Follow me, children,' led the way into the kitchen. At least such was her intention, but when she looked back they had not moved. All stood in the same positions, staring at that spot she had just vacated, motionless again, and she giggled.

'Silly me. They will not be hungry. Food and kitchens mean nothing to them. It is love they need.'

She went back to them and bending down whispered the wonderful message. 'Children, I want you to know you are mine – I am yours from now on. Do you understand? We now belong to each other. Your loneliness is over. So is mine.'

The boy in black moved slightly. His eyes gleamed like sparks floating in the dark.

'Can no one – not a single one of you, give me some sign that you understand?' Celia pleaded. 'Don't let that awful clergyman be right. Please.'

They all vanished. Were switched off. Were no more.

Celia spent the rest of the day looking for them.

The bed had come with the house and was very wide. Celia had always slept in a three foot bed, never having had occasion to require anything larger. This might have been the reason she slept on the left side of this giant and never parted upper from lower sheet on the right. Despite – or maybe because of – the experience of that day, she slept soundly all night; sank into a deep coma of unawareness that drugged every sense, save for the one which has never been explained.

Then she awoke and lay quite still, knowing the unexpected had happened, but unwilling at that moment to open her eyes and discover what shape it had taken.

The senses returned to seventy-five percent normality, the brain expelled the fog of sleep, but still Celia kept her eyes tight closed, conjecture creating mental pictures that were without understanding.

Then hearing recorded a sound. Low childish laughter. Not far off, but near – in this room – by – or on – her bed.

The demand to know would not be denied. Celia opened her eyes.

The window curtains were drawn apart and the room was flooded with silver moonlight and revealed their slender forms in every detail. All five children were seated on her bed. The two small ones, the twins, on the spare pillows, the tall boy and he in brown way down at the foot and he in black lying on his stomach, his head turned in her direction, the black eyes now glittering with an alien intelligence.

Joy came shuffling on reluctant feet, for had they not come to her, sought her out of their own accord, and surely it was not their fault they had so white faces, or that the lad in black should have rather frightening eyes.

They had that death-beauty that rightfully belongs to some vivid nightmare that has long been forgotten by the active mind, but still can be recalled by the sub-conscious at that moment which separated sleep from awakening. Celia thought briefly of sleeping castles where mist formed strange shapes in ruined corridors.

She tried to sit up, but for some reason her body refused to obey the dictates of her brain, although she was permitted to turn her head from side to side, but that was hardly an asset, for some of the joy seeped away every time she met the glittering-eyed gaze of the lad in black.

Then a giggle came from one or maybe all of them; a deep-throated inane giggle that had the suggestion of a squeal, and undiluted fear slid into her mind and she became as one who has encouraged the presence of half-grown tigers. Instinct warned body and mind and she succeeded in sitting up, but as freedom of movement returned to her, so, it would seem, it did to them.

They all drifted off the bed and blanket and sheets went with them. Then the squealing inane giggle blended with the tearing of her nightdress, and they moved, danced, round the bed, while she called out in fear-joy ecstasy:

'No, children, you must not be so naughty. Please . . . please . . . you'll hurt mummy . . .'

The giggling became louder, the five moved faster until they became a whirling mass of coloured mist; a scratch appeared on Celia's right shoulder and seeped a thin trail of blood down her back. Her hair stood on end and she screamed when it was tugged abruptly. Invisible fingers poked at her naked flesh, pinched and punched, while a roaring darkness threatened to engulf her. Then all movement ceased and she was left trembling on the bed, as the dreadful five congregated in the doorway. All had dead white faces now and every one giggled, ejected the inane squealing sound from between lax lips.

Celia raised herself up on her elbows and managed to speak reproachfully with a sob-racked voice.

'You naughty, naughty children. You've hurt and frightened mummy who only wanted to love you.'

The giggling took on a higher-pitched tone and the five turned and fled over the landing and running footsteps could be heard descending the stairs.

Then for a while silence – and loneliness.

For two days Celia dismissed the minor destruction as nothing more than infantile mischief with no sinister intent. All glass jars and bottles were smashed, the refrigerator door refused to stay shut, then ceased to function. 'They don't understand,' she told the empty house. 'If they had been reared in a loving atmosphere, they wouldn't be like this. Never mind, patience and endurance will work the miracle. It must.'

But on the morning of the third day, when she distinctly saw the lad in black dart from under her right elbow and deliberately upset the frying pan in which she was cooking some sausages, thus causing a roaring flame to soar up towards the ceiling and all but set her hair alight, then she very reluctantly accepted that the children were not just mischievous, but had at least some evil propensities.

But it made not the slightest difference.

Beauty can hide any number of imperfections and love can explain away any number of crimes. In an odd sort of way it was rather exciting having to keep one's wits alert as to what trap they had set overnight. The footstool placed at the very top of the stairs, the bare patch on electric wiring, the turned-on gas taps that just needed a lighted match to send her hurtling into eternity. Probably join them in that dimension they inhabited. So far as was possible she experienced surprise at their ingenuity which resulted in the topmost cellar step being transformed into a death hazard by means of spirit of salts (transported from the loo) poured on the wooden supports. Had not her nose transmitted a warning, the undermined tread would have collapsed under her right foot.

'Artful monkeys,' she murmured, after successfully smothering the blast of terror that threatened to destroy beyond repair the bastion of sanity. 'I wonder what they'll think of next?'

If they were capable of thought, there was little for them to think of, for from then on Celia rarely left a chair she had dragged into the hall, this being the place 'her family' were most likely to materialize. She smiled indulgently when the twins removed her shoes and flung them across the room and laughed softly when the Reverend Rodney climbed in through the sitting-room window, then somehow finished up on the topmost cellar step. After the initial scream, he never bothered her again.

'I should have had children,' she announced again and again. 'I should have considered the possibility of having children, long ago. They are such a comfort.'

In fact they gave her more than comfort. More likely satisfaction, fulfillment, a most gratifying understanding that she had not lived her solitary life in vain. For the children grew fatter, particularly the lad in black who became positively bloated. They never acquired the slightest hint of colour, for all their faces retained that rather disconcerting dead-white complexion, but Celia was certain it was a healthy pallor.

For herself – well – occasionally she became aware of her own alarming thinness, the fact that her hands were well nigh transparent and she lacked the strength to do more than sit in her chair. But presently she took little interest in such mundane matters, for the antics of her family demanded all of her time. How they ran up and down stairs, in and out of those rooms she could see from her position in the hall, chasing each other, stopping now and again to plant a burning kiss on bare flesh, a reward out of all proportion to any slight discomfort she might suffer.

And they squealed with joyful excitement. Yes, really squealed with unrestrained joy. And Celia expressed her joy with some such sound, for had she not at last managed to create a happy family?

They came in through the sitting-room window, the one the Reverend Rodney had inadvertently left open. Tall burly men in blue uniforms, followed by a more slender one in a neat grey suit.

He was the only one to be actually sick. One of the others exclaimed: 'Oh, my God!' but generally speaking they were all fairly immune against being upset by the extremely unpleasant. Two made their way to the cellar steps, only to return a few minutes later, when the one with three white chevrons on his right arm, stated briefly:

'The missing parson isn't missing any more. At the bottom of the steps, what's left of him. Oh, my Gawd! Look at them!'

Shouts that expressed horror, disgust and downright loathing, followed five bloated rats as they raced up the stairs.

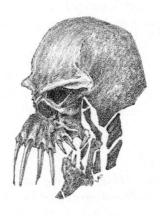

THE BUCK

I WALKED THROUGH A MOONLIT English garden and had good reason to feel pleased with myself. Although only sixteen years had passed since I first saw light of day, it could well have been twenty-six, or one hundred and six, for I was fully grown; tall, slim of waist, broad of shoulder, as handsome a buck that ever took nourishment from bottle or neck.

Age should never be measured by years, but experience. The built-in awareness that is the birthright of every life-form, ranging from a blade of grass to those beings who rule the vast star-lanes and are the font of all knowledge. Aided by the tuition of my wise uncle, I now knew more, understood more and could do far more than a meat-eating male of seventy.

But I still could not walk under the naked sun and this was a disadvantage and sorely tried me.

The count and countess were accepted by county society (together with their presentable nephew) and indeed were social beacons that attracted pleasure-seeking moths from far and wide. Our midnight parties were very popular and I was able to converse with highborn meat-eaters on equal terms. Although many had shallow minds that were incapable of digesting a new idea, a few were gifted with a limited perception that afforded me some intellectual amusement.

To account for my rapid transformation from boy to robust manhood, we had invented a younger brother who paid periodical visits, but was now completing his education in Switzerland. As people could not possibly begin to suspect the truth, this explanation was accepted and I was allowed to 'grow up' with no trouble at all.

I entered the summerhouse and almost bumped into the Hon. Susan Sinclair who stood just inside of the doorway, and had been awaiting my arrival with some impatience. She had the dark – but alas brief – beauty that often made me wish she was one of our kind and a passionate nature that sometimes made me forget she was not. Uncle Erich had warned me not to become too deeply involved with a female meat-eater, stating that such conduct could result in nasty complications, apart from being obscene.

But Susan – her origins and feeding habits notwithstanding – was extremely attractive and I had been for some time aware of an urge to recreate or – to use a people's expression – go through the motions. She wore a white off-the-shoulder evening gown and when this was allied to black hair that framed her pale face, one had a vision that might have strayed from some long forgotten dream.

She said: 'You treat me like nothing at all. I've been waiting here for over an hour.'

I could not explain that an unexpected cloudless evening had kept me confined to the house, to say nothing of Aunt Helena's tears when she found out what I was up to.

I kissed her lightly on the cheek, knowing that even this modest salutation would have incurred Uncle Erich's wrath.

'I am truly sorry, but I just could not get away. Aunt Helena is unwell.'

'Rubbish. I doubt if that woman has ever been ill in her entire life. You don't give a damn if you see me or not.'

I remembered Josie and wished that I could make an uncomplicated playmate of this lovely creature – but alas the innocent days of cubhood were long past.

'That is not true and well you know it, but meeting like this is not – well – not quite the thing.'

She stamped her foot and appeared to be near tears.

'And whose fault is that? You've had dinner invitations galore, but you always find some excuse not to accept. Damn it all, my father is quite prepared for you to practically live at our place, but you shut yourself away here . . . I hate you.'

I sighed deeply and suddenly wanted to be far away in a dense wood, with only the sad shades for company. Then I said quietly:

'You do not hate me. On the contrary, you love me . . .'

'You . . . conceited, self-opinionated . . .'

'Please do not interrupt me when I am speaking. As I was saying you love me and in a way I – well – am very fond of you. But we are separated by a vast gulf that can never be bridged. You really must understand that.'

Not for the first time I saw a glint of fear in her eyes and suspected that this was part of the attraction that drew her to me. Fear of the unknown.

'What on earth are you talking about? Surely not my father's silly title? No one gives a damn about noble birth these days and anyway your uncle is a count and appears to be as rich as Monte Cristo. But there's something else, isn't there? The reason you all hide and rarely pay visits.'

'That really is utter nonsense. We have visited you on several occasions.'

'Only when it rains or is foggy. And you always refuse refreshments. Why? 'Fraid we're going to poison you?'

I turned away so she should not see my eyes.

'Since you insist on talking like a child, I think we had better go into the house.'

Instantly she was contrite, flung her arms about my person and began to behave in a manner that I thought distasteful, even after making allowances for her origin.

'Please don't be angry. I am sorry – really and truly sorry for what I said. I don't care what you may have done. Hide away all you like – but don't be like this. I love you – I do.'

She was bathed in moonlight, a beautiful study in black and white and yes – I felt the burning need that comes to every young male, no matter his species; but there was another desire that I had not experienced for eight long years. I wanted to partake from her.

I was fully aware that both desires sprang from a single font, dark brothers that race along the same road; pleasure and pain, lust and hate – hurt and caress – kiss and drain. I felt the saliva fill my mouth, my fangs slide from their sockets – and my organ began to rise up . . .

I shouted: 'No, it must not be. Do not come near me again,' and ran across the moon-silvered gardens, even as a frightened cub fled from the blood-squad long years before.

My uncle and aunt were entertaining – or being entertained – by Colonel Arthur C. Barton in the great drawing room. I came in through the french window, regained my breath and self control by a supreme effort, then bowed.

'Good evening, sir – aunt and uncle. I trust, Colonel Barton, you are enjoying excellent health?'

Aunt Helena gave me her usual sweet smile and Uncle Erich raised an interrogative eyebrow. The colonel waved a long cigar and stared at me with joyful amazement, while speaking with a sonorous and unnecessarily loud voice.

'That's what gets me about you British – okay, I know you're not British, but you look and sound like 'em – you've got class. There's not one of you that couldn't pass as a head waiter in the plushest joint in town.'

'You are very kind,' Aunt Helena murmured, while Uncle Erich frowned. 'You know how to pay a compliment.'

The colonel smiled complacently. 'Well, you could say I've got class myself. Not in your league of course, but a few rungs down.'

Colonel Arthur C. Barton was an American with whom the count did business; a tall, gaunt old man with a mane of white hair and what meat-eaters call 'a bottle tan', the result of constant imbibing of strong liquor – a weakness that excited my sympathy. He was dressed in a light grey suit, blue shirt, red tie and brown suede shoes. The count, who had been watching me, said quietly:

'Our guest has an empty glass, Carlos. And your aunt and myself would like another bloody-mary.'

I approached the colonel and smiled down into his shrewd blue eyes. 'What are you drinking, sir?'

'Scotch on the rocks, son. And you needn't be too concerned about the rocks.'

I went over to the sideboard, poured a generous measure of whisky over a few cubes of ice, then after a quick backward glance at the colonel, three-quarters filled three glasses with undiluted essence. Placing all four glasses on a gold tray, I first served our guest, then my aunt and uncle, before sinking down into an easy chair. Colonel Barton raised his glass.

'Here's to you. May all your ulcers be little ones.' He half emptied his glass, while we sipped from ours. 'Say, count, ever thought of going back state-side?'

My uncle lit a cigarette and appeared to inhale deeply. Only Aunt Helena and I knew he never swallowed the smoke.

'It has crossed my mind on several occasions. We never intended to stay longer than two years, but it is so peaceful here and a fine place for – for the boy to grow up.'

'Yep, he sure done that. You've got considerable holdings in Amalgamated Meat Products, as I recall.'

The count repressed a shudder and nodded.

'Yes, they have paid off well in recent years.'

'Well, they won't much longer. Meat getting in short supply in some parts. Arizona, for example.'

I could see that my uncle was not all that interested, but politeness demanded that he appeared to be, so he assumed a grave expression and said:

'That is strange. Any idea why?'

'Some sort of disease. Thousands have been slaughtered by government order, then the carcasses burned. Everybody thought it was foot and mouth, but I can't see how it can be. They've taken to killing cats and dogs and burning them too.'

My uncle was interested now, but he still nursed his glass and blew a neat smoke ring towards the ceiling.

'That is really most extraordinary. Are you sure this is not just the result of idle rumour? I cannot remember reading any reports of an epidemic.'

The colonel shuffled in his chair and seemed to be enjoying the prospect of imparting exclusive information.

'Ah, now, that's the point. The shutters are up, the newshounds muzzled, nobody's supposed to know a thing, only a cold breeze that's been blowing down Wall Street for some time now, is fast whipping up to a full force gale. Take my tip, unload your Amalgamated Meat stock, before the roof blows off.'

The count nodded thoughtfully. 'I most certainly will. Thank you for the warning. But why the secrecy?'

Colonel Barton shrugged. 'Search me. Mind you there's been what you might call a mild panic for years. Reports of livestock going mad, unsolved murders, special agents clamping down on news coverage, but I've always put it down to bloody commies – begging your pardon ma'am – spreading alarm and despondency. I don't know, the world's falling to bits and there ain't nobody big enough to pull it together again.'

When his rumbling voice had died away, a dreadful silence descended upon the room and I was at a loss to know why the countess suddenly gripped my uncle's arm, or why he shook it off and shot her a warning glance. Then he asked with a deceptively mild voice.

'What kind of disease can strike cows and cats, but leave men uninfected? It sounds like a lot of nonsense to me.'

The colonel edged his chair forward and actually looked round as though to ensure no one but ourselves was present.

'Now, it sure is strange you asked that. I wasn't going to mention it, because in my opinion it's a lot of ba ... – excuse me, ma'am – hogwash, but they do say men have gone loco all over and they've been burning 'em in piles. Now,' he raised his hand, 'I don't hold with that one little bit. There's no way Washington could cover up a mess like that. No sir.'

'Only by fear,' Uncle Erich murmured.

'What's that, count? I didn't quite hear.'

'I was about to agree with you. There's little fear that such a catastrophe could be kept from the public. Well, we can but hope that this epidemic does not spread.'

'Amen to that.'

It was at that moment that Susan came in through the french windows; a pale, beautiful ghost that I wanted to forget. She drifted across the room without glancing in my direction and smiled sweetly at my aunt, then inclined her head when the count and the colonel rose.

'You must forgive this intrusion, Count Von Holstein, but I have strayed from our garden into yours and seeing the window open ...'

My uncle kissed her hand (and did not seem to observe her shudder) and the colonel shook it most heartily; then my aunt kissed

her cheek and invited her to sit down. The count manufactured
words with his beautiful voice.

'How can one do otherwise than welcome an angel that has
wandered in from the night? Carlos, what are you thinking about?
Ask the beautiful lady if she would like some refreshment?'

I, Carlos Markland, who was so proud of my polished assurance, stood like the merest unlicked cub before a meat-eating
female and almost stammered the formal invitation:

'Gracious lady, what can I get you?'

She did not look up at me, but stared intently at my aunt, who
was still smiling – smiling.

'I will have a gin and tonic, thank you. And lots of gin because I
have got to be very brave and I can't be if I'm cold sober.'

The colonel consulted his wrist watch with an extravagated
concern. 'Good God! It can't be as late as that! I must get back to
town or me lady wife will be playing hell. Be in touch with you,
count, about the Amalgamated stock.'

He began to shake hands all round and I had to put the gin
bottle down and accept his aggressive grip, knowing full well I
could crush every bone in his hand if I so wished. Then he was
gone and I carried a near full glass over to Susan, who promptly
emptied it without pausing for breath, then handed it back to me.

'Again, please and not so much tonic.'

The meat-eaters' need for alcohol has always amazed me, and I
can only assume that their lives are so dull and uninspiring, some
kind of stimulant is an absolute necessity. But although I was aware
that Susan took more than the occasional drink, never had I known
her to over-indulge, and pure kindness prompted me to ask:

'Do you really think you should?'

The count's voice all but hissed his disapproval.

'Carlos, how dare you question a guest's order. Fetch the young
lady her requirement this instant.'

I shrugged and deliberately filled her glass to the brim, adding
but a token drop of tonic water. This time she half-emptied the
glass and stared up at me with a kind of angry defiance.

'Count, would you say I was beautiful?'

'Ask me rather if the moon rides the night sky? Truth cannot be
questioned and therefore requires no answer. You are beautiful.'

'Then tell me this. Why should your nephew fly from me, as though I were a demon out of hell?'

The count narrowed his eyes and gave me an appraising glance, then said:

'Youth is a disease that only time can cure and it often has the effect of making the sufferer do the opposite to that which he intended. I too might fly from your beauty if I feared I was about to perish in its flame.'

Susan took another swig from her glass.

'And you know all about beauty, don't you, count? All three of you are beautiful and no one gives the hell if I get burnt. Beautiful faces, beautiful bodies, beautiful words; a gorgeous show put on for the common herd to gape at. But you know something? I don't think you're real. I've gone quietly mad over the past few years and created the lot of you from my poor, crazy imagination.'

My aunt – still smiling – said gently:

'You are tired, my dear. Everything will seem different tomorrow morning.'

'No it won't. I've been through a thousand tomorrow mornings and always come back to the night before. Let me tell you some-thing else. I'm so in love with your goddarn beautiful nephew, I'd do anything to get so much – or so little – as a smile from him. Sometimes I dream of him beating me, kicking the living daylights out of me. Me, who has half the county willing to lay heart and credit at my feet. And – here's more – he terrifies the guts out of me. All three of you do. Perfect white faces, gleaming teeth, never at a loss for the right word – where the hell did you come from?'

'Erich,' the countess spoke in a low, husky voice, 'I feel the need for some sport. She really is quite delicious – and extremely talkative.'

'Self-indulgence,' the count said gravely, 'can only lead to disaster. Never allow the glands to rule the head.'

He smiled blandly at Susan, who had now emptied her glass and was staring at me with hopeful expectancy.

'My dear child, were it not for our good looks we might appear to be commonplace. But concerning my nephew. If your love was returned and he was able to subdue his basic instinct, you would still die within an hour of your nuptials. Gods cannot mate with mortals.'

Susan peered at him over her empty glass.

'You – are gods?'

The count's smile was an enigma, a question mark on the face of time.

'We are – the exceptional. Go and mate with another of your kind and forget that one with black hair and a white face once allowed you to occupy a brief moment of his existence and ignored the voice of temptation. No greater love has ever been recorded in the annals of eternity. Never speak of what you might suspect, imagine or know.'

'You are threatening me, Count Von Holstein.'

'No, just expressing anxiety for your welfare. Believe me when I say we are exercising great forbearance. It might be well if you left now; went back the way you came and did not dally in moonlight.'

Susan rose rather unsteadily to her feet and began a slow journey towards the french windows. There she stopped and looked back.

'So I'm scared. Fear is a spur that's made many a filly jump over a five-bar gate. Keep pretty boy here – take him to the end of the earth – and I'll be right there beside him.'

She went out into the moonlight and I waited for the recriminations, the so often repeated warnings. But my uncle spoke with a perfectly calm voice.

'How many times must I tell you not to become involved with a female meat-eater? It is necessary for us to mix with them, but to encourage that girl – that creature – is the height of stupidity. It is so easy to start a fire, quite another matter to put it out.'

Aunt Helena sighed. 'Indulgence or scorn will have the same effect. A fevered brain and a talking tongue. Erich, I really do think she should be silenced.'

'And land us in the middle of a police investigation! And do not for one moment think I am unaware where your interest lies. And the answer is an emphatic no. We cannot afford to partake from the locals. In any case we must soon return to the States, the news that Barton gave us is very disquieting. I would like to confer with the grand council.'

'But it has been so peaceful here.'

Uncle Erich gave me a reproachful look.

'It was. Now we have a hysterical female on our hands, to say nothing of a possibly demanding father. No, we must decamp and that quickly.'

'Uncle,' I enquired, 'would there be anything so dreadful about a partaker mating with a female meat-eater?'

For a while it did seem as if Uncle Erich was about to shatter his dignity by a fit of anger. But he succeeded in retaining self-control and speaking in his usual well-moderated voice.

'I seem to remember touching on this question before, but it would appear that I did not make myself clear. I will do so now and trust that the subject is never mentioned again. Apart from the moral aspect there are several practical reasons why such a line of conduct would indeed be dreadful in the extreme.

'One – even a young partaker like yourself has a force of mental energy that can blast minute life-forms and paralyse will power. Should you co-habitate with a female meat-eater, there is no guarantee that you could control this energy at moment of climax. This could well result in your blasting the creature's sanity, turn her into a mindless thing that we would have to put down.'

'I have complete self-control,' I insisted.

'Please – I am speaking. Two – just supposing the creature can get up and walk away still retaining a few faculties that nature has provided, have you considered the possible consequences? A half-breed. Something which belongs neither to one species or the other. The warring instincts would drive it insane.'

I dared to interrupt again.

'But I understand that these days there is no need for . . .'

'That would be an even greater crime, for Beldaza would strike down any partaker who so wasted his seed. Only immortality has so far preserved our race, but what with inroads made by the blood-squad and the occasional sun-blast casualties, it behooves all of us to strive for more cubs. That is why you are so precious and your aunt and myself have taken the trouble to raise and protect you. You are our one hope – our young Prince of Darkness. You will be mated in due course to selected females. Even possibly to your aunt.'

'Aunt Helena!'

The countess's eyes glittered like fire-lit rubies and she made a soft purring sound.

'And why not? She is only your adopted aunt and well propor-
tioned. Beldaza has not seen fit to bless our union, but he may be
more amicably disposed towards your coupling. Your aunt has no
objection.'

'Indeed I have not,' the countess bared her fangs in a far from
engaging smile. 'I am more than ready to do my duty.'

'But that,' the count continued, 'is by the way. Three – and the
most important – to honour a meat-eater is an obscene act. They
are provided by an all-merciful Beldaza for nourishment and that
which fills the belly can never occupy the bed. It is said that in the
beginning one partaker sinned in such a fashion and that is why
they bear a marked resemblance to ourselves. If so, we are even
now being punished for that original transgression, cursed to exist
as a tiny minority, while their multitudes devastate the earth.

'Have I adequately answered your question?'

I bowed my head. 'Yes, gracious uncle.'

'Good. Now let us pass on to more mundane matters. I propose
that we vacate this house seven days from now. During that period
we will let it be known that I am returning to the States to deal
with estates that I own there. Suggestions will be broadcast that
we will shortly return. Is that clear?'

I said, 'Yes, gracious uncle,' and the countess murmured:

'Of course, dear. But I dread going back to America if what
Colonel Barton reported is true.'

Uncle Erich ignored this remark and again turned his attention
to me.

'During the remainder of our residence in this district you will
behave in a manner which befits your station. Treat the young
female with politeness and lofty restraint. Discourage any famil-
iarities and make certain you are never alone with her. Remember
all that I have told you.'

'I will, gracious uncle.'

'Good. Now, I think we would all be better for an early day. May
Beldaza protect us from the evil which stalks the sun-lit hours.'

I bowed my head and murmured: 'B men' before kissing my
aunt's hand and leaving the room.

I stood by my window and looked down over the smooth lawn

which Erasmus mowed on cloudy days, then to the hedge of rhododendron bushes that separated our garden from that of Lord Sinclair's and smiled – then frowned – when a white figure emerged from the trembling shadows.

To toy with danger is the spice which makes life worth living and of late there had been a certain restlessness, an urge to rebel against Uncle Erich's traditional strictures; to partake only from the bottle, avoid close contact with meat-eaters – always remember I was a prince of darkness. And the moon still rode a cloudless sky and the sun had yet to send a warning glow up over the eastern horizon and now (or at least so I told myself) I was in full control of my senses.

I went down the ivy hand over hand, deeming it not wise to demonstrate my ability to jump forty feet and land with effortless grace on the silver grass. I ran to her, then drew back into the shadows, no longer certain of iron self-control, for her white body was making me forget all of Uncle Erich's excellent advice, the crime of co-habiting with a lowly (and hated) meat-eater and Beldaza's ensuing wrath.

She laughed at me, even though her eyes were bright with unshed tears and spoke words that were snatched by the playful breeze and tossed up to the eternal stars.

'So my demon lover has dared to come out! Isn't he afraid of the dreadful uncle?'

I spoke the truth as I knew it.

'I long ago made fear a friend. But I should not be here and neither should you.'

'Shouldn't – shouldn't – shouldn't. I always do the wrong things, that's the only way to live. Carlos, did you know your eyes shine in the dark?'

I edged towards the moonlight. 'Yes, but it might have been better if you had never found out. Now there will be questions that I must not answer.'

'I will never ask questions for the simple reason I would dread the answers. Let me walk through the valley of darkness with only the light of your eyes to guide me.'

I watched a black cat amble across the grass and admired the sinuous grace, the air of superior detachment that would not be affected if every other living creature were to suddenly die and leave it to walk the earth alone. I said:

'You are – I am – and we can never be us. I am leaving soon and then you will forget me, which is as it should be.'

'I'll follow wherever you go. The world is not big enough for you to hide from me. Let's go into the summerhouse.'

'No . . . no I must not . . .'

She grabbed my hand and began to pull me out across the lawn, all the while mocking, her eyes dancing pools of flame.

'Is he a frightened little boy, then? Frightened of losing his precious virginity? I'll be gentle and not hurt his beautiful body – and afterwards he can go home and cry on Auntie's lap – and blame the naughty girl who has no shame.'

I allowed myself to be drawn into the summerhouse, a lamp that would have spared the heedless moth, but was powerless to extinguish its own flame. Lust – love is but a four letter word – ruled her body and brain and Great Beldaza I would not be what I am today if she had not . . .

Her hands moved with terrifying speed and the black dress slipped down . . . down . . . and my eyes saw the unveiled beauty, the perfect, pink-tipped breasts, the flawless skin, the rounded hips and the dark valley between white thighs – and I became as a mighty hunter claiming his prey, a primitive force that scorns restraint: something all-powerful that had come into being at the dawn of time.

I struck her – a resounding slap on each pale cheek – and she crashed to the floor, there to lay looking up at me with dilated eyes, seeing the projecting fangs, the gleaming eyes and recognizing me at last for what I was. Her voice came to me over the vast gulf that would always separate us.

'This is the way I always wanted you to be – a prince of darkness, a nightmare clothed in the flesh of reality. Drink my blood, take my life, for it will be of no value once you have gone. Send my soul down into the pit of damnation, for the world will be dark when I can no longer see the light of your eyes.'

She gave a shuddering cry when my fangs sank into her soft neck, but I did not drink deep for the other lust demanded satisfaction and for a while I knew a savage joy that can only be experienced once in any lifetime, for repetition is the twin brother of boredom. Then I rolled off her and lay for a while purged of all passion, my soul freed from the chains of irresistible temptation. The Hon. Susan Sinclair struggled up on to one elbow, tried to clutch my arm, then fell back – dead. Cause of death – a surfeit of joy.

There was no remorse, no fear – just the sure knowledge that her extinction was the solution to what would have been a tiresome problem for one who had now acquired full buckhood. But of course there was now a minor problem that I did not even attempt to solve – namely how her death would be explained. But I had no doubt that Uncle Erich would handle it with his usual resourcefulness.

For let me now state with praiseworthy honesty, that my recent experience had rid me of that nonsensical appendage that men call a conscience. To be equally frank it had never been a serious handicap; nothing more than a feeling of gratitude to my benefactors, loosely connected with words like duty, doing-the-right-thing, obligations and other such clichés. But now I was free – a new kind of partaker; one who has dared to break the two unbreakable laws.

THOU SHALT NOT DRAIN
THOU SHALT NOT HONOUR A MEAT-EATER

I climbed in through a ground floor window, went into my uncle's (ex-uncle?) study, opened the wall safe, selected two thick wads of American and English banknotes, secured my passport, then left the house the way I had come. The countess's small red car (in which she had taught me to drive) was easy to push until I was far enough from the house to risk starting the engine; five minutes later I was speeding along country lanes, certain of reaching London before the sun had sent its first deadly rays across the eastern sky.

I spent all that day in a hotel room near the East India Docks, then after some quick shopping, embarked on a freighter for New York.

KEEP THE GASLIGHT BURNING

THE WIND WAS SUPREME LORD of the moors. It made the occasional skeletal tree bend its head in cowed submission, lashed the frost-seared heather into a sea of impotent fury, and shrieked with the despairing voices of a million dead.

Maya Griffiths heard them as she sat in the lurching coach, and sensed their ghostly fingers clawing at the tightly closed windows. She shrank back against the well-worn upholstery and tried to curb an imagination that had been fed since childhood on Methodist magazines and the wild stories related by a superstition-ridden servant.

Here, in these open spaces, restless souls wandered for long centuries, forever seeking re-entry into the world of flesh-and-blood bodies. Then there were the great ghost-hounds, that raced before the grim hunter – and heaven help – although it rarely did – anyone who turned and saw his face.

The coach left the rough, pock-pitted road, swung in through an open gateway and presently drew up before the grey house. Maya peered fearfully out at her new home and was not reassured. Built of grey stone, two storeys high, heavily roofed with flags in order to resist the ceaseless attacks of the wind, it was as forbidding and bleak as the surrounding countryside from which it appeared to have sprung. The coachman clambered down from his seat and came round to open the off-side door. There was a look of surly indifference in his small blue eyes.

'Out thou cooms, Miss. This is Blankwall 'Ouse.'

Maya pulled her thin coat tight around her slender shoulder as

she stepped down on to the gravelled drive, and felt the cold grip
of the waiting wind. She quickly took refuge in the shallow porch
and was about to pull a large ornate bell handle, when the door
opened and a tall, raw-boned woman looked down at her with a
look of some concern.

'Come in. Good heavens, the wind cuts like a knife, and it's a
wonder if you're not frozen to the bone.'

Maya allowed herself to be drawn into a large, gloomy hall,
while the woman called out to the coachman in a loud, authoritar-
ian voice: 'Bring the young lady's luggage in, Sugden, and make
haste, man.'

She half closed the door, then turned her head and said: 'Go
down into the kitchen, child. I'll be with you in a moment.'

Maya crossed the hall and found a flight of steps that ran down
to a large stone-floored kitchen: a glorious warm haven with a
gleaming iron-range, rows of copper saucepans that appeared to
wink in the flickering firelight and a giant of a table, covered with
a snow-white cloth. She sank down on the padded seat of an oak
settle that flanked one side of the fireplace, and began to absorb
the gratifying warmth.

Sleep was about to reach out comforting arms when she was
aroused by the clatter of feet descending the stairs, and the tall
woman erupted, rather than entered the kitchen, and shattered
the comforting silence.

'Come, off with your coat. Let's get something warm inside of
you, before Missus starts ringing her blessed bell.'

Maya rose and removed her coat and bonnet, and the woman
eyed the slim figure and unlined face with sardonic amusement.

'Why, you're no more than a child. What was your father thinking of to let you come to this out-of-the-way hole?'

'Please ma'am, I am twenty-two and Father has corresponded
with Mrs Maxwell and was well satisfied with her replies. It is not
a servant I am to be, but a lady's companion.'

'Um! Neither fish nor fowl. What is your name, child?'

Maya, who was feeling a little aggrieved at being called and
treated like a child, raised her head and said quietly, 'Maya Griffiths.
Miss Maya Griffiths.'

'And I am Mrs Duncan, who believe it or not, is a southerner

like yourself and hates this wind-blown place. Now, sit you down. There's stewed beef a-plenty and good solid dumplings to fill up the odd corners.'

Maya was young, healthy and hungry, and the combination enabled her to empty one bowl of stew and start work on the second before Mrs Duncan considered it necessary to speak again.

'It will be just as well if you know what's what before you go upstairs. I'm the housekeeper, Sugden is coachman and man of all work. We are all the staff there is. No one else will stay. Keighley is the nearest town and that's seven miles across the moors. So you won't be bothered by over much company.'

'I've lived in the country all my life,' Maya said with more confidence than she actually felt. 'It . . . it should be peaceful.'

'Peaceful!' Mrs Duncan snorted. 'Not with the wind howling round the house day and night it isn't. Now, about the missus . . .'

'Mrs Maxwell,' Maya corrected.

'Aye – Mrs Maxwell. She's a widow lady who's odd to say the least. I don't see much of her, meself. But you'll be with her most of the day and probably part of the night as well. So you'd best get used to her.'

'I'm sure I'll soon learn my duties,' Maya remarked rather primly.

Mrs Duncan smiled grimly. 'Well, that's more than can be said for the six that came before you. One was gone before she'd unpacked her bag.'

Maya said: 'Oh!' then lapsed into troubled silence.

'Far be it for me to poke me nose into what takes place upstairs,' Mrs Duncan went on, 'but I thought you ought to know it won't be all beer and roses.'

It was then that the bell rang. It resided over the mantelpiece; a large iron affair, suspended on a coiled spring and activated by copper wire that ran round the walls and disappeared up the stairs. It was now swinging violently back and forth and sending out a loud clanging sound.

'She knows you're here,' announced Mrs Duncan with a certain amount of satisfaction. 'And she wants me to take you up.'

This time Maya said 'Oh dear,' as Mrs Duncan rose abruptly and began to march resolutely towards the stairs. They came into the hall, then ascended another staircase that terminated on a large rectangular landing, surrounded on three sides by solid, blank-faced doors, each one equipped with a gleaming glass handle. Mrs Duncan tapped gently on the one that was situated in the left wall, then after a pause, flung it open and announced in a loud voice:

'Miss Griffiths, Madam.'

A voice that was unexpectedly soft and gentle said: 'Tell her to enter.'

Maya reluctantly moved forward, then stopped a few feet beyond the doorway, and endeavoured to accept the scene laid out before her. Although it was only late afternoon and there were still some hours before sunset, heavy red velvet curtains were drawn over the windows, and the room was lit by a splendid suspended gas-lamp. It was made of brass, had three glowing mantles, each one masked with a white globe, and gave out a soft hissing sound that Maya found to be rather alarming.

Neither was she reassured by the atmosphere, that was over-heated by the roaring coal fire and had that sharp, acrid smell that is the result of burning gas. The room was comfortably, even luxuriously furnished, with heavy, well-padded chairs, a mahogany dressing-table, and a vast four-poster bed. In a chair by the fireplace sat a lady attired in a pink dressing-gown.

She may have been in her late fifties; she had a long, almost equine face, brilliant blue eyes, and a pile of beautiful white hair that was dressed high and kept in position by two tortoise-shell combs, one on either side of her head. Apart from a few wrinkles around the eyes and mouth the gently tinted skin was unlined, and Maya was reminded of a carefully nurtured flower.

Mrs Maxwell smiled and her teeth were as white and even as that of an expensive china doll.

'Come and sit by the fire, my dear, and let me have a good look at you. That's right. Don't sit on the edge of the chair, child. Relax.'

Maya tried to obey, but the room, the hissing gas-lamp, were not conducive to relaxation. She said politely: 'Good afternoon, Mrs Maxwell. I am Maya Griffiths.'

Mrs Maxwell laughed. A soft silvery sound, rather like the whisper of church bells heard across a vast expanse of water. 'I did not imagine you were anyone else, my dear. You look very young, but that is an illness from which we all recover. You also appear to be pliable, or perhaps I should say manageable – which I also find to be an asset.'

Maya decided this must be meant as a compliment and said: 'Thank you, Ma'am.'

'Don't Ma'am me. Call me Mrs Maxwell.'

'Yes, Mrs Maxwell.'

'Splendid. Are you easily frightened?'

It was an unexpected question. It was also an alarming question and clearly merited an honest answer.

'I think I am. I don't really know. I've never had occasion to be really frightened.'

Mrs Maxwell nodded slowly and stared thoughtfully into the fire. 'There is nothing shameful in fear. But to be brave, one must be able to see horror staring across a crowded room, and still be able to ask for another cup of tea.'

She raised her head and gave the disquieted girl another brilliant smile. 'But enough of this morbid talk. In this letter your father said you were quite accomplished. Play the pianoforte, I seem to remember, sew and read prettily.'

'Yes, Ma'am – I mean, Mrs Maxwell. I can also cook, make beds, dust and do light work in the garden.'

Again that silvery laugh, which seemed to drift across the room and find an echo somewhere in the far corner by the bed. 'There will be no reason for you to perform such menial tasks. I need someone who will keep me amused – read to me, play the pianoforte when I am bored – dress my hair. Be my little companion. Does the prospect please you, my dear?'

'Yes . . . yes, Mrs Maxwell.'

She lowered her head and once again began to watch the dancing flames of the fire, and the gilt clock on the mantelpiece gently ticked away the minutes while the gas-lamp hissed like a slowly expiring snake. Gradually Maya found a question creeping into her brain; a question moreover that demanded an immediate answer. Twice the words came to the very tip of her tongue, then were hastily swallowed. On the third occasion they seeped over her lips as a strangled whisper.

'Please, Ma'am – Mrs Maxwell – Mrs Duncan said there had been six companions before me. Please – why did they leave?'

Mrs Maxwell did not look up, but continued her intense contemplation of the fire. She spoke softly.

'They were quite unable to ask for another cup of tea.'

The days passed and such is the nature of the human animal that Maya found familiarity bred, if not contempt, at least a feeling of apparent normality. The fact that the gas-lamp in Mrs Maxwell's room was never extinguished, the curtains never drawn, ceased to be thought-provoking wonderment, and sank to a merely puzzling eccentricity.

Mrs Maxwell was never demanding or short tempered, but treated her companion with a slightly condescending kindness, rather as though she were an endearing pet that could be indulged, but never allowed to jump up on to the sofa.

Wonderment of course is the twin sister of curiosity, and Maya began to seek an explanation for Mrs Maxwell's close seclusion, and decided the housekeeper was the ideal person to impart information. She chose one bright winter morning to ask the first question.

'Why does Mrs Maxwell shut herself away? It is really most extraordinary.'

Mrs Duncan wiped her brow with a flour-covered arm.

'I'm sure I don't know. What happens upstairs is none of my business.'

'Yes, but surely you must be curious. What happened to Mr Maxwell?'

'Well, there's them that says he died, and others who maintain he ran off with a creature young enough to be his daughter. But then, there's some people that will say anything.'

'And that gas-lamp. It must have cost a fortune to install. I mean having the pipes laid all the way from Keighley – all for one lamp.'

Mrs Duncan nodded and generally gave the impression she could tell much if she were so minded.

'Aye, it must have cost a pretty penny, and every night I have to feed that meter with a load of pennies, and heaven help us if I forgot.'

'But why?'

The housekeeper raised her head and creased her face into an enigmatic smile, and Maya received the impression that she was revelling in some secret, obscene joke.

'Perhaps she's afraid of the dark, dear. Oil-lamps are all very well, but they are inclined to leave shadows in the far corners of the room. Whereas gas-lamps – especially the one in her room – they don't give even the smallest shadow a ghost of a chance – do they?'

'You mean to say, Mrs Maxwell is afraid of shadows?'

Mrs Duncan bared her teeth in a grin. It was quite the most ferocious grimace that Maya had ever seen.

'Did I say that, dear? Maybe she's more to fear than mere shadows. I guess you're a heavy sleeper.'

The girl shrugged even while an icy chill ran down her spine. 'Yes, I suppose so. Mother used to say that the crack of doom wouldn't wake me. Why?'

Mrs Duncan went back to her task of kneading dough.

'Nothing. Only I'm glad my bed is down here. Now you'd best get back upstairs, or the missus will be ringing that bell.'

Mrs Maxwell kept her up late that night.

She lay on the great four-poster bed, her head propped up by two fat pillows and stared at Maya with disquieting intensity.

'I can't sleep – heaven help me I can't sleep. Read to me, child.'

Maya sorted through the books she had selected from the disused library.

'What would you like? *Jane Eyre* . . . ?'

'Nothing by the Miss Brontës,' Mrs Maxwell instructed. 'They are too coarse. Do you know what I have a fancy for?'

'No, Mrs Maxwell.'

'The Bible. You will find one in the top, left-hand drawer of the dressing-table. Fetch it, child.'

Maya opened the drawer indicated and brought out a leather-bound Bible, and carried it over to her chair by the bedside. Mrs Maxwell's eyes were closed.

'Turn to *Solomon's Song* chapter six, child, and read until I tell you to stop.'

The Bible appeared to fall open at the requested part, and Maya, after clearing her throat, began to read.

Whither is thy beloved gone, O thou fairest among women? Whither is thy beloved turned aside? that we may seek him with thee.

My beloved is gone down into his garden, to the beds of spices, to feed in the gardens, and to gather lilies.

I am my beloved's, and my beloved is mine: he feedeth among the lilies . . .

'That is so true,' Mrs Maxwell interrupted. 'That is so true. Go on, child.'

But Maya was sitting with the open Bible on her lap, while she stared fearfully towards the closed door.

'But – Mrs Maxwell – I can hear someone coming up the stairs.'

'Can you, dear? A little too early I would have thought, but the nights are getting shorter, aren't they? Never mind, it's cosy and bright in here. Please go on.'

Maya glanced at her employer's face, and saw the smile that might have been carved out of granite, and the beautiful eyes that were bright with the sheen of terror. She gasped, but from the parted lips came the harsh command.

'Read, girl. Don't worry your head about what might be on the landing – read.'

Maya again lowered her head and forced her voice to obey.

Thou art beautiful, O my love, as Tirzah, comely as Jerusalem, terrible as an army with banners.

Turn away thine eyes from me, for they have overcome me: thy hair is as a flock of goats that appear from Gilead.

Thy teeth . . .

There came a soft rap on the door. A gentle tap, that after an interval was repeated. Maya looked at Mrs Maxwell and recoiled when she saw the still-smiling mask, the wide-open eyes and the long fingers that clawed at the bedspread.

'Shall . . . shall I see who is there?'

Mrs Maxwell laughed. A harsh bark of a laugh, that momentarily drowned out the, by now, continuous soft tapping on the door. 'By no means, child. Not unless you want your eyes to pop from your head like ripe grapes. Read. Pretend they are not there. They will soon tire of their nonsense.'

'But . . . ?'

Mrs Maxwell sat upright and screamed the single word: '*Read!*'

The need to obey was greater than the demands of fear, and Maya's quavering voice intermingled with the insistent tapping.

Thy teeth are as a flock of sheep which go up from the washing, whereof every one beareth twins, and there is not one barren among them.

As a piece of . . .

The low whisper came from behind the door and Maya's young ears detected every word.

'Matilda – we are lonely. Come down to us . . . come down to us . . . come . . . come . . . come . . .'

Mrs Maxwell very slowly swung her legs off the bed and stood up. Then she began to move towards the door, walking with a strange shuffling motion, as though she was being drawn forward against her will. She stopped at a position about two feet from the door and raised her voice to a kind of shouted whisper.

'Go away. Aren't you tired of this continuous persecution? Go away.' The whispering ceased and after an interval of total silence the footsteps began to retreat along the landing, then slowly descend the stairs. Maya heard the muffled tread, the creak of a loose floorboard, and suddenly realized the eerie sound was being made by two pairs of feet – one heavy, suggesting a man of some weight, the other light, like a child or a slightly-built woman. Presently Mrs Maxwell came back to the bed and lay down in her original position; head propped up by the pillows, hands clasped, eyes staring across the room at the still-smouldering fire. When she spoke her voice was quite calm.

'Maya, dear, put another log on the fire.'

Maya took a log from a wrought-iron basket, placed it on the glowing embers, and waited until the orange flames were consuming the seasoned wood, before asking the all-important question.

'Mrs Maxwell – who were they?'

The woman on the bed did not speak, or display any sign that she had heard, but continued to watch the fire with apparent absorbing interest. Maya dared to take another step along the road of inquiry.

'I know that all the doors are locked, and there is no one else in the house except Mrs Duncan and Sugden. Where did they come from?'

She waited while the fear seethed against the frail barriers of self-control, then when the woman still did not speak, suddenly screamed: 'Please – please – are they ghosts?'

Mrs Maxwell closed, then opened her eyes, and appeared to be marshalling her thoughts into a coherent channel. Suddenly she smiled and patted the seat of the bedside chair.

'Come here, child.'

Maya walked back across the room, then sat down and waited for her employer to explain – perhaps to transform the darkness of irrationality into the comforting light of mundane possibility.

'Maya,' Mrs Maxwell said softly, 'I am very pleased with you. So many of your predecessors have given way to the dictates of fear, and become completely unmanageable. Ghosts, after all, are but talking shadows, sired by fear and born from darkness. If one is able to accept their existence, come to terms with the rules of the macabre game, then – I think I can safely say – life can be endured. Only just, but the floodtide of madness can be kept at bay. That is very important – do you not agree?'

Maya said: 'Yes,' because there was very little else she could say. Mrs Maxwell gave a vast sigh.

'That is most satisfactory. For a girl of your background, you have a certain *sang-froid* that a person of more advanced education might well envy. You of course have nothing to fear. It is me the wretches are after, hoping to wear me down, you understand.' She laughed gently. 'Just as though I would go down with them and spend an eternity in the garden. But I am up to their little tricks . . . You wished to say something, my dear?'

'Please – who are they?'

Mrs Maxwell frowned. 'That is scarcely your business, Maya. Just because I am permitting you a measure of familiarity, it does not mean you are to take liberties. Now, where was I? Oh, yes! Their little tricks. Darkness and loneliness are their allies. The one

I have banished by the gas-lamp, the other – well, dear – why else would I need a companion?'

Maya pondered on this information. She remembered her home where gaslight was a luxury, and her brothers and sisters provided more company than was strictly necessary, and footsteps on the landing were solid, sometimes sleep-murdering, but never ghostly. She came to a decision.

'If you please, Mrs Maxwell – I'd like to go home.'

Mrs Maxwell began to cry. A terrible, body-shaking, paroxysm of grief that was out of character with the aristocratic face and the pile of white hair. The shock produced by this outburst was further enhanced when Maya noticed, that although Mrs Maxwell sobbed, created loud mournful cries, she did not shed tears. She might have been a beautifully manufactured robot that had been programmed to express grief. Presently Maya placed a hand on one trembling shoulder and said: 'Please don't. You mustn't cry, really you must not. It's . . . It's not right.'

Mrs Maxwell began to damp down her sobs and find words in the morass of her distress.

'You must not talk of leaving me. I forbid it. Do you hear? I just cannot face the prospect of being alone again. And there is so much you can do. Promise you will stay.'

'Well . . .'

'You will not leave this room until you have promised.'

Maya was quite unable to resist the mew of a stray cat, the whine of a hungry dog – or an appeal from an unhappy employer. But her soul still shuddered when she said: 'I promise.'

Instantly Mrs Maxwell's eyes sparkled like twin blue lakes reflecting a wind-swept sky, and her slender shoulders became still, while her right hand caressed Maya's dark hair.

'I knew I could rely on you, my dear. Now, run off to bed and dream of mountains bathed in moonlight. The young can always dream, whereas the old must forever look back along the mist-shrouded valley of what might have been.'

Maya quickly retired to her bedroom at the far end of the landing, but was unable to sleep until the first glimmer of morning light had turned the window into a silver screen.

★

Maya was brushing Mrs Maxwell's beautiful white hair. It was like grooming the mane of a thoroughbred horse, thick, long, flecked with a thousand silver lights, it seemed to pulsate with independent life under the girl's administrations, and gave out little, contented crackling sounds. Mrs Maxwell's reflection watched her from the dressing-table mirror.

'How gentle you are, my dear. One might suppose you had been trained in the duties of a lady's maid.'

'I used to brush my mother's hair,' Maya said. 'Hers was not as beautiful as yours, but it was just as thick.'

Mrs Maxwell waited until her hair had been combed back into its customary style, before she spoke again.

'Do you sometimes wonder why I always keep the curtains drawn? Why, no matter the time of day or how bright the sun shines, here in this room, I sit and read by gaslight?'

Maya took a deep breath. Curiosity was hungry for knowledge, but fear wanted to hide behind a curtain of ignorance.

'I have wondered . . . But of course it is none of my business.'

Mrs Maxwell stood up and placed a hand on the girl's arm.

'If you are to help me, you must know. Will you be very brave and do something for me?'

Maya suddenly wanted to be in a far-off place, walking alone with a mind that was wiped clean of all knowledge, memory and the alien thoughts imprinted on it by passing strangers. She said: 'I'm not very brave, Mrs Maxwell. And I believe – although I don't want to – in living shadows.' Mrs Maxwell laughed and clapped her hand.

'What a simply priceless expression! Living shadows! That's what they are – aren't they? But even shadows can bite. Suck. Draw the life essence from the body and grow fat on our screaming souls. Do me this little favour, dear, and as a reward you may have my best cashmere shawl.'

'What . . . what is it you want me to do?'

Mrs Maxwell's smile was so gentle, her voice so coaxing, and her beautiful eyes so appealing, only a deaf and blind man could have resisted her.

'Go to the window, part the curtains ever so slightly – and peer down into the garden.'

Terror came leaping across the room and placed chill hands on Maya's thudding heart. She shook her head.

'I couldn't. Ask me to do anything else . . .'

'But you must. Until you have seen – recovered from the first shock – you will never be able to help me. And you do want to help me – don't you? Don't you? Don't you?'

The walk to the window was a journey across a vast gaslit country, and the thick, draped red curtains, a frail barricade that only just kept the horror-hordes at bay. Her fingers caressed the dusty velvet, then, with courage born from desperation, parted them, so that a long slit of grimy window-pane was exposed.

Mrs Maxwell's voice came from behind her. 'Not too much. They must not think I am surrendering.'

At first, relief. The scene is so familiar – natural – matter-of-fact – there is nothing to fear. Let the eyes rove over the wild moorland where the never-resting wind ripples the tall grass, and the curlew glides smoothly against the steel-blue sky; now lower them, and rejoice that there is nothing more alarming than the low garden wall, with a weed-ridden lawn spread out like a patchwork carpet, between it and the house. Now look directly downwards.

They are standing between two barren flower beds, looking up at the window motionless as marble statues; white and red shadows, that have fed upon fear and guilt, and now are as solid as slabs of rock on a snow-covered mountainside. The man is tall, middle-aged, with greying hair and a thick moustache. His skull has been split and the congealed blood has formed the likeness of a crimson cap. The girl is fair, pretty and very young. But her severed throat is not at all pretty, and a fragment of jagged windpipe gleams like polished ivory in the pale sunlight.

Mrs Maxwell's voice came from over the expanse of limitless space.

'You can see why I could never possibly draw the curtains.'

Maya gave a deep sigh, then fainted.

A blazing sun sent slivers of white heat across a golden desert, and in the far distance stood the still figures of a man and a young girl. Then a loud, harsh whisper came shuddering across the empty waste.

'Maya . . . Maya . . . wake up, child.'

The sun turned into a hissing gas-lamp, and the desert shivered and was gradually transformed into a familiar room. Maya sat up as a spark of memory flared up into a searing flame.

'I saw . . . saw . . . them . . . them . . .'

Mrs Maxwell raised her gently, then propelled her towards the nearest chair. 'Yes, dear, I know. But they weren't all that bad – were they? Would you like a drop of something strong? A glass of sherry, maybe?'

'No thank you. Please – who are they?'

The face of Mrs Maxwell became as rigid as steel. 'That is the second time you have concerned yourself with a matter that is no business of yours. Suffice to say that the man is – was an adulterous husband, and the girl a shameless creature. Their evil lives on.'

Truth was knocking at the door of Maya's mind, but she was not yet willing to face the inevitable. Surely there must be another, more acceptable explanation, or at least fact presented in such a way that it could be dismissed as illusion – the effect of tainted atmosphere. This gaslit room was a pocket of black fantasy, lost in a world of stark reality.

'They look so real,' she said.

'Evil is very real,' Mrs Maxwell replied primly, 'but it can never prevail against determination, single-mindedness and innocence.' She smiled down upon Maya's face. 'You are very innocent, my dear.'

That had been very true. But a single peep through parted curtains had done much to broaden Maya's mind, and she knew her employer was about to request a service that would be most unpleasant.

She whispered: 'No . . . no. Please.'

Mrs Maxwell sank down beside her and began to explain the wherefore, the how-to and the grim possibility.

'They come up every night. In the house it must be dark, you understand. Such creatures cannot bear to see the faces of their victims. Or maybe it is because they died in darkness – I do not know. But if someone with an untainted mind – someone who has not been forced to raise their hand against the ungodly – were to go out . . .'

Maya cried out: 'No . . . no . . .'

'Please do not interrupt me. Were to go out and order them to go down into the eternal darkness – then, they would have to obey.'

Maya shook her head violently from side to side and whimpered like a terrified animal. Mrs Maxwell grabbed her hands and began to plead.

'You must. Don't you realize what it is like to be shut up in here, year after year? Not daring to turn out the light or open the curtains. Once I went out – once only – and they followed me. Do you hear? Actually followed me! You can set me free, and I'll be grateful. So very, very grateful. As much money as you need for the rest of your life, think about that. Just for two minutes of work. If you can call it work. Say yes. Come along, it is such a small word. Yes . . . yes . . .'

'I cannot. Ask me to do anything . . .'

'Yes. Say yes. You can close your eyes when they are near. Come . . . say yes . . .'

'Ye . . . Ye . . . s.'

Mrs Maxwell stood up. 'At last. Really, all that fuss about nothing. I will see that Mrs Duncan and Sugden have the day off. The woman suspects, but she's never been able to prove. But it will be just as well if we have the house to ourselves, particularly as there is bound to be a certain amount of noise. Oh, for heaven's sake, don't start whimpering again.'

Mrs Duncan dumped her packed bags on the kitchen table and glared at Maya.

'Told me to take the day off, she did. And when I told 'er I didn't want no day off, she discharged me. Well, she's in for a shock.'

Maya stared at her with wide-open eyes. 'You mean – you're not coming back?'

'That's the truth of the matter. And if you had the sense you were born with, you'd push off as well. I'm not deaf or blind and I've a fair idea what keeps my lady shut tight in 'er room. Drive down to the station with Sugden and me.'

'Can't. I promised.'

'More fool you. I'm off. But when darkness falls, remember my words. You can't dismiss a guilty conscience.'

★

Just before sunset, Maya summoned up her meagre stock of courage and explored the garden. She walked slowly round to the back of the house and looked tearfully up at the curtained window. It was on this very spot the apparitions had stood, and were she to go upstairs now, and peer down from between a parting in those red curtains, she would undoubtedly see them. But – and she looked anxiously from left to right – there was no one fearful or otherwise in sight. A moorhen called out from its nest far away in the moor, and the wind, being in a playful mood, ruffled her long dark hair. Then a cloud passed over the face of the dying sun and a long black shadow came racing across the garden.

Maya ran back into the house and bolted every door, fastened every window, before ascending to the gaslit room on the first floor.

'I adjure you to get from hence and return no more,' Mrs Maxwell intoned in a loud voice.

'I adjure you to get from hence and return no more,' Maya repeated for the sixth time.

'Wander forever and a day in the black valleys of Hades,' Mrs Maxwell continued, 'where the primates horrific dance in demon-haunted forests.'

'Wander forever . . . Mrs Maxwell – how do you know it will work? I am only an ignorant girl and these words mean nothing to me.'

Mrs Maxwell threw up hands n a gesture of despair.

'Because I do know, girl. I have suspended reason and have replaced it by indisputable knowledge. I know those abandoned creatures are waiting in the garden below. I know they come upstairs every night and try to make me join them. I have succeeded in transmitting this knowledge to you. Therefore, you must accept my assurance that a certain combination of words will send them about their business. Do you understand?'

'Yes – I suppose so.'

'Thank heavens for that. Now, once again: I adjure . . .'

The footsteps began their relentless advance up the stairs, a little after midnight, and Mrs Maxwell became as a cat who welcomes the approach of a long-awaited mouse.

'Get out there, girl. Hurry – the door must not be open when they reach the landing. If we came face to face, who knows what might happen.'

She pushed the trembling girl towards the door, half opened it and sent her stumbling out on to the shadow-haunted landing. An oil-lamp with a frosted globe was suspended from the ceiling and this permitted a circle of yellow light to illuminate most of the landing and the top three stairs. Beyond, in every direction, the darkness seemed to surge against invisible barriers, while throughout the house, windows rattled, doors muttered, as the rising wind thundered its incessant demand for entry.

The approaching footsteps ignored the thick stair carpet, for they made a soft thudding sound, that had not been distinguishable from behind the closed door. A gradual approach of lightly placed feet; the relentless advance of unsated vengeance, that has fed upon the inexhaustible power of the human mind.

They came up into the circle of light, then paused, with them came a seeping coldness that flowed through Maya's limbs and made her into a frozen statue that could neither move nor speak, only see, hear and dimly understand. The man stared with hungry eyes at the closed door. The girl stood a little to his rear; the gaping wound in her throat was like red smiling lips.

Maya sensed the terrible loneliness, the searing guilt that could never be appeased until the third member of the grim trio had been purged of her crime. She heard their voices; the terrible whispered words.

'Matilda . . . come down with us. Come . . . come . . .'

Mrs Maxwell's voice called out from behind the door.

'Maya . . . speak, girl. Order them to go from hence. What's the matter with you?'

But a throat that was clogged with fear could not utter words; it could only croak, make little strangled cries, try vainly to scream, but an articulate incantation was well beyond its immediate powers. On the other hand Mrs Maxwell's vocal range was being greatly extended as the whispered appeal continued.

'In the name of pity speak . . . get rid of them . . . don't let me down. Don't . . .' Her voice died away, and during the ensuing silence the two figures moved slowly towards the door, then became motionless, as though waiting for permission to enter. The scream crashed into the silence and erupted into a torrent of gabbled words.

'The gas . . . the gaslight is going out . . . Mrs Duncan forgot to feed the meter . . . Maya . . . *the gaslight is going out . . .*'

The walls of light that had so far made the fortress invulnerable were falling down, and blind, unreasoning fear made the sole defender fling the door open and come shrieking out on to the landing, where the two shades from a blood-stained yesterday stood waiting.

Some part of Maya that was divorced from the paralysing terror saw a look of disbelief on Mrs Maxwell's face when she at last made visual contact with her ghosts. Fear that had always been hidden from view, left to stare up at curtains that were never opened, identified as a whispered summons from behind a closed door, had over the years assumed a half-real, half-imaginary existence. Now fear was clothed in the cerements of memory, the violent acts of yesterday had sent their vibrations over the frontiers of today, and the lingering remnants of racial superstition grew strong in the flickering light of a dying gas-lamp.

Mrs Maxwell shouted: 'No . . . you're dead. I killed you . . . go from hence . . . go . . . go . . .'

But she lacked the faith that can move mountains, and the last vestige of courage melted under the high noon of fear, and she retreated step by step, as the tall man and young girl slowly advanced into the darkening room.

Before the gas-lamp spluttered into extinction Maya saw three figures standing close together in the center of the room. The man and girl had their arms around Mrs Maxwell and their lips were gently caressing her cold, white cheeks.

Her screams died with the gaslight.

Maya ran across the vast black moorlands. The moon peered round racing cloud-banks, the stunted trees bowed their heads in token submission to the prevailing wind and the tangled heather rippled like the waves of a subterranean sea. She came to rest on the crest of a hill and looked fearfully out across a scene that alternated between silver and ebony as the moon hid, then reappeared from behind the wind-hunted clouds. She prayed when the moon was bright.

'May I not believe. Let me not see, hear or remember. Please, may this be so. Amen.'

The wind seized the pathetic little prayer, hurled it up to the tormented sky, then sent it on an endless journey to the distant stars. Maya waited.

Presently she saw. Nebulous shapes drifted across the moor, wringing transparent hands, forever condemned to roam the limitless plains of time and space.

She heard. Their plaintive cries intermingled with the shrieking wind, and stirred the dust of memory. She believed.

From far off came the bay of hunting hounds.

Presently Maya began to run again.

BIRTH

GURNEY SLADE WAS CUTTING GRASS. The motor-mower hummed
with contentment and so proclaimed its newness as did the lovingly
applied film of oil which coated the working parts. Decapitated
grass-blades leapt into the gleaming green-enamelled box, while a
sweet aroma of newly-mown hay evoked an up-to-now forgotten
memory of Gurney's childhood.

The sun had always shone in those summer afternoons of long
ago.

He remembered lying in the thick grass that had been allowed
to reach full maturity beyond the close-shaved lawn, resting snugly
in that sense-blurred plane where one is neither asleep or awake.
From behind, came the faint clatter of cups on saucers as his
mother laid the table for tea and, away to his front, the distant,
muted roar of a haymaker.

The smell of cut grass bridged the years before an iron hand
gripped his heart and hurled him back on to the smooth green
carpet. The mower became as a body without a brain; it zig-zagged
across the grass, the engine spluttering as though with rising fear,
then crashed into the garden wall, denting the gleaming box,
before lapsing into an abrupt silence.

A soft summer breeze made an old beech tree tremble; a sparrow alighted on the shorn lawn and looked vainly for worms.
From far, far away came the sound of a howling dog.

Gurney got up and looked round. He saw the ruined mower, then
instinctively glanced downwards.

He thought: 'Oh my god!' and knew.

The body lay flat on its back, the sightless eyes staring up at the cloudless sky. Its forehead was smooth, the face unlined, the teeth bared in the death grin, and one hand, the left, was gripping the white shirt front.

'I'm dead.'

There was no brain to form the thought, no tongue to utter the words, only a speck of consciousness that floated some six feet above the ground. But he was aware – existed – knew.

Only one sense remained. Sight. He could not hear, feel, or smell – only see. But emotion still lived. Sadness and fear produced a soundless cry, then merged and gave birth to grief. He mourned the death of his body and all that pertained to it. Eating, drinking, the smell of newly-cut grass, the lash of rain on his face, the smoothness of Caron's white skin . . .

'Caron!'

She was not due back until ten o'clock: six or seven hours away, but the shock of finding this thing – the face fast turning black – could well nigh kill her, or perhaps worse, drive her insane.

His line of vision was suddenly directed towards the cottage: the yellow walls half-veiled by honeysuckle, the windows masked by white nylon curtains – four rooms, a dividing hall and a built-on kitchen called to him, and in a flash he was there, floating along the hall, drifting across the dining-room; a something without dimension.

'She will look for me.' The wordless thoughts went streaking across the small room as invisible waves. 'At first without alarm. She will open doors, call my name, go outside, look in the outhouse . . . Not the garden, it will be too dark. For some time she will not think of going out into the garden . . . The puzzled smile will die, her eyes widen, her voice take on the first grey tones of worry. Red thoughts will come out from her brain like scarlet poppies unfolding over the graves of the long-dead, and she will be as a beautiful moth trapped in a summer storm.'

Like a newly-born colt he quickly learnt how to move from one place to another. He thought 'bedroom' and was there, poised over the large double bed, peering into the long wardrobe mirror that denied his existence. 'Kitchen' was associated with 'sink', and at once he was deep down in a stainless-steel pit, where the gleaming walls towered up to a white, grease-streaked sky.

'Meant . . . to . . . decorate . . .' The thoughts hurled him into the small outhouse where empty tins of paint, brushes nestling in jars of turpentine, a distemper-smeared pair of steps and a rust-flecked saw glared at him with angry reproach.

'Oven . . . oven . . . Caron . . . told . . . me . . . to . . . turn . . . it . . . down.'

He was on the kitchen floor looking up at the grey-white gas stove; little headless snakes of black smoke were creeping shyly out from round the door edges. He mourned the passing of a ruined meal, then spun round in alarm on finding himself in a flame-lit cavern, where a giant casserole bubbled and spat, its surface a blackened face coated with erupting blisters.

'Should . . . have . . . turned . . . it . . . down . . .'

He was in the heart of a blue flame. A glorious, blue bubble of quivering light that streaked out and up to the limitless frontiers of space, and he felt no fear or wonderment, only a serene understanding, that he was not without size or shape. He had reverted to the original spark that had, in the beginning, been thrown out by a mighty cosmic fire.

'She . . . will . . . soon . . . be . . . back . . .'

The thought shot him back into the living-room where he raced round the walls in a frenzy of helpless terror, until at last a kind of tiredness, which had nothing in common with weariness of the body, made him come to rest on the table.

He must accept. Try to understand. He was dead. Dead . . . dead . . . dead. But was he? The essential Gurney Slade was very much alive. He could still think, even move after a fashion. He had not lost the power to reason. Indeed, coming down to basic facts, all he lacked was a body.

He considered this thought for some time, then allowed it to expand. What were the main functions of a physical body? Well, most essential, it must breathe, then it should be able to talk, and, of course – walk.

Walk! What had it been like to walk? Gurney tried to remember. Strange, he had always taken this fundamental action for granted and never actually noted the senses involved. Firstly, there had been a feeling of a hard surface beneath the feet, then the smooth working of leg muscles, plus possibly an automatic swinging of arms. Prompted by an experimental urge, Gurney rose to a height of approximately six feet and started to move slowly across the floor. He tried to imagine a firm surface on which a pair of well-formed feet – suitably shod in stout shoes – were pacing. At once he found himself deep down in the thick pile of the carpet; a table leg soared up above him, like the trunk of a mighty oak. He shot upwards, fired by a blast of irritation.

He adjusted his height and tried again, but now he concentrated on a shape that walked on two legs. This was surely the answer; he must not think of the floor. After all, one didn't – its existence was taken for granted. Now he was in an oval box – in other words, the head – looking out of two small windows, and lower down was a flesh-covered bone cage, which housed a messy collection of bowels, heart, lungs and liver. This was supported by a pair of hinged, movable pillars, and they in turn were attached to flattish, ten-toed objects called feet.

He concentrated his mental power (if this was the right definition) on this desired state of being. The legs were swinging . . . No, they weren't, darn it. The legs were lifting the feet and putting them firmly down on an honest-to-goodness Wilton carpet. The head was looking to its front, the eyes were unblinking, the mouth closed; the heart was beating seventy-two beats to the minute, the lungs knew their business and were breathing in and out, and the bowels were unmoved.

Gurney turned when he reached the doorway and tramped steadily back across the room.

Now, to go over it all again. He was looking through two little windows which had a kind of fringed blind on the outside. His mouth – a lipped slit – was tight shut. The heart was beating soundly, the liver was behaving itself, the lungs inflated before deflating and his bowels rumbled.

Then he bumped into the table.

He stamped solid feet on a carpet-covered floor.

He heard no sound, but there was feeling. Or rather emotion. The joy of one who has created.

He went up the stairs one step at a time, looking straight to his front through those little windows, and there was a great urge to see that which he had made. To take pleasure in his creation.

He came up on to the landing, then turned and entered the bedroom. There was some anxiety because he could not hear, neither could he look to left or right nor, for that matter, up or down. The neck! He had forgotten to hinge the neck. Never mind – the fundamentals must be there, otherwise he would not be able to walk, feel the floor beneath his feet, or see through his little windows.

He stood before the wardrobe mirror and gazed upon his creation. Cold horror rushed in and held the reflected image frozen for an eternity of a second. The face was oval, white, hairless; there was a thin slit that did service for a mouth, but no nose, no ears, and no neck. Two little milk-white windows stared blankly at their creator. The head, if it could so be called, sat on a barrel-shaped – something, and he had forgotten to include arms. Further down he realised he had forgotten something else, but under the circumstances it did not seem important.

The legs were a triumph. Long, muscular, hairy, they had all the hallmarks of a perfectly acceptable pair of masculine legs. Gurney would have gladly taken them anywhere. For the rest . . . The image quivered like a blancmange in a furnace, then quickly dissolved and Gurney Slade was once again a speck of consciousness floating some six feet above the floor.

'How?'

How to take on a perfect reproduction of a flesh-and-blood body? He knew it could be done, but how? How . . . how . . . how . . . ? Of course his will was, so to speak, the flour that made the cake. But whence came the water, the sugar and spice and all things nice? Once he had solved this mystery the next build-up should be a success. He floated through the cottage like an invisible moth, entering dark cupboards, taking a childish delight in oozing through keyholes. He went into the little-used front room, was momentarily lost in a vase of flowers, went back to the kitchen and instantly retreated on finding it full of smoke. Finally he flashed back to the bedroom. It was here, if anywhere, the answer lay. He settled on the bed and thought.

'Why?'

Why the bedroom? One thing was certain, his memory was intact. The loss of his brain had not destroyed his memory pattern; did this also mean the automatic impulses could still be activated? The mental power-unit that had created a thirteen-stone man out of an eight-pound baby? If so . . . He floated upwards, then drifted over to the wardrobe mirror. But there was still the question. Why the bedroom?

Because . . . Thoughts tumbled over each other in their desire for expression. Because it was here he had slept, made love, given out basic, raw passion, that . . . The thoughts collected together, became as a blown-up balloon, then exploded . . . That could not die. The raw passion, the bits and pieces, the wastage of his soul, did not, could not, die. The walls, the floor, the bed, were saturated with them. The personality of Gurney Slade was spread out everywhere. And all he had to do was to pull it together, suck the life-giving essence, build-up slowly bit by bit, forgetting nothing – use his god-darn will.

Outside, darkness was falling, and he knew the congesting shadows would give him strength, help supply that little extra something he needed. He wondered if the rising moon might not be, in some way, responsible, but quickly dismissed the thought as he prepared for the great experiment.

First, his thoughts, like little winged messengers, went out to the walls, floated down to the beds, disturbed the dust-layer of memories.

'. . . Why . . . do you want to eat me? Love is love is love is lust. What is it? The urge to get inside someone and become part of them?'

'This is no time for philosophy.'

'Can't we talk sometimes?'

'Me Great Big Sitting-Bull . . . me no talk . . .'

Then his thoughts became tubes, long tentacles which fastened their suckers on walls, bed, floor, ceiling, and his will was a mighty pump, drawing in the bits, the pieces, the fragments of Gurney Slade.

'You mustn't . . . all right . . . if you want to . . . you've tied it too tight . . . damn . . . indigestion . . . must take bath . . . money . . . lots of lovely money . . . you're hurting . . . plant daffodils tomorrow . . . lovely tits . . . I'll be thirty-five next week . . . getting old . . . bills . . . bloody bills

*. . . flesh . . . white . . . soft . . . legs . . . thighs . . . bum . . . good word
. . . better than buttocks . . . behind . . . arse. . . .'*

The tubes were fat, pulsating, filled with essence, but he must
go carefully. Keep his cool, build up slowly, forget nothing. Lay the
foundations.

In the end and the beginning there were bones. The skeleton.

Gurney Slade watched his skeleton come into being. First as
a faint, slightly phosphorescent outline, then a solid, hard frame-
work of articulated bones, complete with skull, spinal column,
clavicle, scapula, sternum, ribs, humerus, ulna, sacrum, pelvis,
femur, patella, fibula, tibia and cartilages.

Now let the empty places be filled.

A mass of grey matter took possession of the skull; then came
eardrums, glaring eyeballs, pink tongue, blood vessels, teeth, complete with fillings, windpipe, food tube – Gurney could not remember its right name – delicate pink lungs, dark brown liver, mauve,
white-streaked heart, kidneys packed in creamy suet, neatly rolled
coils of intestines . . . Soon Gurney's skeleton was packed tighter
than a holiday-maker's suitcase, and he prepared himself for the
final act.

'Flesh . . . flesh . . . let there be flesh.'

The skeleton was covered by a mist; this quickly merged into a
slimy paste that ran in all directions. It bubbled, seethed, sprouted
raw ears, a wet gleaming nose, then it solidified and acquired a
smooth white skin. The bald skull darkened as a mop of red hair
came into being; eyelashes declared their existence, a five-o'clock
shadow clouded the chin. Colour tinted the cheeks, the full lips,
and a well-built young man gazed upon his body with contentment.

'Life . . . a pint of life in a proper measure.'

The heart took up a steady beat; blood raced through the singing
veins; hearing exploded with a sudden roar – and he was complete.

'I've done it.'

His voice sounded strange, but it was familiar. His body felt
perfect; never had it been so in tune, so free from aches and pains.
But somehow it did not seem right. He was like a man who has
sold his house and has illegally taken possession of it again.

'I'm alive!'

But was he?

He stood in front of the wardrobe mirror and breathed in deeply, then exhaled. His chest rose, then sank, in a most satisfactory manner. He slapped his left thigh with one of Caron's hairbrushes and was almost surprised when the blow stung and the flesh turned pink.

'I did it . . . but I couldn't have done.'

These conflicting thoughts accompanied him to the bathroom and refused to be dispelled even when he cut himself while shaving, and watched the bright red blood trickle down his chin.

'I know how I did it, but I can't believe I did.'

When he was in the bath a more comforting thought made its presence known.

'Perhaps . . . perhaps I never died at all.'

Relief poured in, flooded his brain, drove anxiety into a dark corner, where it waited for the tumult to subside.

'I was never dead. Of all the crack-brained ideas. Bloody imagination run wild. I'm probably going barmy, but I was never dead. Dear God, I was never dead.'

He had donned his best tweed suit, put on his shoes and was knotting his tie, when yet another thought sent its whispered words shuddering down the dark corridors of his brain.

'If you did not die, then there should be nothing lying out there in the garden.'

He seized the evil snake of a thought and thrust it into the bag of forgetfulness. But somehow it got out, and would not – could not – be confined. It began its obscene whispering all over again.

'If one cannot trust memory, where is reality? Dismiss your memories, erase the past, then you are dead, for you have never lived.'

'It did not happen,' Gurney spoke aloud. 'I am alive. How can I be dead in the garden, and stand in this room, breathing, seeing and hearing?'

'Then go out and bury your past in a deep hole.'

'No, if I go out it would deny my existence.'

He went down into the kitchen and turned off the gas oven tap, then opened the window and back door. The acrid smoke drifted out with surly reluctance, while the cool evening air came in to caress his hot face with clammy fingers. He pulled the oven door down and took out the ruined casserole – a black, red-pocked face, that seethed weakly, like a bog digesting its latest victim.

The garden called him with silent, irresistible voice. The urge to go out and face the double-faced head of truth was like that which comes to a man perched on the rim of a high building. Jump – it's the quickest way down.

He shook his head and whispered, 'No!' as he took a torch from the kitchen dresser. He shouted: 'I won't go!' as he shuffled along the garden path. The torch cast a round circle of light which darted across the smooth-cut lawn, revealing the straight lines which marked the passing of the mower.

'Not there . . . not there . . .'

Wild hope mocked him and he knew he was allowing the torch beam to stray to the garden wall, the isolated flower beds, any-where but the dark patch, away over just beyond the garden shed.

'Not there . . . dream . . . madness . . .'

He edged slowly to his right, trying to keep the light beam over to the left, but his treacherous wrist would not be denied. At last, that which he did not wish to see was there – highlighted, revealed in its full ugliness.

He came to it as a rabbit is drawn to a snake. Slowly, inch by inch. And had there been the will, the strength, he would have turned and run back into the darkness. But his feet moved forward remorselessly, and soon, too soon, he was looking down on the black-faced thing that stared up at the now cloud-racked sky with bulging eyes. The teeth were bared in the death-grin; one hand – black – black with sudden death, was still clenched over the shirt front, and Gurney Slade's terror was blended with pity. Pity for the hideous form of his former self.

'She must not see it.'

He went to the garden shed and took out a pick and shovel.

Every man should bury his past.

Caron came home at ten-thirty.

Gurney heard the car growl as she changed gear and turned into the drive. Footsteps on the gravel, the garage door groaned, the engine snarled, and the drawn curtains momentarily blazed with light. Then the garage doors slammed, footsteps came round to the front door, a key clicked into the lock, and she was there – in the hall.

'Gurney?'

Her voice was clear, so familiar, yet it seemed to come from a time that had long since passed.

'Gurney, are you there, darling?'

She laid her cool cheek against his and hugged him gently.

'So sorry I'm late, but mother wasn't well, and I thought I'd better wait until Mildred came home. Did you think I'd never come?'

'Beautiful women are always late,' he said.

'Flatterer.'

She pulled away and went into the living-room, shedding her gloves, her outdoor coat, then adjusted her bright auburn hair in the overmantel mirror.

'Lord, I look a mess. Has the dinner spoiled?'

'Well . . .' he began.

'You did remember to turn the oven down?'

'I sort of . . . forgot . . .'

'You didn't! Great jumping catfish! Honestly, you are the giddy limit. All you had to do was turn a tap. Men! Mother was right, the sooner women learn to lay eggs the better.'

She went into the kitchen and he listened to the little explosive sounds, the bang of a dish on the table, followed almost immediately by a low chuckle.

'Talk about a burnt offering.'

He sank into an armchair, lit a cigarette, took a few puffs, then hurriedly extinguished it in an ashtray. The smoke tasted strangely bitter.

'Eggs and ham,' Caron's voice called out. 'That's all we've got. Will you have 'em poached or fried?'

Gurney had a sudden vision of eggs floating on a bed of melted fat in a frying pan; two dead man's eyes. He swallowed a pang of rising nausea.

'Poached.'

'Right. Poached eggs and ham coming up. What have you been up to while I've been away?'

'Digging.' The rattle of plates, the roar of a gas-ring.

'What on earth have you been digging?'

'Oh,' he shrugged, 'burying some old rubbish.'

Her footsteps were pottering back and forth across the kitchen.

'You don't want to overdo it. I thought you looked rather seedy this morning. Have you had any more of those pains in the chest?'

'No,' he said and smiled. 'No more pains.'

'I expect it was a touch of indigestion. Be an angel and lay the table.'

He covered the table with a blue-edged cloth, carefully placed knives, forks and spoons in their traditional places, then went back to his chair.

He was hungry.

Not a nagging hunger. Not a pleasurable craving for food that makes the mouth water with anticipatory delight, but an urge for immediate nourishment that filled his entire body. Waiting upon this hunger was a growing weakness, that was not a little frightening. How strong, in fact how durable, was this new body which had been manufactured out of the dark wastage of his soul? He got to his feet as Caron entered, pushing a loaded food trolley, and quickly seated himself at the table.

'Is the poor old fellow famished, then?' She placed a plate of ham and poached eggs, with fried potatoes, before him. 'It's your own fault, letting the casserole burn. I can't think what came over you.'

He seized a knife and fork and carved a lump of sizzling ham.

'Got enthralled. Forgot time.'

'Enthralled in cutting grass!' she laughed, a sweet, silvery sound, as Gurney popped a piece of ham into his mouth.

The taste was all wrong. It was as though he were chewing hotted-up long-dead flesh; his stomach heaved and he spat the food out. It lay upon the table cloth as a revolting splodge; the half-chewed meat looked like red worms.

'What the . . .' Caron half rose from her chair and stared at him with astonishment and fear. 'Are you ill? For heaven's sake, what's the matter?'

'The ham.' Gurney gestured with his fork. 'It's rotten. Putrid.'

'Nonsense.' Caron put a small portion into her mouth and

chewed it with an expression of pathetic anxiety. 'It's fine. There's nothing wrong with the ham. It's you. I knew something was wrong the moment I set foot inside the front door. You're ill.'

'Damnation!' Gurney flung down his knife and fork and shuddered. 'There's nothing wrong with me. I feel marvelous and I'm hungry. Bloody hungry, but I can't eat that filth.'

'I think you'd better sit quietly for a few minutes, while I fetch a cloth.'

She walked slowly towards the kitchen, stiff-backed, face carefully averted, and he could sense, almost smell her fear. He stabbed a solitary fried potato and raised it towards his mouth. Instantly his stomach revolted and some automatic impulse forced his hand back upon the table. But the all-prevailing hunger was greater than before.

'Can't eat. I'll starve . . . can't eat . . . What's the good of a new body if I can't eat?'

Caron came back with a glass-cloth and, a bare second before she reached the table, he caught a glimpse of his right hand. With one quick movement he buried it between his legs.

Caron rubbed the tablecloth, then glanced down at him, her pale face a picture of acute anxiety.

'You look dreadful. You'd better go to bed. I expect you've been overdoing it, but if you're not better by tomorrow morning I'll call the doctor.'

'Yes, I expect you're right.'

As he got up he slid his right hand into a trouser pocket.

'I'll be fine after a good night's sleep. Don't worry . . . don't fuss. I'm all right, just tired . . . stomach upset.'

He left her, doing his best to walk erect, but there was a terrible weakness in his legs, and the great hunger had him by the throat – was clamouring for satisfaction. The stairs were a mountain that took him an eternity to climb, the landing a vast desert, and the bedroom door a gateway that led to nowhere.

Gurney Slade sank down upon the bed and slowly withdrew his right hand from its hiding place. He stared at it for a long time, then gradually accepted the unpalatable truth.

The flesh had disappeared from the tip of his right fore-finger. A fragment of gleaming white bone projected from a cylinder of wrinkled skin. After a while he rubbed the other fingers, gently bit the palm. There could be no pretense. His right hand was dying. He began to cry; he sat on the edge of the bed and sobbed like a hurt child. He had snatched a bundle of life from the arms of death, but now the grim reaper was taking back his property. Presently, overcome by weakness, which momentarily made him forget the strange hunger, he climbed out of his clothes and got into bed. He saw that his right toe was turning black, but at that moment it did not seem important, the cool sheets received him, and he sank down into a world where a soft, starlit gloom was forever free from the harsh rays of a devouring sun.

He was gliding over a desolate moor, drifting out of mist-banks, floating in lakes of starlight. An occasional leafless tree lifted back skeleton-arms to a windswept sky, and tall grasses whispered the undying thoughts of the unnumbered dead. The great hunger drove him onward towards a distant horizon and he called out: 'What is it? Must I eat grass, gnaw wood, fill my mouth with black earth?'

The wind laughed; the tall grasses waved their tapered heads, and the black trees shook with obscene merriment. Then he heard the sound of soft footsteps, the opening of a door, and the roar of running water.

He felt better. The hunger was still there, but it had subsided to a dull ache; his new body was relaxed, limp between the sheets, and, for no reason that could be defined, there was a sense of rising excitement.

Caron was taking a bath. The roar of cascading water ceased, to be followed by a soft, splashing sound. She was humming. The tune he did not recognise, but it was irritating, and he felt his heartbeat quicken, while there was a rising warmth in his loins. The humming merged into words, and she began to sing softly as though fearful lest she disturb his sleep. The words and tune were out of keeping with her normal, matter-of-fact self. He could hear every word:

'Oh, wilt thou have my hand, Dear, to lie along in thine?
As a little stone in a running stream, it seems to lie and pine!
Now drop the poor pale hand, Dear . . . unfit to plight with thine.'

It was as though he were peering through a small window in her soul. Who was Caron? He had lived and slept with her for seven years, and yet, he now realised, he had never really known her. The soft voice went on.

'Oh, wilt thou have my cheek, Dear, drawn closer to thine own?
My cheek is white, my cheek is worn, by many a tear run down.
Now leave a little space, Dear, . . . lest it should wet thine own.'

A blast of anger flooded his brain. She had cheated him, deceived him, dared to hide the inner chamber of her soul. He sat up and waved a clenched fist . . . Three fingers were now white, gleaming bone. A fragment of the skeleton to come, unless . . . He growled deep down in this throat, and the growl shattered and became fierce, muttered words.

'Cheat . . . liar . . . you locked a door where I should have entered.'

'Oh, must thou have my soul, Dear, commingled with thy soul?
Red grows the cheek, and warm the hand . . . the part is in the whole!
. . . Nor hands nor cheeks keep separate, when soul is joined to soul.'

A splash, the gurgle of water draining away, the rasp of rough towel on smooth skin, then the approaching pad of naked feet.

Caron came in wrapped in a red bath towel; she looked breathtakingly beautiful and strangely very young. She gave him a quick, searching glance, then sat down before the dressing-table.

'You're awake, then? I hope I didn't disturb you with my cat-yelling.'

He did not answer, only stared at her gleaming shoulders and slim neck with dilated eyes.

'Do you feel better now? You must be more careful. I don't like you doing all that heavy work in the garden. Heavens above knows, we can afford to employ a man.'

The towel was slipping, sliding down to her waist, and the naked flesh was like a white flame, dazzling his eyes, feeding his anger. The great hunger flared up and mingled with anger.

'Tomorrow we'll get Doctor Waterhouse to give you a thorough examination.'

'What was that you were singing?'

He was surprised at the calmness in his voice, the casual way in which he asked the question.

'Oh, that.' She looked smilingly back over one shoulder. 'It's called "Inclusions", by Elizabeth Barrett Browning. Norma Shearer sang it in *The Barrets of Wimpole Street*.'

'I never knew.' He had to swallow – his mouth was filled with anticipatory water. 'I never knew you went in for stuff like that.'

She laughed and he trembled with rage.

'There's a lot of things you don't know about me, my lad.'

He slid his legs out from under the bedclothes and the floor was solid beneath his feet. He rose up to full height, aware of a burning sensation in his gums, while the gleaming bones of his right hand opened and closed, like the claws of a carnivorous spider.

'Come here.'

A growl that rose up from the stomach, tore at the vocal cords and rasped off the tongue. Caron spun round and stared at him in astonishment.

'What!'

'Come here.'

She came towards him slowly, reluctantly, but perhaps with a secret, fearful joy, for was he not magnificent in his rage? And the great hunger peeped out of his glaring, red-tinted eyes.

'What is it? There's no need to look so . . .'

The bones of his right hand crashed across her cheek and she went down to the floor, where she lay downward, her bare shoulders trembling, while she sobbed with pain and bewilderment.

The waist was slender, the back curved up to the white shoulders; above was the slim, beautiful – oh, so beautiful neck. Three weals seeped blood and marred the soft curve of her cheek. His eye-teeth moved, slid down from their gum-sheaths and dimpled his lower lip. He dribbled as he came down to her; he was as a starving man invited to a banquet when those wonderful teeth – fangs – sank into the soft white neck.

Her screams were music, her flailing body, the death struggle of a rightful prey, and her blood, life-giving nectar. It filled his mouth, cascaded down his throat, flooded his stomach, raced through his veins and was quickly transformed into violent, never-to-be-extinguished life. She was an orange, a beautiful white bottle, a carton of juice with her neck as the straw, and he drained her to the very last, precious drop. When he finally rose, the body was limp, whiter than white, a skin-bag filled with bones and bloodless meat.

Gurney Slade placed one foot upon the yielding back, clenched his now fully-fleshed hands, opened his mouth and gave vent to the triumphant roar of a well-fed bull-vampire.

He experienced the remorse of the fully-sated.

'I am alone.'

He pushed the body over on to its back and was revolted by its awesome appearance. The face had shrunk, the eyes protruded, the mouth gaped. He felt sad that it had been necessary to destroy so much beauty, but most of all he missed her.

Presently he rose, took up the limp corpse and carried it out into the garden. He dug his second grave and gave her back to the hungry earth.

He was bored.

He roamed the empty rooms looking for excitement. His stomach rumbled; there was more than a hint of indigestion, for his last meal had been rich, chock-full of vitamins and flesh-building protein, and now that the great hunger was gone, he missed it. He was like a man who is fully sated after the sexual act. All the pleasure had been spent; now there was a faint guilty feeling, a suggestion that he had made a pig of himself. He had eaten his cake, now he wanted it back, complete with white icing.

The hall clock announced three with a silver voice. Gurney knew, with the instinct of his kind, that time was running out. Soon the sun would stretch out golden fingers across the face of night, and long before then his fine new body must disintegrate, become a million invisible atoms that would lie like silver dust in dark corners – waiting for darkness to bring them together again.

A shadow flitted across the floor. A mere streak of darkness that he would not have seen yesterday, but now his eyes had a special keenness, and he knew Caron had come back. He ran up the stairs two at a time, truly alive with love, lust and cynical amusement. In the bedroom the tiny speck of a shadow flitted across the wardrobe mirror, then hurled itself at his face. He laughed and spoke softly.

'Don't be such a little goose. Build up, it's your death right. Don't waste your energies in prancing around like a sex-mad moth. Do you hear me? Stand still.'

After a few more turns round the room, the speck of a shadow came to rest some five foot six inches above the floor, which meant it was in line with Gurney's nose, and between him and the mirror.

'That's better. Now, concentrate. Think of all things dark. Bathe in the black waters of half-forgotten sins; remember all the deeds you'd rather forget, then let your thoughts become tubes that suck . . . That's it. By gosh, you catch on quick, but then, I suppose women have more dark thoughts in their brains . . .'

Her skeleton formed very nicely; the internal organs slipped into place, the flesh squelched over the bones, and in no time at all, she was complete.

Caron took her first deep breath, then quickly rediscovered her tongue.

'You bastard.'

'Now, now.' He raised protesting hands. 'Don't get all worked up . . .'

Suddenly she burst into tears and he drew the beautiful white body into his arms and kissed her gently.

'There . . . there. It's all over now. I missed you so much, and I was lonely. The terrible loneliness of the damned.'

'Why did you do it?' She rubbed her eyes with the back of one hand. 'Why did you do it?'

'Every man drinks the one he loves,' he misquoted. 'You were there, I needed you. I suppose I wanted you to join me.'

'And we will never be parted again?'

He shook his head.

'Never. The night will belong to us for all eternity.'

'No stakes through hearts? No burning?'

He laughed.

'This is a civilised country.'

From the road which bordered their garden came the sound of someone singing. A voice raised as an act of worship to Bacchus. Not a tuneful voice – it was raucous, unkind to the ear – but Caron's eyes glistened with wonderful, beautiful joy.

> *'Nellie Dean, oh, Nellie Dean.*
> *Where the bloody 'ell have you been . . .'*

'A traveller, homeward bound on the waves of wine,' said Gurney softly.

'I'm so hungry,' Caron whispered.

'You've just time for a little snack,' Gurney assured her. 'I'd get stuck in, if I were you.'

'Do you think I dare?'

She tip-toed to the door, a lovely woodland nymph, her eyes shining with girlish anticipation. She paused.

'Won't you join me?'

'Thank you, I've dined.'

He waited. The songster drew nearer; his refrain was a tribute to a fertile imagination.

> *'Oh, Nellie Dean, I'll chase you round.*
> *A bloody great pointed, grassy mound.*
> *You'll jump right up, I'll push you down,*
> *Then I'll . . .'*

'Cor, strike a light!'

'Ah!' Gurney nodded. 'He has seen.'

A short silence. Then:

'Blimey! Starkers! you come along over 'ere . . .'

His scream started on a high note, then descended to a rather nasty gurgle. Gurney lay down on the bed and thought happily of the years to come. They would be buried in a churchyard of course, but that wouldn't matter, and someone else would come to live in the cottage. He hoped it would be a decent family, a large family, the sort of people Caron and he could get along with. Who knows, in time they might be able to build up a thriving community.

Caron came back. Bloody-mouthed, dewy-eyed, her teeth were like red pearls.

'I feel fit to burst,' she confided.

'You look great. Like Aphrodite after she had been chewing on red grapes.'

'Oh, am I in a mess? Please don't say I'm in a mess.'

'Go and wash your face,' he instructed. 'But hurry. Soon it will be sunrise, then we will have to go.'

She went into the bathroom, and he heard the sound of running water. How wrong the old tales were – as though water could do anything else but clean. Wash away the marks of sin, purify the face with beauty, soften the lips, caress the hands.

There was music in his head – pulsating drums, clashing cymbals, throbbing violins – and he was a god of flesh, supreme master of blood, undisputed king of night. He got to his feet and was on his way to the bathroom when Caron gave one strangled cry, and suddenly they were both atoms of consciousness floating across the room.

The first pale fingers of dawn filtered through the curtains, and outside in the garden the rising sun smiled upon the infant day. The shadows retreated slowly, as though seeking protection from the death-dealing light, while a buttercup spread out its yellow petals and rejoiced that night had died.

Way down at the bottom of the garden, under a laburnum tree, where the shadows still lurked unmolested, a starling snatched a writhing worm from a freshly-filled grave.

THE GREAT INDESTRUCTIBLE

I PULLED THE IRON BELL-HANDLE and listened to the mournful clanging sound that took place somewhere deep down in the old house. I waited – not without considerable trepidation – and presently was rewarded by the slip-slop of approaching footsteps. The door groaned its doleful protest as it slid open, and the face of the count's butler peered round the edge. He bared teeth that were too long and sharp for my peace of mind and hissed,

'Y-iss-s?'

I produced my press card. 'Clutcher – *Ghoul Gazette*. I have an appointment with Count Dracula.'

He opened the door to its fullest extent, and I was able to see that his head was tilted over to one side and rested on his right shoulder. A large bump stood out like a monstrous carbuncle on the exposed side of his neck.

'Won't you en-ter, sir? His Excellency is ex-pecting you.'

I entered the hall and noted the picturesque cobwebs that dangled from the ceiling; the friendly rat that sniffed with optimistic expectancy at my ankles; and the bleached skeleton that did service as a hat-stand.

The butler began to pat my pockets and run his green-tinted hands down my person. 'If you would permit, sir. I must ass-ure that you have no cros-ses, sharp stakes or gar-lic. One cannot be too careful.'

Having made certain that I was completely devoid of lethal weapons, he led me towards a fungus-covered door, and after tapping on one spongy panel, turned a handle and announced in a loud voice,

'Mr Hans Clutcher, of *Ghoul Gazette*, your Excell-ency.'

I entered, and there behind a worm-riddled desk stood the Great Indestructible. The Unquenchable Thirst. The Mighty Partaker. Tall, surprisingly thin, long, white face, red-flecked eyes, sleek black hair – he was all that I had expected, and more. He motioned me to an upturned coffin, then bared his fangs in an engaging smile.

'Please be seated, Mr Clutcher. Delighted you could come.'

I sat down and the count nodded to his butler.

'Thank you, that will be all, Carlos, unless . . .' He looked at me with meaningful intent. 'Unless you would care for some light refreshment.'

I hastened to decline this kindly offer. The count seated himself, and when the door was closed, said, 'I would be lost without Carlos. Excellent provider.'

'Where did you find him?' I asked.

'On the gibbet. I expect you have noticed he has a broken neck. Fortunately I was able to get a nip-on-time.'

A short silence followed while I digested this piece of information, then I remembered my mission and produced my notepad.

'Count Dracula, you have been called the Great Indestructible. Would you care to comment?'

He shrugged and tore his fascinated gaze away from a small razor nick on my chin. 'Everyone's had a go – haven't they? I've had a stake through my heart six times. Been left out in the sunlight twice. Been decapitated, smothered in garlic, burnt to a cinder, plunged into running water, and disintegrated by innumerable chanted incantations. But I always come bouncing back.'

I said 'Good Heavens!' and instantly apologised for my lack of tact. 'How do you account for this . . . this continuous resurrection?'

'Fortunately, the world is full of long-nosed idiots who can't mind their own business. There's always someone who will pull a stake out of a grinning skeleton; pour virgin blood over my ashes; hold midnight orgies and gabble unpronounceable words, then scream their fool heads off when I put in an appearance. On one occasion I was revived by a priest's blood. Can you beat that?'

I started to say 'Good G . . . !' but managed to change it to 'Bloody hell!' just in time.

'Yes,' the count put his feet up on the desk and I was able to observe a small hole in the right shoe. 'I was encased in ice at the time. You know, the usual thing – some rotten swine had lured me over a frozen river – thin ice – running water beneath – in I go – become as stiff as a fish finger – and that was that. Then along comes this knee-basher waving a wooden unmentionable – slips on the ice – cuts his text-croaking throat – and I get a mouthful of the red stuff. I was up and about in no time at all.'

It was then that we were interrupted by an ear-splitting scream which seemed to come from somewhere beneath our feet. The count nodded his approval.

'Ah, that must be Carlos drawing off my lunch. Keep a couple of virgins in the cellar, you know. Well, I can't get around so well as I used to. They aren't bad. AB group, 1954 vintage. I suppose you wouldn't care . . . ?'

I shook my head vigorously and the count smiled.

'I won't press you – at least, not yet awhile. Do you know what I've always wanted? The present which would make my eyeballs swivel in their sockets?'

My thoughts toyed with walnut coffins with gold fittings – a central-heated tomb – a new dinner jacket – the one he was wearing was frayed and turning green. Finally I shook my head.

'A magnum of O group,' he stated, while two little rivulets of moisture ran down his trembling chin. 'The last time I wetted my whistle with a drop of O group must have been 1863. Or was it 1849? Anyway, I remember the container was a baker's wife, and I was just getting stuck in when her husband turns up and starts waving two crossed loaves at me. Then the delivery boy shoved a dirty great poker through me gizzard, and the last thing I saw was that precious liquid making a mess of six French rolls and a tray of jam tarts.'

This painful memory seemed to cause him such distress, I could do no less than murmur 'What a bloody shame!'

The Great Indestructible sighed deeply. 'Yes, I've never been what you might call lucky. Scarcely am I up and around, than some interfering busybody has me nailed down again. It's very discouraging.'

I consulted my notes. 'You have had several journeys into the realms of matrimony, I believe?'

'You might call it an invasion. At one time I had three wives
– all at once. Though we shared a common taste, we were not
really compatible. Women are all right in the kitchen – if you get
my meaning – but they're all take and no give.' He was lost in a
maze of melancholy thoughts for some little while. Then he said
softly, 'Greedy cows. There was that young solicitor – what was
his name?'

'Jonathan Harker?' I suggested.

'You may well be right. I remember he had an unfortunate habit
of writing long, detailed letters and keeping a diary. Anyway, I
intended to put him on ice. A little something for a dry night – and
I naturally assumed that he wouldn't be touched. Not a bit of it.
I came home early – there they were – fangs dripping, bibs at the
ready, squawking away like a flock of starved hens, fighting over
a bowl of stewed giblets.' He chuckled. 'I did 'em dirt though. I
drained him drier than last year's orange peel. Did they nag!'

This was an aspect of vampiral matrimonial conduct I had never
considered. 'You mean to say your wives nagged you?'

'What! Did they nag!' He rolled his eyes until they resembled
two milkyglass marbles. 'Evening, midnight and sunrise.' He
raised his voice and began to imitate an indignant woman. ' "You
never bring us anything *nice* home. Not like Baron Carver over
the hill. He gives his wives a couple of fat bankers and a property
speculator every Sunday. All you can do is lie-a-coffin all night and
expect us to wait on you." ' He resumed his normal tone of voice.
'Enough to make you want to spit.'

I was about to ask him if he had any interesting hobbies, when
he erupted again.

'Then there were the mother-in-laws. Great fat, billowing,
parched-throat, bulging-eyed, flap-eared, grasping harridans.
Huddled together like a herd of cows at milking time. "You can't
get round us," they said. "No, but the exercise will do me good,"
I retorted.' He smiled complacently. 'I always had a pretty turn of
wit.'

I frowned. 'Somehow, I can never think of lady vampires having
mothers.'

He bared his fangs in a snarl. 'Did you suppose an owl dropped
'em under a tombstone? They had fathers too. Lazy old has-beens.

"Now we've gained a son, we can all take things easy." Nine of 'em all told I had to cater for. You can't wonder the entire countryside was soon suffering from anaemia. That's why I emigrated.'

I closed my notepad, placed it carefully in my pocket, then stood up. 'Well, this has been most interesting. I am certain the readers of the *Ghoul Gazette* will be thrilled out of their skins.'

The count walked round the desk. I backed away a few paces and bumped into Carlos who had somehow entered the room without making a sound.

I think the attentive butler was brushing some mould from the seat of my trousers and possibly he was a little careless, for I felt a sharp pain on the back of my hand. When I looked round, Carlos was straightening up and doing a fair imitation of an excited wine-taster.

An expression of unholy joy transformed his face into a grimacing mask and he had difficulty in imparting the good news.

'Excell-ency, O-o-o-o . . .'

'Are you in pain, my good Carlos?' the count enquired solicitously.

'No, Excell-ency. O . . . o . . . o group. A comp-lete body of O group.'

The Great Indestructible moved in with single-minded intent. I tried to appeal to his better nature.

'You wouldn't?'

His smile was gentle. 'I would. I will. My dear fellow, you can't expect me to pass up a chance of a hundred lifetimes.'

'It won't be good for you. Too rich – and diluted with whisky . . .'

He nipped my neck. A genteel little nip – a prelude to a good old-fashioned, get-stuck-in bite, but fortunately I had the presence of mind to thrust two crossed pens in his face. He looked rather hurt.

'That's a dirty trick,' he said. 'I expected something better from a gentleman of the press.'

I backed away towards the door, then turned and ran across the hall. The friendly rat looked at me reproachfully.

I know I've been bitten by a vampire. So what? That's no reason for anyone to get worked up about it. As I sit typing this report, my editor is standing in the doorway. He says he's sharpening a pencil.

Well – I've never seen a pencil that size before.

If I'm found skewered in the centre of some crossroads, with a sprig of garlic in my mouth, I want the world to know who is responsible . . .

LOUIS

Letter from Hilda McCarthy to Liza Russell, May 15th 1987

c/o Mrs L. Brand
23 Sea View Avenue
Broadstairs

Dear Liza,

Just a line to let you know I am extending my holiday by at least two weeks. Mrs Brand – my landlady – is quite agreeable, as the season has not really started yet and there are no bookings for my room for at least three weeks. I think I should tell you that the reason for this extension is – well partly – due to my making a new friend down here. His name is Louis Longchamp and to be frank – as I can be to an old friend like yourself – I find we have so much in common. Similar tastes, books, films – the better ones and those made before 1960 – music and a complete hatred for the present government.

Please, Liza, don't get the wrong idea. This is friendship pure and simple and the fact that this new friend happens to be a man, is beside the point. We met at an outdoor exhibition of modern paintings and Louis very kindly explained the finer details, which without his help I would have most certainly missed. During the ensuing conversation it came out we were both down here by ourselves, and – well – as Louis so aptly put it – 'why not be lonely together?'

We've been together every day since and I have to be frank, I've never had such a wonderful time. Not even when Daniel was alive.

I've told Louis about you – how you're my best friend – my only

friend – and he's looking forward to meeting you. Isn't it amazing he only lives a few miles from us – at Hampton Court actually.

Well I'd better finish off now as Louis is waiting to take me to North Foreland Lighthouse, then to lunch afterwards. I'm saving an awful lot of money. He pays for everything. When I objected – well one has to – he said nonsense and when he took his wallet out I noticed it was simply crammed with fifty pound notes. From the way he talks I get the impression he's very well off.

Give my love to Tiddles,
Hilda

Letter from Liza Russell to Hilda McCarthy, 17th May 1987

18 Kingston Gardens,
Twickenham

Dear Hilda,

Thank you for your letter dated the 15th.

Well, the way you carried on about this new friend of yours took my breath away. I can only hope from what you tell me he's everything you'll eventually think he is. But take my advice, Hilda, soak him for a few lunches and dinners, let him have a little kiss and cuddle in one of those glass-sided seating arrangements they have down there, if you feel so inclined, although I would have thought at your age you'd have something better to do; then call it a day. As my mother used to say, you can't beat a nice warm fire, a purring cat, a friend to have a chat with, then a manless double bed, when the years begin to draw in. If you get my meaning.

I might as well mention after all that, that I found Arthur Minns ringing your doorbell two nights ago. When I gave him the good news – you were away for at least two more weeks – he got into a hell of a stew because you hadn't written to him. Not so much as a postcard. I must say, Hilda, I never knew things had gone that far between you two. You never told me if they have.

Tiddles is eating well, but I think she misses you. I found her mewing in the hall when I opened the door yesterday.

Don't stay away too long and be very careful of this Louis.

Lots of love from your friend,
Liza

Letter from Hilda McCarthy to Liza Russell, 20th May 1987

c/o Mrs L. Brand
23 Sea View Avenue
Broadstairs

Dear Liza,

Thank you for your lovely letter.

Arthur had no business ringing my doorbell and complaining because I hadn't written to him. I mean – I've had a couple of coffees with him and a chat about 1984. Nothing more. Some men are so silly and if you just try to be a wee bit friendly, think that's an invitation to come share bed and board. Honestly, he makes me sick. Arthur Minns, I mean.

That's what I like about Louis, he's a real gentleman and never even tries to take advantage. I mean, whenever he asks me out any-where, he always adds: 'If you've nothing better to do.' And if I said – 'yes, I have,' which I never have – I know he wouldn't be in the least put out.

Rather exasperating sometimes.

I must tell you what he looks like. Do you remember Ronald Colman? Well, if you don't, you must have seen him in *The Prisoner of Zenda* on TV. Well he looks like Ronald Colman, only taller. And the same kind of voice only it's got the merest hint of a foreign accent. And Liza, when he puts his hand under my elbow to help me up the steps and sort of half whispers in my left ear: 'May I hope to see you tomorrow?' Liquid fire . . .

Good heavens! How I am raving on! One would think I was infatuated by the man, which I most certainly am not. As you say, dear Liza, at my age – forty-three on the 30th – I have something else to do than play slap and tickle with some man – no matter how attractive he might be. We went to the theatre last night, and saw *Pygmalion* performed by the local rep. Not at all bad, but of course missed the music, forgetting it wasn't *My Fair Lady*.

We had late dinner afterwards in a little restaurant facing the sea and Louis told me how Charles Dickens so loved Broadstairs and lived for a while in Fort House – which is now called Bleak House – so silly don't you think? – which does look like a small fort. Much extended since Dickens's time Louis said.

It is really very sweet of you to look after Tiddles, Liza. And I am most awfully grateful. You must allow me to wine and dine you – as Louis would say – when I get back.

Must finish off now. Louis wants to take me out to the Goodwin Sands while the tide is still out.

Fondly and forever yours,

Hilda

Letter from Liza Russell to Hilda McCarthy, May 23rd 1987

18 Kingston Gardens

Twickenham

Dear Hilda,

Thank you for your most interesting letter.

Dearest, please don't misunderstand what I am about to say, which is for your own good. I mean, dear, we have a rather special friendship and for that reason I can dare give advice and even crit-icize – in the nicest possible way of course – a line of conduct that might land you in an awkward, even dangerous situation.

Hilda, dear, from your letters it is becoming clear to me you are becoming too involved with this Louis. You are indeed.

Look – I am going to be awfully, awfully frank now and you'll most probably hate me now, but bless me in the future.

It would seem this Louis is a real dish. Well, if he looks like Ronald Colman only taller, he must be. And he sounds as if he is a lady killer into the bargain. Now, to me, Hilda, you are the most beautiful person in the whole world, because I know the real you that lies behind – please don't get all hurt and angry, Hilda – behind the rather homely exterior. Before you tear this letter up, go and look into the nearest mirror and ask yourself a really honest ques-tion: 'What have I got a dishy lady killer could possibly want?'

Well, darling Hilda, you have a very nice flat which would fetch a nice sum and a respectable little fortune tucked away in stocks and shares.

Hilda, don't you really think it's about time you came home and let poor old Liza comfort you? I do. Oh, I do. Please think over what I've written and try not to hate me. I couldn't bear that. If I really thought you hated me I'd most likely do away with myself.

Before I forget Arthur Minns has been round again. Wants your holiday address. Of course I refused to give it to him.

Why do you get yourself implicated with these men? I thought we had decided we could do well without any of them.

All my undying love,
Liza

Letter from Hilda McCarthy to Liza Russell, May 25th 1987

c/o Mrs L. Brand
23 Sea View Avenue
Broadstairs

Dear Liza,

Thank you, thank you very much for your very, very kind and most thoughtful letter. It is such a source of happiness to me to know I have a friend who is not afraid to tell me the whole, unvarnished truth. Indeed, I was not aware of the full extent of my 'homely appearance'. As I believe Robbie Burns put it: 'See ourselves as others see us.'

Do you know what I did after reading your so kind letter – I went into the bedroom, as you advised, and took all my clothes off, stripped starkers and stood in front of the wardrobe mirror. And I was not all that displeased with what I saw. And I think my sight is as keen – if not keener – than yours.

No one could fault my breasts – despite my age – which according to you merits a seat by a nice warm fire, a purring cat on my lap and a kind, thoughtful friend to chat to before retiring to an empty double bed. Or am I supposed to share that with the nice, kind thoughtful friend. May I suggest in the nicest possible way, that you, Liza dear, do some soul-searching. And have a good look at your reflection in a mirror.

Although, as you say, Louis may have designs on my worldly wealth, I could see no reason why he shouldn't lust after my body as well. I took the trouble to measure my vital statistics and do you know what I came up with? 38. 35. 37. Not bad for an old crock like me. We can only wonder if you have the courage to take a tape measure to yours, Liza dear. My skin is white and smooth, no sign of wrinkles round eyes and mouth. I know of no one else in *our age group* that can say as much.

Did you know Arthur Minns was raving about my eyes when we had coffee together last? Large and cornflower blue he called them. Louis over dinner last night – 'Auburn hair that frames your heart-shaped face.' And very little tinting. Teeth my own and in good trim. Not many old things like *us* can make that boast.

I can't write anymore. I'm going dancing with that fortune hunter Louis who keeps his repugnance for my homely face under admirable control.

Your one time friend
Hilda

Letter from Liza Russell to Hilda McCarthy, May 26th 1987

18 Kingston Gardens
Twickenham

Dear Hilda,

I have not slept since receiving your cruel letter. How could you even think such awful things about someone who always thought she was your best friend. Dreadful, hurtful words that should never have come from your pen. All because you deliberately – I repeat – deliberately misunderstood my good intentions. I really do believe you have always wanted to grossly insult me, and used my – if you hadn't been so blinded by *hate* for me who has the misfortune to love you – letter that was simply saturated with good intentions, as an excuse to pour out bile upon my super-sensitive soul.

We are finished of course. Absolutely. I will continue to feed Tiddles and clean out her dirt box until you come home, but no more. Please don't write or try to communicate with me again. It would be like drawing a sharp knife across a raw wound.

I wish you well with your *new* friend Louis.

My best regards despite all that has happened.

Liza

Letter from Hilda McCarthy to Liza Russell, May 31st 1987

c/o Mrs L. Brand
23 Sea View Avenue
Broadstairs

Dear Liza,

I was very upset after reading your last letter, but after much thought and deliberation cannot view yours of the 23rd with other than pain. I'm sure this is very silly of me but I just can't do otherwise. I have written to Arthur Minns and given him this address so you should not be bothered by him again. If you are at all interested, Louis is taking me to see his family tomorrow. It would seem they have an estate hereabouts. He gave me a lovely gold bracelet for my birthday, which you may remember was yesterday.

Regards
Hilda

Letter from Liza Russell to Hilda McCarthy, June 3rd 1987

18 Kingston Gardens
Twickenham

Dear Hilda,

This is to acknowledge your letter dated May 31st.

I am not in the least interested where Louis took you and what he gave you for your birthday. I should have hardly thought it wise to give Arthur Minns your present address. If I know him he'll be down there trying to cut your *new* friend out and generally making a nuisance of himself. But perhaps that is what you want. Have two men fighting over you.

But still that is your concern.

Sincerely
Liza

Letter from Hilda McCarthy to Liza Russell, June 10th 1987

The Imperial Hotel
The Parade
Broadstairs

Dear Liza

You will note the change of address. I really just couldn't stay with Mrs Brand any longer, so I moved into the Imperial Hotel. I shall probably stay here for another two weeks – maybe longer. I did not intend to write to you again, especially after the vile insult in your last letter, but I don't like to be at daggers drawn with any-one, least of all with someone whom I at one time held in some esteem.

Besides – there has been some trouble – and I must tell someone about it or I'll go mad. Arthur Minns turned up at Mrs Brand's house four days ago and created an awful scene. I was just going out to dinner with Louis; me in the white off-the-shoulder evening gown – the one you said made me look quite seductive – and Louis in a really well-tailored dinner jacket; when that awful little man suddenly appeared from nowhere and started shouting. Something about me toying with his emotions. Can you imagine? I've never, but never encouraged that man to believe my feelings for him were anything more than casual friendship.

Louis of course behaved like the perfect gentleman he is. Said in that lovely voice of his: 'Will you kindly not embarrass the lady [me], sir. At this time she happens to be my guest.'

That made Arthur really wild. You know of course he's rather coarse on occasion. Well, it's only to be expected, his father kept a fish and chip shop down in Camden Town. That is a fact. Daniel's father knew him. Arthur called Louis a tarted-up ponce. I've never known what a ponce really is, but it must be something very rude, for Louis from being awfully white – which he generally is – went sort of grey and glared at Arthur until I thought his eyes would spit fire. Then he leaned over him and said in a dreadful harsh voice: 'Tonight you are filled with wine and false courage, tomorrow night you will be empty of everything worth having.'

I don't know what he meant by that, but I think Arthur did, for he shrank back and suddenly looked quite old and said to me in a little pathetic voice, 'I never thought you'd do this to me, Hilda. I really didn't,' then slunk off like a rejected dog.

I didn't really enjoy the rest of the evening for I kept remembering Arthur's face and the way Louis spoke and looked at him. I'm still very happy being in Louis's company, for he is really so charming and handsome, but at the same time I'm not all that joyful. What with his family and this awful scene with Arthur. I haven't told you about his family. He took me to see them on Monday . . . But you won't be wanting to hear any more of my troubles.

My very best regards
Hilda

Letter from Liza Russell to Hilda McCarthy, June 12th 1987

18 Kingston Gardens
Twickenham

Dear Hilda,

Thank you for your letter dated June 10th. Your affairs of course are no longer of any concern to me, but I did warn you. Give Arthur Minns your present address, I said, and he'll be down there causing trouble. Far be it for me to say I told you so – but I did. You have only yourself to blame. And as for this Louis – handsome is as handsome does, as my dear mother used to say.

I'll not lay myself open to insult again by giving unsolicited advice – but personally I would chuck both of them and come on home.

But you must please yourself.

Best wishes in so far as they are for your own good,
Liza

P.S. Belatedly – many happy returns of your birthday. The gift I had for you I threw in the dustbin. Wrapping and all. Stupid really. If I had taken it back to the shop I'd most likely have got a refund.

Letter from Hilda McCarthy to Liza Russell, June 14th 1987

The Imperial Hotel
The Parade
Broadstairs

Dear Liza,

I've just got to write to you and hope you will find it in your heart – sooner or later – to forgive if not forget my awful letter of May 25th. The fact is, Liza, I'm sorely troubled and all mixed up and think maybe I'm going mad. I saw Arthur Minns yesterday slinking along the front and I do mean slinking – like a fox that is being hunted by a lot of angry chicken farmers with shot guns. When he saw me he broke into a shambling run and I just had to catch up with him. He looked simply awful. All white and drawn and sort of shrunken. He shuddered when I touched him and said in that common way he has sometimes: 'Keep 'im off me.'

I can only assume he was talking about Louis, but why he should be so frightened of him I just can't understand. Then he ran away and I haven't seen him since.

Liza, I'm going to tell you about Louis's family and if you don't want to read it, don't. Use this letter to line Tiddles' basket. But I must tell someone.

The family estate is way out in the country and is called Wittering Grange and it really is eerie. First of all, we came to a pair of immense iron gates guarded by a dreadful-looking old man with white hair that looked like bleached snakes. He had no teeth and grinned at me with black gums, then flung the gates open as though they weighed nothing at all. Then we drove up a tree-lined drive and came at last to an old house that was a mass of turrets, crouching chimneys, deep embrasured windows and tiny red bricks. You reached a great iron-studded door by means of three black marble steps and went into a hall where all the doors, walls and ceilings were painted black. A black and white stained glass window had a picture of Lucifer (I think that's right) with his left foot on the world.

Two footmen dressed in black satin and white powdered wigs and flowing lace cravats bowed to Louis and said together:

'Welcome, Prince Louis, may your sins be heavy and your conscience light. Glory to the Lord Marcus.'

My heart bounced up to my throat then down again. I mean, I guessed Louis was someone important, but I never dreamed he could be a prince. Right, maybe a foreign prince that isn't like one of ours, but still . . . I mean if he were to get around to popping the question and I was to say yes, then I'd be a princess with people bowing to me and royal highnessing me all over the place. Not bad for a girl whose dad mended windows round Teddington way.

There again I wasn't all that happy about the heavy sins and light conscience part, but dismissed it as some royal protocol business that was part of the tradition his family wallowed in.

Then I met the king-pin – the head of the family – the great Lord Marcus, they all bowed to. A great black and white brute whose eyes gave me the shakes, for I could swear they burnt a hole in my head and were peering into my brain.

The family drank thick red stuff from large balloon glasses and smacked their lips in a most disgusting fashion. In fact I was the only one who ate anything – roast beef, potatoes and Yorkshire pudding, followed by roly-poly pudding with hot jam poured over it. Very nice indeed. But I was rather put out when one little creature who looked as if he had horns poking through his thick black hair, which had to be ridiculous, after watching me eat with marked distaste for some while, clasped hands to his mouth and ran from the room, then made being-sick noises in the hall.

And how they kept looking at me as though I was something they hadn't seen for a long while. Thankfully we didn't stay all that time, just for dinner and a big argument that Louis had with the Lord Marcus afterwards. All about taking some place over as I understood it and how something called a meat-eater with special essence would be so useful, but frankly I was more worried about a horrible little man with a greenish face who kept pinching my arm to take all that notice.

On the drive back Louis didn't say much and for some reason I found myself worrying about Arthur Minns, wondering why he was so frightened of Louis and why he should say, 'Keep 'im off me.' I mean he was an awful pest, but I wouldn't like to think something dreadful had happened to him.

Well, I've let it all pour out and I expect, Liza, you have long ago torn this letter up or twisted it into a spill to light the gas ring. But in case you haven't, let me say this: I'm really and truly sorry about that letter and wish I hadn't written it.

It's up to you to decide if I'm to be forgiven and our former relationship resumed – if you understand me. I'm thinking about coming home soon. Very soon.

If I can.

Your rather sad and just a wee bit frightened,
Hilda

Letter from Liza Russell to Hilda McCarthy, June 17th 1987

18 Kingston Gardens
Twickenham

Dear Hilda,

I read your letter dated June 14th with mixed feelings.

It's all coming out as I thought it would, and that is after making allowance for your hysterical nature and the tendency you have for dramatizing even the most mundane event. The truth is of course you are already getting fed up with your glamour boy and just can't find the courage to bring the entire business to an end. It does sound – if I am to believe what you say – he has some weird relations. Lots of people have. I seem to remember your Uncle George wasn't the kind of person one would willingly introduce to polite company.

The only sensible decision you've made yet is to come home soon. Of course I don't know when soon will be and how firm your *intention* is. Frankly I'm not all that interested. I know. To err is human, to forgive divine, but Hilda you must know I'm not in the tweeniest bit divine. The dreadful things you wrote in your letter have seared my very soul and I honestly can't find it in my heart to forgive yet. *When* you come home I do think it might be well if we don't meet or talk for some while. Maybe an exchange of notes pushed through our respective letter boxes might be in order, until such time as we either decide to have a full reconciliation – (which at this moment I feel to be most unlikely) or – perhaps wisely – make a complete break. In that event I am certain we can both (I know I can) behave like civilised intelligent people and pass the time of day should we meet in the street or lift.

I feel rather sorry for that poor little fool Arthur Minns. He's clearly besotted with you and I cannot help feeling that you have behaved rather brutally in so blatantly encouraging him. I always thought he was rather unbalanced and now from what you tell me, it would seem he has gone right over the edge.

You know, there are times, when I think I am the only rational person on this planet.

Put a note through my letter box when you return.

Regards that are intended to be kind,
Liza

Letter to Liza Russell from Hilda McCarthy, June 20th 1987

The Imperial Hotel
The Parade
Broadstairs

Dear Liza,

I did not know you could be so cruel and heartless. No matter how much I may have hurt you by my unwise letter, there can be no excuse for such calculated unkindness. I am really very upset, which when added to the feeling of approaching menace that cannot be explained by rational thinking, has the effect of driving my confused mind into a kind of madness. I find myself accepting the possibility of something happening to me, in much the same way as a person marooned on the top of a tall burning building, comes to believe that jumping into space is a quick and easy way down.

Yet, I ask myself, what have I to worry about? Louis is charm itself, even though I cannot believe that gleam in his eyes means he has come to love me. Poor homely me – remember? Most certainly he is not after my poor little financial assets, for he is very rich. And his strange family even more so.

Shall I tell you what really worries me? Ever since my early teens

I have always let my brain plan ahead. Usually when I am making up in front of the dressing table mirror, I will do so and so today – and tomorrow such and such a thing will take place. This time next week I will ring Mrs What's-her-name.

I can no longer do that. The brain refuses to even consider the future, as though it can sense a black wall of nothingness, or a future so horrible it must not be even thought about, if sanity is to be maintained until the last possible moment.

Of course you will say I am over-dramatizing, allowing an undisciplined imagination to run wild. I do hope you are right.

But during the day and evening when I am with Louis I am right as rain. His personality seems to drug mine so that fear and foreboding are banished into a painless void.

I have not seen or heard from Arthur Minns and can only hope he has gone home. Yes, you are most possibly right – I did act brutally towards that silly little man, for I did encourage him – at least subconsciously – to inflate my ego. What strange creatures we women are, particularly when we reach a certain age. There was I simulating indignation because Arthur was showing all the signs of imitating a clinging leech, when that was what I was hoping he would do, even if I did not really like him.

Better be worshipped by a beggar than ignored by a king. And you, dear Liza, what kind of satisfaction are you deriving from pretending to be still very hurt and unforgiving? Tell me, do you still pull the wings off blow flies, then watch them running across the table vainly trying to fly? That was your favourite pastime as a child I seem to remember. But now of course you play with much larger victims.

When I finally slip into the slough of despair, you will find brief happiness in pushing my head under. Later of course you will be tortured by remorse and spend the remainder of your life doing good works at the local church.

I am writing this by the window and have just seen Louis running up the front steps. He looks so handsome and distinguished. Some woman has stopped and is now staring at him. They all do. Going into a restaurant with Louis's hand lightly cupping your elbow is equivalent to a triumphant entry into ancient Rome. The only trouble is I don't know which of us is the conqueror.

Don't bother to answer this letter if I've flicked too many raw wounds. I shall fully understand.

Hilda

Letter from Hilda McCarthy to Liza Russell, July 7th 1987

The Imperial Hotel
The Parade
Broadstairs

Dear Liza,

As you can see I am still at the same address – The Imperial.

You have taken advantage of my suggestion that you did not answer my last letter, but I do sincerely hope you will not ignore this one.

Liza, I can't get away. Surrounded by hotel staff and the holiday crowd which is now packing the place, I am as much a prisoner as some poor wretch doing solitary confinement in Dartmoor. Louis is with me even when he is miles away visiting his dreadful family. His eyes are black holes leading to another universe, his mouth the gateway to a particularly vicious kind of hell.

Liza – lips, hands and voice can raise a flame of unendurable pleasure, which so quickly turns to freezing horror.

Teeth in the neck . . . His sink deeper . . . deeper . . . and fire races through the veins and I can hear his tongue splashing liquid against the roof of his mouth and in his eyes I can see a distant view of a misty valley which runs between fire-tipped mountains, with that awful Lord Marcus riding a black horse in the scarlet cloud-covered sky.

It has been such a relief to have written all that even if you do decide I've gone right round the bend.

Another thing – the people in this hotel are more than a bit peculiar, although I'm not all that normal myself. They all seem to be continually talking to each other, without making any sound. As though I am living in a strange dream. All dreams are silent are they not? And I have a feeling they are all watching me, without so much as one head turned in my direction.

Do you know I'm so desperate I tried to telephone you yesterday evening, but the lines must be down or something for all I kept getting was a man's voice saying, 'Last train to Limbo one minute past dark hour.'

I must really make a real effort to get away. This is so silly.

Liza, please contact me. Ring – do anything . . .

Hilda

Telegram sent by Liza Russell to Hilda McCarthy c/o The Imperial Hotel, The Parade, Broadstairs, telephoned 06.45 hours July 8th 1987.

TRIED TO TELEPHONE YOU NO JOY AM COMING DOWN TO BROADSTAIRS BY 09.00 HOURS TRAIN BE PACKED READY TO LEAVE LIZA

Letter from Liza Russell to Hilda McCarthy, July 8th 1987

18 Kingston Gardens
Twickenham

Dear Hilda,

What bloody mad game are you playing? I went down to Broadstairs this morning as I promised in my telegram and went straight to the Imperial Hotel, only to find you are not registered there. The desk clerk remembered my letters being delivered and which he placed on the collect letter board. They apparently all disappeared sometime during the morning. This surely means you go there to collect them, but are living somewhere else. My telegram had been delivered, but that too had gone.

I found Mrs Brand's house and she told me you moved out on June 8th. She hasn't seen you since. She remembered this Louis of yours quite well. She thought he was very handsome, but in her opinion rather sinister. It would seem his eyes did something dreadful to her spine.

Hilda, the tone of your letter and the fact you pretend to be staying at the Imperial Hotel, when you are somewhere else, tells me that either something very dicey is going on or you are really deranged. Now read what I am going to write very carefully.

Get it touch with me at once. Either by telephone or telegram, or if both for some reason are not possible, by express letter. If I do not hear from you by some way or another, I am going to contact the police. You have until the 10th. That is to say the day after tomorrow – Friday.

Yours, very worried,
Liza

Letter from Hilda McCarthy to Liza Russell, July 9th 1987

The Imperial Hotel
The Parade
Broadstairs

Dear Liza,

Has the entire world – including you – combined to drive me mad? I received your telegram and *sat for the entire morning in the IMPERIAL HOTEL foyer waiting for you to turn up.* Even after Louis insisted on giving me lunch in the hotel restaurant, he gave instructions to the desk clerk to let me know the very moment you arrived. But you didn't. Liza, you must have gone to the wrong hotel. Louis says there isn't another Imperial in Broadstairs, but one of the smaller establishments may have called itself something similar and you could well have been mistaken.

But it is very odd about the telephone. I've tried to ring you from the phone in my room and kept getting what must be the railway station for this man keeps on about the last train to Limbo leaving one minute past dark hour.

Half of me still wants to leave and the other half can't bear the thought of being parted from Louis. But, Liza, I seem to be getting weak and frightfully thin.

Which reminds me. I saw Arthur yesterday evening. I was sitting on the balcony which commands a clear view of the beach, when I saw what had to be a skin-covered skeleton trudging through the sand. Hat down over the ears, torn shirt and frayed trousers flapping in the strong breeze, he looked like a walking scarecrow. But there was that personality over-print that often enables us to identify someone we have not seen since childhood, which told me it was Arthur Minns. Suddenly he turned and broke into a shambling run back the way he had come and just after he had disappeared, I saw Louis approaching the hotel. He laughed when I told him about seeing Arthur and teased me on my overwhelming effect on men.

Liza, I am still determined to go home and will, I promise you, break free from this hold Louis has on me. Please forgive me for so hurting you and please try to recapture a little of that regard you once had for me. I still can't get over your visiting Broadstairs, thinking you were in the Imperial and me looking for you all morning. Then there was the matter of your letters and the clerk remembering seeing them. Honestly, it's all beyond me. Unless . . . !

I am not going to get all fanciful again. I'm not, I'm not . . .

Please get in touch with me again – soon – at once – the fact is dear Liza, I'm so very frightened. I am . . . I am.

Yours forever,
Hilda

Letter from Liza Russell to Hilda McCarthy, July 11th 1987

18 Kingston Gardens
Twickenham

Dear Hilda,

I think we both must have been driven mad. Hilda, I was in that foyer at the Imperial Hotel – the one and only Imperial Hotel – on Wednesday last – I questioned the staff, went to see Mrs Brand, then came back to the Imperial where everyone denied ever seeing you. The only reason the clerk knew your name was because he had seen it on the letters I sent you. And the telegram, Hilda, don't try to put me off by a cock and bull story. I have just rung the Imperial – less than five minutes ago – and the manager still maintains no one of your name or appearance is staying there.

Hilda, please stop this playing about and tell me where the hell you are. Or better still, do what you say you want to do, come on home. This is a civilized – well almost – country and no one can be unlawfully stopped from going wherever they wish. Tell this Louis weirdo to go take a running jump. Look, send me a wire if you still can't get through on the telephone and I will hire a car and come and fetch you. Maybe you're sick, I don't know. I'm beginning to feel a wee bit panicky. Oh Gawd! *Tell me where you are. Come on home. Do something positive.*

Your very worried,
Liza

Letter from Hilda McCarthy to Liza Russell, July 13th 1987

The Imperial Hotel
The Parade
Broadstairs

Dear Liza,

Thank you, oh, thank you for your letter. Yes, that's a wonderful idea – hire a car and come and fetch me. Don't worry about not finding me this time. I am at the Imperial – I am. It's the largest hotel which faces the front and I will be sitting on the front steps from nine o'clock onwards. My luggage with me. And Louis will not talk me out of it. This morning I told him I was going home and he didn't object the least bit. Even offered to drive me home in his car. But I'd much rather be with you. With him there would always be the suspicion that just maybe he would take the wrong turning and we'd finish up at Twittering Grange.

I keep noticing things lately. There's a clock tower over an arrangement of glass-sided seats in the pleasure gardens. Well, that clock is going backwards. The little and large hands are moving backwards and that is giving the silly impression that the day is moving backwards too. The sun rises at nine p.m. Sets at six in the morning. The clock in the hotel foyer is misbehaving as well.

Liza, darling, wouldn't it be awful if I was rushing backwards in time? Getting further and further away from each other. But I mustn't think that way.

Louis has just come into the room – he never taps any more – not to be wondered at I suppose. But I must close now.

I'll be on the steps tomorrow morning, I promise. Oh, I do hope this letter reaches you in time. I couldn't send you a wire, I tried, but just couldn't raise telegrams on the phone – or get through to you. Tell you what – if you don't make it tomorrow, I won't panic, but do the same thing the day after. On Wednesday. Can't wait to see you.

Hilda

Letter from Liza Russell to Hilda McCarthy delivered by hand to the reception desk of the Imperial Hotel, Broadstairs, July 15th 1987 09.00 hours

Dear Hilda,

This situation is really mad and I've just about had enough of it. I not only came down here by car yesterday, but having waited for you to put in an appearance – as promised in your letter of the 13th – *took a room in the hotel* – and I do not intend to leave until you stop messing about and come out of hiding.

Hilda, I've seen the hotel register and if you booked in here, then you must have used a different name.

As you seem to have received all the letters I sent you here, I am handing this one in at the reception desk, where I am given to understand, the clerk will put it on the 'Mail to be Collected Board' – the one covered with green baize and triangular tapes – in front of the lift. I am going to seat myself where I can watch the board and grab you or whoever comes to collect it.

Hilda, I am determined to solve this mystery, one way or another, I won't be made a fool of.

Hilda, for God's sake if you're in trouble let me know where you are. I'll do anything to help. Anything at all.

Your devoted friend,
Liza

Letter from Liza Russell to Hilda McCarthy, July 15th 1987. [Placed on mail collection board 11.00 hours. Imperial Hotel, Broadstairs].

Hilda, how the hell did you do it? I swear I did not take my eyes off that board, but suddenly my letter was not there. I've just got to believe I dozed off without realising it. Well, I'm standing by this one. No one is going to get by me. But no one.

Hilda, if you get this one and you are nearby for God's sake shout. Call my name and I'll come a-running.

Your very devoted and worried friend,
Liza

Letter from Hilda McCarthy to Liza Russell, [redirected from 18 Kingston Gardens, Twickenham, to the Imperial Hotel, Broadstairs July 15th 1987. Collected by Liza Russell from letter collection board at 20.15 hours].

Dear Liza,

I'm so frightened and don't know what to do. I collected your letter dated today's date from the letter board and just can't understand anything. I sat on the front steps all day yesterday and Liza, you did not turn up. There is no way you could have got by me without my seeing you. And you are not in the register. And I've been in the foyer all morning as well. I am going to put this letter on the board, so if by chance you are in the hotel, you'll pick it up. I'll even stand by the board so that no one can get at that letter without pushing by me.

Louis is getting a wee bit cross with me and says I'm being very silly and why don't I let him drive me home? There's not much point in him doing so if you are really in Broadstairs. Anyway, I don't believe he means it. I keep seeing members of his awful family coming and going out of the hotel and they all give me a quick glance as though to see if I come up to expectations.

And lately there is a square black car parked in the vicinity in which are seated four dreadful looking creatures that make me think of a picture book I had as a child in which were depicted dogs dressed in big hats and long overcoats. I have a feeling they are watching me as well.

I've been thinking of hiring a cab to take my things to the station and making my own way back to town, but I'm not sure if those awful things that look like dogs will let me. I can't dismiss the thought that I am very important to Louis's family, and they want me for some reason – in a very special place.

Louis told me a while ago that Arthur Minns's body has been found washed up on the beach near North Foreland. Do you know? He chuckled and said poor Arthur was empty of everything worth having and I do believe I heard him say something like that before, but can't remember when or where.

The clocks are all going backwards – even my wrist watch – the one you gave me last Christmas – but that doesn't bother me anymore. Louis is changing and his smile is more gloating than loving and almost becomes a sneer when I talk about catching a train for town. He whispers in my ear: 'Pretty lady is catching the last train to Limbo, that leaves one minute past dark hour.' That's what the man on the telephone said – about the last train for Limbo leaving one minute past the dark hour.

Just before starting this letter I thought I saw you in the foyer, but it turned out to be someone who did not look a bit like you. Oh, Liza, what is going to happen to me? That black car is parked outside of the hotel now and I have a feeling one of those dog-shaped things is standing by my door . . .

Liza, I think that when Louis made me move from Mrs Brand's house, he took me into – another place that is in the same place . . . Oh, I'm not making sense and you'll think I'm over-dramatising again. But my poor little brain has been working day and night on what has happened to me and dimly – very dimly – understands.

Liza, could there be more than one version of the Imperial Hotel? And another version of Broadstairs – another version of our world? The hidden world? The one Louis has taken me to is going backward in our time. And shortly I am going to be forced on to a train that will take me to another hidden place called Limbo.

Liza, there's nothing either of us can do. Louis and his family can go anywhere they wish – you and I only to where we are allowed or taken. Lord Marcus and Prince Louis rule the timeways . . .

I cannot understand how our letters get through, but I do not believe they will much longer. Maybe the wonderful, fabulous, soul-destroying and most evil Louis has overlooked one little loophole. Pray that it remains open so that some other poor wretch in my position can maintain a form of contact with the world that gave them birth. But I cannot hold out much hope. Louis knows we are corresponding.

Oh, Liza, if only we could be together again – with claws sheathed.

Yours forever

Hilda

Letter from Liza Russell to Hilda McCarthy handed into the reception desk Imperial Hotel, Broadstairs at 18.30 hours. Disappeared one hour ten minutes later.

Dear Hilda,

I am willing now to accept truth no matter in what guise it comes to me. I have reported you missing to the police and a search is being made for you everywhere. A plain clothes policeman is on duty round the clock in the foyer of this hotel, watching the post collection board. I can only hope he has more luck than I did. So far as I was concerned, one moment my letter to you was on the board, the next it had disappeared.

Hilda, I have a practical, no-nonsense mind. As a child I never believed in Father Christmas, as an adult I could not accept the concept of life after death. Now I find myself forced to believe a dear friend has somehow been abducted and taken to another dimension. Such knowledge undermines the basic concepts that form the foundation of my being. Already I can feel the grip I have on this form of existence, slackening. Soon – very soon I will be dead. Let us hope that in some unforeseeable future we will find ourselves together at a yet to be imagined destination.

Believe me, dear Hilda, my thoughts will be with you for so long as whatever laws that control the universe permit me to be a rational, remembering, thinking individual.

Liza

Letter from Hilda McCarthy to Liza Russell written on Imperial Hotel notepaper and in a corresponding envelope, which was found on the mail collection board at 06.00 hours, 21st July 1987

Dear, dear Liza,

I found your letter on the board – and one of the dog-faced creatures was watching it – the board I mean. Liza, the police won't find a trace of me, or the remains of poor Arthur Minns. But there must be a way back, there must be . . .

But I must remain calm or you will begin to think I've gone mad and start you looking for me all over again.

Liza, forgive me for anything I may have done and said to hurt you, but a silly vain creature like me cannot always be held responsible for what she does or says. Yes, Liza we will meet again somewhere. On the road to eternity, perhaps.

But it is dark here and the moon is reflected on the sea and I can hear a solitary gull crying and can't help wondering if it is the soul of Arthur Minns calling vainly for help. The four dog-faced creatures are in the room with me, not doing anything but staring with unblinking eyes that are black, with red-red sparks in them . . . sparks that might become flames if I move or do something I must not . . . And Louis is seated on the bed looking so handsome and wonderfully evil . . . And I'm terrified for it's time to go . . . to go and catch the last train to Limbo and I will never see the moon again let alone the sun which will never rise . . . Good . . .

Note: All the letters and one telegram that were exchanged by Mrs Hilda McCarthy and Miss Liza Russell were found in room 16A first floor the Imperial Hotel, Broadstairs, laid out on a bed. There is no explanation at the time of going to press how they came to be there. No traces of Mrs Hilda McCarthy or Mr Arthur Minns have to date been discovered.

Miss Liza Russell died on August 29th of a heart attack.

LOOKING FOR SOMETHING TO SUCK

Whoever, what-so-ever it had been was an open question, but now it was a Shadow.

The night was full of shadows, so no one said: 'What's that?' as a pencil thin line of deeper darkness darted along a gutter, or undulated round the corner of a shop or house. Only a very keen pair of eyes could have detected that quivering line as it streaked away on its unending journey.

The Shadow had a glimmer of intelligence, a flickering awareness of its surroundings, but it did not require intelligence to know that light was the implacable enemy. Light was pain, too much light meant extinction. So it moved only by night, resting by day in some cellar, sewer, or any underground place where light could not penetrate. It resented these forced periods of inactivity, for overriding even the instinct for self-preservation was the urge to keep searching. To frequent the haunts of flesh and blood beings; to sip, to taste – to find the one in a million vessel that could give it tangible life.

The Shadow slid under a neat privet hedge, then moved cautiously into a long narrow flower garden, that bordered a crazy paving path. Extra care must be taken, for this particular night was not ideal; the frosty air was clear, the tiny Sky Lights glittered like a million far off street lamps, and the big Night Sky Light, only a little less feared than the awful Day Sky Light, was scarcely hidden by a tall house.

A front door opened and a slab of light crashed down upon the garden path and flower bed, causing the Shadow to quickly contract. Two flesh and blood beings came out into the frosty night; they stamped their feet, and the Shadow felt their thought waves of discomfort. It sent out a cotton thin tentacle when a nylon clad ankle came within tasting distance, and sipped. A female, her life force three-quarters spent, the vibrations disappointing, lacking power, and suggesting a creature given up to bodily comforts and placid thoughts. The thin tentacle crept upwards, flowed across a fur coated back and found that a hand, belonging to the other creature, was resting lightly on the far shoulder. A male this time, a little more life force, the vibrations stronger, but unable to provide nourishment.

The Shadow withdrew its tentacle, skirted the light slab, and took refuge under the porch step, contracting its length into an oval ball of blackness. Then it began to quiver with anticipation. The vibrations were strong, the life force only just reaching maturity; but there was something more, a vital, unknown something that made the Shadow forget its caution and streak upwards. A blast of light hurled it back again; it elongated, darted up both sides of the porch door, but to no avail. The cold harsh light protected the two figures standing in the doorway with a dazzling oblong shield, and the dim Sky Lights made it shrink back to the friendly darkness under the porch step.

Then just as despair and hunger, for the Shadow had not fed for many days, was causing its consciousness to dim down, a small foot was placed over the doorstep. It was little enough. The mere tip of a shoe, a scrap of leather, but above that was a set of five blood and flesh toes, and above them, a slim leg. The Shadow flowed up to the shoe, moved slowly over the toecap; it was safe so far, the light was on either side, but not here. It almost reached the round kneecap, before the leg was snatched away. Jerked away so quickly that for a fraction of a second the Shadow was left exposed to the full fury of the over-head hall light. Only the fact that half of its length was still protected by the doorstep, saved it from extinction. The three remaining beings were agitated. They sent out alarmed and angry thought waves, then the older ones went away, their vibrations dimmed, then ceased to be. The door slammed, but the light remained on.

Down below the doorstep the Shadow was content. The one in a million vessel had been found, and eventually the light would go out, night was the time when lights slept. Then there was a long thin crack under the door, and inside all would be dark; and inside all that darkness would be the vessel. And in that vessel was – goodness.

'Oh, for Pete's sake shut up,' Jerry Wilton, his face flushed with anger, slammed the dining-room door shut, then flung himself down into a large easy-chair. 'Why the hell don't you grow up?'

Jane leant over him, her face pale, her large blue eyes unnaturally bright. 'Jerry, will you listen to me for a moment?'

'You listen to me for a change.' He pushed her away so that she staggered back against the table. 'You are aware who you have just offended by your childish behaviour, aren't you? That was my managing director and his wife, and the only reason they condescended to eat in our miserable hovel, was because he wanted to sum you up. He wanted to be certain you were the right kind of wife for a prospective board member.'

'Jerry, let me explain.'

'And what do you do? When he put out his hand you suddenly put on an expression of extreme disgust, pulled up your leg as if you were going to kick him, then turn and run. What the hell, he wasn't going to rape you, only shake hands.'

'Jerry, there was something out there.'

'Don't talk such bloody rot.'

'It's not rot. If I'd stood on that porch a second longer I'd have passed out.'

Jerry got up and walked to the fireplace where he stood glowering at her.

'If you felt unwell why didn't you excuse yourself like a civilised being?'

'Because there wasn't time.' Her voice rose to a shout. 'Can't you get it through that thick skull, I couldn't help myself? You've no idea what it's like.'

'What?'

The word was spat out like a bad taste, and Jane knew at that moment he hated her. She sank into the chair he had just vacated, and spoke in a quieter tone.

'Jerry, you've got to accept the fact that I'm different.'

'And how.'

'No, don't interrupt. Please. Some people have a gift for music, others have an aptitude for acting. I have a gift, a curse, call it what you like for psychic phenomena.'

'What, table rapping?' Jerry smiled grimly. 'Pity you didn't put on a show for old Smithers this evening. It couldn't have been worse than the one he was given on the doorstep.'

'I'm serious,' Jane pushed back her blonde hair with a long-fingered hand. 'I once made a – thing materialise.'

'Don't talk such utter bilge.'

'It's not bilge, but cold fact.'

'For instance.'

Their eyes met, then she lowered her gaze and the fear-inspired anger came thundering back.

'For instance,' she thumped one clenched fist down upon the chair arm, 'the house next door to the one where I lived as a child was haunted. Haunted, do you hear? Not the wind moaning down chimneys, not a loose floor board, but bloody well haunted. A woman could be heard crying. An unmistakable, heart choking sobbing. Everybody had a go at her. The local vicar turned up with a prayer book, the Psychic Research Society, the local spooks church, the lot. And she still kept on crying.'

'Can't say I blame her,' Jerry remarked dryly.

'Then I had to put my nose in. I was about sixteen at the time, and I thought the whole thing was a big giggle. It was easy to get into the house, mostly all the windows were broken, and I could hear her sobbing all right. My God I could. I ought to have taken to my heels, like I did tonight, but I hadn't that much sense.'

Jerry frowned and said nothing.

'The sound came from an upper room. It was said some woman hung herself up there years ago. When I got into the room it was empty. Just dusty floor boards, flaking wallpaper, and a window with most of the panes missing. I was scared all right. Make no mistake about it, I was all but dead with fear . . . But at sixteen you're frightened of being afraid, at least I was. She stopped crying, and I couldn't see a thing, but I knew she was still there. Sort of listening. No, that's not right. Feeling is more like it. Then I began to get cold; colder than I've ever been before or since in my entire life. And it started to go out of me.'

'What?' demanded Jerry.

She looked up at him like a bewildered child, and he felt his heart soften; shared a little of that remembered terror.

'I wish I knew. But something vital, something that was essentially mine. A white mist was drifting away from me; coming out of my nose, my mouth, my ears, even from the pores of my skin.

It made itself into a shape, the mist I mean, if it was mist. Then there was no mist, only a little woman with her face all screwed up, and a rope tied tight about her neck. I remember particularly that her tongue was sticking out.'

'I say,' Jerry had, at least for the moment, forgotten their row, 'you're not kidding me, are you?'

'No, I'm not kidding. But what really terrified me was the sudden knowledge that the ghost, whatever it was, was made out of me. An essential part of my body had been used to shape that – thing. It was like seeing someone walking around with an arm you know has been made from your missing leg.'

'What happened?'

'I passed out. When I came to I was home in bed. Someone must have seen me go into the house, for Dad knew where to look. Funny thing is, that woman was never heard crying again.'

'Look.' He sat down on the arm of her chair. 'I'm not saying your story isn't true, although it sounds like auto-suggestion to me, but that happened in a reputed haunted house. This place can't be haunted, it hasn't been built long enough. Nobody died here, and before the estate was built, it was all open fields. So why that nonsense on the porch?'

'I can't explain it,' she shook her head, 'perhaps there are forms of disembodied life that have never died. The only thing I am certain about is, something was drawing the power out of me on that doorstep. There was the same icy feeling, my skin crawled . . . No, Jerry, it wasn't imagination.'

He got up and looked down at her with genuine concern, then he smiled.

'I'm sorry, but it's all beyond me. I think you ought to go to bed, you look all in.'

'Yes,' she rose slowly, her face white and drawn, 'I think you're right. I'll just stack the things on the draining board.'

He followed her into the kitchen and grimaced when he saw the stack of unwashed dishes, then pretended to stagger when she piled six empty milk bottles into his arms.

'Doorstep?' he enquired.

She could not entirely suppress a slight shudder, and he pretended not to notice; fighting down an irritability that she should still be harbouring a memory he was trying to blot out. He opened the dining-room door, frowned when he noticed the hall light was still burning, then walked to, and opened the front door. A blast of cold air made him recoil as he stepped down on to the garden path and, bending over, laid out his milk bottles in a neat line before the porch step. His shadow, foreshortened and grotesque, lay across the path, like, he could not smother the thought, a crouching beast waiting to pounce.

The Shadow sipped. Male, the life force strong, but the vibrations were not in tune; this was not the Vessel. The being moved, and the soft glow cast by the Night Sky Light made the Shadow contract into its former position under the porch step. A small being flashed by; flesh and blood, harsh life force, low vibrations; hunger, a desire for warmth. It sensed the Shadow's presence. Fear. Then the door shut: the light went out.

The Shadow slid over the narrow porch step; under the front door, and into the darkened hall beyond.

Jerry closed the dining-room door and called to Jane whom he could hear moving about in the kitchen.

'The cat's come in.'

Her voice came to him over the rattle of crockery.

'Yes, I know, he's in here. Something seems to have frightened him, his fur's standing on end.'

'Probably frozen. It's damn cold out there.'

'I'll give him something to eat, that should make him happy.'

He heard the cat's demanding cry that ceased when a saucer rattled on the tiled floor, then Jane came into the room.

'Think I'll go up now. Coming?'

He sank into his arm-chair, and took up a leather bound book; the faint feeling of irritability made him determined she should go out into that darkened hall alone, so as to convince herself (and him) there was nothing to fear.

'Let me finish this chapter, and I'll be with you.'

'Right.' Jane only hesitated for a moment, then walked to the door; she looked back over one shoulder, her hand on the door-knob.

'I'm awfully sorry about this evening. Do you think old Smithers was really upset?'

Jerry shrugged, not looking up from his book. 'He wasn't exactly jumping for joy when he left, but he'll probably get over it. After all, the rest of the evening went off all right.'

She was out in the hall, fumbling for the switch.

'Jerry, you turned the light . . .' She screamed, one terrified cry, and Jerry leapt to his feet, flung the book to one side, and ran across the room. Her hand still clutched the light switch; the hall was bright. But there was a shadow under the hat stand, and Jane stood white-faced and trembling against the wall.

'Darling, what's wrong?'

'Something . . .' She looked fearfully round. 'Something . . . just before I turned on the light . . . grabbed my ankle.'

'Not again!' He looked about him helplessly. 'We've no rats, at least . . .'

'Rats don't clutch.' There was a suggestion of hysteria in her voice. 'Rats bite, claw, and mostly run. But they don't clutch. They . . .' She turned her head and looked up at him, her blue eyes expressionless, like one who has already surrendered to the inevitable. '. . . They don't . . . suck.'

'Suck!' He shook her gently, not entirely aware of what he was doing, and began to lead her towards the stairs. 'Let's get you to bed, you'll laugh about this tomorrow morning.'

'Will I, Jerry?'

'Of course you will.' He turned on the stair light, and the shadows rushed away. 'You know what your trouble is, don't you?'

'No, tell me.'

'No self control. The 'orrible thing that clutched your ankle was Timmy. When cats reach an interesting state they are apt to clutch things. I don't know about sucking, but they certainly bite. Timmy probably got you confused with his mother and the Persian next door.'

'You certainly explain things away very cleverly, Jerry,' she said in a tired voice. 'Timmy must be a very lively cat by now.'

'How come?' He laughed as they entered the bedroom.

'He must have at least a quarter of my energy in him.'

'Now, that's quite enough of that.'

Ten minutes later she looked up at him, her pale, young face framed by the blue nylon pillow, and he knew she wanted to hold him back; stop him going down to that lighted hall.

'Jerry, do me a favour.'

'Of course. What is it?'

'Don't turn the lights out until you come to bed.'

'All right,' he nodded.

'Nowhere. Here, or on the landing, or in the hall.'

He smiled indulgently. 'If you say so.'

He kept his promise, but once in the living-room he turned off the ceiling light, contenting himself with the reading lamp that cast a yellow circle round his arm-chair. Just before he took up his book he glanced down at Timmy: the cat was stretched out on the hearthrug, soaking up the heat, a veritable picture of contentment as it blinked up at its owner with sleepy eyes.

'You don't appear to have much energy,' Jerry remarked aloud. The cat blinked again, and Jerry watched with detached interest, as a bright pink tongue moistened a paw; the face and head were thoroughly scrubbed, particular attention being paid to the ears, then the back and flanks were well licked, the fur on the breast bitten and preened. Timmy was just attacking the area between his hind legs when he froze, became a motionless black effigy of a cat, then slowly, very slowly, raised his head. The yellow eyes glittered in the lamp light like two pieces of polished amber; the sleek head stopped its slow movement, and Jerry saw it was watching something hidden from him by the deep shadow surrounding the bureau.

'What's the matter with you?' he demanded.

The cat flowed into gentle motion; when he drew near to the shadows his progress became slower; now his head was moving from side to side, a deep growl emerged from between his parted jaws, then, with a leap he was deep into the shadows. Jerry heard a scuffle, and Timmy was out again, his fur on end, his tail lashing like a tormented snake; then he took refuge under a chair, where he sat spitting and snarling his rage and fear.

Jerry did not know why he tip-toed across the room, his arm reaching out for the light switch; he was aware of the tricks eyes can play when they are suddenly turned from the concentrated glare of a single lamp, but that did not fully explain the mass of seething deeper shadow that was creeping up the far wall. It seemed to be twisting itself into a coil, and there was even a suggestion of a head at one end; then Jerry's hand found the switch and the room was flooded with light.

'Nothing,' he muttered, 'a bloody batty cat, a shadow, and I'm getting to be worse than Jane.'

He tried to coax Timmy out from under the chair, but the cat refused to move; when he lifted the chair the animal gave a cry of protest and streaked under the sideboard.

'Damn you,' he swore, 'stay where you are then.'

But when he opened the hall door and turned out the living-room lights, there was another snarl, and Timmy tore out and made for the front door, where he sat mewing while staring up at the handle.

'Are you sure?' Jerry asked, 'it's damn cold out there.'

The cat clawed at the panels, and did not wait for the door to be fully opened before he was out, racing down the garden path, and disappearing through a hole in the hedge.

Thoughtfully, Jerry mounted the stairs, turning out lights as he went.

Jane was not asleep, but lay on her back, eyes wide open, staring blankly at the ceiling.

'You've turned out all the lights?'

'Of course.'

'Then it's dark downstairs?'

He took his trousers off, folded them neatly, then draped them over a chair back.

'It's always dark when the lights go out.'

He put on his pyjamas, came over to her side of the bed, and looked down at that pale, childlike face.

'Come off it, Jane, you're not ten years of age any more. So it's dark outside. That's what life is all about; turning on lights, switching them off again. So long as nobody turns off the sun, we've nothing to worry about. Go to sleep.'

He went around to his side of the bed, clambered in, kissed her unresponsive lips with the rather casual affection proper to a husband married five years, then asked:

'Sleepy tonight?'

She did not answer, only turned her head away, and he sighed.

'So am I. Nighty, night,' and reached up for the pear-shaped switch which hung down over the headboard.

'No!' she whimpered, 'please don't.'

'Oh, for heaven's sake!'

All the bottled-up fear that had lurked deep down, fear which his reason told him had no foundation in fact, turned sour and came out as anger.

'Look, Jane, if you think I'm going to lay here all night with the bloody light on, you're in for a disappointment. I can put up with so much, but there's a limit. What are you afraid of? Things that go bump in the night? A nasty bogey lurking in the wardrobe?'

She turned her head slowly, and the wide open eyes studied him dispassionately.

'I suppose there's nothing I could say that would make the slightest difference?'

'You bet your sweet life there isn't.'

With the defiance of a frightened child, smothering his own spark of fear with a red blanket of anger, he pressed the pear switch and flooded the room with darkness. Jane gave one little gasp, then was still. He felt for her hand, and was shocked at its coldness.

'Silly little goose,' he whispered, 'you've never been like this before. It isn't as if you were alone. I'm here, aren't I?'

Her tiny, little girl voice came to him.

'It's as though you were a million miles away.'

'That would put me out in deep space,' he forced a chuckle, 'and it would be cold out there. Almost,' he drew nearer to her, 'as cold as you are. Damnation, girl, your feet are like slabs of ice.'

'Are they, Jerry?'

'Yes, they bloody well are. I'll turn the electric blanket on.'

He turned away from her and fumbled for the switch that dangled a little below the mattress; in a few minutes a warm glow began to seep up through the under sheet, and sleep closed down over his consciousness, blotting out the darkened room, so that for a while he was lost in a deep, black space . . .

He did not at first know why he woke suddenly; became all at once wide awake, every sense alert; the short hairs on the back of his neck standing erect, a condition up to that moment he would not have thought possible. He lay perfectly still and listened; his ears strained to detect the faintest sound. Far away, possibly on the main road, a motor car sent a faint hum through the cold night, and for a moment he clung to this transient line of contact with a homeward bound stranger. Then the sound died away, and a dreadful silence descended upon the darkness; became part of it, pressed down on him, and it seemed as if the electric blanket, conditioned by its thermostatic control to maintain an even temperature, wanted to keep all the warmth to itself. He was cold, very cold, as if he were sharing the bed with a block of ice. Then, just as he was about to stir and put on the light, the sound began, or rather, restarted, for he knew now, this was the reason for his sudden awakening.

The fear and cold held him in an icy grip, and he could only lie still and listen; try to find a rational explanation; fit the sound into a mundane frame; associate it with water pipes, a creaking window, the wind moaning down a chimney, or possibly, and now Jerry relaxed slightly, Jane snoring. That must be it. The sound grew louder. He defined it gradually, taking each part in turn and trying to make a pattern of the whole. First there was a drawing in; a slightly hoarse, breath-gasping guggle, then a harsh, obscene, blowing out. This was followed by an entirely unexplainable slithering, like dough being rubbed on a pastry board; then the process was repeated, only now, somewhat faster. The pattern was complete, Jerry placed the combination of sounds into their right category. It was a sucking noise, as though a baby with an abnormal appetite, and an outsized pair of lips, was taking overdue nourishment from a feeding bottle. Once the bed trembled slightly, and Jerry reached out for Jane's hand.

'Wake up, darling,' he spoke only just above a whisper, 'you're snoring like hell.'

He found her hand, just where he had released it before turning on the electric blanket; it was cold, very bony, and felt as if it were loosely wrapped in silk. As he fumbled for the pear switch something crashed to the floor on the far side of the room, followed almost at once by a thud on the carpet by Jane's side of the bed. He found a switch, pressed, and the darkness exploded; was

shattered into a thousand splinters by a blast of light; the wreck-
age lay all round the room, a rectangle of shadow under the dressing table, a broken slab of blackness on one side of the wardrobe,
a long smear along the picture rail; all else was light. Jerry tried
to understand what his eyes told him, fought to repel the bitter
bile that rose to his throat, and stared blandly at the thing that
was coiled round the dressing table, curved gracefully down to
the floor; a long, white length that rippled gently; and at places
rubbed its white roundness against the wainscoting, then curled
into a loop, its extremity hidden from sight by the bed. It was all
of thirty feet long, and perhaps a foot in circumference; a long
snake, or more likely, a worm; covered with a beautiful white delicate skin such as might grace a woman's shoulder. In places there
was a faint pink flush; a sign of health on a woman's cheek, or perhaps an emblem of modesty, dawning love, or anger; on the white
worm those coyish pink hues were the final epitome of obscen-
ity. Jerry sought blindly for Jane's shoulder, alive to a childish need
for someone to share this nightmare, but his hand only found the
pillow, still crumpled and hollow where her head had rested. But
Jane was gone; was down on the floor – with that thing.

He cried out, calling her name, and the worm shrieked in
response. A head came up over the edge of the bed; a round
caricature of Jane's face, smooth, veined like a gooseberry, with
thick lips that were parted, displaying a line of pink toothless
gums. It shrieked again, then fell back on to the carpet, the entire
white length quivered as though in great agony, the tail uncoiled
itself from the dressing table and threshed wildly against the wall.
The head came up again and attempted to smash the overhead
electric bulb, but missed and fell across the bed. Jerry screamed
as the wide open blue eyes gaped at him, then flinging back the
bedclothes tore across the room stumbling over a white coil that
felt soft and warm like a woman's arm. He clambered to his feet,
found the wall switch, and the ceiling lamp sent its shadow-killing
rays round the room, making the worm writhe and contract in its
futile efforts to escape. Jane was lying on the bedside rug, her face
was turned away, the bright blonde hair was disarrayed, and she
looked like a broken doll, discarded by a destructive child. Jerry
crawled over those threshing coils, forgetful for the moment of

the white-skinned horror – remembering that he had laughed at her fears, had ignored the warning sent out by his own brain – and prayed that the worst had not happened.

'Darling,' he called softly, 'can you hear me?'

The crumpled figure did not stir, so he gripped the blue satin sleeve of her pyjama jacket, and pulled gently. She rocked slightly, as though half asleep, annoyed at being disturbed, then he pulled harder, and the pyjama jacket seemed to collapse, took on a network of creases and ridges. A feeling of complete despair and horror made him forget the dying monster whose hissing screams were growing fainter; he rose up on to his knees, and gave one last violent jerk. Jane flopped over, and he looked down on to what had been her face. It was a skull covered with loose skin; he ripped the pyjama jacket open – and found that was all that remained of a once beautiful, young body; a pile of bones in a skin bag; a deflated balloon; a hideous bundle. The soft flesh, the satin skin, the wide open blue eyes; Jane's very essence lay stretched out across the room, thumping its white roundness on the carpet, trying to smash its head against the electric bulbs. He took the skeleton into his arms, smoothed back the tousled blonde hair, and muttered words of comfort.

'The lights are on baby, I'll never turn the lights off again. Don't be afraid . . .'

The white worm reared up, making one last effort to reach the ceiling lamp, then came crashing down; the round, veined head lay a few inches from Jerry and he stared at it without emotion. Presently the thought came unbidden, tumbling into his mind, and forced itself out as words.

'It sucked – it sucked all the goodness out of her.'

GREAT-GRANDAD WALKS AGAIN

WHEN GREAT-GRANDAD DIED Great-Grandma was real upset. She said: 'I don't like the idea of putting him in a hole in the ground. He wouldn't have wished it.'

Mother put on her best 'eat it, it's good for you' look: 'Now, Granny, don't carry on so, he'll be nice and comfy. I mean he'll be in one of the best spots in the churchyard, way on the eastside, gets the sun first thing in the morning and nice and sheltered.'

'Besides,' Uncle George looked worried, I think he was afraid the funeral might be canceled and he likes funerals, or rather the booze-up that follows funerals down our way – wetting the corpse's shroud it's called, 'he'll be in good company. Cousin Albert lies only a few feet away.'

'He never liked Cousin Albert.' Great-Granny refused to be put off. 'Said he was vulgar. Drank his beer straight from the bottle.'

Uncle George looked startled as though surprised to learn there was any other way and mother quickly intervened. 'It's no use arguing, Granny, buried he must be and buried he will be, so let's have no more fuss.'

Great-Granny said: 'Why?', and everybody put down their glass, with the exception of Uncle George who believed that a man and his glass should never be parted.

'Why?' Mother echoed the words, and Father, who always made it a point to follow her lead, said: 'Ah!', just to show he had a mind of his own. 'Because he must be buried. After all – he's dead.'

'No reason at all,' Great-Granny muttered, and one could see she was in a real cantankerous mood.

'But, Granny,' Mother spoke very slowly, 'dead people are always buried. If they weren't – well, life would become very unpleasant.'

'Mummies ain't,' Great-Granny insisted, 'propped up in the British Museum they are. I've seen 'em.'

'That's different,' Uncle George hastened to air his knowledge, 'they's yer ancient royalty, ain't they. Embalmed they are. I mean Grandad might have been ancient, but he weren't no royalty.'

'Better,' Great-Granny looked real narked, 'a smelly old Pharaoh couldn't hold a candle to 'im. No, me mind's made up, I won't have him buried in no churchyard. I want him where I can see him, where he's been these ninety years.' She banged her stick on the floor. Right here in this house. So if you wants what yer thinks should come to you after I'm gone, put yer thinking caps on.'

That put paid to any further argument. Her real estate alone ranged from a grocer's shop in the Fulham Road to a couple of dubious houses in Paddington, not to mention what's stacked away in half a dozen bank accounts. Mother went as pale as Great-Grandad in the next room.

'Granny, you wouldn't?'

'Cat's Home,' pronounced Great-Granny, 'the lot,' and without a further word she trotted off to her room clutching a full bottle of gin.

Uncle George sat down, that being the safest thing for him to do, and Father watched Mother rather like a private soldier anxious to please his sergeant-major. Mother thoughtfully drank three Bloody Marys, that being in her opinion the only respectful drink under the circumstances, and I sucked my gin and tonic through a straw, not being old enough, you understand, to sup straight from a glass like an adult. Presently Mother nodded, refilled her glass, forgetting however to add the tomato juice.

'We must pickle him,' she said.

I don't know if you have ever pickled a corpse, but if you have, you must agree it's no easy job. Mother knew all about pickling onions and she could see no good reason why we could not do Great-Grandad in the same manner, only Uncle George pointed out finding a jar large enough might be an insurmountable problem, and anyway, Great-Granny mightn't go for a bottled Great-Grandad stuck up at one end of the table. Then he had an idea.

'Whisky!'

'Help yourself,' Mother said absent-mindedly, 'you don't have to ask.'

'No, pickle him in whisky. Fill the bath-tub and leave him to have a good soak. Come to think of it, the job's half done anyway, when you remember the gallons of the stuff he put away during his lifetime.'

'Be expensive,' Mother objected.

'There's the insurance,' Uncle George pointed out, 'and we'll save on a tombstone. Let me see, we'll need about eight gallons to fill the bath, that's sixty-four bottles at two pound ten per bottle, which comes to . . .'

'One hundred and sixty pounds,' I said in a flash and Mother looked real proud; then she frowned.

'A lot of money to pour down the drain.'

'Look upon it as an investment,' Uncle George urged, 'besides it needn't all be wasted. We can always rebottle it, seal the caps back careful like, and flog it back to the off-licence at say two pound a bottle. Say it was surplus to requirements.'

Mother nodded her approval.

'You've a good head on yer shoulders, I'll say that. Well, you'd better get cracking. George, you take the pram and Alfie can follow with his go-kart. I expect you'll have to make the rounds as I doubt if Higginbottom has sixty-four bottles in stock. And you'll want some money.'

She got her old carpet bag from behind the dresser and dished out three fat wads of notes, the Prudential having coughed up the day before.

'You'd better get receipts,' she added, 'we might be able to fiddle a tax dodge somehow.'

She then turned on Father who retreated a few steps.

'You rustle up a load of bricks.'

'Bricks!' He wasn't very quick on the uptake.

'Yeah, bricks. The things they build houses with. We can't bury an empty coffin, can we? It wouldn't be right. You can take my shopping bag.'

I must say buying sixty-four bottles of whisky isn't such a simple operation as you might imagine. Old Higginbottom wanted to know if we were going to float a battleship, and Uncle George said: 'Any more lip and I'll float you one in the gizzard,' but we got two dozen bottles out of him, which was about as much as the pram could hold, then we got a dozen more from The Dog and Duck, which filled my go-kart. Then Uncle George said we'd better go home to unload, but perhaps he'd sample a drop just in case it hadn't got the right embalming quality needed to keep Great-Grandad nice and fresh. So, purely in the interest of scientific investigation, he took a man-sized swig, pronounced it to be good stuff, then dropped the bottle and stood staring sadly down at a brown pool that formed in a convenient hole in the road. However, it wasn't wasted, because about five minutes later a large tom-cat went staggering by, who looked as if he were prepared to take on anything from a mouse to an alsatian.

We managed to collect sixty-four bottles by closing time and in the meantime Mother and Father had not been idle. Great-Grandad was out of his coffin, half reclining on the sitting-room sofa, his legs sticking straight out, and one arm for some reason raised upright, as though he were either giving the Nazi salute or asking permission to leave the room. His long flannel nightgown was rucked up above his bony knees, and the bandage had slipped from around his chin so that his mouth was wide open. Mother kept telling Father to: 'Push his false teeth back in, do,' but Father rather funked the job, so of course I had to do it, Mother being of the opinion that kids should never be idle.

Father had found some bricks, but not very good ones, being mostly broken halves, and a fair mixture of stones, and there wasn't enough. Mother said he was bone idle and Great-Grandad had more life in him now than Father had, but I had the idea of packing the bricks with soil from the back garden, and Mother said I was real clever, and that I must have got my brains from her side of the family.

Then came the important part. Getting Great-Grandad pickled. Uncle George was all for dumping him straight into the bath and pouring the whisky over him, but Mother said no, not just yet.

'First we ought to fill his inside, get it all circulated round, then put him in to soak.'

'How do we do that?' Uncle George scratched his head, 'he's in no condition to take it down natural-like.'

'I can't think of everything,' Mother complained, 'and with two men in the house, I shouldn't have to.'

'My bicycle pump,' I suggested, and mother patted my head.

'Takes after me old dad,' she said proudly, 'run along ducks and get yer old pump.'

When I got back Great-Grandad was laid out in the bath, and I must say he looked a sight, what with his gaping mouth and the arm which just wouldn't go down, although Uncle George had several goes at anchoring it with the lavatory chain, but when he got a swipe under the chin with Great-Grandad's bony knuckles, he gave up.

Take my tip, never try to fill a corpse with whisky by a bicycle pump, it's dead hopeless. I filled the pump, stuck the connection down the old man's throat, and pushed. Some whisky came out of his nose, some out of his ears, but none went where it was supposed to, so finally we gave up, filled the bath, put two flat-irons on Great-Grandad's chest and left him.

Next day Great-Grandma was real narked when she found out what we had done, said it was a criminal waste of whisky when methylated spirits would have been much cheaper. But Mother said meths wasn't respectful and couldn't be used afterwards. Great-Granny said: 'No, what about window cleaning, and why not buy a nice spirit stove and save on gas?' and for a while there was a real old barney, then it was time for the funeral.

The pallbearers had quite a time lugging that coffinload of bricks to the churchyard, and Mr Carter the butcher said Great-Grandad must have a couple of birds in there with him, to make the bloody thing so heavy. Great-Granny said he was to keep a civil tongue in his head or she'd bash him with her umbrella, and any road, Great-Grandad had never been a lustful man – for his age.

When they lowered the coffin into the grave the ropes broke, and you've never heard such a rattling and thumping that took place when the box landed. Mr Carter said: 'Blimey, the old bastard has come apart,' and Great-Granny took a swipe at him, missed and almost fell into the grave herself.

Everybody came back to the house for the shroud-wetting and

there was a fine old sing-song afterwards. Mother didn't think *Knees Up Mother Brown* was respectful, so Uncle George gave a roof-raising rendering of *Eskimo Nell*, and Great-Granny, who could remember the first world war, sang *Three German Officers Crossed The Line* in her sweet old quavering voice. Altogether it was a great shroud-wetting.

Now it is no use asking me why Great-Grandad started to walk. Uncle George, who fancies himself as a man of learning, having taken the *Sunday Mirror* all his life, said it was something to do with the whisky fermenting, but Great-Granny muttered dark words about the old chap's ancestors. It appears a Great-Great-Somebody was related to the nobility out Trans-somewhere, and in that part of the world dead people don't lay down natural-like, as they do in more civilised countries. That as may be, the fact remains Great-Grandad clambered up out of that bath and, dripping whisky over the almost new stair-carpet, made a bee-line for Uncle George's bedroom. I heard him coming upstairs as a matter of fact, but of course never guessed who it was; the footsteps were a bit slow and heavy, then a door opened and next thing I knew, Uncle George was yelling like a tom-cat that's missed out on its operation.

I jumped out of bed, flew across the landing, and turned into the next room. There was Great-Grandad, still dripping whisky, his right arm stuck up for fine weather, with his false teeth clamped fast into Uncle George's neck. He pulled himself free just as I entered and the National Health choppers came out of Great-Grandad's mouth like an oyster leaving its shell. Mother and Father came in then, and what with them yelling and Uncle George running round the room with the false teeth still stuck in his neck, and with Great-Grandad standing stiff as a poker with his eyes bulging, his arm raised and his shrivelled gums gaping, it was all I could do to keep a straight face.

Uncle George finally got the false teeth out of his neck and the sight of blood set Great-Grandad off again, for he lurched forward, stiff-legged, and we all high-tailed it down to the cellar. The old man soon smelt us out, and all night he was bumping about outside the door, glaring at us with his bulging eyes, through the cracks.

'This is too much of a bad thing,' Mother was saying, trying to make herself comfy on a stack of smokeless fuel, 'we ought to have buried him respectable like.'

Great-Granny, who had been first into the cellar, sniffed.

'He ain't doing no harm. Without his teeth he can't bite nobody, only suck.'

'I'm not having him suck me,' Mother said, ''t'ain't decent. He's turned into a vampire, that's what he's done.'

'We'll have to drive a stake through his heart,' pronounced Uncle George, 'then cut off his head and put a twig of garlic in his mouth.'

This riled Great-Granny again.

'There'll be no sticking of stakes through 'earts in my house,' she said firmly, 'not if those expect, think they'll get. You might think of a poor old widow woman who's got nobody. It'll be company for me to have him round the house after dark, and if he wants a drop of wet stuff to moisten his lips, what's the harm? That husband of yours has got enough and some to spare, by the look of him.'

Everyone looked at Father who was doing his best to hide behind a disused mangle, and Mother had a kind of thoughtful look.

'Not on your nelly,' said Father, and you could see he wasn't keen, 'I'm not going to be a meal ticket to a week-old corpse.' Mother raised sorrowing eyes towards the ceiling.

'Calls himself a man,' she addressed an old bicycle tyre, 'takes everything, and never gives.'

Just before dawn we heard Great-Grandad mount the cellar stairs, then a little later, there was a loud splash.

'Gone back to his resting place,' announced Great-Granny solemnly, 'they 'as to, you know. Now he'll be safely bedded down in his whisky until sunset.'

It's funny how you can get used to anything, and after a few nights we took Great-Grandad's wandering about the house as a matter of course. Uncle George had to get all clever like and went to the local cinema where they were showing *Dracula's Bath Night*. He tried to find some garlic leaves, but no shop seemed to stock them, so bought seven pound of ripe onions instead. He strung these over our bedroom doors and painted red crosses on the panels, but Great-Grandad simply ignored the lot and strutted through any doorway that was open, looking with his raised arm like Hitler come for his old age pension. It was all rather sad really, because Uncle George hung on to the old chap's false teeth and no vampire can get down to a job of blood sucking with his bare gums; rather like a housewife who's lost her can opener. Mother, who's got a soft heart, made him some black puddings, and I think he liked those, but it wasn't the real thing, and Father got all bolshy whenever anyone suggested he cough up a couple pints of blood.

I don't know how it would have ended if Uncle George hadn't met this film producer in the pub. Seems he was making a film called *Dracula's Brother*, and the chap they had signed up for the lead had gone sick with toothache. Uncle George told him about Great-Grandad and how we were having trouble getting him proper nourishment, and the film chap said he might be interested if the price was right. So he came round one night and the minute he saw Great-Grandad stalking around with his raised arm and toothless gums, he went berserk.

'Lovely, dear boy,' he actually put his arm round Great-Grandad, who instantly tried to get a fix on his neck, 'makes Christopher Lee look like Santa Claus.'

'Two thousand pound down,' said Great-Granny, 'and five per cent of the gross, plus as much blood as he can drink.'

When the contract was signed the film producer found he'd got Great-Granny as well, so he cast her as Dracula's mother. The film was called *I Was A Nazi Vampire* and it should be round your way quite soon.

You'll notice the extras all look a bit anaemic, which is only to be expected, and the lead has no dialogue worth mentioning. Also the leading lady screams a lot. That's only to be expected too.

By the way, we had to get a new bath. The old one was the only place Great-Grandad would go back to at sunrise. They top it up with whisky every night.

THE FUNDAMENTAL ELEMENTAL

THE VALLEY APPEARED to be not less than three miles long and was flanked on either side by fire-capped mountains. Francis St Clare, the world's only practising psychic detective, almost forgot himself and swore.

'Your friend is a curse on the face of seven dimensions and she should have her bottom soundly spanked!'

Fredrica Masters, commonly known as Fred, shrugged her white shoulders and grimaced.

'Rowena has already suffered at the hands of brutal men and most certainly needs no further attention from you!'

Francis kicked a long-tailed, but otherwise small dragon from a rock and then watched its slow departure. 'I must decline any interest in the wench, save to find her and get back to my body beautiful.'

Fred creased her smooth forehead into a frown.

'I'm not certain. Where and what are we?'

'We are, dear child, in your subconscious. Way over there can be seen what appears to be a low cave opening which gives entrance to the Universal Mind. An awesome place to be.'

'And we?' Fred enquired, retreating from a slightly larger dragon. 'What are we?'

'We are in our astral bodies while we seek out the wench Rowena Bradley. Not forgetting that our common or garden, nosh-consuming bodies are in our virginal beds way up there on the earthly plane, most likely snoring their heads off.'

'Speak for yourself,' Fred protested. 'I never snore.'

Francis raised a slim eyebrow. 'You do when there's an "r" in the month!'

Fred shrugged. 'I'm not responsible for what you get up to when I'm wandering the Upper Planes – you filthy beast.'

'I bath every day . . . Hell, a fire bomb is coming!'

From high up in the pale pink sky, a bright red fireball came shrieking down onto the valley floor, where it landed with a massive explosion. It soon began to cool off, revealing a surface that had much in common with red human skin.

'Everything in the Seven Universes is related to us,' Francis murmured. 'We are grit on the wind, an avalanche on a mountain side, a caterpillar making a long journey along a blade of grass . . .'

'You talk too much,' Fred complained. 'You say things that I do not understand.'

'But I do,' said Francis, 'and that's what's important.'

'You're mad.'

'I am one of the very few sane people on this planet,' he replied. 'And when I start my last and most essential journey on the Great Road, then there will be no more.'

'Why? You said you were one of the few. Some of them could outlive you.'

Francis shook his head. 'Never. I will live to a terrible old age.'

'Why terrible?'

'Because I will become bored.'

'You could amuse yourself playing with the stars.'

'The Light Lords will never permit that.'

'Why?'

'Don't use that terrible little word.'

'Why?'

'Because sooner or later I would discover the secret of the Universes, and then Man will destroy the Light Lords.'

'Can the Light Lords be destroyed?'

'They can be robbed of light and power. With these two basic elements, death will reign supreme.'

'But you have always maintained that there is no death,' argued Fred.

'Only change,' replied Francis. 'But if you transform bone into ash, then there must be one hundred percent change. Although, of course, the main elements are still there.'

Then a joyful smile lit up Fred's face. 'Here comes Rowena! She was not lost – only missing.'

A tall girl, with shoulder-length auburn hair that stood out in complete contrast to Fred's dazzling blonde beauty, limped to a halt and gave the psychic detective a dazzling smile.

'Sorry if I've dragged you down here for no good purpose, but believe it or not, I strayed out onto the Universal Mind and all but got myself lost. All because I saw something awful going through your dimensional trap, or should I call it your dimensional lock?'

Francis rubbed his hands together, for it had suddenly grown cold in Fred's subconscious. 'Let's wait until we are back in earth-base. Fred is eager to get back to her body beautiful.'

'Too true,' Fred nodded, 'I want me nosh. But why are you limping, Rowena?'

'I stumbled over a mini-dragon and twisted my ankle,' replied the girl.

Fred began hopping from one foot to another. 'I can't wait. Rowena, what did you see?'

'A tall old man dressed in black. I followed him all the way from your earth-base.'

Francis grunted: 'People are thin on the ground down here. Quite a few of them must look like tall lean old men dressed all in black.'

Rowena grimaced. 'I know a vampire when I see one.'

'Let's get our muttons straight,' said Francis. 'Fred and I were called in to investigate an alleged vampire break-in. That's if there is any such thing, living or dead, as a vampire. Even down here in Fred's subconscious we are still investigating, but that doesn't mean we believe in the existence of vampires.'

'Yep!' Fred nodded vigorously. 'And I'm not at all keen to investigate a vampire in my brain.'

Francis put his head on to one side and asked Fred: 'Your what?'

'Pig!' she accused.

'A much maligned animal,' retorted Francis. 'But wait a tiny minute – I took up the trail of something that could have been a blood sucker in Rowena's house. Now the bloody thing appears to have found its way through my dimensional lock and into my hired help's so-called brain . . .'

'I hate you very much,' interrupted Fred.

'It's hard to believe,' continued Francis. 'I mean, if she has a brain then it's in her stomach.'

Rowena expelled her breath in a vast sigh. 'Let's stop the in-fighting until we are back in earth bodies?'

They made their way back along the valley until they came to the cave opening. It was dimly lit by a green luminescence, which rather gave the impression it was a tank of dirty green water.

'In and up,' Francis ordered. 'Let us leave the shades of Hades behind us.'

The psychic detective turned slowly and faced Rowena Bradley. 'Up you go, and may the Light Lords go with you . . .'

Francis and Fred had made this entrance to the Hidden World. There was no air that needed to be inhaled, merely the will to ascend. Rowena stepped into the green light and rapidly rose to the surface, which was situated in Francis's bedroom.

In less than five minutes, three transparent beings stood by their earth bodies, each laying on a three-foot bed. They floated down and became a streak of green light that merged into a sleeping body. Fred was the first to stand up.

'Wakey-wakey! Lead me to the nosh and drinkies.'

Presently, three young people filed into the dining-room where a cold collation was laid out on a long table.

Fred rubbed her hands together. 'Tudor salad, sliced ham and ice cold perry. And nobody is going to talk me out of it.'

Francis seated himself at the head of the table.

'No one will try. And when we have satisfied the inner man – or woman – we will listen to Rowena tell us why she thinks she has a vampire on her trail and how come she found her way down into Fred's subconscious.'

Rowena took a deep breath. 'Well . . .'

'Nosh first,' Fred explained, 'and spare not your tummy. It's not often that his Lordship lets you eat your fill.'

Francis shrugged, 'I think it wise to reinforce the blood supply. One can't be too careful if a vampire – or some creature that is akin to it – sinks fangs into one or other of us.'

Fred dropped her knife and fork. 'You horrible . . . thing. I rather hoped you would protect us helpless women against a blood drinker. I say, that's rather good – a blood drinker!'

Francis speared a boiled potato. 'I prefer a partaker. A partaker of blood – it's more refined.'

'Ugh! Why can't we be a partaker of meat and veg?' asked Fred.

'Plain meat and veg suffice for us,' explained Francis. 'Assuming we are on the trail of a real partaker, one has to be careful of names and titles. After all, where I lead others will follow.'

'His modesty is rather moving.' Fred pulled the salad bowl towards her and smiled at Rowena. 'Why?'

Rowena nodded. 'Are you asking why I came to the world's only practising psychic detective, and then went swanning after you in your own subconscious?'

'Something like that.'

'Well, I've always been able to visit the Hidden World in my sleeping time. Even up to the Seventh Plane.'

Francis pulled the cream jug from beyond Fred's reach. 'That can be dangerous if you don't take proper precautions . . . you could have dropped Fred and I in the manure.'

'I'm sorry, I never thought you two would ever be in any kind of danger. After all, Fred is the world's greatest materialistic medium.'

'Precisely,' replied Francis. 'Every nasty in the Seven Universes would like to get their sticky claws on her. She's reasonably safe now because she's under my control.'

Fred made some interesting noises and pulled the trifle bowl towards her. She seized a large dessert spoon and proceeded to demolish the trifle unaided.

'By the Light Lords, I'm hungry,' she said. 'I'm either suffering from an attack of tapeworms or lack of love and attention.'

'You've only to ask,' Francis said dryly. 'You've got a tongue in your head.'

'I can never remember if there's an "r" in the month.'

'I never seem to find one,' smiled Francis.

Rowena frowned. 'What's all this about an "r" in the month? I always thought . . .'

'Not in the front of the child,' Francis warned. 'I don't encourage her . . . The rank and file can soon mutiny if they imagine they are not getting their rights.'

Fred pushed the empty trifle bowl towards Francis, then asked: 'Can we talk about the 'orrible vampire that may be coiled up in my brain?'

'There would not be much room for the poor thing to move around,' replied Francis. 'Of course . . .'

The two girls waited for him to complete the sentence. Presently he continued in a lower tone of voice. '. . . Of course, down there in Fred's subconscious – always supposing a vamp's astral body is equipped with fangs . . .'

Fred clamped her hands over her ears. 'I don't want to hear. Anyway, it's not possible.'

'How do you know?'

'Astral bodies don't have blood.'

'They have some green essence which is blood in all but name. Mind you, your special essence might suit a vamp's system, or possibly not. Remember Van Helsing gave that poor girl three different blood types and strangely she didn't appear to suffer any ill effects . . .'

'Still,' Fred shrugged her indifference, 'what kills me will put paid to vammie.'

Francis smiled his complete approval. 'I like that – prepared to give your all in the Young Master's service. The lower orders are finding their rightful place at last. But please remember this, I can think of no way that a vampire can be killed while down in anyone's subconscious. And if tradition is to be believed, the damn thing can also change shape. Fred, imagine a little wolf crawling up your throat and taking a nibble from your tonsils . . .'

'I haven't got any tonsils.'

'Aren't you a lucky girl?'

'Don't you dare . . .'

'I was only wondering if it would be possible to get pointed stakes and a ton of garlic down into your subconscious. Then we'd have a fine old time.'

For the first time Fred began to show signs of strain. She glared at her employer and knocked over a silver condiment set. Her voice lost its attractive lilting tone.

'This may be funny to you, but from where I'm sitting it's nothing short of horrific.'

Francis laid a placating hand on her shoulder.

'Don't let the kettle boil over. I must confess to being enthralled by the situation. I mean to say, supposing there is a vammie down there and it suddenly expounds (right word, Fred?) into normal size, will Fred's earth body explode – be smeared over walls and ceiling? What an interesting case!'

'Francis,' Rowena spoke softly, 'Fred's turning green.'

'She's not!' He patted her shoulder in no gentle fashion. 'Come on Fred, pull yourself together. It's always fun and games with us. Once we become all serious like, the nasties will move in. Think about this: once any foreign intruder grows above a certain size, the earth body will reject it.'

Fred patted her forehead with a man-sized red handkerchief.

'You swine! You mouldy bacon. You . . . you . . .'

'Rat in a jack-boot?' Francis suggested.

'Only the size which pinched your corns.'

'I suppose you haven't got any corns?' responded Francis. 'There's no justice in this world. But please, let's treat this matter seriously. Let vammie be given the stake, garlic and head cutting off treatment.'

'Running water . . . ?' added Fred.

'I understand from those who know these things, that running water has never been tested,' replied Francis. 'Anyway, let's get the bloody thing out of Fred and up here. Then we can give it the works.'

'That's all right with me,' Fred declared.

'And me,' Rowena agreed. 'But the number one question is – *how* do we get it out of Fred and up here?'

'Easy, once you think constructively.'

Fred nodded very slowly, then changed her mind and shook her head instead. 'Easy, just drop Fred in the mess.'

'Listen to the Young Master: firstly we accept that there is a vampire bedded down in Fred's subconscious. We know for a fact it is there. In other words, we have faith.'

The two girls said 'Umm . . .' together. Then they followed it up with '*faith?*'

'Yes,' said Francis. 'The stuff which we are given to understand can move mountains.'

'Carry on,' Fred said. 'Although I may yet weep.'

'Now hark you. Once faith has convinced us that Fred has an inner vampire, then we make certain that the vampire knows what she looks like. We arouse its lust, get it drooling, Beldaza bless us!'

'I'm really interested,' Fred stated with undoubted conviction. 'Curiosity will possibly kill me, but I must know . . .'

'But,' the psychic detective raised an elegant hand, 'first I want Rowena to again tell us how a dazzling person like herself came to be concerned about a common or garden vampire.'

Rowena pulled her white shirt down a few more inches, then cleared her throat. 'Well, as you know, I inherited my house from my grandmother and I hadn't been in it more than a few days before I was informed it was haunted . . .'

Francis cleared his throat in turn. 'You say informed. By whom?'

'The postman; the daily who comes to oblige who wouldn't go into certain rooms by herself; the window cleaner who said he had seen a tall old man dressed in black looking at him through the third floor back window. The local vicar also saw the same old man – or one very much like him – standing early one morning by the front gate. He offered to pray for us, but no more. It appears that an exorcism service had resulted in the vicar being thrown down the stairs.'

Francis made a grotesque face. 'How very off-putting. Fred, we've met that type before.'

'Yes, horror under the bed-springs.'

'The Young Master was about to quote,' continued Francis. 'Rowena, carry on. So far your story has proved most interesting.'

Rowena blushed. 'Thank you. Well, for the first month I saw nothing . . .'

'You can't see nothing,' Fred pointed out. 'I don't know why, but you can't.'

Francis sighed very deeply. 'The Young Master rather hoped someone would spot the deliberate mistake. Now someone has, he – the Young Master – further hopes that someone will not make a song and dance about it. Can Rowena continue with her story?'

'She can,' replied Fred, 'and I have no doubt that she will.'

'Yes, well . . . ,' said Rowena. 'Although I did not see the unusual – I heard it . . . The sound of a man on the stairs who found it necessary to clear his throat. Do you know what I mean? Not so much as a hint that a man is there – you are certain that no one other than yourself is in the house – then you hear a throat clearing just beyond the wide open door.'

'Very disturbing,' Francis declared. 'What did you do?'

'Got out of bed, put on a dressing gown and went out on to the landing.'

'Only to find that no one was there . . .'

'Wrong. A tall old man attired all in black was standing by the bathroom door. He was completely motionless. He just stood there staring at me, then turned and walked towards the stairs and went down to the hall below. There he must have vanished, for when I followed a few minutes later there was neither sight nor sound of him.'

Francis did not speak for some little while, then he asked Rowena, 'What was your impression? Was his appearance disturbing?'

'That is the understatement of the year.'

'Well, why was his appearance disturbing?'

'He was so white. Corpse-white. Black hair, bright red lips. But dress him in black drain-pipe trousers, black top hat – and you'd have Abraham Lincoln.'

'Surely you're not suggesting . . . ?'

'Of course not. But I've been given to understand that a full-blooded buck vampire often has a resemblance to the great man.'

Fred gave her considered opinion. 'An undertaker. A top class, Park Avenue undertaker.'

Rowena grimaced. 'Yes, but the kind who lets the corpse bury the coffin.'

'A good description,' Francis admitted. 'But the important thing is that this creature is inside Fred, and Rowena has some inner essence that attracts vampires. Faith demands that we accept the existence of at least one blood drinker. Fred, strip off!'

'What! This is not the time or place . . .'

'Strictly business. Strip off. Vammie must see, lust, and insist on making contact.'

Fred voiced her objection. 'Not on your nellie. I will not be a thinny-goat. *You* strip off.'

'Vampires are strictly heterosexual.'

'You never know your luck. Maybe this is one who has strayed from the straight and narrow.'

'Fred – strip off!'

Fred began to unbutton and unzip. 'Always the same. Any kinky business, any manure-dropping-in, and poor old Fred is in it up to her bloody neck. Must it be everything?'

'Yes. I did think just a torn slip . . . but let's go the full hog. I don't know why you are making all this fuss, there's damn all to come off. I mean, bra and knicks and that's it.'

'Oh yeah! And what about the black mesh stockings?'

'I see what you mean! Keep those on, Beldaza be praised! Your split pea-sized brain does sometimes come up with something not connected with food.'

Fred shouted in an effort to make herself understood. 'I didn't mean leave them on! You won't be able to control a sex-mad vampire.'

'Never mind. So long as we can get him out of your sub and within stake-stabbing distance, this case can be brought to a successful conclusion.'

'What about *me* being brought to an unsuccessful conclusion?'

'Have faith in the Young Master and all will be well.'

'Oh my Gawd!'

Francis St Clare gazed upon the unclad form of his assistant and nodded his approval. 'Fine. Now stand to the left and in front of that tall mirror, then raise your hands above your head. Great! Marvellous!'

'Are you expressing professional appreciation,' Fred enquired, 'or merely drooling?'

'The Young Master never drools. Now turn very slowly and look towards the window and think lustful thoughts.'

'Think what! Let me tell you Francis St Clare, my mum told me to maintain a clean body and a pure mind. Think of the Archbishop of Canterbury taking a bath was her advice, and I've always done that.'

'Well, don't do it now. Think of Rasputin let loose in a nunnery.'

'Who was Rasputin?'

'He was in the monk business himself.'

Fred must have succeeded in creating some kind of unholy thoughts, for presently she emitted a gasping cry.

'There's . . . there's something moving in my subconscious.'

Francis rubbed his hands together. 'We're hitting pay dirt! Well done Fred. You'd better shut down now. A closed mind will mean that he will not be able to get any bigger.'

'I shouldn't have allowed you to talk me into this.'

Rowena clasped both hands over her mouth when the naked form of Fred began to writhe and then was forced back against the window, while her series of cries reminded Francis of his own pain and anguish when he was once shut up in a dark room with hungry rats attacking his feet.

'Shut down completely,' he ordered. 'Fill your mind with blue mist. Blue light. Blue anything. Then dismiss him. He won't go, but it will keep him occupied. Can you get his image?'

Fred's voice was weak but audible. 'Tall, dark . . . strong unlined face . . . and he's after me . . . it will be rape of both bodies . . . I'll be defenceless afterwards . . . Francis help me . . . you know how.'

Francis was all but cheerful. 'By Beldaza! I've done it. Now to get him out without hurting Fred. It's worth trying.'

As though in answer to his wish, Fred's body walked over to his single bed and lay down. Francis grabbed a blanket and completely covered the motionless body while crying out, 'Got you! Well done. Now Fred, let's see if we can get a full materialization from a prone position.'

He crouched down beside the bed until his voice spoke into Fred's left ear. 'Fred, you know what must be done. Get cracking with the ectoplasm.'

There came from the thick blanket the sound of Fred's voice. 'You bastard!'

'Fred, curse me later, but now . . .'

Again a long period of silence made St Clare wonder if the miracle would not take place, that maybe he had asked too much from Fred. Then the blanket began to crease, to form hills and valleys, until from the bottom a stream of white light slid out and built up into a hooded image. Gradually it took on the complete likeness of a tall man, dark of face, strong of feature, attired in black, even to the top hat and drainpipe trousers. He spoke with the voice and tone of an educated North American.

'Well, stranger! Have you called me up to feed my other self? If so, I am grateful, but I doubt it.'

Rowena had described the figure well, and Francis shuddered when he realised that he was in the presence of a vampire. Moreover, a vampire that was comprised of Fred's essence and he, the world's only practising psychic detective, must find some way of destroying this creature . . .

Rowena spoke with a very soft voice. 'The doings are under your bed. The one nearest to you.'

'Who the hell put them there?' Francis asked in much the same tone of voice.

'You did,' Rowena replied, never taking her gaze from the blood drinker's grinning face. 'If and when Fred returns to base, she will be talking about a fine old muck-up, even possibly using stronger language.'

'I have trained my assistant not to use crude words. They sear my sensitive soul.'

The vampire was now smiling gently.

'That glorious creature will soon grow tired and I am planning to drain her of all she has, both blood and essence. Later the empty shell can be thrown to the Shiver Makers. And you, Mr St Clare, think of what a beneficial draught it will be – I'll become ten times the being I am now, and I will render thanks to the Lord Beldaza for this wonderful state of affairs. Well, Mr St Clare – do you believe in vampires now?'

Francis made the only answer that was possible to a man who had blundered so badly.

'I will believe when the stake is driven home, the blood spurts up, and your ego is freed from the chains of flesh.'

The vampire emitted a chuckle that seemed to come from deep within in his chest.

'You speak well and make impressive sounds that smother the pitiful squeals that originate from Celestial vermin. Ah! I see that flicks a raw wound. But you are worthy foes and I will be most happy to add your bodies to my collection. Yes, indeed. I have spent much time and energy in building up my human staircase. Even the Lord Marcus rejoices when he hears each scream as his feet tread on a tender step. His august feet are heavy.'

'Francis,' Rowena pleaded, 'do something. And do something quickly.'

The vampire's chuckle was now merging into a long drawn out growl. 'Good advice, my dear, but I fear there is no way that the great Francis St Clare can follow it. He is toying with the idea of jumping on me, making an attempt to grab at least one of those pointed stakes and the other nonsense that is under his bed. But such dreams can only be found in the pages of fiction . . .'

Francis St Clare nodded. 'True. But there are some people who maintain that the great Lord Dracula only exists in the pages of fiction. That he has no claim to a flesh and blood life.'

An expression that could have been one of alarm passed over the harsh features of the vampire, but one of derision quickly erased it.

Francis St Clare took a deep breath. 'Yes, I have studied old documents, talked with those who say they have seen, heard, and know, but not one word of proof has even suggested that the Lord Dracula ever walked the earth. True, there was one crude monster who had a penchant for impaling his enemies on pointed stakes, but he was by no means a blood-drinking aristocrat.'

The vampire studied his fingernails with deep interest. 'Very well, I will agree that Dracula may have been a legend based on fact, but today there are many of my kind who are spreading across the face of the planet.'

Francis began to wonder how much longer Fred could maintain the body she had created, bearing in mind that the vampire had his own means of prolonging life.

Suddenly he spoke. 'What is your name?'

The vampire stared at him with dilated eyes. 'My name is Diabolus,' he replied.

Francis smiled. 'Another name for your master. You have just grabbed it from the rag-bag of memory. I ask you again, what is your name?'

'My name is not important. I am . . . I . . . am . . .'

'Who is Beldaza?'

'Supreme Lord of the Vampires.'

'How do you know?'

'It is written . . .'

'Where?'

'I will not answer any more of these time-wasting questions. I know your purpose is to keep me occupied until this glorious creature draws back the body she has created.'

Francis St Clare drew himself up to his full height and shouted his questions. 'Where is it written that Beldaza is Supreme Lord of the Vampires?'

'In the *Book of Forbidden Knowledge.*'

'Where will I find this book?'

'I will not answer that. You are trying to force me back into the Hidden World. But it will not work, my friend.'

The solution to this very complicated problem came to Francis St Clare in a soul-searing flash, and he began to laugh as he came to understand how very simple it was.

'I have one more question to ask,' he said when he was in a condition to speak again, 'and you will answer it.'

'Why?' the vampire asked. 'Why must I answer any question that disturbs your mind?'

'Answer my last question and then you will know.'

Rowena could not be certain if the being that looked like a man shrank a few inches from his height, or that his eyes suddenly acquired a reddish glow. But one factor was clear – fear peered from behind those eyes.

'Very well – ask your question.'

Francis St Clare took a deep breath, then asked: 'Who created the Hidden World?'

That dead-white face gradually assumed a greyish tinge, the long-fingered hands began to tremble. But he still retained control of his voice.

'Beldaza,' replied the vampire.

The psychic detective sighed again, only now he sounded very sad. 'Come, you can do better than that, Count Carlos . . .'

The Count's head jerked up. 'I have a name . . . ?'

'Yes, you have. I decided to give you one. Again – who created the Hidden World? Who created everything pertaining to the Hidden World?'

'I cannot recall . . .'

'You lie! Who is the great Creator? Answer me, I so order you – who?'

The vampire sank slowly to his knees and gave his creator the only possible answer.

'You.'

'At last! The only life you have ever known came from my brain.'

The vampire pleaded. 'Have mercy. My need is small – little more than a pint of blood a day.'

'I cannot afford pity,' replied Francis. 'That which I made, I can also destroy. Count Carlos, vampire – cease to exist! Such is my will.'

Fred was seated at the other side of the table. Rowena was on her right. Francis St Clare occupied his usual place at the head of the table.

Fred sat looking at a plate of roast beef, roast potatoes and brussel sprouts. She made no effort to take up her knife and fork. Francis sipped from a glass of white wine, then he addressed Rowena.

'Never again will a vampire cross your threshold.'

The girl grimaced. 'That I accept. But how did you do it? Getting shot of it, I mean. Mr St Clare – what are you?'

'A psychic detective who writes in his spare time,' Francis replied.

'Yes, I know, and you are entitled to destroy anything you have created. Even *anyone*, so long as that anyone was born in your brain. But Francis – Mr St Clare – where does fiction end and reality begin?'

Francis took up a goblet filled with red wine. He took an appreciative sip. 'The Seven Universes are made up of unnumbered quivering lines. They can take any shape. All things are possible to all people . . .'

Rowena pushed her chair back and rose to her feet. 'It's all beyond me. Well, I'll go and pack, and . . . oh yes, write out a cheque . . .'

Fred and her employer sat in silence for some little while, then the young girl cried out: 'Francis, if you could, you wouldn't – would you?'

His voice was tender, his eyes loving. 'Not unless there's an "r" in the month . . .'

THE WEREWOLF AND THE VAMPIRE

GEORGE HARDCASTLE'S DOWNFALL undoubtedly originated in his love for dogs. He could not pass one without stopping and patting its head. A flea-bitten mongrel had only to turn the corner of the street and he was whistling, calling out: 'Come on, boy. Come on then,' and behaving in the altogether outrageous fashion that is peculiar to the devoted animal lover.

Tragedy may still have been averted had he not decided to spend a day in the Greensand Hills. Here in the region of Clandon Down, where dwarf oaks, pale birches and dark firs spread up in a long sweep to the northern heights, was a vast hiding place where many forms of often invisible life lurked in the dense undergrowth. But George, like many before him, knew nothing about this, and tramped happily up the slope, aware only that the air was fresh, the silence absolute and he was young.

The howl of what he supposed to be a dog brought him to an immediate standstill and for a while he listened, trying to determine from which direction the sound came. Afterwards he had reason to remember that none of the conditions laid down by legend and superstition prevailed. It was mid-afternoon and in consequence there was not, so far as he was aware, a full moon. The sun was sending golden spears of light through the thick foliage and all around was a warm, almost overpowering atmosphere, tainted with the aroma of decaying undergrowth. The setting was so commonplace and he was such an ordinary young man – not very bright perhaps, but gifted with good health and clean boyish good looks, the kind of Saxon comeliness that goes with a clear skin and blond hair.

The howl rang out again, a long, drawn-out cry of canine anguish, and now it was easily located. Way over to his left, somewhere in the midst of, or just beyond a curtain of, saplings and
low, thick bushes. Without thought of danger, George turned off
the beaten track and plunged into the dim twilight that held perpetual domain during the summer months under the interlocked
higher branches. Imagination supplied a mental picture of a gin-
trap and a tortured animal that was lost in a maze of pain. Pity lent
speed to his feet and made him ignore the stinging offshoots that
whipped at his face and hands, while brambles tore his trousers
and coiled round his ankles. The howl came again, now a little to
his right, but this time it was followed by a deep throated growl,
and if George had not been the person he was, he might have paid
heed to this warning note of danger.

For some fifteen minutes, he ran first in one direction, then
another, finally coming to rest under a giant oak which stood in
a small clearing. For the first time fear came to him in the surrounding gloom. It did not seem possible that one could get lost
in an English wood, but here, in the semi-light, he conceived the
ridiculous notion that night left its guardians in the wood during
the day, which would at any moment move in and smother him
with shadows.

He moved away from the protection of the oak tree and began
to walk in the direction he thought he had come, when the growl
erupted from a few yards to his left. Pity fled like a leaf before
a raging wind, and stark terror fired his brain with blind, unreasoning panic. He ran, fell, got up and ran again, and from behind
came the sound of a heavy body crashing through undergrowth,
the rasp of laboured breathing, the bestial growl of some enraged
being. Reason had gone, coherent thought had been replaced by
an animal instinct for survival; he knew that whatever ran behind
him was closing the gap.

Soon, and he dare not turn his head, it was but a few feet away.
There was snuffling, whining, terribly eager growling, and suddenly he shrieked as a fierce, burning pain seared his right thigh.
Then he was down on the ground and the agony rose up to become
a scarlet flame, until it was blotted out by a merciful darkness.

An hour passed, perhaps more, before George Hardcastle returned to consciousness. He lay quite still and tried to remember why he should be lying on the ground in a dense wood, while a dull ache held mastery over his right leg. Then memory sent its first cold tentacles shuddering across his brain and he dared to sit up and face reality.

The light had faded: night was slowly reinforcing its advance guard, but he was still able to see the dead man who lay but a few feet away. He shrank back with a little muffled cry and tried to dispel this vision of a purple face and bulging eyes, by the simple act of closing his own. But this was not a wise action for the image of that awful countenance was etched upon his brain, and the memory was even more macabre than the reality. He opened his eyes again, and there it was: a man in late middle life, with grey, close cropped hair, a long moustache and yellow teeth, that were bared in a death grin. The purple face suggested he had died of a sudden heart attack.

The next hour was a dimly remembered nightmare. George dragged himself through the undergrowth and by sheer good fortune emerged out on to one of the main paths.

He was found next morning by a team of boy scouts.

Police and an army of enthusiastic volunteers scoured the woods, but no trace of a ferocious wild beast was found. But they did find the dead man, and he proved to be a farm worker who had a reputation locally of being a person of solitary habits. An autopsy revealed he had died of a heart attack, and it was assumed that this had been the result of his efforts in trying to assist the injured boy.

The entire episode assumed the proportions of a nine-day wonder, and then was forgotten.

Mrs Hardcastle prided herself on being a mother who, while combating illness, did not pamper it. She had George back on his feet within three weeks and despatched him on prolonged walks. Being an obedient youth he followed these instructions to the letter, and so, on one overcast day, found himself at Hampton Court. As the first drops of rain were caressing his face, he decided to make a long-desired tour of the staterooms. He wandered from room to room, examined pictures, admired four-poster beds, then listened

to a guide who was explaining the finer points to a crowd of tour-
ists. By the time he had reached the Queen's Audience Room, he
felt tired, so seated himself on one of the convenient window-
seats. For some while he sat looking out at the rain-drenched gardens, then with a yawn, he turned and gave a quick glance along
the long corridor that ran through a series of open doorways.

Suddenly his attention was captured by a figure approaching
over the long carpet. It was that of a girl in a black dress; she was
a beautiful study in black and white. Black hair, white face and
hands, black dress. Not that there was anything sinister about her,
for as she drew nearer he could see the look of indescribable sadness in the large, black eyes, and the almost timid way she looked
round each room. Her appearance was outstanding, so vivid, like
a black and white photograph that had come to life.

She entered the Queen's Audience Room and now he could
hear the light tread of her feet, the whisper of her dress, and even
those small sounds seemed unreal. She walked round the room,
looking earnestly at the pictures, then as though arrested by a
sudden sound, she stopped. Suddenly the lovely eyes came round
and stared straight at George.

They held an expression of alarmed surprise, that gradually
changed to one of dawning wonderment. For a moment George
could only suppose she recognised him, although how he had
come to forget her, was beyond his comprehension. She glided
towards him, and as she came a small smile parted her lips. She
sank down on the far end of the seat and watched him with those
dark, wondering eyes.

She said: 'Hullo. I'm Carola.'

No girl had made such an obvious advance towards George
before, and shyness, not to mention shock, robbed him of speech.
Carola seemed to be reassured by his reticence, for her smile deep-
ened and when she spoke her voice held a gentle bantering tone.

'What's the matter? Cat got your tongue?'

This impertinent probe succeeded in freeing him from the
chains of shyness and he ventured to make a similar retort.

'I can speak when I want to.'

'That's better. I recognised the link at once. We have certain
family connections, really. Don't you think so?'

This question was enough to dry up his powers of communication for some time, but presently he was able to breathe one word. 'Family!'

'Yes.' She nodded and her hair trembled like black silk in sunlight. 'We must be at least distantly related in the allegorical sense. But don't let's talk about that. I am so pleased to be able to walk about in daylight. It is so dreary at night, and besides, I'm not really myself then.'

George came to the conclusion that this beautiful creature was at least slightly mad, and therefore made a mundane, but what he thought must be a safe remark.

'Isn't it awful weather?'

She frowned slightly and he got the impression he had committed a breach of good taste.

'Don't be so silly. You know it's lovely weather. Lots of beautiful cloud.'

He decided this must be a joke. There could be no other interpretation. He capped it by another.

'Yes, and soon the awful sun will come out.'

She flinched as though he had hit her, and there was the threat of tears in the lovely eyes.

'You beast. How could you say a dreadful thing like that? There won't be any sun, the weather forecast said so. I thought you were nice, but all you want to do is frighten me.'

And she dabbed her eyes with a black lace handkerchief, while George tried to find his way out of a mental labyrinth where every word seemed to have a double meaning.

'I am sorry. But I didn't mean . . .'

She stifled a tiny sob. 'How would you like it if I said – silver bullets?'

He scratched his head, wrinkled his brow and then made a wry grimace.

'I wouldn't know what you meant, but I wouldn't mind.'

She replaced the lace handkerchief in a small handbag, then got up and walked quickly away. George watched her retreating figure until it disappeared round the corner in the direction of the long gallery. He muttered: 'Potty. Stark raving potty.'

On reflection he decided it was a great pity that her behaviour was so erratic, because he would have dearly liked to have known her better. In fact, when he remembered the black hair and white face, he was aware of a deep disappointment, a sense of loss, and he had to subdue an urge to run after her. He remained seated in the window bay and when he looked out on to the gardens, he saw the rain had ceased, but thick cloud banks were billowing across the sky. He smiled gently and murmured, 'Lovely clouds – horrible sunshine.'

George was half way across Anne Boleyn's courtyard when a light touch on his shoulder made him turn, and there was Carola of the white face and black hair, with a sad smile parting her lips.

'Look,' she said, 'I'm sorry I got into a huff back there, but I can't bear to be teased about – well, you know what. But you are one of us, and we mustn't quarrel. All forgiven?'

George said, 'Yes, I'm sorry I offended you. But I didn't mean to.' And at that moment he was so happy, so ridiculously elated, he was prepared to apologise for breathing.

'Good.' She sighed and took hold of his arm as though it were the most natural action in the world. 'We'll forget all about it. But, please, don't joke about such things again.'

'No. Absolutely not.' George had not the slightest idea what it was he must not joke about, but made a mental note to avoid mention of the weather and silver bullets.

'You must come and meet my parents,' Carola insisted, 'they'll be awfully pleased to see you. I bet they won't believe their noses.'

This remark was in the nature of a setback, but George's newly found happiness enabled him to ignore it – pretend it must be a slip of the tongue.

'That's very kind of you, but won't it be a bit sudden? I mean, are you sure it will be convenient?'

She laughed, a lovely little silver sound and, if possible, his happiness increased.

'You are a funny boy. They'll be tickled pink, and so they should be. For the first time for years, we won't have to be careful of what we say in front of a visitor.'

George had a little mental conference and came to the conclusion that this was meant to be a compliment. So he said cheerfully, 'I don't mind what people say. I like them to be natural.'

Carola thought that was a very funny remark and tightened her grip on his arm, while laughing in a most enchanting fashion.

'You have a most wonderful sense of humour. Wait until I tell daddy that one. I like them to be natural . . .'

And she collapsed into a fit of helpless laughter in which George joined, although he was rather at a loss to know what he had said that was so funny. Suddenly the laugh was cut short, was killed by a gasp of alarm, and Carola was staring at the western sky where the clouds had taken on a brighter hue. The words came out as a strangled whisper.

'The sun! Oh, Lucifer, the sun is coming out.'

'Is it?' George looked up and examined the sky with assumed interest. 'I wouldn't be surprised if you're not right . . .' Then he stopped and looked down at his lovely companion with concern. 'I'm sorry, you . . . you don't like the sun, do you?'

Her face was a mask of terror and she gave a terrible little cry of anguish. George's former suspicion of insanity returned, but she was still appealing – still a flawless pearl on black velvet. He put his arm round the slim shoulders, and she hid her eyes against his coat. The muffled, tremulous whisper came to him.

'Please take me home. Quickly.'

He felt great joy in the fact that he was able to bring comfort.

'There's no sign of sunlight. Look, it was only a temporary break in the clouds.'

Slowly the dark head was raised, and the eyes, so bright with unshed tears, again looked up at the western sky. Now, George was rewarded, for her lips parted, the skin round her eyes crinkled and her entire face was transformed by a wonderful, glorious smile.

'Oh, how beautiful! Lovely, lovely, *lovely* clouds. The wind is up there, you know. A big, fat wind-god, who blows out great bellows of mist, so that we may not be destroyed by demon-sun. And sometimes he shrieks his rage across the sky; at others he whispers soft comforting words and tells us to have faith. The bleak night of loneliness is not without end.'

George was acutely embarrassed, not knowing what to make of this allegorical outburst. But the love and compassion he had so far extended to dogs, was now enlarged and channelled towards the lovely, if strange, young girl by his side.

'Come,' he said, 'let me take you home.'

George pulled open a trellis iron gate and allowed Carola to pre-
cede him up a crazy-paved path, which led to a house that gleamed
with new paint and well-cleaned windows. Such a house could
have been found in any one of a thousand streets in the London
suburbs, and brashly proclaimed that here lived a woman who
took pride in the crisp whiteness of her curtains, and a man who
was no novice in the art of wielding a paint brush. They had barely
entered the tiny porch, where the red tiles shone like a pool at
sunset, when the door was flung open and a plump, grey-haired
woman clasped Carola in her arms.

'Ee, love, me and yer dad were that worried. We thought you'd
got caught in a sun-storm.'

Carola kissed her mother gently, on what George noted was
another dead-white cheek, then turned and looked back at him
with shining eyes.

'Mummy, this . . .' She giggled and shook her head. 'It's silly, but
I don't know your name.'

'George. George Hardcastle.'

To say Carola's mother looked alarmed is a gross understatement. For a moment she appeared to be terrified, and clutched her
daughter as though they were both confronted by a man-eating
tiger. Then Carola laughed softly and whispered into her mother's
ear. George watched the elder woman's expression change to one
of incredulity and dawning pleasure.

'You don't say so, love? Where on earth did you find him?'

'In the Palace,' Carola announced proudly. 'He was sitting in
the Queen's Audience Room.'

Mummy almost ran forward and after clasping the startled
George with both hands, kissed him soundly on either cheek.
Then she stood back and examined him with obvious pleasure.

'I ought to have known,' she said, nodding her head as though
with sincere conviction. 'Been out of touch for too long. But what
will you think of me manners? Come in, love. Father will be that
pleased. It's not much of a death for him, with just us two women
around.'

Again George was aware of a strange slip of the tongue, which he could only assume was a family failing. So he beamed with the affability that is expected from a stranger who is the recipient of sudden hospitality, and allowed himself to be pulled into a newly decorated hall, and relieved of his coat. Then Mummy opened a door and ordered in a shouted whisper: 'Father, put yer tie on, we've got company.' There was a startled snort, as though some-one had been awakened from a fireside sleep, and Mummy turned a bright smile on George.

'Would you like to go upstairs and wash yer hands, like? Make yourself comfy, if you get my meaning.'

'No, thank you. Very kind, I'm sure.'

'Well then, you'd best come into parlour.'

The 'parlour' had a very nice paper on the walls, bright pink lamps, a well stuffed sofa and matching armchairs, a large televi-sion set, a low, imitation walnut table, a record player, some awful coloured prints, and an artificial log electric fire. A stout man with thinning grey hair struggled up from the sofa, while he completed the adjustment of a tie that was more eye-catching than taste-ful.

'Father,' Mummy looked quickly round the room as though to seek reassurance that nothing was out of place, 'this is George. A young man that Carola has brought home, like.' Then she added in an undertone, 'He's all right. No need to worry.'

Father advanced with outstretched hand and announced in a loud, very hearty voice: 'Ee, I'm pleased to meet ye, lad. I've always said it's about time the lass found 'erself a young spark. But the reet sort is 'ard to come by, and that's a fact.'

Father's hand was unpleasantly cold and flabby, but he radiated such an air of goodwill, George was inclined to overlook it.

'Now, Father, you're embarrassing our Carola,' Mummy said. And indeed the girl did appear to be somewhat disconcerted, only her cheeks instead of blushing, had assumed a greyish tinge. 'Now, George, don't stand around, lad. Sit yerself down and make yerself at 'ome. We don't stand on ceremony here.'

George found himself on the sofa next to Father, who would insist on winking, whenever their glances met. In the meanwhile Mummy expressed solicitous anxiety regarding his well-being.

'Have you supped lately? I know you young doggies don't 'ave to watch yer diet like we do, so just say what you fancy. I've a nice piece of 'am in t' fridge, and I can fry that with eggs, in no time at all.'

George knew that somewhere in that kindly invitation there had been another slip of the tongue, but he resolutely did not think about it.

'That's very kind of you, but really . . .'

'Let 'er do a bit of cooking, lad,' Father pleaded. 'She don't get much opportunity, if I can speak without dotting me Is and crossing me Ts.'

'If you are sure it will be no trouble.'

Mummy made a strange neighing sound. 'Trouble! 'Ow you carry on. It's time for us to have a glass of something rich, anyway.'

Mother and daughter departed for the kitchen and George was left alone with Father who was watching him with an embarrassing interest.

'Been on 'olidays yet, lad?' he enquired.

'No, it's a bit late now . . .'

Father sighed with the satisfaction of a man who is recalling a pleasant memory. 'We 'ad smashing time in Clacton. Ee, the weather was summat greet. Two weeks of thick fog – couldn't see 'and in front of face.'

George said, 'Oh, dear,' then lapsed into silence while he digested this piece of information. Presently he was aware of an elbow nudging his ribs.

'I know it's delicate question, lad, so don't answer if you'd rather not. But – 'ow often do you change?'

George thought it was a very delicate question, and could only think of a very indelicate reason why it had been asked. But his conception of politeness demanded he answer.

'Well . . . every Friday actually. After I've had a bath.'

Father gasped with astonishment. 'As often as that! I'm surprised. The last lad I knew in your condition only changed when the moon was full.'

George said, 'Goodness gracious!' and then tried to ask a very pertinent question. 'Why, do I . . .'

Father nodded. 'There's a goodish pong. But don't let it worry you. We can smell it, because we've the reet kind of noses.'

An extremely miserable, not to say self-conscious, young man was presently led across the hall and into the dining-room, where one place was set with knife, fork and spoon, and three with glass and drinking straw. He was too dejected to pay particular heed to this strange and unequal arrangement, and neither was he able to really enjoy the plate of fried eggs and ham that Mummy put down before him, with the remark: 'Here you are, lad, get wrapped round that, and you'll not starve.'

The family shared the contents of a glass jug between them, and as this was thick and red, George could only suppose it to be tomato juice. They all sucked through straws; Carola, as was to be expected, daintily, Mummy with some anxiety, and Father greedily. When he had emptied his glass, he presented it for a refill and said: 'You know Mother, that's as fine a jug of AB as you've ever served up.'

Mummy sighed. 'It's not so bad. Mind you, youngsters don't get what I call top grade nourishment, these days. There's nothing like getting yer teeth stuck into the real thing. This stuff 'as lost the natural goodness.'

Father belched and made a disgusting noise with his straw.

'We must be thankful, Mother. There's many who 'asn't a drop to wet their lips, and be pleased to sup from tin.'

George could not subdue a natural curiosity and the question slipped out before he had time to really think about it.

'Excuse me, but don't you ever eat anything?'

The shocked silence which followed told him he had committed a well nigh unforgivable sin. Father dropped his glass and Carola said, 'Oh, George,' in a very reproachful voice, while Mummy creased her brow into a very deep frown.

'George, haven't you ever been taught manners?'

It was easy to see she spoke more in sorrow than anger, and although the exact nature of his transgression was not quite clear to George, he instantly apologised.

'I am very sorry, but . . .'

'I should think so, indeed.' Mummy continued to speak gently but firmly. 'I never expected to hear a question like that at my table. After all, you wouldn't like it if I were to ask who or what you chewed up on one of your moonlight strolls. Well, I've said me piece, and now we'll forget that certain words were ever said. Have some chocolate pudding.'

Even while George smarted under this rebuke, he was aware that once again, not so much a slip of the tongue, as a sentence that demanded thought had been inserted between an admonishment and a pardon. There was also a growing feeling of resentment. It seemed that whatever he said to this remarkable family, gave offence, and his supply of apologies was running low. He waited until Mummy had served him with a generous helping of chocolate pudding, and then replenished the three glasses from the jug, before he relieved his mind.

'I don't chew anyone.'

Mummy gave Father an eloquent glance, and he cleared his throat.

'Listen, lad, there are some things you don't mention in front of ladies. What you do in change period is between you and black man. So let's change subject.'

Like all peace-loving people George sometimes reached a point where war, or to be more precise, attack seemed to be the only course of action. Father's little tirade brought him to such a point. He flung down his knife and fork and voiced his complaints.

'Look here, I'm fed up. If I mention the weather, I'm ticked off. If I ask why you never eat, I'm in trouble. I've been asked when I change, told that I stink. Now, after being accused of chewing people, I'm told I mustn't mention it. Now, I'll tell you something. I think you're all round the bend.'

Carola burst into tears and ran from the room: Father swore, or rather he said, 'Satan's necktie,' which was presumably the same thing, and Mummy looked very concerned.

'Just a minute, son,' she raised a white, rather wrinkled forefinger, 'you're trying to tell us you don't know the score?'

'I haven't the slightest idea what you're talking about,' George retorted.

Mummy and Father looked at each other for some little while, then as though prompted by a single thought, they both spoke in unison.

'He's a just bittener.'

'Someone should tell 'im,' Mummy stated, after she had watched the, by now, very frightened George for an entire minute. 'It should come from a man.'

'If 'e 'ad gumption he were born with, 'e'd know,' Father said, his face becoming quite grey with embarrassment. 'Hell's bells, my dad didn't 'ave to tell me I were vampire.'

'Yes, but you can see he's none too bright,' Mummy pointed out. 'We can't all 'ave your brains. No doubt the lad has 'eart, and I say 'eart is better than brains any day. Been bitten lately, lad?'

George could only nod and look longingly at the door.

'Big long thing, with a wet snout, I wouldn't be surprised. It's a werewolf you are, son. You can't deceive the noses of we vamps: yer glands are beginning to play up – give out a bit of smell, see? I should think . . . What's the state of the moon, Father?'

'Seven eighths.'

Mummy nodded with grim relish. 'I should think you're due for a change round about Friday night. Got any open space round your way?'

'There's . . .' George took a deep breath, 'there's Clapham Common.'

'Well, I should go for a run round there. Make sure you cover your face up. Normal people go all funny like when they first lays eyes on a werewolf. Start yelling their 'eads off, mostly.'

George was on his feet and edging his way towards the door. He was praying for the priceless gift of disbelief. Mummy was again displaying signs of annoyance.

'Now there's no need to carry on like that. You must 'ave known we were all vampires – what did you think we were drinking? Raspberry juice? And let me tell you this. We're the best friends you've got. No one else will want to know you, once full moon is peeping over barn door. So don't get all lawn tennis with us . . .'

But George was gone. Running across the hall, out of the front door, down the crazy-paving path, and finally along the pavement. People turned their heads as he shouted: 'They're mad . . . mad . . . mad . . .'

There came to George – as the moon waxed full – a strange restlessness. It began with insomnia, which rocketed him out of a deep sleep into a strange, instant wakefulness. He became aware

of an urge to go for long moonlit walks; and when he had surrendered to this temptation, an overwhelming need to run, leap, roll
over and over down a grassy bank, anything that would enable him
to break down the hated walls of human convention – and express.
A great joy – greater than he had ever known – came to him when
he leaped and danced on the common, and could only be released
by a shrill, doglike howl that rose up from the sleeping suburbs and
went out, swift as a beam of light, to the face of mother-moon.

This joy had to be paid for. When the sun sent its first enquiring
rays in through George's window, sanity returned and demanded
a reckoning. He examined his face and hands with fearful expectancy. So far as he was aware there had been no terrible change,
as yet. But these were early days – or was it nights? Sometimes he
would fling himself down on his bed and cry out his great desire
for disbelief.

'It can't happen. Mad people are sending me mad.'

The growing strangeness of his behaviour could not go unde-
tected. He was becoming withdrawn, apt to start at every sound
and betrayed a certain distrust of strangers by an eerie widening
of his eyes, and later, the baring of his teeth in a mirthless grin.
His mother commented on these peculiarities in forcible language.

'I think you're going up the pole. Honest I do. The milkman
told me yesterday, he saw you snarling at Mrs Redfern's dog.'

'It jumped out at me,' George explained. 'You might have done
the same.'

Mrs Hardcastle shook her head. 'No. I can honestly say I've
never snarled at a dog in my life. You never inherited snarling from
me.'

'I'm all right.' George pleaded for reassurance. 'I'm not turning
into – anything.'

'Well, you should know.' George could not help thinking that
his mother was regarding him with academic interest, rather than
concern. 'Do you go out at nights after I'm asleep?'

He found it impossible to lie convincingly, so he countered one
question with another. 'Why should I do that?'

'Don't ask me. But some nut has been seen prancing round the
common at three o'clock in the morning. I just wondered.'

The physical change came gradually. One night he woke with

a severe pain in his right hand and lay still for a while, not daring to examine it. Then he switched on the bedside lamp with his left hand and after further hesitation, brought its right counterpart out from the sheets. A thick down had spread over the entire palm and he found the fingers would not straighten. They had curved and the nails were thicker and longer than he remembered. After a while the fear – the loathing – went away, and it seemed most natural for him to have claws for fingers and hair-covered hands. Next morning his right hand was as normal as his left, and at that period he was still able to dismiss, even if with little conviction, the episode as a bad dream.

But one night there was a dream – a nightmare of the blackest kind, where fantasy blended with fact and George was unable to distinguish one from the other. He was running over the common, bounding with long, graceful leaps, and there was a wonderful joy in his heart and a limitless freedom in his head. He was in a black and white world. Black grass, white tinted trees, grey sky, white moon. But with all the joy, all the freedom, there was a subtle, ever-present knowledge, that this was an unnatural experience, that he should be utilising all his senses to dispel. Once his brain, that part which was still unoccupied territory, screamed: 'Wake up,' but he was awake, for did not the black grass crunch beneath his feet, and the night breeze ruffled his fur? A large cat was running in front, trying to escape – up trees – across the roofs – round bushes – he finally trapped it in a hole. Shrieks – scratching claws – warm blood – tearing teeth . . . It was good. He was fulfilled.

Next morning when he awoke in his own bed, it could have been dismissed as a mad dream, were it not for the scratches on his face and hands and the blood in his hair. He thought of psychiatrists, asylums, priests, religion, and at last came to the only possible conclusion. There was, so far as he knew, only one set of people on earth who could explain and understand.

Mummy let George in. Father shook him firmly by the hand. Carola kissed him gently and put an arm round his shoulders when he started to cry.

'We don't ask to be what we are,' she whispered. 'We keep more horror than we give away.'

'We all 'ave our place in the great graveyard,' Father said. 'You hunt, we sup, ghouls tear, shaddies lick, mocks blow, and fortunately shadmocks can only whistle.'

'Will I always be – what I am?' George asked.

They all nodded. Mummy grimly, Father knowingly, Carola sadly.

'Until the moon leaves the sky,' they all chanted.

'Or you are struck in the heart by a silver bullet,' Carola whispered, 'fired by one who has only thought about sin. Or maybe when you are very, very old, the heart may give out after a transformation . . .'

'Don't be morbid,' Mummy ordered. 'Poor lad's got enough on plate without you adding to it. Make him a nice cup of tea. And you can mix us a jug of something rich while you're about it. Don't be too 'eavy handed on the O group.'

They sat round the artificial log fire, drinking tea, absorbing nourishment, three giving, one receiving advice, and there was a measure of cosiness.

'All "M's" should keep away from churches, parsons and boy scouts,' Father said.

'Run from a cross and fly from a prayer,' intoned Mummy.

'Two can run better than one,' Carola observed shyly.

Next day George told his mother he intended to leave home and set up house for himself. Mrs Hardcastle did not argue as strongly as she might have had a few weeks earlier. What with one thing and another, there was a distinct feeling that the George, who was standing so grim and white faced in the kitchen doorway, was not the one she had started out with. She said, 'Right, then. I'd say it's about time,' and helped him to pack.

Father, who knew someone in the building line, found George a four-roomed cottage that was situated on the edge of a churchyard, and this he furnished with a few odds and ends that the family were willing to part with. The end product was by no means as elegant or deceptive as the house at Hampton Court, but it was somewhere for George to come back to after his midnight run.

He found the old legends had been embellished, for he experienced no urge to rend or even bite. There was no reason why he should; the body was well fed and the animal kingdom only hunts when goaded by hunger. It was sufficient for him to run, leap, chase his tail by moonlight, and sometimes howl with the pure joy of living. And it is pleasant to record that his joy grew day by day.

For obvious reasons the wedding took place in a registry office, and it seemed that the dark gods smiled down upon the union, for there was a thick fog that lasted from dawn to sunset. The wedding-supper and the reception which followed were, of necessity, simple affairs. There was a wedding cake for those that could eat it: a beautiful, three-tier structure, covered with pink icing, and studded with what George hoped were glacé cherries. He of course had invited no guests, for there was much that might have alarmed or embarrassed the uninitiated. Three ghouls in starched, white shrouds, sat gnawing something that was best left undescribed. The bride and her family sipped a basic beverage from red goblets, and as the bridegroom was due for a turn, he snarled when asked to pass the salt. Then there was Uncle Deitmark, a vampire of the old school, who kept demanding a trussed-up victim, so that he could take his nourishment direct from the neck.

But finally the happy couple were allowed to depart, and Mummy and Father wept as they threw the traditional coffin nails after the departing hearse. 'Ee, it were champion,' Father exclaimed, wiping his eyes on the back of his hand. 'Best blood-up I've seen for many a day. You did 'em proud, Mother.'

'I believe in giving the young 'uns a good send off,' Mummy said. 'Now they must open their own vein, as the saying goes.'

Carola and George watched the moon come up over the church steeple, which was a little dangerous for it threw the cross into strong relief, but on that one night they would have defied the very pope of Rome himself.

'We are no longer alone,' Carola whispered. 'We love and are loved, and that surely has transformed us from monsters into gods.'

'If happiness can transform a tumbledown cottage into paradise,' George said, running his as yet uncurved fingers through her hair, 'then I guess we are gods.'

But he forgot that every paradise must have its snake, and their particular serpent was disguised in the rotund shape of the Reverend John Cole. This worthy cleric had an allegorical nose for smelling out hypothetical evil, and it was not long before he was considering the inhabitants of the house by the churchyard with a speculative eye.

He called when George was out and invited Carola to join the young wives' altar dressing committee. She turned grey and begged to be excused. Mr Cole then suggested she partake in a brief reading from holy scripture, and Carola shrank from the proffered Bible, even as a rabbit recoils from a hooded cobra. Then the Reverend John Cole accidentally dropped his crucifix on to her lap, and she screamed like one who is in great pain, before falling to the floor in a deathlike faint. And the holy minister departed with the great joy that comes to the sadist who knows he is only doing his duty.

Next day George met the Reverend Cole, who was hastening to the death bed of a sinful woman, and laid a not too gentle hand on the flabby arm.

'I understand you frightened my wife, when I was out yesterday.'

The clergyman bared his teeth and although George was now in the shape with which he had been born, they resembled two dogs preparing to fight.

'I'm wondering,' the Reverend Cole said, 'what kind of woman recoils from the good book and screams when the crucifix touches her.'

'Well, it's like this,' George tightened his grip on the black-clad arm, 'we are both allergic to bibles, crosses and nosy parsons. I am apt to burn one, break two, and pulverise three. Am I getting through?'

'And I have a duty before God and man,' John Cole said, looking down at the retaining hand with marked distaste, 'and that is to stamp out evil wherever it be found. And may I add, with whatever means that are at my disposal.'

They parted in mutual hate, and George in his innocence decided to use fear as an offensive weapon, not realising that its wounds strengthen resistance more often than they weaken. One night, when the moon was full, turning the graveyard into a gothic wonderland, the Reverend John Cole met something that robbed him of speech for nigh on twelve hours. It walked on bent hindlegs, and had two very long arms which terminated in talons that seemed hungry for the ecclesiastical throat, and a nightmare face whose predominant feature was a long, slavering snout.

At the same time, Mrs Cole, a very timid lady who had yet to learn of the protective virtues of two pieces of crossed wood, was trying so hard not to scream as a white-faced young woman advanced across the bedroom. The reaction of husband and wife was typical of their individual characters. The Reverend John Cole after the initial cry did not stop running until he was safely barricaded in the church with a processional cross jammed across the doorway. Mrs Cole, being unable to scream, promptly fainted, and hence fared worse than her fleetfooted spouse. John Cole, after his run was a little short of breath: Mary Cole, when she returned to consciousness, was a little short of blood.

Mr Cole was an erratic man who often preached sermons guaranteed to raise the scalps of the most urbane congregation, if that is to say, they took the trouble to listen. The tirade which was poured out from the pulpit on the Sunday after Mrs Cole's loss and Mr Cole's fright, woke three slumbering worshippers, and caused a choirboy to swallow his chewing-gum.

'The devil has planted his emissaries in our midst,' the vicar proclaimed. 'Aye, do they dwell in the church precincts and do appear to the God-fearing in their bestial form.'

The chewing-gum bereft choirboy giggled, and Mr Cole's wrath rose and erupted into admonishing words.

'Laugh not. I say to you of little faith, laugh not. For did I not come face to face – aye, but a few yards from where you now sit – with a fearsome beast that did drool and nuzzle, and I feared that my windpipe might soon lie upon my shirt-front. But, and this be the truth, which did turn my bowels to water, there was the certain knowledge that I was in the presence of a creature that is without precedence in Satan's hierarchy – the one – the only – the black angel of hell – the dreaded werewolf.'

At least ten people in the congregation thought their vicar had at last turned the corner and become stark raving mad. Twenty more did not understand what he was talking about, and one old lady assumed she was listening to a brilliant interpretation of Revelation, chapter XIII, verses 1 to 3. The remainder of the congregation had not been listening, but noted the vicar was in fine fettle, roaring and pounding the pulpit with his customary gusto. His next disclosure suffered roughly the same reception.

'My dear wife – my helpmeet, who has walked by my side these past twenty years – was visited in her chamber by a female of the species . . .' Mr Cole nodded bitterly. 'A vampire, an unclean thing that has crept from its foul grave, and did take from my dear one, that which she could ill afford to lose . . .'

Ignorance, inattention, Mr Cole's words fell on very stony ground and no one believed – save Willie Mitcham. Willie did believe in vampires, werewolves and, in fact, also accepted the existence of banshees, demons, poltergeists, ghosts of every description, monsters of every shape and form, and the long wriggly thing, which as everyone knows, has yet to be named. As Willie was only twelve years of age, he naturally revelled in his belief, and moreover made himself an expert on demonology. To his father's secret delectation and his mother's openly expressed horror, he had an entire cupboard filled with literature that dwelt on every aspect of the subject. He knew, for example, that the only sure way of getting a banshee off your back is to spit three times into an open grave, bow three times to the moon, then chant in a loud voice:

> Go to the north, go to the south,
> Go to the devil, but shut your mouth.
> Scream not by day, or howl by night,
> But gibber alone by candlelight.

He also knew, for had not the facts been advertised by printed page, television set and cinema screen, that the only sure way of killing a vampire is to drive a sharp pointed object through its heart between the hours of sunrise and sunset. He was also joyfully aware of the fatal consequences that attend the arrival of a silver bullet in a werewolf's hairy chest. So it was that Willie listened to the Reverend John Cole with ears that heard and understood, and he wanted so desperately to shout out the simple and time honoured cures, the withal, the ways and means, the full, glorious and gory details. But his mother nudged him in the ribs and told him to stop fidgeting, so he could only sit and seethe with well-nigh uncontrollable impatience.

One bright morning in early March the total population of the graveyard cottage was increased by one. The newly risen sun peeped in through the neatly curtained windows and gazed down upon, what it is to be hoped, was the first baby werevamp. It was like all newly born infants, small, wrinkled, extremely ugly, and favoured its mother in so far as it had been born with two prominent eye-teeth. Instead of crying it made a harsh hissing sound, not unlike that of an infant king-cobra, and was apt to bite anything that moved.

'Isn't he sweet?' Carola sighed, then waved a finger at her off-spring, who promptly curled back an upper lip and made a hissing snarl. 'Yes he is . . . he's a sweet 'ickle diddums . . . he's mummy's 'ickle diddums . . .'

'I think he's going to be awfully clever,' George stated after a while. 'What with that broad forehead and those dark eyes, one can see there is a great potential for intelligence. He's got your mouth, darling.'

'Not yet he hasn't,' Carola retorted, 'but he soon will have, if I'm not careful. I suppose he's in his humvamp period now, but when the moon is full, he'll have sweet little hairy talons, and a dinky-winky little tail.'

Events proved her to be absolutely correct.

The Reverend John Cole allowed several weeks to pass before he made an official call on the young parents. During this time he reinforced his courage, of which it must be confessed he had an abundance; sought advice from his superiors, who were not at all helpful, and tried to convince anyone who would listen of the danger in their midst. His congregation shrank, people crossed the road whenever he came into view, and he was constantly badgered by a wretched little boy, who poured out a torrent of nauseating information. But at last the vicar was as ready for the fatal encounter as he ever would be, and so, armed with a crucifix, faith and a small bottle of whisky, he went forth to do battle. From his bedroom window that overlooked the vicarage, Willie Mitcham watched the black figure as it trudged along the road. He flung the window open and shouted: 'Yer daft coot. It's a full moon.'

No one answered Mr Cole's thunderous assault on the front door. This was not surprising as Carola was paying Mrs Cole another visit, and George was chasing a very disturbed sheep across a stretch of open moorland. Baby had not yet reached the age when answering doors would be numbered among his accomplishments. At last the reverend gentleman opened the door and after crossing himself with great fervour, entered the cottage.

He found himself in the living-room, a cosy little den with whitewashed walls, two ancient chairs, a folding table, and some very nice rugs on the floor. There was also a banked up fire, and a beautiful old ceiling oil-lamp that George had cleverly adapted for electricity. Mr Cole called out: 'Anyone there?' and receiving no answer, sank down into one of the chairs to wait. Presently, the chair being comfortable, the room warm, the clergyman felt his caution dissolve into a hazy atmosphere of well-being. His head nodded, his eyelids flickered, his mouth fell open and in no time at all, a series of gentle snores filled the room with their even cadence.

It is right to say Mr Cole fell asleep reluctantly, and while he slept he displayed a certain amount of dignity. But he awoke with a shriek and began to thresh about in a most undignified manner. There was a searing pain in his right ankle, and when he moved something soft and rather heavy flopped over his right foot and at the same time made a strange hissing sound. The vicar screamed again and kicked out with all his strength, and that which clung to his ankle went hurling across the room and landed on a rug near the window. It hissed, yelped, then turning over, began to crawl back towards the near prostrate clergyman. He tried to close his eyes, but they insisted in remaining open and so permitted him to see something that a person with a depraved sense of humour might have called a baby. A tiny, little white – oh, so white – face, which had two microscopic fangs jutting out over the lower lip. But for the rest it was very hairy; had two wee claws, and a proudly erect, minute tail, that was at this particular moment in time, lashing angrily from side to side. Its little hind legs acted as projectors and enabled the hair-covered torso to leap along at quite an amazing speed. There was also a smear of Mr Cole's blood round the mouth; and the eyes held an expression that suggested the ecclesiastial fluid was appealing to the taste-buds, and their owner could hardly wait to get back to the fount of nourishment.

Mr Cole released three long drawn out screams, then, remembering that legs have a decided and basic purpose, leaped for the door. It was truly an awe-inspiring sight to see a portly clergyman who had more than reached the years of discretion, running between graves, leaping over tombstones, and sprinting along paths. Baby-werevamp squatted on his hind legs and looked as wistfully as his visage permitted after the swiftly retreating cleric. After a while, baby set up a prolonged howl, and thumped the floor with clenched claws. His distress was understandable. He had just seen a well-filled feeding bottle go running out of the door.

Willie Mitcham had at last got through. One of the stupid, blind, not to mention thick-headed adults had been finally shocked into seeing the light. When Willie found the Reverend John Cole entangled in a hawthorn bush, he also stumbled on a man who was willing to listen to advice from any source. He had also retreated from the frontiers of sanity, and was therefore in a position to be driven, rather than to command.

'I saw 'im.' Willie was possibly the happiest boy in the world at that moment. 'I saw 'im with his 'orrible fangs and he went leaping towards the moors.'

Mr Cole said, 'Ah!' and began to count his fingers.

'And I saw 'er,' Willie went on. 'She went to your house and drifted up to the main bedroom window. Just like in the film *The Mark of the Vampire.*'

'Destroy all evil,' the Reverend Cole shouted. 'Root it out. Cut into . . .'

'Its 'eart,' Willie breathed. 'The way to kill a vampire is drive a stake through its 'eart. And a werewolf must be shot with a silver bullet fired by 'im who has only thought about sin.'

'From what authority do you quote this information?' the vicar demanded.

'Me 'orror comics,' Willie explained. 'They give all the details, and if you go and see the *Vampire of 'Ackney Wick*, you'll see a 'oly father cut off the vampire's 'ead and put a sprig of garlic in its mouth.'

'Where are these documents?' the clergyman enquired.

Mr and Mrs Mitcham were surprised and perhaps a little alarmed when their small son conducted the vicar through the kitchen and after a perfunctory: 'It's all right, mum, parson wants to see me 'orror comics,' led the frozen-faced clergyman upstairs to the attic.

It was there that Mr Cole's education was completed. Assisted by lurid pictures and sensational text, he learned of the conception, habits, hobbies and disposal procedures of vampires, werewolves and other breathing or non-breathing creatures that had attended the same school.

'Where do we get . . . ?' he began.

'A tent peg and mum's coal 'ammer will do fine,' Willie was quick to give expert advice.

'But a silver bullet,' the vicar shook his head. 'I cannot believe there is a great demand . . .'

'Two of grandad's silver collar studs melted down with a soldering iron, and a cartridge from dad's old .22 rifle. Mr Cole; please say we can do it. I promise never to miss Sunday school again, if you'll say we can do it.'

The Reverend John Cole did not consider the problem very long. A bite from a baby werevamp is a great decision maker.

'Yes,' he nodded, 'we have been chosen. Let us gird up our loins, gather the sinews of battle, and go forth to destroy the evil ones.'

'Coo!' Willie nodded vigorously. 'All that blood. Can I cut 'er 'ead off?'

If anyone had been taking the air at two o'clock next morning, they might have seen an interesting sight. A large clergyman, armed with a crucifix and a coal hammer was creeping across the churchyard, followed by a small boy with a tent peg in one hand and a light hunting rifle in the other.

They came to the cottage and Mr Cole first turned the handle, then pushed the door open with his crucifix. The room beyond was warm and cosy, firelight painted a dancing pattern on the ceiling, the brass lamp twinkled and glittered like a suspended star, and it was as though a brightly designed nest had been carved out of the surrounding darkness. John Cole strode into the room like a black marble angel of doom, and raising his crucifix bellowed: 'I have come to drive out the iniquity, burn out the sin. For, thus saith the Lord, cursed be you who hanker after darkness.'

There was a sigh, a whimper – maybe a hissing whimper. Carola was crouched in one corner, her face whiter than a slab of snow in moonlight, her eyes dark pools of terror, her lips deep, deep red, as though they had been brought to life by a million, blood-tinted kisses, and her hands were pale ghost-moths, beating out their life against the invisible wall of intolerance. The vicar lowered his cross and the whimper grew up and became a cry of despair.

'Why?'

'Where is the foul babe that did bite my ankle?'

Carola's staring eyes never left the crucifix towering over her.

'I took him . . . took him . . . to his grandmother.'

'There is more of your kind? Are you legion? Has the devil's spawn been hatched?'

'We are on the verge of extinction.'

The soul of the Reverend John Cole rejoiced when he saw the deep terror in the lovely eyes, and he tasted the fruits of true happiness when she shrieked. He bunched the front of her dress up between trembling fingers and jerked her first upright, then down across the table. She made a little hissing sound; an instinctive token of defiance, and for a moment the delicate ivory fangs were bared and nipped the clergyman's hand, but that was all. There was no savage fight for existence, no calling on the dark gods; just a token resistance, the shedding of a tiny dribble of blood, then complete surrender. She lay back across the table, her long, black hair brushing the floor, as though this were the inevitable conclusion from which she had been too long withheld. The vicar placed the tip of the tent peg over her heart, and taking the coal hammer from the overjoyed Willie, shouted the traditional words.

'Get thee to hell. Burn for ever and a day. May thy foul carcase be food for jackals, and thy blood drink for pariah dogs.'

The first blow sent the tent peg in three or four inches, and the sound of a snapping rib grated on the clergyman's ear, so that for a moment he turned his head aside in revulsion. Then, as though alarmed lest his resolve weaken, he struck again, and the blood rose up in a scarlet fountain; a cascade of dancing rubies, each one reflecting the room with its starlike lamp, and the dripping, drenched face of a man with a raised coal hammer. The hammer, like the mailed hand of fate, fell again, and the ruby fountain sank low, then collapsed into a weakly gushing pool. Carola released her life in one long, drawn out sigh, then became a black and white study in still life.

'You gotta cut 'er 'ead off,' Willie screamed. 'Ain't no good, unless you cut 'er 'ead off and put a sprig of garlic in 'er mouth.'

But Mr Cole had, at least temporarily, had a surfeit of blood. It matted his hair, clogged his eyes, salted his mouth, drenched his clothes from neck to waist, and transformed his hands into scarlet claws.

Willie was fumbling in his jacket pocket.

'I've got me mum's bread knife here, somewhere. Should go through 'er neck a treat.'

The reverend gentleman wiped a film of red from his eyes and then daintily shook his fingers.

'Truly is it said a little child shall lead them. Had I been more mindful of the Lord's business, I would have brought me a tenon saw.'

He was not more than half way through his appointed task, when the door was flung back and George entered. He was on the turn. He was either about to 'become', or return to 'as was'. His silhouette filled the moonlit doorway, and he became still; a black menace that was no less dangerous because it did not move. Then he glided across the room, round the table and the Reverend John Cole retreated before him.

George gathered up the mutilated remains of his beloved, then raised agony-filled eyes.

'We loved – she and I. Surely, that should have forgiven us much. Death we would have welcomed – for what is death, but a glorious reward for having to live. But this . . .'

He pointed to the jutting tent peg, the half-severed head, then looked up questioningly at the clergyman. Then the Reverend John Cole took up his cross and holding it before him he called out in a voice that had been made harsh by the dust of centuries.

'I am Alpha and Omega saith the Lord, and into the pit which is before the beginning and after the end, shall ye be cast. For you and your kind are a stench and an abomination, and whatever evil is done unto you, shall be deemed good in my sight.'

The face of George Hardcastle became like an effigy carved from rock. Then it seemed to shimmer, the lines dissolved and ran one into the other; the hairline advanced, while the eyes retreated into deep sockets, and the jaw and nose merged and slithered into a long, pointed snout. The werewolf dropped the mangled remains of its mate and advanced upon her killer.

'Satanus Avaunt.'

The Reverend Cole thrust his crucifix forward as though it were a weapon of offence, only to have it wrenched from his grasp and broken by a quick jerk of hair covered wrists. The werewolf tossed the pieces to one side, then with a howl leaped forward and buried his long fangs into the vicar's shoulder.

The two locked figures, one representing good, the other evil, swayed back and forth in the lamplight, and there was no room in either hate-fear filled brain for the image of one small boy, armed with a rifle. The sharp little cracking sound could barely be heard above the grunting, snarling battle that was being raged near the hanging brass lamp, but the result was soon apparent. The werewolf shrieked, before twisting round and staring at the exuberant Willie, as though in dumb reproach. Then it crashed to the floor. When the clergyman had recovered sufficiently to look down, he saw the dead face of George Hardcastle, and had he been a little to the right of the sanity frontier, there might well have been terrible doubts.

'Are you going to finish cutting off 'er head?' Willie enquired.

They put the Reverend John Cole in a quiet house surrounded by a beautiful garden. Willie Mitcham they placed in a home, as a juvenile court decided in its wisdom, that he was in need of care and protection. The remains of George and Carola they buried in the churchyard and said some beautiful words over their graves.

It is a great pity they did not listen to Willie, who after all knew what he was talking about when it came to a certain subject.

One evening, when the moon was full, two gentlemen who were employed in the house surrounded by the beautiful garden, opened the door, behind which resided all that remained of the Reverend John Cole. They both entered the room and prepared to talk. They never did. One dropped dead from pure, cold terror, and the other achieved a state of insanity which had so far not been reached by one of his patients.

The Reverend John Cole had been bitten by a baby werevamp, nipped by a female vampire, and clawed and bitten by a full-blooded, buck werewolf.

Only the good Lord above, and the bad one below, knew what he was.

ABOUT THE AUTHOR

RONALD HENRY GLYNN CHETWYND-HAYES was born in Isleworth, west London, in 1919. He grew up a film fan, and in between working odd jobs appeared as an extra in several pictures, including *A Yank at Oxford* (1938), which starred Lionel Barrymore, Vivien Leigh, and Maureen O'Sullivan, and *Goodbye, Mr. Chips* (1939). He served during the Second World War, and after demobilization returned to London and worked in furniture sales. He sold his first short story in 1953, and his first novel, a science fiction tale, *The Man from the Bomb*, was published in 1959. He went on to write some 200 short stories and a dozen novels and also edited anthologies, including twelve volumes of the *Fontana Book of Great Ghost Stories*. Known as 'Britain's Prince of Chill', Chetwynd-Hayes developed a reputation and a large fan base for his old-fashioned ghost stories and his tongue-in-cheek monster tales. Though Chetwynd-Hayes's works were not always huge sellers, his books were always in high demand with library patrons, and he was consistently among Britain's top earners of public lending rights. In 1989, he received the Horror Writers of America's lifetime achievement award and also won an award from the British Fantasy Society for contributions to the genre. He died in 2001.

ABOUT THE EDITOR

STEPHEN JONES lives in London, England. A Hugo Award nominee, he is the winner of three World Fantasy Awards, three International Horror Guild Awards, four Bram Stoker Awards, twenty-one British Fantasy Awards and a Lifetime Achievement Award from the World Horror Association. One of Britain's most acclaimed horror and dark fantasy writers and editors, he has more than 130 books to his credit. You can visit his web site at www.stephenjoneseditor.com or follow him on Facebook at Stephen Jones–Editor.

CPSIA information can be obtained
at www.ICGtesting.com
Printed in the USA
BVOW08s0304260118
505518BV00001B/119/P